CRA

# A PRESENCE IN HER LIFE

*Recent Titles by Louise Brindley from Severn House Large Print*

TIME REMEMBERED
VIEW FROM A BALCONY

# A PRESENCE
# IN HER LIFE

## Louise Brindley

**Severn House Large Print**
London & New York

This first large print edition published in Great Britain 2003 by
SEVERN HOUSE LARGE PRINT BOOKS LTD of
9-15, High Street, Sutton, Surrey, SM1 1DF.
First world regular print edition published 2002 by
Severn House Publishers, London and New York.
This first large print edition published in the USA 2003 by
SEVERN HOUSE PUBLISHERS INC., of
595 Madison Avenue, New York, NY 10022

British Library Cataloguing in Publication Data

Brindley,  Louise
    A presence in her life  -  Large print ed.
    1.  Haunted houses  -  England  -  Yorkshire  -  Fiction
    2.  Large type books
    I.  Title
    823.9'14 [F]

ISBN 0-7278-7226-5

Printed and bound in Great Britain by
MPG Books Ltd, Bodmin, Cornwall.

For Muriel Gallon,
and Lis, with thanks
for a lifetime of
golden memories.
From – Lou.

# Prologue

**1930s**

As daylight faded to dusk on warm summer evenings by the sea, came a feeling of enchantment. Lamplight threaded the branches of trees, fairy lights glimmered along the shore. The sky paled imperceptibly from blue and gold to grey; a tremulous star appeared, a slip of a moon. The colour of the sky deepened to indigo. The sea seemed fuller, deeper, mysterious, remote; sounds and movement became muted in the passing of the day; a kind of slow cotillion of life danced to the music of time.

In the springtime of her life, the girl with golden hair had waltzed home from work to help her mother dish up the visitors' evening meal, to clear the dining tables and lend a hand with the washing-up, whilst her father relaid the tables for breakfast and had a word with the guests on their way out to see a show or whatever they had planned for that evening.

It was the feeling of security that Lara would remember most of all in the years ahead, the glorious sense of homecoming from the library where she had worked since leaving school, of being close to those she loved in a place she loved; that sublime, youthful expectation of happiness without end in the simple pleasures of life, come winter or summer, rain or shine, springtime or autumn.

Come winter, the first snowfall, she would walk alone in the snow, her cheeks stung crimson by the cold, thinking of Christmas and coal fires, of firelight dancing warmly on walls and ceilings, the scent of roast goose and hot mince pies from the kitchen on Christmas morning, of helping her mother to peel potatoes and sprouts, her father to lay the table in readiness for their one o'clock dinner; the fun and laughter derived from opening their presents to one another; her mother's obvious delight in a watch-shaped bottle of 4711 eau-de-cologne, her father's in a leather wallet stamped with his initials, a new tie, or a fountain pen.

Thereafter, springtime would herald the cleaning of the house from top to bottom in readiness for Easter and the first influx of visitors from the West Riding, in dire need of fresh sea air and good simple home-cooked food, of fun and laughter after their winter of discontent in the smoke-grimed atmosphere of Leeds, Wakefield, Bradford or Huddersfield.

Memorably, there was also a man from Middlesbrough, who came at bank holidays and remained aloof from his fellow boarders, choosing to dine alone at a table near the door, eating quickly then going out, presumably for solitary walks along the seashore.

Busy about her kitchen, Mary Harte, plump and serene, never one to pass judgement unkindly, said if the man preferred his own company that was his business, not theirs. He was no trouble at all so far as she was concerned, eating everything set before him, keeping his room immaculate, making his own bed, cleaning the washbasin, drying his shaving brush after use, folding the towels, unlike some people she could mention, with a quizzical glance in her husband's direction.

Lara laughed, so did her father. And this was what she had loved so much in the springtime of her life, that warm sunlit kitchen of home; shared laughter, her mother making pastry, Dad, who did the shopping, writing a list of Mum's requirements, his glasses perched on the end of his nose, herself making a mid-morning pot of tea, forgetful of the strange behaviour of the man from Middlesbrough who made his own bed and dried his shaving brush so as not to leave a wet mark on the glass shelf above the washbasin, whose name she could not for the life of her remember.

Something to do with furniture. Mr Chesterfield? Mr Canterbury? She asked her father.

'Oh, you mean Mr Davenport?' he replied, more concerned about his shopping list than the surname of the man he'd dubbed 'The Lone Ranger'. 'Now where was I? Sugar, tea, milk, eggs, bacon, bread, cornflakes, potatoes. Are you sure that's all, Mary?'

'Yes, quite sure. In any case, there's always tomorrow, isn't there?' Mary said placidly, adding the finishing touches to the steak and kidney pies she was making for the visitors' evening meal and popping them into the oven to bake, never thinking for one moment that, one not so far distant day, tomorrow might never come.

It had happened so suddenly, so shockingly. On an evening stroll along the promenade, Mary and William Harte had died instantly when a drunk driver, his vehicle out of control, had mounted the pavement and struck them, head on, before hitting a lamp post. A terrible accident in which the car driver had also died instantaneously.

The idiosyncratic 'Lone Ranger', Charles

Davenport, had been staying in the house that August bank holiday when the accident occurred: had been beside Lara in the hall when the police arrived on the doorstep, grim-faced yet kindly, to break to her the dreadful news; the deaths of her parents.

Too stunned to speak, too shocked to weep. Lara recalled that Charles had acted on her behalf. 'I'm a friend of the family,' he'd explained to the police, ushering them into the dining room to question them closely about the accident, wanting to know every detail, exactly where and how it had happened; standing behind Lara's chair, his hands on her shoulders. Comforting hands.

And how odd, she had thought bemusedly, Charles's description of himself as a friend of the family. Was that really true? She supposed it must be, since he'd been a regular visitor to the house these past three years and she had been with him, that evening, to a concert in the Spa Grand Hall.

Mum and Dad had teased her unmercifully about her occasional outings with Mr Davenport, she recalled, and they would laugh about this later, when they came home from their evening stroll – except that they wouldn't be coming home. Never. Not ever again...

'I should send for a doctor if I was you, sir,' the kindly police sergeant advised quietly. 'The poor young lady being in need of a sedative, summat to get her over the shock of losing both her parents so suddenly.'

'Yes, of course, sergeant,' Charles replied levelly. 'I'll do as you suggest. Meanwhile, if there's anything more I can do...'

'Well, sir, there's the matter of identification.'

'Naturally. When?'

'The sooner the better. Later on tonight, perhaps? After the doctor's visit?'

Beginning to shake violently, they're talking about Mum and Dad and me, Lara realized dully, numb with grief; making decisions on my behalf as if I were blind, deaf or dumb, a mental incompetent, a cipher, a nonentity.

Rising unsteadily to her feet, speaking for the first time since the police had entered the house, she said huskily, 'You don't understand. I don't need a doctor. I need to see my parents.'

Afterwards, faced with a well-nigh impossible situation, a house full of summer visitors at a time of mourning, with no one to cook or clean for them, reluctantly Lara had hung a 'No Vacancies' sign in the dining-room window when all but one of the visitors had departed. The one remaining was Charles Davenport, to whom she'd confessed the impossibility of staying on in Scarborough close to the scene of an

12

accident which had robbed her, not only of her loved ones, but also of her home, albeit a rented house far too big for just one person, which, on her meagre salary as an assistant Librarian, she could not afford to rent anyway.

In desperate need of someone to talk to, confiding in Charles Davenport, who had proved to be a tower of strength before, during and after her parents' funeral, had seemed the natural thing to do.

Friends, neighbours and relatives had been kind and supportive at the funeral; aunts, uncles and various cousins, had come to Scarborough to pay their last respects to William and Mary. Nice, well-meaning folk who had sent her Christmas and birthday cards. 'With love from Auntie Grace, Uncle Fred, Mabel and Caroline', or from 'Aunt Bessie, Uncle George, Pauline, Phil, Elizabeth and Muriel'. Dim and distant figures with their own lives to lead south of the Watford Gap. Lives to which they had returned, thankfully, Lara had suspected, after the funeral. None of whom had understood the extent of her grief, her sense of loss, her fears for the future, robbed of the two people about whom her life had so far revolved, without whom the future appeared as pointless as a book without pages, an unwritten sonnet, a concerto without music, a night without stars.

When Charles Davenport had asked her to marry him, she'd stared at him as if he had taken leave of his senses. '*Marry* you? But I scarcely know you!'

'Even so, I want you to consider my proposal very carefully before reaching a decision. I am not without means, I assure you. I have an important job, a home of my own in Middlesbrough. I'm a widower. My wife died five years ago, the reason for my frequent visits to Scarborough. An attempt to come to terms with her loss. That I have done so is largely due to you and – your family.' Speaking in a kind of verbal short-hand, he continued. 'I'm offering you a secure future, a home of your own. An escape from your present dilemma. Think about it. When you've thought about it, give me your answer.'

All that had happened twenty-five years ago. And now...

# One

No need to feel nervous, Lara reminded herself. This was simply an outing to meet a lady in need of a house minder for the summer months while she went to America to visit her family.

Even so, long accustomed to feelings of inadequacy, and at a low ebb both physically and mentally following the sudden death of her husband, the trauma of the funeral and the sale of her home, she wished she'd been honest enough to admit to her estate-agent friend, Rory McAllister, that she could scarcely cope with her own problems at the moment, let alone shoulder the responsibility of someone else's.

She was, after all, comfortably established in a pleasant en suite room at the Windsor Hotel, being cosseted and cared for by its owners, Johnny and Jill Carstairs, and their staff, not having to worry about shopping, cooking and cleaning any more since quitting that semi-detached villa on the outskirts of Middlesbrough which, throughout the twenty-odd years of her marriage to an impossibly demanding husband, she had come to regard as more of a prison than a home.

As if reading her mind, Rory said sympathetically, 'No need to worry unduly. If you'd rather not meet Joan Prewett, just say so and I'll drive you back to your hotel in time for lunch.'

He continued, keeping a wary eye on the road ahead to avoid ewes and their lambs, oblivious to the traffic, straying across unfenced land in search of pastures new. 'I can see now that it was presumptuous of me to suggest a meeting with Mrs Prewett. My only excuse is that Joan desperately needs someone trustworthy to look after her property during her absence, and you sprang to mind as being that person.'

The woman beside him smiled wistfully. Gazing out of the car window at the passing scenery, Lara saw broad vistas of moorland dotted here and there with farm buildings, spinneys of trees, gorse bushes in bloom, thrusting fronds of green bracken beneath a watercolour April sky, clouds of white-winged seagulls hovering about the tractors preparing fields for their summer harvest of barley.

She said, 'You mustn't blame yourself, and it would be churlish of me to turn back now. Or would cowardly be a more fitting adjective? You see, Rory, there are reasons why I could not bear to live anywhere near the sea

16

again. Not ever. May I explain why not?'

'Sure. Go ahead. I'm listening.'

When Lara had finished speaking, albeit haltingly, of her dread of revisiting Scarborough ever again; the scene of so many unhappy memories linked to the deaths of her parents, Rory reminded her gently that Joan Prewett's house was situated several miles further down the coast in Carnelian Bay, a picturesque fishing village. Even so, if she hated the sea so much, there seemed little point or purpose in continuing their journey.

But it was not the sea she hated at all, Lara realized, her mysterious companion of many a long-gone summer evening when she had caught her breath in wonderment at the sight of moonlight on water. What she could not face was that stretch of roadway, in Scarborough, where her parents had been killed; the reason why she had accepted Charles's proposal of marriage, to put the past behind her. Not that she had succeeded. Marriage to a man old enough to be her father had been a disaster from beginning to end.

'I know you want me to look after Mrs Prewett's property during her absence. I wish I knew why. I'm no longer short of money. I'm happy at the Windsor Hotel, where I can afford to stay indefinitely, thanks to you...'

'For selling your home at its proper market value, you mean?' Rory interrupted brusquely. 'When, if left to your own devices, you'd have probably given it away?'

'Yes, but...'

'But nothing! You called me in to assess the house and its contents at their true worth, which I did, which any estate agent worth his salt would have done!'

'Rory, why are you so angry with me all of a sudden?'

'I'm not ... angry, just a bit disappointed that a woman in the prime of life, with her future before her, should choose to stay indefinitely in a backwater hotel, no matter how comfortable. The word indefinitely really bothers me, Lara. So what are you going to do? Keep on clinging to the past or look ahead to the future?'

'It's not that cut and dried. Not that simple.'

'Is anything nowadays?' He frowned. Then, 'I'm sorry, Lara. I shouldn't have said what I did. It is up to you to live your own life as you see fit. So how about Carnelian Bay? Do you want to go there or not?'

And, 'Yes,' Lara replied, pulling herself together. 'Yes, I do. Very much.'

The moorland road behind them, Rory pointed the car downhill past a signpost marked 'Carnelian Bay 10 miles'. He said gruffly, ashamed of his recent outburst, 'In case you're wondering, Joan Prewett and I are friends of long standing. She, too, is a widow. After the death of her husband, and her daughter's marriage to an American and the daughter's departure to live with him in New York, she asked me to find her a smaller house, preferably near the sea.' He smiled reminiscently. 'She fell in love with Stella Maris at first sight.'

' "Stella Maris"? That means "Star of the Sea", doesn't it?' Lara said eagerly, remembering a book she had once read in her assistant-librarian days in Scarborough. Who had written that book she hadn't the foggiest idea, but she had never forgotten the name of the heroine, Stella Maris, or its derivation, 'Star of the Sea'.

Rory said, 'You know, Lara, you never cease to amaze me. How a woman of your sensitivity endured twenty-odd years of marriage to a man like Charles Davenport beggars belief. Forgive me, but why didn't you simply up and leave him? Tell him to go to hell, or words to that effect?'

Laura said simply, 'Because he was my husband.'

On the outskirts of Carnelian Bay, passing an imposing Victorian mansion, iron-gated and with high stone walls, reminiscent of a prison, 'What is that?' Lara asked nervously, disliking the look of it.

'Nothing sinister, I assure you,' Rory explained light heartedly. 'The direct opposite, in fact. It's a war veterans' nursing home for the mentally sick and disabled, administered by a charity organization in aid of poor devils desperately in need of good food and fresh sea air, plus employment, if possible, as decorators, gardeners or whatever to encourage their eventual return to normality.'

'Oh, I see.' Lara breathed a sigh of relief. 'I thought it was some kind of penitentiary.'

Suddenly, catching the scent of sea air and hearing the crying of gulls wheeling in the blue arc of the April sky, it seemed that the years between had fallen from her shoulders like a beggar's cloak, and she was young once more, a girl on the cusp of her life – hurrying home. Home! Tears filled her eyes.

Mistily she discerned, on the downhill road to the harbour, the pantiled roofs of fishermen's cottages clustered about a scene of quiet activity: two grey stone jetties, between which fishing vessels lay lopsidedly at anchor, awaiting the turn of the tide to refloat them. She saw patient old men unhurriedly mending fishing nets and lobster pots; younger men swabbing decks; heard the sound of their laughter as they called out to one another between one sloping deck and the next. Happy men, friends and neighbours, possibly brethren, awaiting the turn of the tide, a sailing forth, at eventide, to bring home the bounty of the sea.

This being a one-way street for obvious reasons, far too narrow to admit the passage of two-way traffic, at the harbour mouth, Rory nosed the bonnet of the car towards a lower promenade and a steep one-way road leading to the cliff tops overlooking the whole of Carnelian Bay.

En route, Lara noticed gaily painted beach huts with tiny verandahs, a café and a gift shop, closed and shuttered at this time of year. On the upward incline to the cliff top, houses advertising bed, breakfast and evening meals, in anticipation of an influx of summer visitors who, more than likely, came to Carnelian Bay year after year in search of peace and quiet far removed from the rush and bustle of the busy resorts farther along the coast. Scarborough, for instance...

'You're shivering, Lara. Are you cold?' Rory asked concernedly. And, 'Yes,' she replied. 'My fault entirely, I should have worn something warmer than a jumper and skirt and a lightweight anorak.'

'Not to worry,' he advised her. 'Stella Maris isn't far now, and Joan Prewett is bound to have had the kettle on the boil, all morning, for a nice hot cuppa, awaiting our arrival.'

Rory had ground the car to a halt on a car park close to a parade of shops, including a butchers', greengrocers', a bakery, a fish-mongers', a hairdressing salon, a chemists' and a library. A library, actually a library, Lara thought happily, stepping from the car on to the roughly pebbled car park, and following Rory towards a Private road fronting a small enclave of detached Victorian villas, at the end of which stood Stella Maris, Star of the Sea.

This was a graciously proportioned house, bay and sash windowed, with peaked dormers, presumably attic windows, on the third storey. Lara's heart sank. It was much bigger than she'd imagined it would be, with a sizeable garden surrounded with tall beech hedges, poplar trees, horse chestnuts and hornbeams.

Assailed by a sudden panic attack, imagining what it would feel like to be alone in a house of that size, 'I'm sorry, Rory,' she said breathlessly; heart hammering against her ribs. 'I can't face it. I really can't!'

At that moment, the front door opened and a smiling lady wearing a tweed skirt and an Aran sweater, bespectacled and with wispy grey hair blowing about her thin, intelligent face, tripped down the garden path, hands outstretched to greet them.

'Rory, my dear,' she said, standing on tiptoe to kiss his cheek. 'How good it is to see you again. And you must be Lara. I'm Joan Prewett. Call me Joan. Now, please do come in. We mustn't stand here catching cold. After all, "April is the cruellest month", as some poet or other once said, though I can't for the life of me remember which one.'

'I think it was T.S. Eliot,' Lara said softly as her heart resumed its normal rhythm; relaxing in the warmth of Joan Prewett's unorthodox personality, realizing that here was a woman she could trust implicitly. The kind of friend she'd always longed for and never had in what she thought of as her Middlesbrough days...

'All right now?' Rory asked her concernedly, tucking a hand into the crook of her elbow as they followed Joan into the house. And, 'Yes,' she replied gratefully, glad of his presence in her life, thinking that if she'd had a son by Charles Davenport, she'd have wanted him to be like Rory McAllister. But Charles hadn't wanted children. Sex, most certainly, but not children.

Entering Stella Maris, Lara saw, ahead of her, a broad, red-carpeted staircase rising to the upper landings, a passage leading, presumably, to the kitchen quarters, and doors to left and right of the hall, one of which stood open to reveal a magnificently furnished drawing room, overlooking the sea.

'Sit down, Rory dear, and make yourself at

home,' Joan advised him mischievously, 'as if you wouldn't anyway, knowing you, whilst I introduce Lara to her fellow inmates and rustle up sandwiches and coffee. OK?'

'Fellow inmates?' Lara queried bemusedly, following Joan to the kitchen quarters. 'I'm sorry, I don't understand. I assumed that, if you, that is, we, came to some conclusion about my taking care of your home for the summer, I'd be living here alone.'

Joan chuckled infectiously as a golden labrador arose from its basket near the Aga cooker, wagging its tail, and a tortoiseshell cat jumped down from the window sill to rub about her ankles before rolling on its back to have its tummy tickled. 'I'd like you to meet Buster and Cleo, my two guardian angels. Yours also, I imagine, if you decide to come here to live.'

She added more seriously, 'I do so hope that you will, Lara, otherwise I'll cancel my trip to America. No way am I prepared to go away leaving my home and my animals in charge of someone I couldn't trust implicitly to take care of them. So far as I'm concerned, you *are* that right person. I knew it from the first moment I saw you. No, please don't commit yourself until you've seen the rest of the house and we've had time to discuss my domestic arrangements.

'I have, you see, a wonderful cleaning lady

called Iris Smith, who comes in on Mondays, Wednesdays and Fridays, to attend to the vacuuming, dusting and polishing; also, a peripatetic gardener called Ben, who comes, when he feels like it, to bring in fuel for the Aga, dependent upon the state of his back muscles, usually a bit dodgy, I'm sorry to say, the poor old man, but I haven't the heart to sack him. What I mean is, he relies on his wages to pay for his beer and baccy. And why not? He's a human being, for God's sake, not a plaster saint!'

Putting the kettle on to boil, Joan continued, 'I send all my washing and dry-cleaning to the laundry. The van man calls on a Monday and delivers on a Friday. If and when you come here to live, Lara, you'll find that my household expenditure has been well taken care of in advance, via a lump sum paid into a separate bank account, to which, as my named representative, you would have immediate access, in the event of an emergency.'

Weighing up the pros and cons, Lara said anxiously, 'But aren't we jumping the gun a little, since you haven't shown me the whole of the house yet? Besides which, to be entirely and totally honest with you, I'm in a poor state of health at the moment.'

'I know that, Rory told me,' Joan replied, making a cafetière of coffee. 'I was in the same boat after the death of my husband, at

25

a very low ebb. The reason why I came here to live, to make a fresh start. I might have stayed on in Leeds if my daughter, Becky, hadn't met an American and announced her intention of marrying him and going with him to New York after the wedding.

'It was a low-key ceremony in a registrar's office. Low key because of the recent death of her father. Naturally, I'd envisaged a church wedding for my only child; lots of flowers, a champagne reception afterwards, a three-tier wedding cake.' Joan's eyes filled with tears momentarily. Brushing them aside, she continued, 'But life has a way of dealing out body blows when least expected. My one consolation was that I approved wholeheartedly her choice of a husband. Scott Barnaby, my son-in-law, is one of the kindest people I've ever met. Now, as you can imagine, I'm longing to visit New York, to see my three grandchildren – two boys and a girl – for the very first time, while I'm still fit enough to travel.

'You see, Lara my dear, I'm in the early stages of multiple sclerosis, which means that sooner or later I'll be confined to a wheelchair, unable to walk, much less travel.

'Becky has no idea, and I have no intention of telling her. In fact, apart from myself, my doctor, now you, no one else knows. Not even Rory. So, promise me that you won't breathe a word.'

'Of course not,' Lara promised, deeply shocked by Joan Prewett's revelations regarding her state of health. 'And you have my word that I'll do everything I can to help you achieve your trip to New York. So, when do you intend going?'

'Later this month,' Joan replied shakily, attempting to pick up the tray containing the cups and saucers and the freshly made cafetière of coffee.

'Please, let me carry the tray for you,' Lara said quietly, feeling needed, really *needed*, for the first time since she had waltzed home, in the springtime of her life, to help her mother with the washing-up.

# Two

She had given the Carstairs a fortnight's notice of her intention to vacate her room at the Windsor for the summer months, saying she hoped to return to the hotel in September. She would let them know the exact date, dependent on Mrs Prewett's return from America.

'We'll miss you, Mrs Davenport,' Jill said wistfully. 'It's been a real pleasure looking

27

after you, but I can't say I blame you for wanting to get away from Middlesbrough for a while. Besides, the sea air will do you a world of good. It's just what you need after all you've been through recently; losing your husband so suddenly, I mean, and parting with your home.' She sighed deeply. 'I guess I'd want to part with the Windsor if anything happened to Johnny, which God forbid. It's the memories, isn't it? I'd see him every which way I turned, remembering the good times. I guess that's how you felt when you lost Mr Davenport.'

'Something like that,' Lara replied quietly, not about to reveal the truth, that she had sold her home because there were no good times to remember, and she could not have borne to stay in it a moment longer than necessary, after Charles's funeral.

At least his demise had given her, for the first time in her life, a modicum of financial security via the sale of the house and the payment of an insurance policy, taken out by Charles in his younger days, of which she had known nothing until a cheque in excess of ten thousand pounds had fallen on to her doormat.

Fortunately, Charles had left a will in her favour, as his sole beneficiary in the event of his death. Moreover, his employers had written to her offering a lump sum in respect of his pension rights, or monthly payments into her bank account for the forseeable future, whichever she preferred. Cannily, Lara had chosen the latter.

Two days prior to her departure to Carnelian Bay, taking a taxi to the town centre of Middlesbrough, Lara had bought presents for her friends at the Windsor Hotel: a cashmere twinset for Jill, a box of cigars for Johnny, a bottle of malt whisky for the chef, chocolates for the waitresses; gift vouchers for the cleaners; plus a comfortable dressing gown, a bottle of Estée Lauder's Youth Dew and several pairs of silk stockings for herself. Money no problem, although she still felt guilty about spending money on herself, on what Charles would have termed 'needless luxuries'.

Delighted at her acceptance of Joan Prewett's house-minding proposition, Rory had asked Lara, on their way home from Carnelian Bay, what arrangements had been arrived at regarding her guardianship of Stella Maris.

When Lara explained that Joan's cleaning lady, Iris Smith, would be there, on the Saturday morning of her arrival, to acquaint her more fully with the running of the household, he'd suggested his driving her there to help with her luggage and to see her safely settled in her new surroundings, an offer which Lara gratefully accepted. 'If you have nothing better to do,' she'd added diffidently. 'I mean – on your weekend off–' thinking that a handsome man like Rory McAllister should have something better to do with his time off than wasting it on herself.

He said dismissively, keeping an eye on the road, 'I had once. No longer, I'm sorry to say. Not since my wife left me for another man, whose child she happened to be carrying at the time. There was nothing I could do about it except agree to a divorce.'

'Oh Rory, I'm so sorry. I had no idea...'

'Well, that's life, isn't it? A body blow beneath the belt when least expected.'

And so, when the time came, Lara had arrived at Stella Maris with Rory in tow, hefting her luggage from the boot of his car to the front steps of her summertime abode, when the front door opened to reveal a slightly-built elderly lady, wearing a nylon overall, a kind of turban to hide her roller-embellished hair, who said brusquely, 'I'm Mrs Smith! You're late! I expected you an hour ago! Well, you'd best come in! *I* ain't got time to waste even if *you* have!'

Lara's heart sank to her shoes. She said, 'I'm so sorry, Mrs Smith, we were late setting off from Middlesbrough,' thinking just her luck that she had got off on the wrong foot with Joan's cleaning lady.

Rory said equably, 'Oh, come off your high horse, Iris! What's an hour between friends? The delay was all my fault! So why not put the kettle on for a nice hot cuppa, then show Mrs Davenport the way to her room? She is, after all, here on Mrs Prewett's behalf to take care of the house during her absence, in case you've forgotten, so a little kindness wouldn't come amiss, wouldn't you agree?'

Lara said, 'There's no need to show me the way, Mrs Smith, and *I'll* put the kettle on.' She smiled. 'I really am sorry for the delay.'

'Ah well!' Iris shrugged her shoulders. 'If you say so. I don't come in on Saturdays as a rule. It's just that madam asked me to give you the keys an' tell you about the Aga.'

They went through to the kitchen together, where Iris explained the ritual involved in keeping the cooker stoked up from the coke bunker near the back door, the riddling of ashes and so forth. 'Give me a nice clean electric cooker any day of the week,' she grumbled, 'but madam won't hear of it cos of the animals. Spoilt rotten they are, if you ask me.'

Lara patted Buster's head surreptitiously. Cleo was fast asleep on the window sill. Mrs Smith continued, 'There's plenty of food in the fridge; milk, butter, bacon, eggs an' so on. The tinned stuff's in the larder along with the veggies an' dog biscuits.'

'Thank you, Mrs Smith,' Lara said, feeling exhausted, wishing the woman would go away. 'I'm sure I'll manage fine.'

'Right then, I'll be on my way.' Iris removed her overall and hung it behind the door, adding, as she put on her outdoor things, 'I come first thing Mondays, Wednesdays an' Fridays, think on.' A threat or a promise? Lara wondered as Mrs Smith marched down the front steps, complete with turban and rollers, and pulling a plaid shopping trolley behind her.

'Not the most endearing personality in the world,' Rory remarked when she'd gone. 'I hope she didn't upset you, speaking to you the way she did. She wouldn't have dared if Joan had been here. Now, let me take your luggage upstairs, and while you're getting settled I'll make some coffee.'

'I'm glad you came with me,' Lara confessed, following him to the first landing. 'I'd have felt lost without you.'

'I could stay over, if you like,' he suggested, sensing her nervousness at finding herself alone in the house when darkness came. 'I've done so before, at Joan's invitation, when she was feeling low for whatever reason. Come Sunday morning I'd cook breakfast, take Buster for a walk along the prom to relieve his feelings, so to speak, feed the cat, then drive Joan to church. Afterwards, likelier than not, we'd have lunch together at the Golf Club Hotel, following which I'd drive her home and pack my duds in readiness for my return to the fleshpots of Middlesbrough.'

'Then please do stay over,' Lara said gratefully. 'If you've a mind to.'

'Your wish is my command,' he replied light-heartedly. 'And, in case you're wondering, I'm fully house-trained and utterly reliable, which is more than I can say for Buster, at times, if Mother Nature happens to get the better of him!'

Unpacking her belongings in the second-best bedroom, Rory was such fun to be with, Lara thought happily, a source of laughter long denied her during her disastrous marriage to Charles Davenport, with whom every day that dawned had been fraught with guilt that she might not live up to his expectations of perfection in a wife – or a housekeeper. – in a house filled to overflowing with his first wife, Freda's, furniture and photographs, none of which he would part with, until, after his death, guilt-ridden and desperately unhappy, she, Lara, had called in a firm of estate agents with a view to ridding herself of the house and its contents – her predecessor's furniture and effects – as quickly as possible – apart from the photographs of Freda Davenport, which she had, God forgive her, torn up and burned in a back garden bonfire.

Assessing the property, Rory McAllister, a partner with the firm of Greenall and Ellis, had advised her that the various items of Victorian furniture, china and paintings to be included in the sale were worth a great deal of money, at the same time strongly advising her to sell the house and its contents separately, not as a going concern.

And so, drawn towards his warm, out-going personality, heeding his advice, she had sent Freda Davenport's wardrobes, chests of drawers, brass bedsteads, whatnots and gilt-framed paintings to a saleroom, where they had sold for a sum of money far beyond her expectations. So, eventually, had the semi-detached villa in which she had squandered twenty-odd years of her life catering to the demands of a man who no longer dried his shaving brushes after use, but expected her to do so on his behalf.

All in the past now. Even so, Lara realized, the day-to-day humiliation she had suffered during her marriage to Charles Davenport, had robbed her of self-esteem. More importantly, of her health and hope for the future. What future? Life in a backwater hotel, as Rory had recently reminded her? As the temporary custodian of another woman's home and belongings? Then what? A return to the Windsor Hotel? Only time would tell.

Would real, lasting happiness ever come again, of the kind she had known in the springtime of her life? Or was she destined to sink, without trace, into a future devoid of happiness or hope? Would she ever meet a man who really loved her, whom she could love and trust implicitly?

It was then she heard Rory calling upstairs to her that coffee was ready and waiting in the drawing room, when, squaring her shoulders, and smiling, she walked downstairs, grateful to him for the momentary respite he'd given her to wash her hands and comb her hair; to make herself presentable, as her mother would have said to her when, after long walks in the wind and rain, she'd come home looking as if she'd been dragged through a hedge backwards.

Rory said, pouring the coffee, 'Is there anything you'd like to do before lunch? Is there anything more you need in the way of food?'

'No, I don't think so, but I should like to go to the library, and to visit the church, if possible.'

'But of course. No problem.' Handing her a cup of coffee: 'What denomination are you, by the way?'

'Church of England,' she replied wistfully. 'But I haven't been inside a C of E church since – heaven knows when. Charles was a staunch Methodist, you see.'

Rory saw only too clearly the pattern of Lara's life with a man whose word was law, even to the extent of denying his wife the comfort of her own religion. Not that he was qualified to judge either way, believing himself to be an atheist, though he did believe, at times, there must be a guiding hand somewhere in the universe. Not necessarily a being in a flowing white gown of the Old Testament ilk. But *someone*! A presence of some kind in the lives of every man!

Ye gods, what had come over him? he wondered. For one brief moment he'd imagined the vague outline of a man, in uniform, standing near the bay window, looking out to sea. A mental aberration of some kind, he reckoned, linked to his present problems concerning his personal life; his forthcoming divorce from his wife, Georgina, about to give birth to another man's child...

'Are you all right, Rory?' Lara asked anxiously. 'You look as if you'd seen a ghost!' she added compassionately. 'No need for pretence with me, of all people. So why not go up to your room, lie down and try to sleep? I'll be fine on my own for a while. Well, not quite on my own, with Buster and Cleo for company.'

'Thanks, Lara. I am a bit tired, come to think of it.'

Deeply concerned about Rory, Lara thought that he drove himself far too hard on other people's behalf. Now she was beginning to understand why. He had spoken briefly about the breakdown of his marriage, but it could not have been easy for him, a handsome, hard-working man, to discover his wife was pregnant by another man and to have the decency to free her from a loveless marriage.

What had gone wrong between them? she wondered. How little one really knew about other people's lives, the dark secrets often hidden behind an apparently normal façade, recalling Joan Prewett's decision to hide her illness from her family, her own attempts to persuade herself, and others – particularly Charles's elderly coterie of colleagues, their wives and members of the Church Council he'd insisted on inviting to dinner occasionally – that they, she and Charles, were a happily married couple.

Making up her mind in an instant, knowing that Rory would sleep for a while, taking Buster to his basket near the Aga and seeing Cleo safely ensconced on her window sill, then putting on her outdoor things, Lara walked along to the library, where, crossing the threshold, an old familiar smell of beeswax polish tickled her nostrils, recalling memories of her springtime years in Scarborough, of all the books she had meant to read then, before handing in her notice, and giving up a job she had loved to marry a man who had regarded reading as a waste of time.

Glancing about her, albeit nervously at first, then more determinedly approaching the counter, she asked the librarian if she might have access to the shelves.

The woman, middle-aged and glamorous in appearance, in no way a stereotype librarian, said pleasantly, 'Yes, of course you may. Just fill in this card giving your name, address and so on, and you'll be registered right away. So go ahead and choose the books you want, and I'll stamp them on your way out.'

Lara chose an anthology of John Betjeman's poems, a biography of the Brownings, Robert and Elizabeth; *The Pickwick Papers* by Charles Dickens, *Rebecca* by Daphne Du Maurier, and *The Hound of the Baskervilles* by Sir Arthur Conan Doyle.

'Hmmm, an eclectic choice, if I may say so,' the librarian opined, stamping the books. 'Oh, please forgive me, Mrs Davenport, but I knew at once, from your address, that you must be the lady in charge of Stella Maris during my friend Joan Prewett's absence. My name is Amanda Fielding, by the way. We're bound to meet socially sooner or later, this being a close-knit community.'

'Thank you. You've been very kind.' Lara left the library, warmed by the feeling that she had made at least one friend in Carnelian Bay, despite the woman's bizarre appearance.

Returning to Stella Maris with her precious burden of books, Buster barked a warning, hearing footsteps in the hall. Entering the kitchen, 'All right, sweetheart, it's only me,' she laughed as he lumbered, tail thumping madly, from his basket. 'Friend, not foe. I'll whistle in future, shall I?' Pursing her lips, she whistled a snatch of 'Danny Boy', though why that particular tune had entered her head, she hadn't the faintest idea.

Rory emerged from his room later that afternoon, explaining shamefacedly that he had slept far longer than he had intended; apologizing profusely for having left her alone for so long, for missing their trip to the church and the library, not to mention luncheon, which he'd intended treating her to at a fish restaurant near the harbour.

'No need to worry,' Lara said lightly. 'I've been to the library, and we can visit the church tomorrow morning. As for lunch, I wasn't all that hungry anyway. In any case, what does time matter? We'll have supper instead. Not that I'm much of a cook, but I can manage a couple of omelettes given half a chance. So why don't you take Buster for a short walk along the prom, and supper will be ready and waiting when you return.'

After supper – mushroom omelettes, chips, and a smidgin of green salad, eaten in the kitchen – Rory said appreciatively, helping Lara with the washing-up, 'I thought you said you weren't much of a cook? Where on earth did you get that idea? That was the best mushroom omelette I've ever tasted, and the chips were nothing short of perfection, crisp on the outside, floury on the inside.'

Lara smiled reminiscently. 'Ah well, that's a little secret taught to me by my mother, who cooked divinely. It was Charles who didn't care much for my cooking. He preferred his meat and vegetables well cooked, you see? A bone of contention between us, I'm afraid, among many another, resulting in my lack of confidence to even cook his breakfast bacon and eggs to his liking. Either the bacon was too crisp or not crisp enough, the eggs too hard or too runny. In the end, I gave up trying to please him, knowing that nothing I did for him was right no matter how hard I tried.' By which time her smile had faded to a grimace of despair that she had failed so miserably to please a husband who, to Rory's way of thinking, deserved not a lovely wife such as Lara, but a harridan who would have belted him over the head with the frying pan, eggs, bacon and all.

He said gently, 'You mustn't blame yourself, Lara. None of that was your fault. You married the wrong man, that's all, just as I, apparently, married the wrong woman. I should have realized that Georgina wasn't the domestic type. I've just put my own home on the market, as a matter of fact. It seemed pointless carrying on with the mortgage when I could manage better in a small rented flat.'

He continued reflectively, 'Things might have been different had we started our married life in rented accommodation. But no, I wanted a house, a home to feel proud of. Georgie, on the other hand, wanted lots of parties, fun and laughter, not a house mortgaged to the hilt. I explained to her that we couldn't afford both the house and the parties on my salary: that the household bills must come first. The cause of our first quarrel.

'Gradually things went from bad to worse. She called me mean and narrow-minded. I called her scatterbrained and flighty. When the other man entered her life, I have no idea. All I know is, she seemed much happier all of a sudden, and I thought ... Well, what matter what I thought? All water under the bridge now. When she told me she was pregnant – by the other man in her life –

and begged me to divorce her, what else could I have done except agree to her request? The devil of it is, I'm still in love with her, God help me!' He smiled awkwardly. 'Life's a bitch, at times, isn't it?'

Lara said quietly, encouragingly, 'The thing to remember is that you are still capable of creating a new future for yourself.'

'And you are not, I suppose?' he replied, tongue-in-cheek.

'Oh come on, Rory, be fair,' Lara adjured him sharply. 'I married, not for love but security. You married for love. I lived over twenty years with a man I wasn't in love with. Besides which, I'm long past thinking in terms of some pie-in-the-sky romance which will never happen. Even if I wanted it to, which I *don't*! Frankly, all I want is peace of mind, to live the rest of my life as quietly as possible. Is that so difficult to understand?'

'I guess not,' Rory said contritely. 'So where do we go from here? Would you prefer a stroll along the prom, or an evening watching television?'

'Neither, if you don't mind–' putting away the last of the supper dishes. 'It's been a long day, and I am rather tired. I'm off to bed now. So goodnight, Rory, and God bless. See you in the morning?'

# Three

There came times, Lara realized, when even physical exhaustion precluded a good night's sleep.

All she needed to do, to push her racing mind to rest, was to swallow a sleeping pill from the bottle her doctor had prescribed for her. Somehow she couldn't bring herself to do that. She needed to think; *wanted* to think clearly and lucidly about her present situation, not to blur her intellect with sleep-inducing drugs, to wake up next morning in a state of semi-consciousness, unable to cope with the day ahead of her.

Her bed was comfortable, and she could hear, in the distance, the old familiar sound of the sea washing in on the shore, as she had done, long ago, in her room in Scarborough.

She had lain awake many a long night then, recalling the delights of the evening before: canoeing on Peasholm Park lake, for instance, in company with the laughing companions of her girlhood days, filled to overflowing with the sheer exuberance of youth and happiness, scarcely able to await the dawning of a new day.

Now, here she was, a middle-aged woman, lying in bed in a strange room in a strange house, a shadow of her former self, beset with worries about the future, wondering how she would cope alone when Rory returned to Middlesbrough.

Anxiety was part and parcel of sudden shock, the doctor had explained to her after Charles's funeral. Charles had been a patient of his for many years, something of a hypochondriac, in his opinion, overly fussy about his health, faddy about his diet, demanding frequent blood pressure tests, imagining occasional bouts of dyspepsia as something more sinister – stomach ulcers, heart murmurings, liver malfunction – or whatever.

Dr Roberts had reassured his touchy patient that there was nothing physically wrong with him apart from nervous tension, exacerbated by the nature of his employment as Chief Accountant with a long-established engineering firm of which, as Head of Department, he was responsible for the annual tax returns submitted to the Inland Revenue, with every last penny accounted for. A soul-destroying job if ever there was one, in Dr Roberts' opinion.

Curiously enough, the 'old boy' had died, not of physical ailments, but accidentally, from a backward fall down a flight of stairs at his place of employment. A blood clot on the brain as a result of his fall had led to his death, an hour afterwards, in the emergency ward of the local hospital.

There had been an inquest, of course – very distressing for his widow – but the coroner, after weighing up all the evidence, had recorded a death by misadventure verdict in the case of an elderly man with failing eyesight, not wearing glasses at the time, who, having obviously misjudged the distance between one step and the next, had reeled backwards down the stairs to strike his head on the ground below.

Gareth Roberts had been surprised, not to say pleased, when Lara Davenport had come to his surgery to seek his help and advice. A thoroughly dull woman, in his view, whose life with an elderly hypochondriac old enough to be her father could not have been a bed of roses. Why she had married him in the first place, he could not begin to imagine. But that, strictly speaking, was none of his business. The woman was obviously in a distressed state of mind, and it was up to him to prescribe suitable medicine to alleviate her distress, including sleeping pills to ensure the switching off of her mind at bedtime.

He'd found her to be an intelligent person though curiously reticent about her life with

Charles, unwilling even to discuss the death of her husband, as if she had got it into her head that she was somehow responsible for it.

That day in his surgery, 'Is there something you're not telling me?' he'd asked. 'If so, you may rest assured that I shall not betray a confidence which could have a bearing on my diagnosis of your condition and the best course of treatment to prescribe for you.'

She said bleakly, 'I did something dreadful, unforgiveable. I can't stop thinking about it.' A long pause had ensued. 'I – I lit a bonfire in the garden and I – I burned his late wife's photographs. Worst of all, I enjoyed doing it. I could never live up to her, you see, and I knew it! I must have been mad at the time! Perhaps I still am – mad, I mean, in need of restraint for my own good!'

So that was it! He said calmly, 'No, of course not. Human beings, in a state of shock, react in much the same way, given the provocation. A means of release, if you like, from a seemingly intolerable situation, especially in the event of the death of someone close and dear to them.'

'But you don't understand, Doctor,' Lara said bemusedly, staring into the past. 'My husband wasn't dear and close to me at all. I hated him, and I'm glad, not sorry, that he's dead!'

And this was the burden of guilt she had lived with ever since the day of his funeral, and would continue to do so until, God willing, she had discovered some means of salvation apart from the obvious solution of painkilling drugs to calm her troubled spirit.

Up early on Sunday morning, Rory had taken Buster for his constitutional, stoked the Aga, set the kitchen table for breakfast, fed the cat, listened to the weather forecast on the radio, removed his overnight stubble, showered and washed his hair in readiness for Lara's appearance to enjoy the bacon and eggs, coffee, toast and marmalade he intended to prepare for her on this bright, shining April morning.

He had slept well in his single room on the top landing, near to a door behind which lay a short flight of stairs leading to the attics: three rooms in which Joan kept surplus household furniture, rolls of carpet, tea chests and cardboard boxes containing unwanted china, pots and pans and obsolete electrical equipment; rooms which had most probably been the servants' quarters in the Victorian era.

Wealthy families of that era would have employed at least three servants to keep their household cart on its wheels. Rory knew, from careful perusal of the deeds of

47

the house, prior to Joan's purchase of the property, that Stella Maris had been built by a woollen-mill owner from the West Riding as a retirement home for himself, his wife and daughters, in the last quarter of the nineteenth century, around 1885. He couldn't be certain of the exact date, but he remembered the name of the mill owner quite clearly, a patriarch rejoicing in the name of Joshua Daniel Stonehouse, whom he'd envisaged, in his mind's eye, as a fierce, bewhiskered old gentleman, as shrewd as a monkey in matters financial, keeping a sharp eye on the workmen engaged in building his cliff-top eyrie overlooking Carnelian Bay, intent on not being diddled out of so much as a penny, if he could help it.

The shrewd old devil had certainly built a house to feel proud of, Rory reckoned, glancing at his wristwatch, wondering what had happened to Lara. Past ten o'clock, and there was still no sign of her. Perhaps she'd overslept? Should he go upstairs to her room to find out? Take her breakfast on a tray? But no, better not to intrude on her privacy, he decided. Far better to leave her to her own devices. If only he knew what was really troubling her, the root cause of her present distressed state of mind, apart from the deaths of her parents two decades ago, the more recent death of her husband and the sale of their marital home; her apparent reluctance to even contemplate a new relationship with any man who really cared about her.

But if not, why not? Rory wondered. Lara Davenport, in his view, was a very attractive woman in her early forties at a rough guess – possessed of a clear, unlined complexion, a slender figure, touches of gold in her hair, despite her present unbecoming hairstyle scraped back into a bun at the nape of her neck.

He had just poured himself a second cup of coffee when she came into the kitchen, dressed for going out; looking anxious. 'Oh, Rory, am I too late? Shall we make the service in time?'

Realizing she meant matins, 'Sure, if we get a move on,' he said brightly. 'Will you be warm enough?'

'Yes, I'm wearing a thicker jumper and skirt, and this jacket is much warmer than my anorak.'

There was something touchingly naive and innocent about her, he thought, tucking his hand into her elbow as they hurried down the front steps. He said, 'You must feel hungry. You haven't had anything to eat. I would have brought breakfast to your room, but I didn't want to disturb you.'

'I seldom feel hungry nowadays. In any case, I want to take Communion,' Lara replied mistily. 'The first time since ... What

49

is the name of the church, by the way?'

'St Mary's. It's old and very beautiful. The kind one sees on Christmas cards, with a lychgate; an ancient churchyard. There'll be lots of daffodils now, I shouldn't wonder. Such happy, hopeful flowers, daffodils, don't you agree?'

Lara said quietly, 'You are one of the kindest people I've ever met. Thank you for staying over last night. You'll never know how much that meant to me.'

'I'll stay over again next weekend, if you want me to,' he suggested. 'And I'll phone you every evening to make sure you're OK.' He added cheerfully. 'Besides which, tomorrow morning you'll have the pleasure of Iris Smith's company. Just don't let her bully you, that's all.'

Rory was right about the church, Lara thought, as they walked up the path to the open doors, it *was* beautiful: old and grey, with lichened gravestones, ancient cedars and yew trees, and high elms in which a colony of cawing rooks were building their nests; the ground beneath ablaze with golden-trumpeted daffodils.

Entering the church, to the sound of organ music, sunlight shining down from the stained-glass windows, creating stepping stones of red, blue and gold down the central aisle of St Mary's, Lara felt that this was a kind of homecoming, an essential part of her life so long withheld that she had half forgotten the comfort of her own religion, just as she had half forgotten the order of the service; the responses, the sacred ritual of Communion, which, at the last moment, she refused to accept, believing herself to be not good enough, preferring to remain in her pew, head bent, tears trickling down her cheeks.

Deeply aware of her distress, quietly Rory handed her a clean hanky from his breast pocket, on which to dry her eyes, knowing she needed more time to come to terms with her painful memories of the past, just as he needed time to come to terms with his own.

As they were seated towards the back of the church, Rory ushered Lara into the fresh air during the final hymn. The last thing she'd want was to meet the vicar face to face in the porch, after the service, or to engage in conversation.

'I'm sorry. I made a fool of myself.'

Rory smiled. 'Not to worry. These things take time. You could always come along to evensong during the week; get the feel of the place. Now, how about a cup of coffee? I'll take Buster for a walk, then we could have lunch at the Golf Club Hotel, if you feel up to it. If not, we'll have brunch in the kitchen.'

Secretly worried about her appearance, that she was scarcely dressed well enough to appear in a hotel dining room, at the same time aware that Rory would need a decent meal inside him before his return journey to Middlesbrough, she said, 'No, lunch at the golf club sounds fine to me. It's just that you look so smart and I look so – dowdy. I haven't many clothes, you see, apart from jumpers and skirts.'

Not wanting to sound presumptuous, he said carefully, 'Then why not splash out on a new wardrobe? Whitby's a good shopping centre, I've heard, and there's a good bus service, or so I believe. Joan often went to Whitby to replenish her wardrobe, especially in preparation for her trip to New York. She showed me some pretty snazzy outfits, I can tell you. A couple of cocktail dresses, smart jersey-wool suits, tailored blouses and so on.'

He continued, on their way to Stella Maris, 'Think about it, Lara. A spending spree would do you the world of good, and who knows, you might feel the urge to dress up once in a while. The folk hereabouts are a pretty gregarious lot on the whole, fond of 'drinky-pooh' parties, and so on, so a few well-cut trouser suits, tailored sweaters, silk scarves and a few items of junk jewellery wouldn't come amiss. Possibly even a new hairdo.'

Lara stared at him aghast. 'But I'm not that kind of person at all! I've never touched alcohol in my life, and I'd be out of my element in a room full of strangers! No, it's out of the question!'

And yet Lara knew, in her heart of hearts, that what Rory had told her was true – a spending spree, the ditching of her dowdy image, a new hairdo, might well pave the way to a renewed feeling of self-confidence after her years of misery tied to a husband who had never encouraged her to squander money on her appearance; had utterly refused to allow her to cut her hair, which he had loosened, night after night, at bedtime, as a prelude to his clumsy love-making.

The Golf Club Hotel dining room was not busy when the waiter showed Lara and her escort to a table near the window, overlooking the links. The majority of diners came in after the nineteenth hole, he explained, recognizing Rory from his previous visits with Joan Prewett. Odd, he thought, that such a good-looking bloke always had elderly women in tow. Was he one of them 'giggy' whatsits? The kind that battened on dotty old dames for what he could get out of them? Ah well, none of his business, he decided, handing them the menus.

53

He'd bet a hundred pounds to a hayseed that 'giggy's' present companion would order fruit juice for starters, fish, chicken or lasagne, vanilla ice cream for afters, whilst 'giggy' would go for the minestrone soup, roast beef and Yorkshire pudding, the apple pie and custard. What's more, he wasn't far wrong, as usual, except that the 'old dame' with the bun chose not fish, chicken or lasagne, but steak-and-kidney pie for her main course. (Anyone over the age of forty was old in the eyes of a twenty-year-old waiter.)

Feeling suddenly quite desperately hungry, Lara tucked into her steak-and-kidney pie until, her meagre appetite appeased, she laid down her knife and fork on the plate amid a welter of scarcely tasted carrots, sprouts and roast potatoes, apologizing as she did so for the waste of so much uneaten food.

Rory said concernedly, 'Rule Number One, Lara. Stop being apologetic. Remember that you are a free agent now, at liberty to decide for yourself exactly how much you feel inclined to eat, or not to eat, as the case may be.' He smiled. 'Not to worry, you'll get the hang of it sooner or later when you begin to realize that you are no one's slave, but your own person at last. Did you enjoy your steak-and-kidney pie, by the way?'

'Oh yes,' Lara smiled back at him. 'It was

very nearly as good as the ones my mother used to make.'

Rory said, 'You have a great deal going for you right now, Lara. Financial independence for one thing. A whole new future ahead of you. My advice is, make the most of your summer in Carnelian Bay: get to know people, get into the swing of things in a new environment, take more exercise, get more fresh air into your lungs. Do something ... outré. You'll find it will pay!'

'Like buying lots of new clothes and having my hair cut, for instance?'

'Well, yes, if you like. At the same time making time for your own pursuits, such as reading, churchgoing. Can you sing, by the way? And are you any good at flower arranging?'

'Oh, Rory, I really don't know!'

'Then find out,' he advised her. 'Just as Joan Prewett found out when she joined the church choir and became a stalwart of the St Mary's Mothers' Union, deeply involved in their activities...' He added awkwardly, 'Oh lord, I'm so sorry, Lara, I'd completely forgotten that—'

'I've never been a mother?' she queried gently. 'If only I had been. I desperately wanted children, you see. Lots of children. How different my life might have been if only that one wish of mine had been granted. Now it's too late.'

She added mistily, 'Shall we go now? I didn't sleep very well last night, and I am rather tired. What time will you be leaving, by the way?'

Rory said bleakly, 'After I've seen you back to Stella Maris, fed and exercised Buster, stripped my bed and packed my duds. Around two thirty, I imagine.'

Beset by the dreadful feeling that he had somehow failed to live up to her expectations, he said, at the moment of their leave-taking, on the front steps of Stella Maris, 'I meant what I said. I'll come back next weekend. If you want me to.'

Smiling up at him, 'Of course I do. The clean bedlinen should be back from the laundry by then, and I'll make certain that Mrs Smith has your room in apple-pie order in readiness for your return.' When he had gone, Lara went back into the house alone, first switching on the radio as a source of comfort, and encouraging Buster and Cleo to sit beside her, on the settee as darkness fell on the world outside. Then it was time to go upstairs to her lonely room on the upper landing, taking with her the anthology of John Betjeman's poems for company.

Awaking suddenly, in the early hours of next morning, the book having slipped from her fingers to the floor beneath her bed, Lara heard the sound of footsteps overhead: treading softly the floorboards of the attic rooms above the upper landing.

Half frozen with terror, slipping on her dressing gown, plucking up every ounce of her courage, silently she mounted the stairs to the upper landing, switching on the lights as she went, calling out, 'Who's there?'

No reply, and yet she knew, beyond a shadow of doubt, that she was not alone in the house, that someone was up there, in the attic rooms, pacing up and down, up and down, up and down. But no, that was impossible! The door leading to the attics was securely locked from the outside, the attics being a 'no-go' area so far as Joan Prewett was concerned, the key to which reposed on the ring of household keys which Iris Smith had handed to Lara on Saturday morning.

Had she been dreaming? Imagining the footsteps? Quite possibly, Lara thought returning to her room. And yet she could have sworn ... Was she going mad, after all, she wondered, getting back into bed ... She could have sworn that she had caught the softly whistled opening notes of 'Danny Boy'.

# Four

Iris Smith was in the kitchen next morning when Lara came downstairs. 'Oh, there you are! I thought you must have overslept,' she said self-righteously, placing undue emphasis on the word *there*.

Rory had told Lara not to let Mrs Smith bully her, but it was impossible not to feel intimidated by this woman's presence in the house. 'I'm sorry, I wasn't sure what time you'd be here.'

'Eight o'clock sharp!'

Glancing at the kitchen clock, 'But it's only five past now,' Lara ventured.

Iris bridled. 'Oh, well, if that's your attitude! But I'm a stickler for time, I am. Better early than late is my motto! The laundry man comes at nine, so I'd best get your bed stripped an' sort out the bathroom towels...'

Lara said guiltily, 'Mr McAllister stayed over on Saturday night, so his bed will also need stripping.'

'No skin off my nose, I'm sure,' Iris said nastily, her nose fairly peeling, putting two

58

and two together and coming up with the wrong answer. 'I thought he might, seeing as how anxious he were to help you indoors with your luggage.'

Lara's cheeks reddened. 'If you are implying...' This was intolerable. If this evil-minded home help thought for one moment that there was anything improper in her friendship with Rory, the sooner that notion was nipped in the bud, the better. 'I am right in thinking that Mr McAllister has often stayed overnight before?' she said. 'At Mrs Prewett's invitation?' Knowing, even as she spoke, that she was making the situation between herself and Iris Smith worse not better.

Oh God, she thought bleakly, if only she'd had the sense to ignore Mrs Smith's snide remark. Too late now. The damage was done; the situation saved only by Buster's emergence from his basket, tail thumping madly, to lick her hands, Cleo's jumping down from her window sill to have her tummy tickled. 'If you'll show me where Buster's lead is kept, I'll take him for a walk.'

What the hell had she let herself in for, she wondered, quitting the house with Buster straining at his leash. The last thing she'd envisaged was a war of nerves with a female counterpart of her late husband, seemingly every bit as critical, judgemental and narrow-minded as he had been.

Underlying all this were the events of last night, the footsteps and the whistling she'd imagined. What other explanation could there be? Joan had told her the first time she had come to Stella Maris, when she had shown her round the house, that she kept the door to the attics locked, so no one could possibly have been up there. As for the whistling, it could have been the sound of the wind sighing about the windows, couldn't it?

Floorboards in old houses often did creak for no apparent reason. Perhaps houses, like people, grew rheumaticky with age? Glancing back at Stella Maris, Lara wondered when it had been built, and by whom? An interesting subject for research. Obviously the house had been modernized in recent years, tastefully modernized, but she'd enjoy finding out more about it as a means of occupying her time between Iris Smith's thrice weekly visits, which she dreaded.

Walking Buster as far as the road leading down to the prom, as Rory called it, she stood for a while gazing down at the fishing village below. Strands of hair blowing about her face in the cool breeze coming inshore from the sea, she remembered, with a deep feeling of relief, that Rory would be on the phone to her this evening, that she'd be seeing him again next Saturday – and let Iris Smith make of it what she would ... The worst, most probably – that she and Rory were engaged in a passionate love affair and he had crumpled his bedlinen on purpose to suggest otherwise.

Enjoying the feel of the wind on her face, and brushing back strands of hair from her forehead, with a sudden, unaccustomed uplifting of her spirits, why not give the old girl something to really sink her – dentures – into, Lara wondered, by way of a wardrobe of smart new clothes and a gamine haircut? After all, what had she to lose apart from her maiden-aunt image, too much hair, and a preponderance of dowdy jumpers and skirts fit only for a jumble sale?

Returning to the house, she walked through to the kitchen, filled the kettle and cut two slices of bread in readiness for the toaster. Then, unhooking Buster's lead, she went into the pantry to find tins of dog and cat food, opened the tins, and forked the contents into the animals' separate bowls, smiling as she did so at their eager anticipation of a good breakfast. She would have hers at the kitchen table, when she had replenished Buster's water bowl and given Cleo a saucer of milk. Two slices of toast, marmalade, and a pot of tea wouldn't come amiss after her walk in the fresh air.

The kettle had just boiled and the toast was ready for buttering when Iris Smith walked into the kitchen. 'What ever are you doing?' she demanded irately. 'Them animals ain't supposed to be fed yet. Not till six o'clock! The dog's due a few biscuits at midday, so is the cat. Nowt till then!'

'Oh. I'm sorry, I didn't know,' Lara added innocently. 'About the rota. What time am I supposed to be fed?'

'Madam allus has her breakfust at nine sharp,' Iris said sourly.

Glancing at the clock, the hands of which stood at a minute to nine, 'So, I appear to have got something right, for once,' Lara replied equably, refusing to be browbeaten. 'A minute to go. But as you yourself remarked so wisely, better early than late.' Tilting her head slightly: 'Was that the doorbell I just heard? Must be the laundry man. Dead on time!'

Quaking inwardly, pretended savoire faire was all very well, Lara thought, but what if Mrs Smith handed in her notice and marched out of the house, trundling her shopping trolley behind her? If only! In which eventuality, Lara decided, she would do the housework herself. But where would that leave Joan Prewett on her return from the USA?

Feeling suddenly deflated, her appetite for toast and marmalade diminished, Lara drank a cup of tea and wandered aimlessly through to the drawing room to the droning sound of a vacuum cleaner in the room above. The master bedroom, Joan Prewett's bedroom. So, Iris Smith was still extant, and would remain so until she had finished her dusting, polishing and cleaning when, presumably, she would go back to where she belonged. But where did she belong?

Staring out to sea from a richly curtained bay window – lined turquoise velvet complementing the turquoise and cream carpet – it seemed ridiculous to Lara that she should be at daggers drawn with a comparative stranger. Surely it was up to her to discover something of Iris Smith's background instead of condemning the woman out of hand, at least to make overtures of friendship towards her.

And so, with the best of intentions, Lara called up to her, 'Mrs Smith, would you care for a cup of coffee?'

The woman appeared, red-faced, on the landing. She said, 'I don't drink coffee, but I wouldn't say no to a cup of tea. Mind you, it's a bit early. I don't usually have one till half ten, an' I'm not one to take liberties.' Again came that self-righteous tone of voice.

'Neither am I. The reason is I need to talk to you about the running of the house. Is it possible you feel resentful of my being here? Please be honest with me...'

'Oh, calling me dishonest now, are you? Well, I'll have you know—'

'I meant nothing of the kind,' Lara interrupted. 'What's more, you know it, don't you? I just want to know why you dislike me, what I've done to upset you – apart from my late arrival on Saturday morning.'

'I'm sure I don't know what you mean!' Iris angled her shoulders. 'If madam chose to hire a stranger to take care of her property, that was her business, not mine! No skin off my nose! I have enough on my plate as it is, what with my hubby an' grandkids to see to an' working Tuesdays an' Thursdays up at the nut-house; cleaning the wards, helping with the cooking an' washing-up. An' a fat lot to show for it, I must say! But my hubby's not a well man, an' the kids are allus wanting this an' that, new clothes, new football gear, an' playing hell up if they don't get 'em.'

'I see,' Lara said thoughtfully, pouring boiling water into the teapot. 'By the "nut-house", I imagine you're referring to the war veterans' hospital? But it isn't an insane asylum, is it?' Wanting to get things straight in her mind, setting out the cups and saucers, sugar basin and milk jug, she added, 'So what you're really getting at is working all hours for very little money? And you think I'm here, doing nothing, and being well paid for it?'

64

'Well, aren't you?' Iris thrust back at her, revealing an inner core of jealous resentment against the new incumbent of Stella Maris.

'No, as a matter of fact, I'm not,' Lara replied quietly. 'The reason I'm here is because I've been ill recently and needed employment of some kind to – oh, it's difficult to explain. Not a paid job, as such, but a change of environment to help me overcome the recent death of my husband. Mrs Prewett was kind enough to offer me help in that direction, for which I am more than grateful. Payment didn't enter into it. I'm here because I *need* to be here, to get my life back on track, if at all possible, with or without your cooperation. So now you know! Well, are you going to help me, or not?'

Mrs Smith said grudgingly, 'You're making a helluva mess pouring that tea! Best let me do it, my hands are steadier than yours!'

Having poured the tea to her satisfaction, Iris sat down to drink it, elbows propped on the table, the cup held in her hands. She said, 'I reckon that's the reason for all them pills on your bedside table. No wonder you can't get going of a morning with that lot inside you.'

'I thought I had got going,' Lara reminded her. 'I was up and doing when you came to work. Besides, if you take a closer look next time, you'll see that most of the bottles are unopened.'

'Take a closer look? Huh, I'm not one to pry into other folks' affairs,' Iris retorted, 'if that's what you're getting at. The very idea! I have better things to do with my time than waste it reading the labels on medicine bottles! I'd get shot of the lot of them if I was you!'

Facing a no-win conversation, Lara tried another tack. 'You mentioned your husband and grandchildren. How many children?'

'Two boys, Ernie an' Sid, an' right limbs of Satan they are an' all, allus skiving off school, getting into mischief. I've told my hubby time an' time again he should tek 'em in hand, but he wain't. He just laughs an' says boys will be boys, leaving everything to me. It just don't seem fair somehow, him sat there in front of t' telly day in, day out, an' me slaving me guts out to earn a living, apart from all the cooking an' cleaning I has to do when I gets home of an evening.'

At last, at last, Lara rejoiced inwardly, she had begun to crack Iris Smith's hostile façade, her resentment and jealousy, to discover the rebellious human being beneath that carapace of self-righteous indignation when she felt herself to be underestimated and undervalued by her peers, for want of a better description.

She said, matter-of-factly, not wanting to sound patronizing or too sympathetic,

'What does your work here entail, apart from vacuuming, dusting and polishing? What I mean is, have you a rota? If so, would you mind explaining it to me, so that I shan't interfere with it in any way? Rather to help you, if possible, in seeing to my own room, for instance, cleaning the silver, or whatever.'

'Why? Do you think I'm not up to my job?' Iris flung back at her. Rising quickly to her feet, 'Oh, I daresay you'd like that fine, wouldn't you, Mrs whatever your name is...'

'My name is Lara,' she responded gently. 'A fellow member of the human race, believe it or not. Now, do you want to wash the tea things, or shall I?'

'Please yourself, I'm sure,' Iris said defiantly. 'No skin off my nose!'

Washing the breakfast pots, the animals' feeding bowls and dishcloths, it occurred to Lara that her conversation with Iris had been a waste of time. There had been no softening of the woman's antagonism towards her in the long run. More than likely, Mrs Smith now had her earmarked as a drug addict, having made it her business to read the labels on her medicine bottles, Lara surmised from Iris's heated denial of prying into other folks' affairs. The very idea!

The wonder was that Mrs Smith had any skin left on her nose at all, from sticking it into other people's business, and this propensity of hers, allied to a waspish tongue and a mile-wide streak of jealousy running through her like print in a stick of Scarborough rock, might well prove a dangerous combination so far as her own, Lara's, reputation was concerned. But what to do about it, apart from leaving Mrs Smith to her own devices from now on, she hadn't the faintest idea.

In any event, did it really matter? The summer months over and done with, she would be free to return to the Windsor Hotel to be cared for and cosseted by Jill and Johnny Carstairs, to sink back into her role as a semi-invalid, no longer required to think or act on her own behalf. A consummation devoutly to be wished. And yet...

When the phone rang at seven o'clock that evening, picking up the receiver, hearing Rory's voice on the line, she replied to his question, 'How are you doing, Lara?'

'Not too badly, on the whole! I caught a bus to Whitby, this afternoon, would you believe? And what I did there was spend lots of money on new clothes, not to mention a new hairdo!'

'Tell me about it!'

'Well, first of all I treated myself to a fish-and-chip lunch at a restaurant near the harbour. Then I made a four o'clock

appointment to have my hair cut; meanwhile, I bought myself lots of smart outfits;
two rather fetching jersey-wool suits, several
new skirts and lambswool sweaters, a camel-
hair coat and a – cocktail dress. So, tell me
I'm mad, why don't you?'

Rory responded quietly, 'But you are not,
are you? In my estimation, you are one of
the sanest people I've ever met in this crazy
world of today. So, how are you feeling,
right now, shorn of your locks?'

Lara laughed. 'Light-headed, to say the
least!'

'And how did you make out with the
redoubtable Iris Smith?' he enquired.

'Not too well, I'm afraid. We are still at
loggerheads, to put it mildly.'

Rory chuckled. 'I'm not entirely surprised.
Had Joan Prewett told Iris Smith that she
intended to cross the Atlantic Ocean on
foot, she'd have believed her! Can *you* walk
on water, by the way?'

'Not so far as I know. Can *you*?'

Hanging up the receiver, this had been a
heart-warming phone conversation, Lara
thought happily, getting up from the
drawing-room sofa to close the turquoise
velvet curtains against the darkness of the
world outside, lit only with intermittent
street lamps evenly spaced along the head-
land overlooking Carnelian Bay.

Next, going through to the kitchen to

make certain that Buster and Cleo were safe and secure, after saying goodnight to them, Lara went upstairs to her room, albeit nervously, half expecting to hear the creaking of floorboards from the attics overhead, the softly whistled opening bars of 'Danny Boy' in the sighing of the wind round the casements of Stella Maris.

But there was nothing more than the comforting sound of the sea washing in on the shore beneath her bedroom window, to the lullaby of which she, Lara, fell fast into a deep, dreamless sleep of utter and complete physical and mental exhaustion, totally unaware of a presence in her life. A man who silently kept watch over her as she slept. A woman he had loved during his brief lifetime on earth, and would keep on loving for all eternity.

# Five

She awoke early next morning feeling strangely alert and light-headed, curiously happy. Getting out of bed, slipping into her dressing gown, she hurried downstairs to the kitchen, where she received a rapturous greeting from Buster and Cleo, and remembered, with a deep feeling of relief, that this was a Smith-free morning.

The redoubtable Iris, she imagined, would have a fit if she could see her now, improperly dressed, gazing into the Aga to see if it was still functioning as a source of heat; which, thankfully, it was, though it would need stoking and riddling in due course, when she'd exchanged her dressing gown for an old jumper and skirt – of the jumble-sale variety.

Meanwhile, catering to Buster's need of ... self-expression, she bundled him out of doors to commune with nature in the back garden, safe in the knowledge that Cleo could commune with nature whenever she felt so inclined, by means of her cat flap. She filled the kettle for an early morning cuppa and went through to the drawing room to open the curtains and gaze out of the window at the glorious expanse of sea beyond the cliff edge, the whole of Carnelian Bay resembling a watercolour painting by a master hand, touched here and there with white-capped waves beneath a cloud-flecked April sky.

Impossible to believe, on a morning such as this, that she had ever felt remotely nervous of staying alone in Stella Maris. It was such a lovely house. Glancing about her, she noticed the exquisite antique furniture, the peach shaded lamps on the side tables near the fireplace, the comfortable armchairs and sofas, upholstered in a deeper shade of peach velvet which should have clashed with the turquoise curtains and the carpet, but somehow did not. Rather, they enhanced the sheen and patina of the chestnut colours trapped in marquetry of a bygone age, whilst the colour turquoise predominated the room in a painting, over the fireplace, depicting Paris by night; the Arc de Triomphe adumbrated against a sky shading from a clear eggshell blue to a deep glowing turquoise, threaded here and there with shafts of golden light indicating the setting of the sun in that breathlessly held moment in time before darkness fell and the turquoise light faded.

Paris, Lara thought wistfully, which she

felt she knew like the back of her hand from George du Maurier's enchanting novel, *Trilby* – read in her assistant-librarian days, arousing in her a desperate longing to one day visit the city of her dreams; to see with her own eyes Notre Dame, Monmartre, the Sacré Coeur, the Cimetière du Père Lachaise, the Artists' Quarter, the bookstalls on the left bank of the Seine, when she had saved up enough for her fare, and board and lodgings. And she might well have done so had she not married in haste and repented at leisure...

The picture above the drawing-room mantelpiece had reawakened memories of her girlhood days, the thrill of saving a few shillings a week from her wages to achieve what had proved to be an impossible dream in the long run. Charles had utterly refused to travel abroad, and so they had spent their summer holidays in the Lake District, Cromer or Sandsend, in various cheap boarding houses, where the food they ate was every bit as uninspiring as their environment, where the bath water ran tepid, if not cold. Just as long as Charles could champ his way through full English breakfasts and lamb or roast-beef dinners, complaining if the food was not to his liking.

Ah well, all in the past now, Lara reminded herself. So much for her girlhood dreams of one day tucking into steaming bowls of onion soup, baguettes, croissants, or coq-au-vin on the Left Bank of the Seine, in bistros inhabited by students of the Sorbonne intent on feeding themselves as cheaply as possible, according to their means. Whatever they ate secondary to their discussions on art, music or politics, she imagined, ideas, not food, coming uppermost in their minds. Just as ideas, not food, had always come uppermost in her own mind. Even now, despite her recent debilitating illness and her lack of self-confidence, she still longed to visit Paris, her city of dreams – but as what? A middle-aged tourist, a member of a coach party being shown the sights by some smart young courier or other? No, that was unthinkable. She must go to Paris alone, or not at all. In her present circumstances, the latter seemed the greater likelihood. But she could dream, couldn't she?

Never a vain person, she had almost forgotten her new hairstyle. It came as something of a shock when she caught sight of herself in the bathroom mirror. No wonder she felt light-headed, the hairdresser had certainly been to town with his scissors, taking years off her appearance in the process, revealing a natural curl which she'd half forgotten when her hair was scragged back from her face.

Wearing one of her old skirts and a jumper preparatory to doing battle with the Aga, she took a satisfying peep at her new garments in the wardrobe, loving the colours of the jersey-wool suits – one a deep, glowing red, the other moss green – the softness and texture of the lambs-wool sweaters, the tailored skirts, one the colour of autumn leaves, the second charcoal grey, a third checked in muted shades of heather and lilac, carefully chosen to complement the sweaters. Clothes of which Charles would have strongly disapproved, especially the cocktail dress, black, with a cowl neckline sewn with sparkling silver paillettes matching a similar motif at the hemline of the garment. As for the camel-hair coat, Lara had fallen in love with it the moment she had seen it, feeling the warmth and silkiness of the stand-up collar about her face and knotting its belt about her waist.

Even now, she sensed his disapproval in the air about her, as if he was watching her from beyond the grave. Closing the wardrobe door, but that was ridiculous, Lara reminded herself severely, the dead did not come back to haunt the living...

Letting Buster off his lead on the beach below the promenade, she watched him race into the sea in search of the stick she had thrown him, laughing delightedly when he came back to her carrying the stick in his mouth, wagging his tail as he laid it at her feet, beseeching her with his eyes to continue the game, but the wind was cold, and the tide was coming in.

She said affectionately, 'No, that's it for today, old lad. Almost supper time. Besides, look at the state of you, wet through. My fault, I know, but I don't want you catching your death of cold, so it's a good rub down for you, my lad, a good feed and a fresh bowl of water, a strong cup of coffee and a couple of boiled eggs for me. So let's go home, shall we?'

Home, she thought, as they made their way back to Stella Maris. She was beginning to think of it as such, but she mustn't. Stella Maris was not her home, and it never would be. The thought occurred, as she crossed the threshold, that she no longer had a home of her own, that when the summertime was over, she would be returning to her en suite bed-sitting room at the Windsor Hotel.

True to his promise, Rory telephoned her later that evening. Sensing that something was wrong, 'What is it?' she asked concernedly.

He said dejectedly, 'I heard from my solicitor this morning. My divorce will be finalized in six months from now. Meanwhile, I've been granted a decree nisi. Oh God, Lara, I really didn't want this to happen! I'd got it into my head that somehow it wouldn't happen, that Georgie would come back to me, and I'd have welcomed her with open arms, her and the baby...'

'Oh, Rory, I'm so sorry. Is there anything I can do to help?'

He paused momentarily, then, 'Well yes, perhaps there is. I'm due a week's leave. Would you mind very much if I spent it with you, at Stella Maris?'

'No, of course not. I'll be glad of your company.'

'Pretty poor company, I'm afraid.'

'As I told you once before, you don't need to put on an act with me. How soon can you come?'

'Tomorrow afternoon?'

'Yes, that'll be fine with me. I'll make up your bed myself, shop for food in the morning while Iris is buzzing about with her vacuum cleaner. She'll be gone by the time you arrive, thank God.'

'Thanks, Lara,' Rory said huskily. 'See you tomorrow, then?'

'Yes,' Lara replied quietly. 'See you tomorrow.'

The shopping precinct was intriguing, Lara thought, quiet and peaceful, unlike those in the town centre of Middlesbrough from which she had emerged, exhausted, lumbered with plastic carriers, to await the next bus home. Little wonder she had loathed shopping so much, constantly worried lest she had forgotten something of importance necessary to keep her domestic cart on its wheels.

Now, she looked forward to restocking the refrigerator with fresh vegetables, lettuce, tomatoes and cucumber, with lamb chops and dry-cured bacon, sausages and free-range eggs, bearing in mind that Rory would need good food to sustain him.

Catching the scent of freshly baked bread, she entered the bakery to buy a wholemeal loaf, a veal-and-ham pie, a fruit loaf, and an apple tart. From the fishmongers, she purchased a sizeable fillet of haddock, two fillets of plaice and a wing of skate, determined that her house guest should not fade away from lack of sustenance.

Prior to her shopping spree, she had taken Buster for a walk along the prom after bidding Iris Smith a cheerful good morning, to which she'd received the daunting reply, 'What's good about it, I should like to know! An' what the 'ell have you done with your hair? Humph, talk about mutton dressed as lamb!'

To kill time till midday, Lara went into the library, knowing that Iris would leave Stella Maris at twelve o'clock precisely, dragging her plaid shopping trolley behind her.

'Oh, hello, Mrs Davenport,' Amanda Fielding said warmly, looking far too glamorous for a librarian. 'It's good to see you again. How are you settling in Carnelian Bay?' Tilting her head a little to one side, she added, 'There's something different about you. No, don't tell me, let me guess. You've had your hair cut! Very nice it looks too, if you don't mind my saying so.'

'No, as a matter of fact,' Lara replied, 'since someone has just told me I look like mutton dressed as lamb.'

'If you mean Iris Smith,' Amanda said astutely, 'take no notice. That woman's a menace. Never happy unless she's miserable and making everyone else feel miserable too. Mind you, she hasn't much going for her, has she? Not with that feckless husband of hers coming the old-soldier act since he had the good fortune to break a leg in a fall from a ladder in what he's pleased to refer to as an industrial accident, though he shouldn't have been up the ladder in the first place, having been warned it was unsafe. Now he's blaming the hospital for not having set his leg properly; his employers for the state of the ladder. Well, you get the picture? But enough of that. What can I do to help you?'

'I just wondered, have you any information about the history of Carnelian Bay, and

Stella Maris in particular?' Lara asked, wishing the subject of her new hairstyle had not arisen. As if it mattered a damn one way or the other that she had got rid of her bun; beginning to wish that she had not.

'Of course,' Amanda said brightly. 'Everything you need is in the archives. The material isn't for loan, but you are welcome to make use of it as often as you like. Just give me a moment to find the key, and I'll take you through right away.'

'No, another time, if you don't mind,' Lara demurred, glancing at her wristwatch, not wanting to embark on research when she needed time to make up the spare room bed in readiness for Rory's arrival. 'Tomorrow, perhaps, or the day after.'

'Whenever,' Amanda replied charmingly. 'By the way, my husband and I are planning a small drinks party at the weekend. Please say you'll come. I'll be in touch later, shall I?'

'That's very kind of you,' Lara prevaricated, 'but I may be otherwise engaged. Sorry, but I really must go now.'

Rory arrived mid afternoon, looking utterly weary and dejected. Opening the door to him, 'Come in, my dear,' Lara said softly, compassionately. 'Your room is ready and waiting for you, so why not go upstairs and unpack? Meanwhile I'll put the kettle on for a cuppa. Which would you prefer, tea or coffee?'

'Tea would be nice,' he murmured gratefully on his way upstairs. Then, looking down at her from the landing, 'I'm really sorry to burden you with all this, but I didn't know who else to turn to for help. Please forgive me, Lara, for being such a nuisance; imposing myself on you so suddenly.'

He'd been sleeping badly, he explained later over tea and fruit loaf; had been bullied into taking a week off work by his colleagues, Frank Greenall and Ted Ellis. Not that he'd taken much persuading. He grinned wryly. 'Talk about a zombie! I knew they were right in wanting to see the back of me. That's when I thought about Stella Maris – and you. The reason why I'm here, making a damn fool of myself, I daresay. I mean, a grown man in need of tea and sympathy.'

Understanding those needs precisely, Lara said, 'I'm glad you're here, Rory. Now, if I'm not mistaken, Buster's in need of his afternoon constitutional. A breath of sea air will do you both the world of good. So, hop it while I get on with my cooking and spud-bashing, as my dad referred to it. A boring but necessary occupation with a fish pie in mind. Tell me, Rory, when did you last have a good square meal inside you? No, don't tell me, let me guess. Last Sunday at the Golf Club Hotel. So, what have you been living on since then, sandwiches and coffee?'

'Mainly coffee,' he confessed shamefacedly, clipping Buster's lead to its collar. 'And cigarettes.'

'Huh, no wonder you've been sleeping badly,' Lara remarked as he hurried down the front steps with Buster in tow.

They ate supper in the kitchen. 'That fish pie was delicious,' Rory said. 'And may I add how nice you're looking. I like your new hairdo. It does things for you.'

Lara laughed. 'Iris said I looked like mutton dressed as lamb.'

'Ah well, *she* would, wouldn't she? Does she know I'm here, by the way?'

'No.' Lara pulled a face. 'I daren't tell her.'

'Oh lor', does that mean I'll have to go into hiding?'

'You could try, but she'd find you as sure as eggs. Iris has a way of finding things. I daresay she's already had a good look at my new clothes. Heaven only knows what she thought when she saw the cocktail dress, but I'm sure to find out sooner or later.

'By the way, I had a dinner invitation this morning, from a Mrs Fielding, a friend of Joan Prewett, which I managed to avoid accepting. She said she'd be in touch later, but I'm not quite ready for drinks parties at the moment.'

'Oh, Amanda? We have met occasionally. A rather fulsome lady, heavy on the charm; married to a consultant. Joan can't stand her, her husband or their drinks parties.' Rory smiled reflectively. 'But then, Joan can spot a phoney from a mile off, the reason why she liked you so much, because she knew at a glance that you were the real McCoy. So how did you meet the fair Amanda?'

'In the library, the day we came here. Remember, you were feeling tired and went to your room for a lie down? Well, I walked along to the library, and there she was.'

'And I'll bet any money you thought what a nice, charming person.'

'Well yes, I did. I had no reason to think otherwise. I saw her again this morning, as a matter of fact, to find out more about Carnelian Bay and this house in particular and, to be entirely honest, to kill time till twelve o'clock, when I knew that Iris would be on her way home. When Amanda offered me access to the archives, and proffered the drinks invitation, I just mumbled something about being otherwise engaged, and hurried home.'

'Hmmm, and did Iris Smith arise as a topic of conversation? I'd be surprised if she didn't. You see, Amanda and Iris are at daggers drawn because of Iris's husband, who holds Fielding responsible for his present state of immobility. The row has been going on for two years now, and may well continue indefinitely. It's the reason why Joan Prewett engaged Mrs Smith in the first place, because she felt sorry for the woman. Besides which, she's a damn good worker, despite her lack of charm-school qualifications. So, there you have it in a nutshell.'

Rising to his feet to begin the washing-up, Rory added, 'No, you sit down and rest, Lara. Leave the clearing away to me.' She looked tired and strained, he thought, and no wonder. Despite her new hairdo and her improved appearance, she was still in a precarious state of health, in need of kindness and consideration. A pity about her fraught relationship with Iris Smith, and that she had fallen into the clutches of Amanda Fielding, who, having sunk her claws into someone whom she regarded as worth cultivating, seldom let go.

He had seen this happen with Joan Prewett, had once heard Joan mutter, sotto-voce, 'Oh lord, no! The Fielding woman is coming up the path! You answer the bell, Rory. Tell her I'm out, ill, in the bath. Tell her anything, but don't let her in. I'll never get rid of her if you do!'

'Why? What's wrong with her?' he'd asked

on the first occasion he'd been detailed as a bodyguard, faintly amused by Joan's reaction to a visit from a friendly neighbour.

'Because I can't stand humbugs, pseudo-intellectuals, or being bored to the back teeth, that's why!'

Meeting Amanda, Rory had known exactly what Joan meant. Could the woman really be a librarian? She looked more like an ageing chorus girl.

Lara said, when the washing-up was done, the Aga refuelled, and the kitchen curtains had been closed against the deepening shadows of an April evening, 'Thanks, Rory, but there's no need to handle me with kid gloves. I'm not really tired. You're the one in need of rest, remember? And to think I've been sitting here, watching you work, when I could have been helping you with the washing-up.'

'Ah, but *you* did the spud-bashing and cooking, as I recall. So, a fair division of labour, wouldn't you agree?' He smiled. 'Now I'd best take Buster for a stroll along the prom.' Bending down to fondle the creature's ears. 'Yes, I'm talking about you, old son!'

'Would you mind if I came with you?' Lara asked diffidently, not wanting to be a nuisance. 'I could do with a breath of sea air before bedtime.'

'My dear girl, of course not,' Rory assured

her warmly. 'We'd be delighted, wouldn't we, Buster?'

'Then I'll be down in just a minute, if you don't mind waiting.'

Upstairs in her room, Lara ran a comb through her hair and put on her camel-hair coat, turning up the collar and tucking into its neckline the paisley silk scarf the saleslady had talked her into buying to complement the garment, finally knotting its belt about her narrow waistline.

Returning to the kitchen, she said, 'Well, I'm ready! How do I look?'

Filled with admiration for the sheer pluck and spirit of the woman, 'You look absolutely wonderful,' he said. And he meant it, seeing her as the pretty girl she must have been, twenty years ago.

# Six

Never would Lara forget the way she felt that evening, walking beside Rory in her new coat, seeing the lights of Carnelian Bay clustered about the harbour; the riding lights of the fishing vessels heading out to sea; the panoply of stars overhead, as if the pages of time had flicked back and she was young and hopeful once more.

She said softly, as they stood together for a while near a spinney of birches overlooking the promenade, 'I'd half forgotten there was so much beauty in the world, so much – peace.'

Smiling down at her, he said reflectively, 'You know, Lara, it has crossed my mind to leave Middlesbrough after – I mean, when my divorce is finalized. Perhaps the time has come to move on, to make a fresh start, find myself a new job in some quiet country town in the Cotswolds or Wiltshire. What do you think?'

Lara responded thoughtfully, 'I felt the same way when Charles died, when I realized that I couldn't bear to go on living in my so-called marital home a moment longer than necessary. So, yes, I'd go for it if I were you. Just take your time; explore the territory beforehand, don't let circumstances force you into making a hasty decision which you might regret later.'

'You mean that you regret staying on in Middlesbrough?' he asked. 'But I thought you were happily settled in the Windsor Hotel.'

Weighing the pros and cons, attempting to come to terms with her feelings regarding her immediate past, wanting to be entirely truthful with herself and Rory, she said haltingly, 'Had I been physically fit at the time, I'd have shaken the dust of Middlesbrough from my feet and gone on holiday to – Paris. But that just wasn't possible, so I settled for the Windsor Hotel instead.'

Smiling up at him, she continued, 'But you are fit and strong, Rory, in the prime of life, and you should make the most of it: "Gather ye rosebuds while ye may", as the poet Robert Herrick once wrote. I'd take his advice, if I were in your shoes.'

'Thanks, Lara,' Rory said warmly, tucking his hand into the crook of her arm on their way back to Stella Maris. 'By the way, I have an apology to make. About Amanda Fielding. I shouldn't have said what I did about her. It wasn't very gentlemanly of me, and I'm sorry.'

'I don't think you said anything bad about her. You simply expressed an opinion,' Lara replied lightly. 'All you said was, "A rather fulsome lady, heavy on the charm." What's wrong with that?'

'Rather more than that, as I recall,' he said wryly, opening the front door for Lara and Buster, who, having climbed the steps ahead of them, lumbered through to the kitchen for a good drink of water. I shouldn't have brought Iris Smith into the conversation, or that she holds Fielding responsible for her husband's present disability. That was hitting below the belt.'

'Look, Rory,' Lara said patiently. 'I wasn't born yesterday. I, too, can spot a phoney when I meet up with one! I've met up with several in my time, believe it or not. In Middlesbrough, for instance, a next-door neighbour, all pretended sweetness and light, who begged me to join her flower-arranging club because she thought it would do me good to take up a hobby, when I knew all along that what she was really after was a good old pry into my marital affairs. Not to mention those stalwarts of church coffee mornings, jumble sales, and so on, who treated me like dirt because I wasn't one of them, who made it perfectly clear to me, without actually saying so in my hearing, that Charles must have been mad to marry a nonentity like me, after the estimable Freda, his first wife.'

'Oh, Lara, I'm so sorry!'

'What ever for?'

'For reminding you of the past; making you unhappy.'

'*Unhappy*? If that's what you think, forget it! I mean what I say, Rory! Seldom before have I felt happier than I have done today, thanks to you. Shopping and cooking for you; making up your bed; rejoicing in the pleasure of your company.'

Lara was in the kitchen cooking eggs and bacon when Iris came to work next morning. Meeting trouble head on, she said pleasantly, 'I have a house guest. Mr McAllister is staying for a few days. I'm cooking his breakfast.'

'Ha, so you're turning madam's home into a boarding house, are you?' Iris said scathingly. 'Fine goings on, I must say! Next thing you'll be taking it up to him on a tray, I shouldn't wonder.'

'No, not at all. He's out at the moment, taking Buster for a walk on the beach. By the way, I've stripped my bed and sorted the towels ready for the laundry man, to save you the time and trouble.'

Mrs Smith's reaction shocked Lara. Trembling from head to foot, cheeks aflame with anger, 'Well that does it!' she cried in a high-pitched voice. 'If you think I'm staying here a minute longer to be insulted by the likes of you, you've got another think coming! Just who the 'ell do you think you are? You may have tekken over madam's house, but you ain't takin' *me* over, no sir! I'm leavin' right now, an' I shall be wantin' a month's wages in lieu of notice, think on!'

Rory, who had entered the hall unnoticed and had heard the woman's outburst, said firmly, standing near the kitchen door behind the irate Iris, 'But you haven't been given notice, have you? You're quitting your job of your own accord.'

Startled, Iris turned to face him. 'Oh, trust you to take her side,' she screeched hoarsely. 'An' just how long have you been standing there, eavesdropping? Creeping about the place as if you owned it! Well you don't own it, an' neither does *she*!'

'My dear Mrs Smith,' Rory reminded her. 'If I owned the place, I'd scarcely be creeping about in it, would I? As for Mrs Davenport, you seem to forget that she is acting on Mrs Prewett's behalf in taking care of the house and has every right to be here. As for "insulting" you, I fail to understand your reasoning. How could stripping her bed and making up a bag of washing ready for the laundry possibly be construed as an insult?'

'Cos she's had it in for me ever since she came here,' Iris retorted wildly. 'Accusing me of spying an' such like. Poking her nose into my business; callin' me dishonest!'

Pushing aside the frying pan before the contents burnt black, 'That simply isn't true,' Lara protested, close to tears of frustration. 'But what's the use?'

'Oh, that's right, turn on the waterworks,' Iris uttered fiercely. 'But tears won't wash with me! The world's full of silly, rich bitches like you an' that Amanda Fielding, though you dress poorer than most, despite a wardrobe stuffed with posh clothes, bought with your fancy man in mind, I shouldn't wonder!'

'All right, Iris,' Rory said levelly. 'That's quite enough! Just take your trolley and your overall, and leave as quickly as possible. Your own choice, remember?' He smiled grimly. 'Apart from "silly, rich bitches", the world, I imagine, is also full of part-time cleaners such as yourself. Hopefully far better mannered!'

When she had gone, 'I'm so sorry, Lara,' Rory said concernedly. 'But I suppose it was bound to happen sooner or later and, to be honest, I'm rather pleased that it has; that I was here to lend you my help and support, for what it's worth.'

Drawing in a deep breath, squaring her shoulders and brushing aside her tears, Lara said, unexpectedly, 'Might as well ditch this lot,' shovelling the ruined breakfast into the pedal bin near the Aga, to Buster's distress, who would have gladly eaten a kizzened egg and two rashers of bacon, given the chance. 'So let's settle for toast and marmalade, shall we?'

Within a short space of time, after Iris's hasty departure, Lara learned more about where things were kept than she had done since she had come to Stella Maris. Information Mrs Smith might have given her had she dared ask without being made to feel like an interloper by that touchy guardian of the vacuum cleaner.

At least she knew the whereabouts of that particular household appliance – in the cupboard under the stairs. 'You know, Rory,' she said, trundling it into the hall. 'Until now I've felt like a guest in a luxury hotel, or that girl in Daphne Du Maurier's *Rebecca*, scarcely daring to make a move, with Mrs Danvers breathing down her neck, waiting to pounce. Apart from my own room, the kitchen and the drawing room, there are rooms I've never been in or looked at closely, simply glimpsed when Joan showed me round the house the first time I came here.'

Rory laughed. 'Here, let me give you a hand with that,' he said. 'But surely you're not thinking of vacuuming, are you?'

'Why not? Someone's got to do it. Thank God it's an upright model, not one of those cylinder thingies – all buzz and no suck!'

'Even so, this is a big house, and I don't want you tired out attempting the impossible. Now that Iris and her trolley have disappeared into the wild yonder, the sooner we advertise for a replacement, the better, wouldn't you agree?'

'No, Rory. I'm sorry but I'd like to get to know the house better, if that makes sense. Realistically, how could I explain her duties to a stranger? Seemingly silly unimportant things – where the cleaning materials are kept, and so on – when I don't know myself?'

'Yes, I see what you mean, and you are right,' he conceded thoughtfully. 'Perhaps I could help?' He smiled encouragingly. 'Let's go on a voyage of discovery, shall we?'

'Oh yes, let's do just that,' Lara replied happily, with a deep inner feeling of relief that she had seen the back of a woman whose presence in the house had hung over her like a cloud.

Switching on a light in the cupboard under the stairs, squinting inside, Rory exclaimed boyishly, 'Ha-ha! Success! Cleaning materials all present and correct! Come and take a look! Cans of spray-on furniture polish, bottles of washing-up liquid, boxes of Brillo pads, silver polish, carpet shampoo, bin liners, masses of dusters and Jay Cloths; not to mention buckets and mops. A veritable Aladdin's Cave of household treasures. That wretched Mrs Smith should have shown you! I'm sure that was Joan's intention when she asked her to meet you on the day of your arrival. Not simply to hand over the keys and explain the workings of the Aga.'

'Yes, I'm sure you're right,' Lara replied hesitantly. 'Oh, Rory, what if Iris has a set of keys to the house?'

'Damn! I should have thought of that.' Rory frowned. 'But not to worry, I'll see about it.' He smiled. 'You really love Stella Maris, don't you? A pity it has been altered so drastically in recent years, but modernization is the name of the game nowadays. I'd give anything to see it the way it was when old Joshua Stonehouse brought his family to live here, way back in the late 1800s,' changing the subject to take Lara's mind off the keys.

'Please, go on. Tell me more.' Lara perched on the second step of the stairs, Rory beside her.

'This was the first house to be built here, on this strip of land. The other five followed in due course, though I daresay old Joshua fought tooth and nail against further development of his territory, or what he regarded as such.

'Doubtless he, his wife and two daughters arrived by horse-drawn carriage to take

95

possession of Stella Maris, accompanied by a small retinue of servants, almost certainly a cook, lady's maids and a manservant. More than likely, women from the village came in to do the washing, ironing and cleaning, what was known as the "rough".' He grinned. 'Victorian counterparts of Iris Smith. Mind you, the cook would rule the roost in the kitchen, the helpers would have to toe the line, or else! I'll bet any money she was a very large lady, guarding her territory as jealously as Iris guarded the cupboard under the stairs.'

Lara saw it all in her mind's eye as clearly as if she had been there at the time: the black-leaded kitchen range, the well-scrubbed table on which the food was prepared; stone sinks and wooden draining boards; gleaming copper pans; household china, plates, meat dishes and tureens arrayed on a Welsh dresser.

'Is there a dining room?' Lara asked. 'I've only used the kitchen so far. It just occurred to me that you might like to dine in state this evening.'

Rory laughed. 'No thanks, I'm quite at home in the kitchen. It's nice and warm near the Aga. In any case, there isn't a dining room as such. Joan does her entertaining, as and when necessary, in what she calls the conservatory. Come, I'll show you.'

He led the way to what had once been the

dining room, behind the door of which lay a passage leading to a small room with a bay window, used by Joan as a winter retreat where she could cosy-up to the fire, read or listen to music. Next door to this was a modern cloakroom, at the end of the passage was the conservatory, a room filled to overflowing with pot plants, trailing ivy and other vegetation, with cane basket chairs and a long marble side table on which, Rory explained, buffet food was set out when Joan felt it necessary to proffer hospitality to the vicar and his wife and members of the Church Council, the choir and ladies of the flower arranging group in an atmosphere lacking formality, which she loathed and detested. Joan disliked formality intensely, he recalled.

'The marble side table was a feature of the original dining room,' Rory said, 'from which the footman served the food, I imagine, when the Stonehouses had dinner guests or weekend visitors. They entertained quite lavishly according to the account books of that era. You name it: ducks, geese, capons, salmon, lobsters, venison, beef, pork, lamb, not to mention champagne and caviar; a far cry from Joan's informal buffet parties. I'm surprised she didn't introduce you to what she refers to as her "inner sanctum" on your first visit. I wonder why not?'

Lara said quickly, 'She probably did, but I was too confused at the time to notice,' blaming herself, not Joan, knowing that the woman had not been feeling at all well that day, despite her brave attempts to appear her usual happy-go-lucky self in Rory's presence.

'Yes, I guess you're right,' he acknowledged. 'By the way, these plants look a bit droopy to me, in need of watering, wouldn't you say? You hang on here a sec. I'll nip through to the kitchen to fetch some water. Joan'll have a fit if she comes home to find her beloved plants have perished for the want of a bit of tender, loving care.'

Alone in the conservatory, which, to her certain knowledge, Lara had never seen before, she sensed a presence in the room. Possibly that of a young footman carefully placing tureens of vegetables on the marble-topped side table, scared of losing his employment if, perchance, a stray sprout, escaping from a tureen, rolled across the dinner table and ended up in a lady's lap, recalling that a similar occurrence had once happened to herself, in the Middlesbrough house, when, hands shaking with nervous tension, she had carelessly let go of a brimming gravy boat, the contents of which had dripped relentlessly into the lap of the minister's wife.

Coldly angry, after that disastrous dinner

party, Charles had accused Lara of deliber-
ately wanting to show him up in front of his
friends and colleagues, calling her clumsy,
inept and malicious, a poor housekeeper, a
brainless idiot, and a rotten cook into the
bargain, reducing her to tears of despair,
knowing that none of the things he said was
true. Clumsy, well, yes, perhaps there was a
grain of truth in that, but malicious? A
brainless idiot, a poor housekeeper, a rotten
cook? To add insult to injury, he had then
referred, in glowing terms, to his first wife,
Freda, a splendid housekeeper, hostess and
cook, who would never have dreamt of
serving half-cooked meat and vegetables to
their guests, much less have spilt gravy into
the lap of the Reverend Claude Grayson's
wife, to the ruination of the woman's evening dress finery and the distress of her
husband, whose decision to return her to
The Manse as quickly as possible had virtually put paid to that ghastly dinner party,
when the other guests had also drifted away
in view of the gravy-soaked tablecloth, the
al-dente vegetables and the undercooked
roast leg of lamb which she, Lara, had
provided for the meal.

Little wonder that Charles had been so
angry with her, Lara considered ruefully,
awaiting Rory's return to the conservatory
with the water. But Charles was dead and
gone now, the past behind her. Or was it? If

99

so, why the gut feeling that she had been here before, in Stella Maris, long before its present-day modernization, when a black-leaded kitchen range had occupied the space now allotted to an Aga cooker? Why her feeling of affinity with a long-dead-and-gone young footman who had once waited on table in the original dining room.

The thought occurred that she was still not as well as she had imagined herself or pretended to be, that her mind was playing tricks on her. But no, she reminded herself sharply, that could not possibly be true. Any minute now, Rory would return from the kitchen with a bucket of water to revive the drooping plants in Joan Prewett's conservatory, and everything would be back to normal. And yet...

On Rory's return, she asked curiously, 'About those account books you mentioned, of the Victorian era, how did you come across them?'

'Oh? I didn't, Joan did, in one of the attics, in an old cabin trunk, I believe,' Rory replied, assiduously watering her plants.

'What happened to that trunk?' Lara insisted.

'Huh?' Rory straightened his back. 'It's still up there, so far as I know. For some reason, Joan took a dislike to the attics; said they gave her the creeps. Not that there was anything sinister about them. In fact, the architect responsible for modernizing the dining-room – this area – had suggested knocking the three attics into one to create a kind of studio flat to add value to the property. But Joan wouldn't hear of it. She simply stowed away, up there, surplus furniture from her Leeds home, locked the landing door and virtually threw away the key.' He frowned slightly. 'Why the sudden interest? We can go up and take a scout round, if you like, seeing we're on a voyage of discovery.'

'No, I'd rather not, if you don't mind.' Glancing at her wristwatch: 'It's time for elevenses. High time Buster went out for a walk to relieve his feelings. Will you take him, or shall I?'

Rory laughed. 'Gosh, is that the time?' Glancing at his own watch: 'A quarter past eleven already! Poor old Buster! Anyway, the plants are well and truly watered, so I'll take him for a short walk on a long lead, meanwhile, you make the coffee, and I'll be back to drink it in two shakes.'

When he had gone, filling the kettle, Lara thought about that cabin trunk and wondered what else it might contain.

Cursing himself inwardly for not ensuring the return of the front door key from Iris Smith before she marched, head-in-air, down the steps, muttering threats – saying that if 'that woman' – meaning Lara – thought she'd got the better of her, she had another think coming – Rory decided to pay Iris a visit that afternoon to settle the matter of the key and to warn her against more troublemaking.

The last thing he wanted was for Lara to feel threatened or insecure in any way. He'd have the locks changed, if necessary, as a safety precaution, before his return to Middlesbrough.

Explaining his mission to Lara, over coffee, to his surprise she elected to go with him, after lunch, to confront the redoubtable Iris. A brave decision on her part, considering Mrs Smith's scarcely concealed enmity towards her.

'There's really no need,' Rory said gently, wanting to spare her the trauma of what might prove to be a slanging match, to put it mildly.

Lara replied wistfully, 'No need to at least try to convince Iris that I was never her enemy? Frankly, Rory, I'm just beginning to realize that, had I been more forceful, less cowardly from the outset, this situation might never have arisen in the first place. So, I'm coming with you this afternoon, whether you want me to or not!'

# Seven

The Cramer Industrial and Housing Estate lay three miles inland from Carnelian Bay, a sprawling, ugly development cheek-by-jowl with a football stadium, garages, super-markets whose windows were plastered with cut-price posters, an ambulance station, several modern pubs advertising bar snacks, a fish-and-chip shop and a bookies'.

Dispirited-looking women stood in bus shelters, drably dressed and lumbered with plastic shopping bags, reminding Lara of herself in her Middlesbrough days. Now she regretted wearing her new camel-hair coat to visit the Smiths' house – one of a maze of pebble-dashed semis in criss crossing streets beyond the main thoroughfare – with narrow paths leading to violently coloured front doors, neglected front gardens, and net-curtained windows as a means of con-cealment from the prying eyes of the nosy neighbours across the way; or so she pre-sumed, disliking the set-up intensely. Soul-destroying, to put it mildly.

As if reading her mind, Rory said, 'You'd

best wait here in the car, Lara. Leave me to tackle the lioness in her den.'

'Thanks, Rory, but I'm not about to take the coward's way out. Mrs Smith's quarrel is with me, not you! How do you think I'd feel allowing you to shoulder the blame for a situation that is all my fault?'

'Very well then,' he conceded patiently. 'Have it your way. But you may well be in for a rough ride, and the last thing I want is to see you hurt or upset in any way in confrontation with a woman of Iris Smith's mentality on her own territory! Think about it, Lara! She'll eat you alive, I shouldn't wonder!'

Getting out of the car, squaring her shoulders, determined to stand her ground, 'Well, let's see, shall we?' Lara said, pushing open the gate leading to the Smiths' front door.

Rory rang the doorbell. Seconds later, a rough-looking man sporting a two-day's growth of stubble, leaning heavily on a walking stick, dressed in a collarless flannel shirt, trousers upheld with braces, and wearing carpet slippers, appeared on the doorstep.

'Mr Smith?' Rory enquired politely.

'Yeah, so what if I am? Who the 'ell are you, an' whaddayou want?' he asked suspiciously.

'A word with your wife, if you don't mind,' Rory replied pleasantly. 'My name is McAl-

104

lister, and this is a friend of mine, Mrs Davenport.

'*What*? Well, you've got a nerve an' no mistake! Comin' 'ere as large as life after what you done to my missis! Come 'ome cryin' 'er eyes out, she did, after you'd given her the sack! Now she's gone out shopping, so you'd best clear off, the pair of you!'

'Without her trolley?' Lara frowned, catching sight of it in the narrow hallway.

The kitchen door opened suddenly. Iris marched out, eyes blazing. 'Oh, get back to the telly, Fred,' she uttered scornfully, 'an' leave this to me! I have a score to settle with these two; especially with *her*.' Glaring at Lara: 'A bit of a jumped-up nobody, givin' me orders; callin' me a thief an' a liar, or as good as. Sacking me for no good reason 'cept that I knew too much about her an' her "fancy man".

'Huh, no wonder you wanted me out of the way in a hurry, my fine lady, when I sussed what was going on between you an' *him*! Well, I call it damn well disgusting, a woman of your age carrying on under madam's roof. So why have you come 'ere, the pair of you? Come to ask me to go easy on you? Is that it? If so, you're wasting your time!'

Lara said quietly, 'No, Mrs Smith, I simply came here to collect the key to Mrs Prewett's property, which you neglected to return to me when you left Stella Maris so abruptly this morning!'

'Oh, is *that* all?' Fiddling in her overall pocket, Iris handed over the key, smiling nastily as she did so.

Lara said levelly, 'Well, not *quite* all, I'm afraid. You see, if you persist in spreading scurrilous rumours regarding my friendship with Mr McAllister, I shall not hesitate to consult a solicitor. Defamation of character is a serious offence. Do I make myself clear?'

'Oh, lah-di-dah,' Iris scoffed. 'You could give it a try, I suppose, but it'd be your word against mine. I'm entitled to an opinion, an' it's my opinion that you an' him 'ave been up to no good. Huh! Why else would you 'ave bought all them fakey new clothes an' had a tarty hairdo into the bargain? I weren't born yesterday, think on.'

'Then stop fantasizing and face facts,' Rory said brusquely, worried that Lara was feeling the strain of the encounter. 'Everything you've said so far is totally untrue, a figment of your warped imagination. Obviously you derive satisfaction from hurting others, Mrs Davenport in particular. Prompted by what, I wonder? Could it be jealousy?'

'Please don't, Rory,' Lara beseeched him. 'We've got what we came for, the key to Stella Maris. Let's leave it at that, shall we?

I'd like to go home now.'

'Yes, of course.' Tucking his hand into the crook of her elbow, Rory led her back to the car.

Iris called after them, her voice high-pitched with a kind of volatile excitement expressive of her unbalanced state of mind, *'Home?* But Stella Maris ain't your home, is it? You're nowt but a jumped-up nobody who pinched a job that should've been mine by right, if you 'adn't stuck your nose in where it didn't bloody well belong!'

In the car, Rory said apologetically, 'I'm so sorry, Lara. I'd have given anything to have spared you the past half hour.'

Shivering slightly as he nosed the bonnet of the car away from the Cramer Estate, 'You mustn't blame yourself,' Lara said thoughtfully. 'Truth to tell, I can't help feeling sorry for the Iris Smiths of this world, waking up every morning with nothing more to look forward to than a soul-destroying round of cooking, cleaning and shopping. And I should know, having been there myself, remember? The difference being that my marital home hadn't a purple front door, pebble-dashed walls, or a weedy front garden. Oh no, far from. Nevertheless, I awoke each and every morning with a feeling of imprisonment, a sense of dread of the day ahead, lest I failed to live up to my husband's expectations of me as – a jack of all trades – which I did, all too often, I'm afraid.'

'I know, Lara, and I'm truly sorry. But the past is over and done with now,' Rory reminded her gently, heading the car towards Carnelian Bay, and Stella Maris – if not her permanent, at least her spiritual home for the time being – as if she somehow belonged there, as if she had lived there before, in another age, another century, perhaps? A bloody crazy notion if ever there was one. Even so, had he really seen, or imagined he had seen, the ghostly outline of a man, in uniform, standing near the drawing-room window that day he had first come to Stella Maris with Lara, to help her to settle into her new surroundings.

Later, wanting to take Lara's mind off the bizarre events of the day, Rory suggested having an early dinner at the Golf Club Hotel, before the dining room filled up with 'nineteenth holers' from the cocktail bar, further suggesting that she might wear one of her new jersey-wool suits; pleased by her warm response to his invitation.

Seated at a table overlooking the links, wearing the mulberry suit, feeling happy and relaxed in his company, Lara noticed the appearance of the first star of evening above the treetops, glad of the companionable silence between them.

Aware of Lara's need for contemplation, peace of mind after a long, difficult day, glancing at her across the table with its pink-shaded lamps, he thought how well she had handled her confrontation with Iris Smith, how pretty and youthful she looked in her new suit, a far cry from the downtrodden woman he had first encountered on the doorstep of that semi-detached villa in Middlesbrough after the death of her husband, when she had appeared to him as a plain, nerve-ridden wreck, too scared to say boo to a goose.

Now, against all the odds, she had begun to emerge as a person in her own right since her occupancy of Stella Maris. Even so, he could not help wondering what would happen to her on Joan Prewett's return from New York, when she would be called upon to carve out a new future for herself. Would she return to the Windsor Hotel, or venture further afield?

It also occurred to Rory to wonder how she would manage on her own, in a few days from now, when his leave of absence was over and he must, albeit reluctantly, return to his desk at Greenall and Ellis's Estate Agency.

In one sense he was glad the rumpus with Iris had erupted before he went away, that he had been present to help and support

Lara when she had needed a male presence in her life. Even so, he felt a sense of unease regarding Iris. Difficult to pinpoint, to do with handing over the key, the malicious smile on her narrow lips as she had done so. Anticipating a storm of protest, he'd felt suspicious of her compliance, so at odds with her usual vitriolic verbal outbursts. Or was he letting his imagination run away with him?

They had dined simply, but well, he on steak, spring vegetables and minted new potatoes, Lara on grilled plaice and a green salad with a vinaigrette dressing. About to ask her if she would prefer ice cream or a more substantial dessert, his question remained in mid-air as the dining-room door opened suddenly to admit, of all people, Amanda Fielding, her husband and a gaggle of their friends from the cocktail bar, in search of a window table.

'Oh God, no,' he uttered despairingly, keeping his head down, perusing the menu, praying to heaven that Amanda hadn't spotted himself and Lara dining together. In vain. Uttering a high-pitched cry of pleasure, sailing towards them, hands extended, breaking in on their privacy, Amanda called out, 'Well, what a pleasant surprise! How lovely to see you again, Rory. You too, Lara! You simply *must* join our table! I refuse to take no for an answer!'

Rising courteously to his feet, Rory said pleasantly but firmly. 'Thank you so much, Amanda, but Mrs Davenport and I have already eaten. Another time, perhaps?' Then, taking Lara's elbow, he escorted her from the room, aware of Amanda's muttered remark, 'Well, really!' – knowing he had deeply offended the woman.

Outside, in the fresh air, he said apologetically, 'I'm sorry, Lara! The simple truth is, I couldn't have borne a minute longer in the company of Amanda, much less her friends. There's something about that woman that sets my teeth on edge. Even so, I shouldn't have dragged you away so abruptly, without a by your leave! For all I knew, you might have enjoyed finishing your meal in the company of Mrs Fielding and her entourage.'

'By the same token, pigs might fly,' Lara assured him, tongue-in-cheek. 'So, let's go home now, shall we? You take Buster for a walk, meanwhile I'll make a pot of coffee. Don't know about you, but I'm more than ready to call it a day. An odd kind of day one way and another, wouldn't you say?'

When Rory had gone off with Buster, Lara filled the kettle, poured Cleo a saucer of milk, and went to the pantry to fetch tins of dog and cat food, Cleo purring about her ankles as she did so.

In the pantry, aware of a draught of cool night air on her face, startled, Lara noticed that the pantry window, usually closed and latched, had been partially opened. Heart pounding, she closed it and pressed home the latch. As a further precaution, she locked the pantry door behind her. But what about other windows in the downstairs rooms? Hardly likely an intruder would be deterred by a locked pantry door.

On his return, Rory said grimly, 'No need to worry unduly. Apart from the pantry, all the windows are fitted with burglar alarms. Joan saw to that. I'm surprised she didn't tell you. Unlike her not to have done so, not to have put your mind at rest regarding security.' He sounded angry, upset.

Lara said placatingly, 'She had a lot on her mind at the time and, let's face it, everything was done in a hurry; my taking over here, I mean!'

'Yes, of course. I'm sorry.' He smiled. 'I'm feeling a bit on edge, that's all, having made a damn fool of myself one way and another, being rude to Amanda, hustling you out of the dining room the way I did, behaving like a teenager rather than a responsible adult. Huh, no wonder Georgina wanted rid of me!'

'Don't be too hard on yourself,' Lara said softly. 'We all say and do things we regret later. What happened in the dining room wasn't your fault entirely. Amanda should have known better than to approach you – us – so blatantly. I daresay she'd had a drop too much to drink, that she has forgotten all about it now, in the company of her friends.'

She paused. 'But there's more to it than that, isn't there? It's Georgina you're really worried about, not Amanda; feeling yourself to blame for the breakdown of your marriage. But you could be wrong about that, just as I was wrong about the breakdown of mine. I couldn't see it at the time, but I can now, thanks to you, and Stella Maris.

'Coming here is the best thing that has ever happened to me: gaining a whole new aspect on life, thinking in terms of the future, not the past, beginning to feel happy once more. Oh, not all the time, that isn't possible. No one feels happy all the time, there'd be something wrong with them if they did. Perhaps I'm mistaking happiness for hope? Hope of future happiness? Something warm and comforting to cling to, far removed from past failures and despair. If only you felt that way too, Rory. I'd give anything in the world to blot out the past for you as you have succeeded in blotting out mine.' She smiled wistfully. 'Well, almost, at any rate.'

He replied truthfully, 'What's really

bothering me is the thought of returning to Middlesbrough, leaving you here alone to fend for yourself, being denied the pleasure of your company.'

'In which case,' Lara said, 'you'd best spend your weekends here, at Stella Maris, to keep an eye on me, Buster and Cleo, for the forseeable future, to help with the shopping, cleaning and cooking. Can you cook, by the way?'

'No. But I'm willing to learn.'

'Fair enough! Now, I'm dog-tired, so are you. So goodnight, Rory. See you in the morning.'

Going upstairs to her room, Lara wondered if there was a seed of truth in Iris Smith's allegations of a romantic liaison between herself and Rory McAllister. No, of course not, she told herself severely, and yet she knew, in her heart of hearts, that their friendship was fast developing into something deeper – dependancy, for want of a better description – understandable under the circumstances, her dependance on Rory's comforting presence in her life and vice-versa. Even so, the day would come when they must face their separate futures alone.

Next morning, a letter addressed to Lara landed on the doormat. Joan Prewett had written briefly to say she was having a marvellous time in New York. Her flight had gone smoothly, her son-in-law had met her at the airport and driven her to the family home in Greenwich Village, where she had received a rapturous welcome from her daughter and grandchildren.

She was feeling well, happy and relaxed; had been sightseeing and shopping, buying lots of new clothes, and presents for her family; spending money hand-over-fist; at the same time missing Buster and Cleo, not to mention Stella Maris. She'd ended the letter with the words: 'I can't thank you enough, Lara, for making this trip possible for me; for your understanding and discretion in a sensitive situation. Yours gratefully, Joan'.

Reading the letter, which Lara had handed to him across the breakfast table, Rory said, frowning slightly, 'In a sensitive situation? What "sensitive situation"?'

'My taking on Stella Maris at such short notice, I imagine,' Lara responded quickly, light-heartedly. 'More coffee, by the way?'

'Later, perhaps,' he said, handing back the letter. 'When I've seen to the Aga and taken Buster for his constitutional.'

Suddenly, the doorbell rang. 'That'll be the laundry man,' Lara guessed correctly, 'come for last week's money. Spot on, as usual!' At least, she thought, with a deep feeling of relief, this Friday morning had not included the daunting presence of Iris Smith and her buzzing vacuum cleaner.

From now on, Lara had decided, she would derive infinite pleasure from cleaning Stella Maris herself; dusting and polishing furniture, cleaning silver, washing paintwork, stripping and remaking her own bed, and Rory's, and, after his departure on Sunday afternoon, cleaning and re-stoking the Aga, exercizing Buster, shopping for food to replenish the pantry and the refrigerator; cooking simple meals for herself; watering plants – in short, fulfilling her role as a housekeeper, harking back to her Middlesbrough days. The difference being that now, blessedly, there would be no one to please but herself. Not even Rory. But how much she would miss him when he had gone.

To be on the safe side, Rory had shown Lara where the burglar alarm was situated and explained that an alarm call would be conveyed automatically to the local police station and acted on without delay.

He'd slept badly last night, worrying about that open pantry window, his return to Middlesbrough the day after tomorrow, about Georgina, whose baby was due any time now, praying to God that her new partner would take care of her and the child. Poor Georgie. Little more than a child herself, slightly built and emotionally immature, she might well resent being saddled with an infant which would effectively put paid to her butterfly approach to life. Unable to support the restraining bonds of a mortgage, how would she support the restraining bonds of a baby?

None of his business now, he thought bitterly, since his marriage to Georgie was virtually over and done with. Even so, memories of their wedding day, when she had drifted down the aisle towards him, a vision of loveliness in a white satin gown, a diaphanous veil, and carrying a bouquet of Madonna lilies, remained indestructible. Loving her as much as he had done then, never for one moment had he envisaged the shocking conclusion of what he had imagined to be a lifelong relationship with the woman he loved.

Of course, he was jealous, bitterly resentful of the man who had superceded him in Georgina's life, the reason why, perhaps, he felt safe and secure in the company of more mature women – Joan Prewett and Lara Davenport, for instance. And yet he regarded them differently. Joan, he'd realized, attempting to come to terms with his mixed emotions during a sleepless night, had never come as close to him as Lara had done. Lara, his Funny-Valentine friend who had somehow, despite her own deep-seated emotional problems, managed to imbue his own life with a new sense of purpose, who had extended a hand of friendship in inviting him to Stella Maris to feed, cosset and care for him, when he had stood in dire need of being cared for.

On Friday afternoon, Lara said quietly, not beating about the bush, 'Look, Rory, I have books to return to the library. Why not come with me? Meet Amanda Fielding face to face? Buy her a bunch of flowers? Make your peace with her? Meanwhile, I'll push off to attend evensong, as you once suggested, remember?'

Rory laughed. 'OK, Lara, you win! What kind of flowers, by the way?'

'How about daffodils?' Lara replied, tongue-in-cheek. 'Since they appear to be the "in thing" at the moment.'

'But what the hell shall I say to Amanda?'

'Oh, *that*.' Lara frowned momentarily. 'Just tell her that I was in need of a breath of fresh air.'

Lara had really enjoyed evensong; the dimly lit church, the minister's words, the renewed sense of belonging to her former Church of England religion, so long denied her by Charles's adherence to his own, far stricter religious beliefs including penury and self-denial. Comfort lay in the well-known order of service, the familiar texts and prayers, a kind of spiritual refreshment.

Emerging from the church, she found Rory waiting for her. 'How did it go with Amanda?' she asked, falling into step beside him. He pulled a face. 'Rather too well,' he admitted ruefully. 'I'm afraid she talked me into one of her drinks parties.'

'Oh lord. When?'

'Tomorrow evening. Sorry, Lara, I said we'd go. Hadn't much choice, had I? Not after an apology and three bunches of daffs. I did say we couldn't stay long because of Buster. Oh, blast the woman and her parties! Why doesn't she have an early night once in a while?'

Lara smiled. She said discerningly, 'And waste her sweetness on the desert air? Women like Amanda need to be seen and admired, the centre of attention, to show off their clothes and jewellery, I imagine; their homes and their possessions.' She added teasingly, 'You must admit, Rory, that she's a very attractive woman, a bit like one of those old Hollywood movie stars: glamour personified, not a hair nor an eyelash out of place.'

He said, 'She certainly doesn't look like my idea of a librarian. Know what I'd really like now? A fish supper from a chippie near the harbour; haddock and chips tangy with salt and vinegar, eaten outdoors, with our fingers, direct from the parcels; sitting on a wall overlooking the sea. How about you?'

'I can think of nothing I'd like better,' she replied happily.

It was a magical evening, cool but not cold. Lights from the quayside glimmered down into the harbour and gleamed on cobblestones, wet after a brief April shower. Narrow streets winding up from the harbour were lined with picturesque, pantiled cottages. There were lighted windows bespeaking warm interiors, families busy about their daily lives, the homeliness of a closely-knit community, of the kind she, Lara, had known in her childhood.

The fish shop, strategically sited on a street corner, obviously a mecca for the fishermen's wives queueing up for their Friday-night suppers, was redolent with the scent of cod and haddock cooking, hot steam and bubbling fat, vinegar and mushy peas. Joining the queue, when their turn came, Rory ordered haddock and chips for two, to take out, and they walked along the jetty to eat them, laughing like teenagers, revelling in a sense of freedom, hearing the slap of the tide against the harbour wall, the creaking of the cobles moored alongside as they rose and fell gently to the movement of the water beneath their keels.

Glancing up at the sky, Lara saw that it

was littered with stars, and knew that no matter what the future might hold in store for her, she would never forget tonight.

# Eight

Opening the front door, Amanda appeared on the threshold in a red and gold kaftan, numerous gold chains, bracelets and dangling gold earrings, exuding an overpoweringly musky perfume, and swaying slightly on high-heeled sandals. At least in the library she wore tailored suits and little jewellery, Lara thought.

Resting her hands on Rory's shoulders, to his intense embarrassment, she kissed him full on the lips before turning her attention to Lara, who instinctively moved away slightly from the woman's embrace, realizing that she had already drunk more than was good for her, and beginning to wish, with all her heart, that Rory had turned down Amanda's party invitation. Too late now, and how could she possibly blame Rory since it had been her own idea that he should make his peace with her?

A high price to pay, she thought ruefully, for three bunches of daffodils.

The Fieldings' house, of the same vintage as Stella Maris, had been more blatantly modernized to include an open-plan stair-case totally out of character with the age of the building, and sliding glass doors to separate the drawing room from the kitchen. Obviously designed with partying in mind, what Amanda termed 'the lounge' had a built-in cocktail bar, a bewildering number of settees, armchairs and occasional tables. There were also modernistic table lamps with conical orange shades, cubist paintings on the walls, Lara noticed enter-ing the room, no soft edges anywhere. Feel-ing out of place in so alien an atmosphere, longing for the charm and quietude of Stella Maris, she wondered how long she could survive the thump-thumping of the back-ground music, the high-pitched voices of her fellow guests, their inane chatter and laughter, before running for home.

The situation worsened when Amanda, drawing her towards the bar, asked in a loud voice what she'd have to drink. 'Gin, vodka, whisky?'

'Orange juice, please,' Lara replied.

*'Orange juice?* You have to be joking! This is a drinks party, for God's sake, not a church social. For heaven's sake, woman, loosen up. Have you signed the pledge by any chance?' Insulting words uttered carelessly by an

insensitive woman who had already drunk far more than was good for her; meant as a joke, Lara realized, aware that Rory, who was standing beside her, grim-faced and angry, regarded Amanda's remarks in a more serious light, as an intolerable breach of good manners towards a guest beneath her roof, and seemed likely to say so in no uncertain terms, adding to the tension of this ghastly occasion.

Laying a restraining hand on Rory's arm, glancing up at him beseechingly, she said quietly to Amanda, 'No, nothing so dramatic as signing the pledge; I just happen to be taking medicine, which prohibits my consumption of alcohol, hence my request for orange juice, though mineral water would do just as well.'

Rory had never admired Lara more than he did at that moment, lying through her teeth to prevent him making a damn fool of himself in a roomful of gawping strangers, knowing full well that she had recently consigned her various pills and potions to her bathroom lavatory – sleeping pills, pep pills, aspirin, the whole bang-shoot – born of her determination to get well in her own way, as a free spirit, not a drug addict. An addiction to which she had now confessed to explain her preference for – orange juice. More importantly, to allay his strong desire to shake Amanda Fielding until her teeth rattled.

A slightly built man, bespectacled, with greying hair, had moved closer to the bar. He said coolly, 'Not everyone possesses my wife's capacity for alcohol, myself included. I am Mark Fielding, by the way. Now, Mrs Davenport, would you prefer your orange juice neat, or with ice?'

Glaring at her husband, having received what amounted to a verbal slap in the eye, Amanda shrugged her shoulders dismissively and turned her attention to handing round nibbles to her less inhibited guests, laughing loudly and swaying tipsily as she did so, making a spectacle of herself, Lara thought regretfully, feeling sorry for the woman's frantic desire to be the centre of attention, the life and soul of the party, her joie de vivre no longer fuelled by youth, but alcohol. Tears filled her eyes.

She murmured apologetically, 'I'm sorry, Mr Fielding, I'm not quite up to socializing for the time being, I'm afraid. Please forgive me.'

'My dear lady, there's nothing to forgive,' Mark assured her gently. 'I am, after all, a member of the medical profession, and my best advice to you is to forget about socializing, to return home, and to get a good night's sleep.' He smiled charmingly. 'Things will look a whole lot better in the morning.'

Rory interposed gratefully, 'Thank you, Mr Fielding. Now, with your permission, Mrs Davenport and I will bid you goodnight. Meanwhile, many thanks for you and your wife's hospitality.'

Escorting Lara to the front door, accompanied by Fielding, suddenly the doorbell rang.

Opening the door to a man standing on the doorstep, 'Oh, here you are at last!' Mark laughed light-heartedly. 'I thought you'd changed your mind about coming, after all! Well, don't just stand there! Come indoors, my dear chap!'

The 'dear chap' on the doorstep Lara recognized instantly as none other than her Middlesbrough physician, Gareth Roberts, whose recognition of herself was far from instantaneous. 'Mrs Davenport?' he murmured disbelievingly, unable to equate, immediately, the woman he had last seen wearing a baggy tweed skirt, a shapeless sweater, and with her hair skewered into a heavy bun at the nape of her neck, with a short-haired lady wearing an attractive cocktail dress, about to be helped into a camel-hair coat by, presumably, her escort, a tall, handsome man, immaculately dressed in a well-cut grey lounge suit, silk shirt and a pin-neat collar and tie.

And, 'Yes,' Lara replied coolly, despite her inner turmoil at this unexpected encounter with a man she had hoped never to see again once she had left his Middlesbrough surgery to create a new life for herself. A man to whom she had once confessed her hatred of her late husband, the burning of his former wife's photographs on a garden bonfire, the feeling she'd had, then, that she was losing her grip on reality, going slowly but surely out of her mind with anxiety.

Now here she was, faced with the man on the Fieldings' doorstep, about to quit a so-called party at which, presumably, he, Gareth Roberts, would assume his role as a guest of honour in the Fielding household, judging by Mark Fielding's warm welcome towards him.

Roberts said quietly, admiringly, 'Well done, Mrs Davenport, for taking your life into your own hands, at last!' He added, 'I take it that you are still taking the medicine I prescribed for you?' At which point, Amanda appeared on the scene to throw her arms around Dr Roberts, during which diversion Lara and Rory slipped away, unnoticed.

Rory said disconsolately, 'What a shambles! Can you ever forgive me?'

'For what?' Lara smiled, bending to fondle Buster's ears. 'No harm done. We're home and dry and the night is still young. Why not take this young man for a walk? Meanwhile, I'll rid myself of my finery, make sandwiches and coffee. Then I'd like to talk about tomorrow. The last thing I want is for you to leave here feeling guilty when there's no need.'

On his return, after the animals had been fed, Rory carried the coffee and sandwiches to the drawing room, closely followed by Buster and Cleo, who, settling down on the hearth rug, fell blissfully asleep in the warmth of the fire. 'Feeling better now?' Lara asked him, pouring the coffee.

'A little,' he admitted wryly. 'Thanks to you.'

'*Me*? Why? What did I do?'

'Think about it, Lara. If it hadn't been for your tarradiddle about medicine to explain away your preference for orange juice, I'd have probably told Amanda exactly what I thought of her. Humiliating you the way she did was – unforgiveable.'

'Oh, *that*!' Lara said dismissively. 'It seemed the lesser of two evils at the time, lying through my teeth or allowing a first-class row in a room full of strangers. Amanda was very drunk at the time, remember. You, on the other hand, were not. So who would have emerged the loser, in the long run? Not Amanda, that's for sure. She was among friends. We were merely interlopers.'

'You are right, of course,' Rory admitted,

viewing the evening in retrospect, shuddering slightly as he did so at the memory of Amanda's lips on his, the overpowering perfume she was wearing, the even stronger reek of alcohol on her breath. Above all, disturbingly, shockingly, that her tongue between his lips had indicated her desire for a physical relationship between them. The message was unmistakeable; in this case, sickening, unthinkable, disgusting.

He said, 'Mark Fielding must be a remarkably tolerant man to put up with his wife's behaviour. I'd pictured him as being a much taller, well-built man. The bluff and hearty type, a bit of a rough diamond!'

'Well, they do say that opposites attract,' Lara responded thoughtfully, 'although I sensed a degree of intolerance on his part, watching Amanda making a fool of herself. Frankly, I felt sorry for the man. I imagine it troubles him a great deal knowing of his wife's increasing dependence on alcohol as a source of forgetfulness, the loss of her youthful beauty and ebullience. She must have been remarkably lovely in her heyday. Middle age must have come as quite a shock to her.' She added wistfully, 'There, but for the grace of God, go I, and every other middle-aged woman in the world, I daresay, faced with the prospect of growing old.'

'That all depends on the woman, doesn't it?' Rory said. 'Her outlook on life. Her plans for the future. Looking forward, not back.' He hesitated momentarily, then, broaching the subject of the man they had briefly encountered on the Fieldings' doorstep, he continued, 'Tell me to mind my own business, if you like, but Fielding's friend, as I recall, failed to recognize you, at first, though you had obviously recognized him at first glance. Then he spoke warmly, admiringly, of your decision to take your life in your own hands. Who was that man?'

'His name is Roberts, Gareth Roberts. He was Charles's doctor, and mine, in Middlesbrough. It was he who signed Charles's death certificate, who later prescribed quantities of drugs for me to alleviate a stressful period of my life. Sleeping pills, painkillers, pep pills; high-blood-pressure tablets, vitamin supplements. Need I say more?'

'No, of course not! I'm sorry, Lara. I didn't mean to pry.'

Lara laughed, 'Of course you did. And why not? Now, let's forget about tonight and talk about tomorrow. Our last day together for the time being, so let's make the most of it.'

'Your wish is my command,' he said gallantly, biting into a ham sandwich, feeling suddenly ravenously hungry, having missed out on the nibbles at the Fieldings' party. 'Just tell me what you have in mind.'

Lara said unexpectedly, 'I'd like you to drive me to Scarborough, to revisit the scene of my parents' deaths, then to the cemetery, to lay flowers on their graves. Afterwards, to walk along the sands as I used to when I was a girl, then have a bite to eat at a fish-and-chip restaurant on the foreshore before returning home to Stella Maris.

'You see, Rory, with you beside me, I believe that I would have the courage to come to terms with the past, to lay to rest the horror of my parents' deaths once and for all. Or am I asking too much?'

Rory said quietly, 'I shall feel honoured.'

Buster went with them. Lara put his drinking bowl and a bottle of water in the boot of the car, and his bedding on the back seat, praying that he wasn't prone to travel sickness. Rory said that was a chance they'd have to take. No way could they have left him alone in the house, unable to relieve his feelings when he felt like it. He'd probably get his head stuck in Cleo's cat flap, if they did.

Shared laughter eased Lara's anxiety over the journey she was about to make, a build-up of nervous tension born of uncertainty as to her reactions revisiting the scene of the accident which had caused the deaths of her parents. What if, at the last minute, she couldn't go through with it, much less visit their graves?

Reading her mind, Rory said quietly, 'Please don't worry. If you don't feel up to it, just say so and we'll give Scarborough a miss; go inland instead; head towards Helmsley, have lunch at the Black Swan.'

'Take the coward's way out, you mean? Thanks, Rory, but this is something I must face, sooner or later, for my parents' sake, and mine. I feel so guilty having left them alone all these years, as if I didn't care. But I *do* care. I always have done, and I want them to know that. They were so very special and precious to me...' Tears filled her eyes. 'If only I'd refused Charles's proposal of marriage, had stayed on, in Scarborough, to make my own way, had not taken what appeared to be, at the time, the only solution to my problem of loneliness.'

'In which case, Scarborough, here we come,' Rory said gently. 'I'd half forgotten what a lovely place it is.' He was speaking reassuringly, sensing her unhappiness. 'Don't be sad, Lara. Look about you, remember the happy times. Think of today as a homecoming, a new beginning.'

Stopping the car on the Esplanade, he opened the door for her. 'Aren't you coming with me?' she asked. He smiled encouragingly. 'No, this is your time. We'll wait for you, Buster and I.'

Returning to Stella Maris around four o'clock in the afternoon, going upstairs to his room to pack his belongings, Rory recalled, with admiration, Lara's bravery in coming to terms with her past.

He had watched, from a distance, her visit to her parents' graves, marvelling at her composure as she filled the vases with fresh water, then daffodils, bought from a florists' van parked near the gates of the cemetery.

Afterwards, they had walked together near the sea of Scarborough's South Bay, throwing stones for the dog, scarcely speaking to one another. No need of words, simply deriving pleasure from each other's company, then tucking into parcels of fish and chips bought from a seafood café along the way, with an extra portion of haddock for Buster, wolfed down in less than a second, tail wagging, pleading for more with those soulful eyes of his.

This had been a marvellous day, he thought, a richly fulfilling day for himself and Lara, a day of blue skies, of white-capped waves, fresh sea air and golden sand. A day to remember when, in an hour or so from now, he would find himself on the outskirts of Middlesbrough, returning to an empty flat, devoid of comfort, warmth and laughter.

Lara was in the hall when he came

downstairs. 'I've made sandwiches for you,' she said. 'And packed you a bottle of milk, cornflakes, a loaf of bread, some butter, eggs and bacon, a jar of coffee,' handing him a carrier bag. 'Promise you won't go to work on an empty stomach?'

'I promise,' he said huskily, touched by her thoughtfulness, dreading saying goodbye to her, to Stella Maris, to Carnelian Bay. 'I can't begin to thank you for all you have done for me,' he murmured.

She smiled. 'Then don't even try. Just take good care of yourself, and come home again soon.'

Bending down, he brushed her cheek with his lips. And when he had gone, Lara went indoors, cradling his kiss with the palm of her hand.

# Nine

Monday morning. Laundry morning. The van man asked if Iris was 'poorly', obviously surprised to see Lara wearing an overall, her sleeves rolled up to her elbows, his money in one hand, a duster in the other, and the new laundry parcel all ready and waiting.

No use prevaricating, Lara realized. 'Iris isn't here any longer, but she appeared perfectly well the last time I saw her.'

'Huh, better in health than temper, I shouldn't wonder,' the man remarked sagaciously. 'Not what I'd describe as a cheerful personality, more of a doom-and-gloom merchant, if you want my opinion. But then, some folk are never happy unless they're miserable.' He added brightly, pocketing his money after signing the receipt, 'Any news of Mrs Prewett, by the way?'

'Yes. She's having a marvellous time in New York, with her family,' Lara replied warmly, glad of a switch of conversation away from that of Iris Smith, sensing an ally in the fresh-faced young delivery man on the doorstep.

'Oh, I'm glad of that,' he enthused. 'My name's Jeff Cogill, by the way. Spelt with a J not a G, an' if ever you need help, just give me a ring. My number's in the phone book.'

'How kind, how very kind of you,' Lara said gratefully. 'Thanks, Jeff, I'll remember.'

When he had gone, closing the door behind him, Lara felt suddenly lonely and bereft in a big, empty house, shorn of Rory's comforting presence in her life. But there was work to be done, carpets to be vacuumed, silver to polish, the Aga to be cleaned and replenished; animals to see to, plants to water, beds to make, food to buy and cook; memories to mull over. Memories of yesterday, in particular, of her return visit to Scarborough.

Strange how one could feel so uplifted one day, so downcast thereafter, as if life were a kind of carousel ride of painted horses on the merry-go-round of human existence, up one moment, down the next...

Yesterday, she had come to terms with the deaths of her parents. Today, she doubted her ability to come to terms, not with the past, but with her own future role in life. As what, exactly? A temporary housekeeper of another woman's property? A long-term resident of the Windsor Hotel? Or as a free spirit intent on making the most of life;

squandering her inheritance on foreign travel? Seeing, with her own eyes, the painting of La Giaconda in the Louvre Museum, in Paris; the Eiffel Tower, the Arc de Triomphe at sunset; Notre Dame, and the Ile de la Cité; the River Seine; Sacré Coeur, the Cimetière du Père Lachaise; the Tuileries Gardens.

Time, which had passed so quickly in Rory's company, hung heavy on her hands now. After lunch, she walked to the library, determined to clear the air between herself and Amanda, if necessary. Not that she had any intention of going armed for a confrontation – the last thing on earth she wanted.

She might have known that Amanda would bypass the matter, or possibly she retained no memory of her appallingly bad behaviour of Saturday night? In the event, she greeted Lara as if nothing untoward had happened between them the night before last, switching on the charm full blast – and yet ... Her opening gambit, 'I do hope you are feeling better now,' betrayed the fact that she *did* remember Lara's taradiddle about medicine, and her early departure from the drinks party.

Making matters worse, not better, Amanda continued archly, 'I really had no idea you'd been so ill recently. A patient of

Gareth Roberts', no less.'

'He told you that?' Lara's lips tightened imperceptibly, feeling her anger rise at his betrayal of doctor/patient confidentiality.

'Not in so many words,' Amanda babbled. 'Realizing you'd met before, I simply put two and two together. And, as I recall, he did mention the medicine he'd prescribed for you!' She continued mindlessly, 'Dear Gareth. He and Mark have been friends for simply ages, ever since they attended Medical School together. They are off to Scarborough, this afternoon, to attend some bloody boring medical conference or other, leaving poor little me all on my ownio! Doesn't seem fair, does it? Men have all the fun.'

A pause for breath, then, 'Where's Rory, by the way? Quite an item, aren't you? Couldn't help noticing, the other evening at the Golf Club. Huh, quite touchy he was when I invited him, and you, of course, to join our table. And, hello, I thought, a little more going on there than meets the eye. Not that I'm blaming you, of course. Lots of men prefer mature women, and "gather ye rosebuds while ye may", has always been my motto.'

Disliking the woman intensely, Lara said levelly, 'I'm sure it has. As one mature woman to another, our rosebud gathering days are over and done with now, wouldn't you say? At least, I hope so. You see, Amanda, in my view there is nothing sadder than women of our age trying, in vain, to recapture their lost youth; making damn fools of themselves into the bargain.'

So saying, she walked out of the library, head held high, eyes smarting with tears that her warm friendship with Rory had been so villified, so misunderstood by a middle-aged alcoholic who should have known better than to tar her with the same brush as herself.

One thing was for certain, she would never visit the library again, despite her love of books – poetry, autobiographies, contemporary novels – to keep her company, often in the dark watches of the night, when sleep would not come and she needed some gripping yarn or other to cling to, till morning came, anything rather than swallowing sleeping pills to dull her mind into a state of unconsciousness, quenching her awareness of life. *Life.* The only gift, apart from love, worth having.

There were other libraries close at hand, in Whitby for instance, and bookshops galore. She had always meant to start a collection of her own favourite books, and perhaps she would do so one day, when she had somewhere to put them; possibly a little place of her own, when she had come to terms with the future.

* * *

She was standing near the drawing-room window, worrying vaguely about the state of the garden, the length of the grass, which badly needed cutting, and wondering if she possessed the physical energy to tackle it herself, when a gnarled, elderly man in overalls and wearing a flat cap hobbled up the path, mounted the front steps, and rang the doorbell.

His face, Lara decided, resembled a baked russet apple, wrinkled yet rosy. Doffing his cap, 'Good day, my lady,' he said respectfully. 'Happen you've heard of me? My name's Ben Adams, from up yonder,' nodding vaguely in the direction of the war veterans' home on the hill. 'I'se come about the garden. I'd hev come afore, but me back's bin playing me up summat cruel this past month or more. Still, here I is, ready, willin' an' able, if you needs me, that is.'

'Need you? I'll say I do,' Lara responded gratefully. 'Come in, Mr Adams.'

'Nay, my lady, I wain't come in the front way on account of me mucky boots. Ah'll just nip round the back, get me gear from t' shed, an' mek a start moaning the grass, lessun you wants me to do summat else fust.'

'No, the grass will be fine for the time being,' she assured him. 'I'm just so pleased that you've come. I trust your back is

139

better now.'

'Why? Does it show?' he enquired anxiously.

'Does *what* show?'

'Me truss.' He sighed deeply. 'The doc up yonder tould me it'd ease me back, but he didn't mention nowt about me front. Just fancy, a man of my age wearin' a corset!'

Keeping a straight face, Lara said, 'Tell you what, Ben, before you start work, how would you fancy a nice cup of tea? I'll pop the kettle on, shall I?'

'Well, I wouldn't say no, my lady.' Ben fairly beamed, displaying a mouthful of tobacco-stained teeth. 'Three sugars an' not much milk.'

It seemed providential, Lara thought, Ben turning up when he did to relieve her anxiety about the garden. He said, nursing a mug of strong sweet tea, 'Happen them borders'll need a good seein' to afore long, wi everything sproutin' so fast at this time o't year. I could get one o't younger fellers ti gie me an 'and if that's all right by you?'

'By all means. Tell me, Ben, are you well looked after – up yonder?'

'Oh aye. It's all kep' nice an' clean. We sleeps in dormitories, six beds to a room, wi' 'anging space for us clothes, an' lockers atween t' beds. There's what they calls a "common room" on t' ground floor, wi plenty o' chairs an' tables effen we feels like a game o' dominoes or whativer, an' a TV lounge for them as wants ti watch.

'The grub's a bit rough, like, but plentiful. We gets porridge an' toast an' jam fer breakfast; eggs an' bacon come Sundays; bangers an' mash, shepherd's pie, or summat similar, at midday, mainly taters.' He pulled a face. 'If there's owt I hates, it's spud-bashing, but we has ti tek us turns ti save the domesticates the trouble an' cut down on t' over' eads.' He sighed deeply. 'Stands ti reason, I suppose. Them women 'ave enough on keepin' the place clean an' doin' the washing-up.'

His face brightened. 'But we does get a nice evenin' meal. Soup fust, then mebbe a slice or two of roast belly pork, or a lamb chop wi plenty o' vegetables, follered by a steamed pudd'n an' custard, so we dain't go ti bed 'ungry. Then, on Sundays, we has roast beef an' Yorkshire pudd'ns wi' plenty of onion gravy an' roast pertaters, wi' mebbe rice, tapioca or semolina pudd'n ter foller, an' what they calls a high tea for us evenin' meals: baked beans, sardines or spaghetti on toast, jam an' bread an' cakes, usually spiced loaf or rock buns. So, you see, my lady, we've no cause fer complaints. We'se tret fair an' square on the whole, an' damn glad of an 'ome to call us own.' He added wistfully, swallowing his last mouthful of tea, 'Mind you, my lady, I'd leave 'ere like a shot effen

141

I 'ad elsewhere ti go. But I 'aven't. So I'd mun make the best of a job, 'adn't I?'

Lara's heart went out to him. She said gently, slipping him a five-pound note from her purse, 'Here, take this, Ben. Treat yourself to a packet of cigarettes, a couple of pints of beer, or whatever. Now, hadn't you best be getting on with mowing the grass? What I mean is, whilst there's still light enough left to see what you're doing?'

The shades of an April evening were fast falling when Ben departed, having mown the grass of the front lawn, albeit raggedly, and returned his gear to the garden shed.

This had been a fraught day, on the whole, Lara realized, recalling her meeting with Amanda Fielding; that odd-ball librarian; her feelings of contempt, pity and dislike for the woman, a tangled web of emotions impossible to untangle until she'd had time to think about it more clearly. Possibly she had expended too much physical energy in shopping, cooking and cleaning to weigh up the pros and cons for the time being. A tired mind in a tired body was scarcely conducive to clear-sightedness.

Suddenly, the phone rang. Rory was on the line. Relief flooded through her at the sound of his voice. She asked anxiously, 'Are you all right? What kind of a day have you had?'

'Fraught,' he said tautly. 'And you?'

'Much the same,' she confessed. 'But never mind about me. Tell me about yourself.'

'Well, for starters, lots of work piled up on my desk: clients to see, questions to answer, properties to survey; appointments to be kept, traffic snarl-ups, playing the role of a bright-eyed, bushy-tailed executive. Feeling more dead than alive. Returning home, so-called, to discover my immersion heater's on the blink, so no hot water to wash away the cares of the day. Worse still, there won't be any tomorrow morning either. What a bloody life, eh?'

'Yes, isn't it just?'

'So, what's with you?' he asked concernedly. 'You haven't been overdoing things, have you?'

'Not really. Just housework, that's all, though I did have a bit of a showdown with Amanda this morning.'

'Tell me about it.'

'There's nothing much to tell. We – exchanged views – as they say in political circles. In fact, I gave her a piece of my mind...'

'Good for you! About time someone did,' Rory commented drily. 'Then what?'

'A man from the war veterans' hospital came to cut the grass. When he had gone, I took Buster for a short walk along the prom, came home, made myself a cup of tea and a slice of toast, and here I am, ready for bed, and, dare I say it, a good soak in a hot bath beforehand.'

Rory chuckled softly. Then I'd best not keep you from your ablutions. Just one thing, before I go. I'd give all I possess, right now, to be back in Carnelian Bay with you, Buster and Cleo. Meanwhile, goodnight, Lara, and God bless. Sleep well, and don't worry about me. I'll be fine, just fine, hot water or no hot water. I'll probably start growing a beard!'

'Goodnight, Rory, and God bless you, too,' Lara murmured, hanging up the receiver, feeling suddenly at peace with the world, knowing beyond a shadow of doubt that she was falling slowly but surely in love with Rory McAllister, that it didn't matter at all whether or not he loved her in return, because, after all, he would never know, never even begin to suspect her feelings towards him.

Suddenly, the phone rang again. Startled, Lara answered the call. A wrong number, perhaps? But it wasn't a wrong number. She would have known that voice, with its faint Welsh inflexion, anywhere, as the voice of Gareth Roberts. The last person on earth she wished to talk to.

'Why are you ringing me? What do you want?' Her voice shook slightly.

'You sound worried, Lara. Are you

unwell?' Roberts asked.

'A bit tired, that's all. I'm sorry. I didn't mean to snap.'

'The reason why I'm ringing – I had hoped for a word or two on Saturday evening. Unfortunately there wasn't time to pursue the matter of your new lifestyle, which appears to suit you very well.' He paused. 'I'll be in the vicinity of Carnelian Bay for a day or so until my return to Middlesbrough on Friday. Meanwhile, I'd be grateful if you could lunch with me – whenever – at a time and place convenient to yourself. Please say that you will.'

'To discuss my illness, you mean?' Lara responded sharply. 'No, I'm sorry, Dr Roberts. I'm here, in Carnelian Bay, to forget about illness, not to talk about it over a luncheon engagement.'

'You mistake my motives,' he said. 'I find myself in a pleasant place on the map at the moment, with a certain amount of time on my hands now that I have fulfilled most of my reasons for being here in the first place, and I can think of nothing nicer than having lunch in the company of – not a patient of mine, but a friend.'

Put like that, how could Lara have refused his invitation without seeming churlish? She said, 'Very well then. Shall we make it tomorrow at twelve thirty?'

'Splendid! I'll call for you. We'll take it

from there.'

Going upstairs to her room, Lara wondered what she had let herself in for. Knowing practically nothing about Dr Roberts, what on earth would she talk about? The weather? Oh, drat the man! She was not, and never had been, a friend of his, merely his patient, so why pick on her?

'You mistrust my motives,' he'd said, but what exactly *were* his motives?

She might have known he'd arrive precisely on time. She said awkwardly, 'Good afternoon, Dr Roberts.'

He smiled, 'Please call me Gareth.' Escorting her to his car: 'May I say how well you're looking? Sorry, how attractive you look? How well your new hairstyle becomes you. Frankly, I scarcely recognized you at first glance, the other evening on the Fieldings' doorstep.'

'My hair? Oh, it's far less trouble this way,' she responded warily. 'Short, I mean. It took ages to dry before.'

Slipping into the driver's seat, he said, 'So where are we heading for lunch? You'll need to direct me. I'm not quite au fait with this neck of the woods, though I have been here before, quite often, as a matter of fact, as a guest of the Fieldings, Mark being a golfing companion of mine, with a penchant for dining at the Golf Club Hotel.'

'Oh, that's where I'd thought of for lunch,' Lara said breathlessly, ungrammatically, feeling tongue-tied and stupid in the presence of the man behind the steering wheel of his sleek, silver-grey Mercedes.

She blurted, 'It's been a lovely month, so far.'

'Yes, hasn't it?' He seemed faintly amused by her opening gambit. 'Very pleasant for the time of year, and the forecast for May is quite good, so I'm told.'

'Is it? I hadn't heard.' Oh God, she thought, what had become of her lately discovered self-confidence in Rory's company? But this man, despite his undoubted good looks, regular features, grey-blue eyes and his mop of dark-brown hair brushed back from his high forehead, possessed none of Rory's inate charm of manner and his relaxed attitude to life, his ready laughter and boyish enthusiasm for living. Never, for one moment, could Lara imagine Dr Roberts eating fish and chips from a parcel, for instance, re-stoking a recalcitrant Aga cooker, watering plants, or standing up for her in a battle of wills between herself and the redoubtable Iris Smith.

Perhaps comparisons were odious? Possibly she was wrong in drawing parallels between Gareth Roberts and Rory McAllister, to the former's detriment? And did it matter all that much, anyway? Hopefully, after lunch at the golf Club Hotel, Dr Roberts would drive her back to Stella Maris, thank her politely for her company, and return to his Scarborough conference, à toûte vitesse. The sooner the better, so far as she was concerned.

The dining room was quiet, almost deserted at a quarter to one on a Tuesday afternoon. Inevitably, a young waiter offered them a window table overlooking the links. Seated, studying the menu, feeling that even the smallest amount of food would choke her, Lara ordered a glass of orange juice and a mushroom omelette.

Glancing at her across the table, 'Not dieting, are you?' Gareth enquired briskly. And, 'No, not at all,' she replied defensively. 'I'm just not very hungry, that's all! Why? Is there a law against that?'

He said placatingly, 'Of course not.' Handing the menus back to the waiter: 'Orange juice and mushroom omelettes for two, please, plus a portion of chips and a green salad.'

When the waiter had gone, Gareth said brusquely, I'm sorry, Lara, I should have known better than to invite you to lunch with me. Obviously you still regard me, not as a friend but a physician, someone who metes out pills and potions which you no longer feel necessary to your future health and well-being. That's true, isn't it?'

And, 'Yes,' she admitted softly. 'I'm sorry, Dr Roberts, but friendship between us is – impossible, I'm afraid. You *do* see that, don't you?'

'As a doctor and patient, most certainly,' he acquiesced. 'But what price a man-to-woman relationship once the patient has decided to part company with her physician?'

'I'm sorry,' Lara replied confusedly. 'I don't quite understand the gist of this conversation, unless...'

'Unless *what*, Lara?' Gareth persisted intently. 'Unless I believed that we were destined for some kind of future together, you and I?'

'Are you out of your mind?' Rising swiftly to her feet, about to quit the dining room in a hurry, so *this* was Dr Robert's hidden motive, she thought bitterly, a blatant attempt at seduction!

A future together indeed! A sexual liaison more like!

'Sit down, Lara,' Roberts said impatiently, 'and hear me out. Sorry if I shocked you, but I meant what I said. The fact is, I've thought about you often since our first meeting, after the death of your husband; wondered how you were, if you were well and happy. Meeting you briefly on the Fieldings' doorstep, I knew that you were –

149

quite radiant, in fact.

'For what it's worth, I felt strongly attracted to the new look Lara Davenport. You see, my wife died seven years ago, since when I've lived a pretty lonely existence, wishing I could meet someone to dispel my loneliness. Then I met *you*! Can you blame me for wanting to renew an old acquaintance with someone I admire?'

'I suppose not,' Lara murmured, out of her depth in the company of this comparative stranger looking at her intently across a dining-room table. 'Except that I haven't the remotest desire to become romantically involved with anyone, ever again.'

'Especially not with me?' he suggested, as the waiter brought their food to the table.

When the youngster had gone, 'I'm afraid not,' Lara said.

'Am I allowed to know why?' Gareth asked. 'Because of my profession?'

'I'm sorry, I can't explain. I've scarcely come to terms with my past yet, let alone the future.'

# Ten

Aware that she had mishandled a delicate situation, Lara spent a restless night wishing she'd been less dogmatic, more understanding of Gareth Roberts' motives. He had, after all, expressed honourable intentions, admiration for her, scarcely warranting the harsh treatment she had meted out to him.

After lunch, he had escorted her back to Stella Maris, apologized for having wasted her time, and driven away without a backward glance, feeling, no doubt, as wretched as she did, and with good reason. She had behaved badly and she knew it. But what, if anything, could she do about it? Write him an apology? Saying what, exactly? That she hadn't meant what she said? But she *had* meant it. At no time in the future could she envisage a romantic liaison with Dr Roberts.

To add to her worries, Rory had not rung, as he usually would, after supper, leaving her in a state of turmoil, wondering why not. Had he been taken ill? Was he in trouble of some kind? Or had he simply decided not to create a precedent in ringing her every evening at a certain time? The last thing Lara wanted was to feel herself a mill-stone round any man's neck, especially Rory's.

Up and doing early next morning, Lara bathed and dressed quickly, and hurried downstairs to take Buster for his constitu-tional along the prom and back. Approach-ing home, she noticed, in the front garden, the figure of a man kneeling beside a flower bed. Presumably Ben Adams' colleague from the war veterans' hospital.

'Hello there,' she called out to him, approaching the garden gate. 'I'm Lara Davenport. Who are you?' But entering the garden, to her dismay, she saw that it was empty. The handsome gardener had simply disappeared into thin air, or he appeared to have done so. But that was not possible. He must be somewhere or other, possibly in the garden shed? But no, there was no sign of him anywhere. So, was she slowly but surely going out of her mind? Women of a certain age had a tendency to lose touch with reality. So far she had experienced no symp-toms of a mid-life crisis, indeed, since com-ing to Carnelian Bay she had felt acutely a new awareness of the reality of life.

She was in the kitchen making toast and

coffee when Ben appeared at the back door. 'Good morning, my lady,' he said, sniffing the air. 'Thowt as 'ow I'd mek an early start on t' back lawn effen that's what you want.'

'Yes, fine, Ben. Just one thing first. I saw a man in the front garden half an hour ago. I called out to him but he – disappeared without trace.'

Ben chuckled. 'Oh, that'd be Beau, I reckon. A queer kind o' bloke, a bit light in t' upper storey, poor lad, scared stiff o' strangers, bein' as 'e 'as summat called am — am— amnasthesius.'

'You mean – amnesia? Loss of memory?' Lara prompted him gently.

'Aye, that's it! Dunno who 'e is nor where 'e cum frum, 'cept America, by all accounts, cos of 'is accent. A damn shame reely, 'im not 'avin' no one ti claim 'im, as it were. No kinfolk, no visitors. By t' way, that toast smells good!'

'All right, Ben, I get the message. Come in and sit down.'

'Ta very much, my lady. I does feel a bit peckish, come ti think of it.'

'Help yourself to butter and marmalade.' Not that he needed reminding, he had already done so. 'And I suppose you wouldn't say no to a mug of coffee?'

'Well, since you asks, though I'se rather hev tea effen it ain't too much trubble.'

'No trouble at all. Don't tell me, let me

153

guess, three sugars and not much milk?' Re-boiling the kettle: 'Now, tell me more about – Beau.'

'There ain't much more ti tell.'

'How long has he been – up yonder?'

Ben screwed up his forehead. 'Danged if I knows! Since t' end o' t' war, ah reckons; since t' Yanks entered t' conflagration. 'E were there afore me, that's fer sure. T' doctors seem baffled-like ti' know that ti do wi' 'im, seein' as they can't find out now't about 'im, an' 'im wi' an 'ole in 'is 'ead where 'is brain-box should be.'

'And you think he ran away, when I spoke to him, because he was – scared of me?' Lara asked, handing Ben a mug of tea.

'Ah reckons so, but ah ain't sure. A law unto hisself, that 'un,' Ben replied, helping himself to more marmalade.

'Now listen to me, Ben, and listen care-fully,' Lara said briskly. 'The next time you see Beau, tell him from me to come back here tomorrow morning. Tell him I won't speak to him or bother him in any way as long as he gets on with his work. Promise, Ben! Promise me that you'll pass on my message!'

'Right then, my lady, I will!' Ben appeared slightly hurt by her insistence. 'There's nowt wrong wi' *my* brain-box!' He added hope-fully, 'Any chance of another cuppa? I'se feelin' fair parched this morning.'

Feeling at a loose end after her sleepless night, yesterday's brief encounter with Gareth Roberts and staying up late awaiting Rory's phone call which had never come, scarcely knowing what to do with herself to fill in time, apart from housework, exercising Buster, watering plants and keeping a weather eye on Ben 'moaning' the back lawn. After lunch – consisting of a banana and a slice of brown bread and butter – when Ben had returned the 'moaner' to its shed and departed 'up yonder' to partake of bangers and mash, shepherd's pie or whatever, with a strange feeling of excitement in the pit of her stomach, Lara walked slowly upstairs to the top landing of Stella Maris where, unearthing the key of the attic from the bunch in her possession and nervously unlocking the door, she slowly mounted another flight of stairs to a remote world of rafters and shadows pierced, here and there, by rays of sunlight slanting down from gothic windows of a bygone age.

Curiously, she felt suddenly at peace, no longer nervous, as if she had been here before, long ago, in a different age, a different dimension, had known happiness here, beneath this roof, these rafters; had seen, in times long gone, sunlight streaming down from these selfsame windows. Impossible, and yet...

Suddenly she remembered the day Rory had told her about the account books of the Victorian era, discovered by Joan Prewett in a trunk in the attic, asking him what had become of that trunk; his reply, 'It's still up there for all I know.'

And so it was. A handsome cabin trunk fashioned from strong green canvas bound with sturdy leather hoops, and fastened with a hasp of solid brass, and a matching brass key in its lock, standing there, safe and secure, in a beam of sunlight slanting down from one of the high Victorian windows.

With a swiftly beating heart, kneeling beside the trunk, turning the key in its lock; lifting its lid, looking inside at its contents, Lara saw there a veritable wealth of old manuscripts, architects' drawings pertaining to the birth of Stella Maris. Above all, sepia daguerrotypes of the man who had built the house in the first place, taken with his wife, son and daughters grouped about him and, at the bottom of the trunk, several of what appeared to be scrapbooks, journals and bundles of correspondence.

Closing the lid, leaving the contents of the trunk undisturbed for the time being, she went downstairs feeling that she had discovered a treasure trove, to be examined not hastily but leisurely, item by item, day by day, as a source of satisfaction in finding out, first-hand, more about the history of

Stella Maris and the family and servants who had once lived here.

Realistically, here and now, she had the animals to see to, supper to cook. Suddenly hungry, she recollected that she had eaten practically nothing these past few days, and decided to cook herself a chicken breast, new potatoes and spring cabbage, if only to keep body and soul together.

Yesterday's luncheon with Gareth Roberts had been a disaster. She had scarcely touched her mushroom omelette; this morning, Ben had quickly demolished her toast-and-marmalade breakfast, and all she'd eaten since was a banana and a slice of bread and butter. No wonder she had an aching void in the pit of her stomach.

About to carry her supper tray to the drawing room, suddenly the phone rang. Forgetting about the tray, she dumped it on the kitchen table and hurried to answer the phone. Rory was on the line. She knew at once, by his voice, that something was wrong.

He said hoarsely, 'Sorry, Lara, it's bad news, I'm afraid. Georgie's in hospital. Her baby was stillborn, its father has left her in the lurch. She's been crying out for me, and I must go to her as quickly as possible, the poor kid. I'm leaving immediately, which is why I'm ringing early. I just wanted you to know that I may not be able to make it to

Carnelian Bay at the weekend after all.'

'Oh, Rory, I'm so sorry.' Her heart went out to him. 'Where is Georgie at the moment?'

'In Hull Royal Infirmary, within striking distance at least.'

'And has the man in question really left her alone?'

'So it would appear,' Rory said grimly.

'And has she no close relatives – parents, friends?'

'Yes, but she has never seen eye to eye with her parents. In any case, they're abroad right now, so I'm the only person close to her. Oh, Lara, I scarcely know which way to turn. I can't stay with her and, when she leaves hospital, I couldn't very well bring her back to my flat. She'd hate that, being cooped up all day in a confined space with no one to take care of her, and I couldn't possibly afford a nursing home.'

Lara said thoughtfully, 'How about the Windsor Hotel? The Carstairs would take care of her just fine, as they took care of me. She'd have a pleasant room, good food, and you'd be able to visit her as often as possible.'

'Thanks, Lara,' he murmured gratefully. 'Yes, of course, that would seem an ideal solution. Trust you to come up with an answer. Right now, I'd give anything to be back in Carnelian Bay. If only.'

158

'I know,' she responded quietly. 'And I'd give anything to have you here. So would Buster and Cleo. But one weekend, perhaps, when Georgie is feeling well enough to travel, you could possibly bring her with you for a breath of sea air?'

'Perhaps. Who knows?' he said wearily. 'Frankly, Georgie isn't a breath-of-sea-air person, nor do I imagine her taking kindly to a room at the Windsor Hotel. All that I can do, for the time being, is – play it by ear.'

'That's the most anyone can do, isn't it? What my mother often referred to as "making the best of a bad job". Just one thing, Rory, never forget that I am here if ever you stand in need of help of any kind. So, please keep in touch with me, won't you? Promise?'

'Of course I will,' he assured her. 'You see, Lara, I shall always regard you as the best friend I've ever had.'

Returning to the kitchen, she discovered that her supper had gone cold, that Buster and Cleo had possessed the good manners not to eat it during her absence, whereupon she shared it between them, chicken breasts, new potatoes and cabbage, in short the whole bang-shoot, no longer hungry herself, just worried sick about Rory in his present dilemma, still head-over-heels in love with Georgina, despite all the grief, misery and pain she had caused him.

Perhaps pain was a necessary part of loving? Georgie had called out for Rory and he had heeded that call. In time they might well make a fresh start together if the man Georgie had run off with had really left her. One thing seemed abundantly clear: that Rory's life, her own and Georgie's would never be the same again. Rory picking up the pieces of Georgie's life, Georgie faced with the loss of her child and the man she loved.

As for herself, the new-found happiness she had discovered in Rory's company would never come again. From now on she must start picking up the pieces of her own life akin to slotting together a jigsaw puzzle with half the components missing.

At least, she thought wistfully, she had garnered a handful of shining memories along the way. Memories of fun and laughter, sunlit days and star-lit nights, the joy of caring for a fellow human being when Rory had turned to her for help and she had shared with him, for a little while, more happiness than some women had in a lifetime. And yet, curiously, she had known, deep down, that such happiness could not last, remembering the many times she had told herself, Whatever happens in the future, I shall never forget this night, this moment in time.

★ ★ ★

Up early next morning, glancing out of her bedroom window at the garden below, she saw the figure of a man, trowel in hand, weeding a flower bed. Presumably the man called Beau. So Ben had kept his promise after all. Now she must keep hers not to speak to him, to let him get on with his work uninterrupted.

Going downstairs, opening the back door for Buster, she saw, to her surprise, a basketful of logs near the door of the shed. Meanwhile, Buster had disappeared out of sight round the corner of the house, wagging his tail and barking excitedly, and, 'Come back Buster,' she called out to him, to no avail, until, to her amazement, Beau appeared, Buster trotting happily beside him and, 'Not to worry, ma'am,' the man said quietly. 'He didn't bother me none. I'm fond of animals.' Words spoken in an unmistakeable American accent. 'It's people I'm scared of, not animals.'

Looking at him intently, Lara saw a tanned face beneath a thatch of greying blond hair, deep-set blue eyes, a mobile mouth revealing splendidly strong white teeth – real teeth, not dentures – a resolute chin, a handsome face, that of a young man grown old before his time.

She said warily, 'And are you scared of me?'

161

'I was yesterday, but not today,' he replied. 'Not since Ben gave me your message. I kinda figured what a nice lady you were from his description, promising not to talk to me just as long as I got on with my work. So I'd best get on with it, hadn't I?'

'Yes, of course. Thanks for the logs, by the way, and please feel free to come indoors to make yourself a cup of coffee, whenever. It has been a real pleasure meeting you, Beau, but I have other things to see to, so no need to talk to me if you'd rather not. Just come and go as you please.'

Feeling tense, unsettled, she decided to take Buster for a good long walk along the beach to blow away her mental cobwebs. Walking past the beach bungalows on the lower promenade, she noticed that workmen were busy cleaning and painting the interiors in readiness for the summer influx of visitors, and realized that today was the first of May. May Day, she thought. Blossom time, lilac and laburnum time, softer air and longer days and nights now that daffodil time was over and done with, wondering if she might possibly rent one of the bungalows as a kind of bolt hole for the summer months.

Approaching the overseer in charge of the workmen, she asked him how she should set about doing so. He said politely, 'You'll need to enquire at the Information Bureau

162

near the coble landing. Mind you, they're snapped up pretty quick, so you'd best make haste.'

'Thanks, I shall. I'll go there at once!'

The woman in charge of the Information Bureau, glancing at her list of chalet bookings, said briskly that only one of the bungalows was available for the summer season, due to a recent cancellation; a deposit was due in advance, since this was one of the more spacious bungalows on offer, with a sink, cooking facilities, a table and chairs, crockery and cutlery laid on.

'Thanks, I'll take it,' Lara responded gratefully, producing a cheque book and pen from her shoulder bag. 'How soon may I take possession?'

'Well, not until the workmen have finished painting it,' the woman advised her. 'Shall we say the week after next?'

'Yes, fine by me,' Lara agreed, writing a cheque for the required deposit, the balance of which was payable on possession, the woman told her, curious about her client's identity, her eagerness to rent a beach bungalow for the summer season. After all, what was so special about a wooden shack containing nothing more than a stone sink, a cold water tap and a Baby Belling cooker the size of a postage stamp, a rickety table, a few deckchairs and a cupboard full of zinc spoons and several Woolworth's cups, plates and saucers?

But hers not to reason why. All she knew was that she suddenly felt much happier having encountered a lady called – with a quick glance at the name on the cheque – Lara Davenport. She said, 'My name is Marcia Matthews, by the way.' They exchanged smiles, then, 'I hope we'll meet again some day,' Marcia added.

'Thank you.' Wary of friendly strangers since her encounter with Amanda Fielding, Lara smiled and went on her way, mulling over the possibilities of the beach bungalow as an escape route where, on summer days, she could rest and read to her heart's content in closer proximity to the sea, the lullaby of the waves washing in on the beach below the promenade, as an alternative to the loneliness of Stella Maris without week-ends with Rory to look forward to.

Returning home, she saw, propped up on the kitchen table, a note from Beau, which read: 'I have taken the liberty of re-stoking your cooker and emptying the ash can to save you the trouble. Yours respectfully, Beauregard Jackson.'

Deeply touched by the message, thinking what an attractive man, yet emotionally threadbare for the time being, sitting down at the kitchen table, burying her face in her hands, Lara gave way to tears borne of loneliness and regret that nothing in earth or heaven came as it had come before. Especially not happiness and peace of mind.

Then, resolutely drying her eyes and rising to her feet, she set about feeding Buster and Cleo, who relied on her for sustenance – and love – whose tail-waggings and purrings enriched her life immeasureably by their faith in her as an unfailing purveyor of food, milk, water and affection.

Rory rang briefly at six o'clock. Sounding tired, he told her he was on his way to Hull to see Georgie, whose condition was causing concern, the reason why she was being kept under observation for the time being.

'She's physically weak,' he explained. 'But there's more to it than that. It's her state of mind that's so worrying. She can't come to terms with the loss of her child – and its father. She's got it into her head that he's gone off somewhere, taking the child with him. It's heartbreaking, Lara, and I don't know what the hell to do about it. I feel so helpless, so utterly useless. She won't talk to me; doesn't even notice I'm there, apparently.'

'But you *are* there, and that's what really matters,' Lara reminded him. 'The poor girl's in a state of shock, but she's in safe hands, receiving treatment for her condition, and that is what you must cling to right now.'

'I know,' he said dejectedly. 'And I'm doing my best. My best just isn't good enough. Sorry, I must go now, I have a long evening ahead of me.'

Lara knew what he meant, a journey to Hull, after work; visiting hours fitted in before the journey back to Middlesbrough. Was he getting enough to eat? she wondered, or living on hastily snatched sandwiches and meat pies? Hardly likely he'd have the time or inclination to cook himself proper meals. Chances were he wasn't getting much sleep either.

A thought struck her. She said, 'On your way home tonight, why not make a detour? Your bed's ready and waiting, and I'll have a good hot meal in the oven. Something that won't spoil, a beef casserole. What do you think?'

'*Think*? Oh, Lara, I'd love to, but I couldn't put you to so much trouble, and I'd need to set off at the crack of dawn tomorrow, to get to work on time.'

'Fine. That's settled then.' She breathed a sigh of relief. 'I'll see you later.'

Going through to the kitchen to start preparations for Rory's supper, happily she took from the refrigerator the pound of steak and kidney she'd purchased that morning, which she duly coated with flour and browned first in the frying pan, before popping it into the oven to begin cooking.

Next came the vegetables: carrots, onions, baby turnips, and celery, which she peeled and sliced in readiness to complement the casserole, and which, when they were done, she added to the contents of the earthenware pot in the oven, before turning her attention to spud bashing, and mixing together self-raising flour and shredded suet, pepper and salt, plus a modicum of cold water in readiness for the dumplings she planned to pop atop the casserole when Rory made his appearance. Creamy mashed potatoes, with lots of butter, would accompany the meal, she decided, her housewifely instincts coming to the fore, enjoying to the full the very thought of providing sustenance for a beloved guest – a hungry man in need of heart-warming food to sustain him after a long journey.

Resisting the strong temptation to throw her arms about him when he appeared on her doorstep, she simply held out her hands to him, and said, 'Oh, Rory, I'm so pleased to see you.'

'And I you, Lara,' he responded gratefully. 'How much, you'll never know.'

She said lightly, 'Come in. Supper's almost ready. Would you care to freshen up first?' Thinking how tired he looked, how strained and unhappy. And, 'Yes,' he replied.

'I do feel a bit hot and sticky, come to think of it.'

When he came downstairs a quarter of an hour later and entered the kitchen, Buster, mad with joy at seeing him again, barked furiously, wagging his tail ecstatically, and Cleo, jumping down from her window sill, purred about his ankles, bringing tears to Rory's eyes at their display of affection towards him. He said bleakly, 'God, how much I've missed all this – and you, Lara. Above all, you.'

'I know, Rory,' she said quietly. 'Now, sit down and have your supper.' Bustling the food on to the table, she served him a plateful of the beef casserole, vegetables, baked dumplings and mashed potatoes she had so lovingly prepared for him, a much smaller portion for herself, and, seated opposite, noticed his obvious enjoyment of the meal, which he devoured like a starving man, relishing every mouthful that passed his lips.

Smiling inwardly, she remembered a saying of her mother's: 'Food, given without love, has no flavour.' A wise woman, her mother, whose daughter now knew, beyond a shadow of doubt, that she had fallen deeply in love with Rory McAllister. No pretence, no prevarication, no guilt feelings whatever, just the plain and simple fact that she loved him. Nothing whatever to do with the fact that he was head-over-heels in love with someone else, simply an awareness, an acceptance of her feelings towards him, a kind of warmth, deep inside her, at his presence in her life, demanding nothing in return except that, somehow, he would always remain a presence in her life.

The meal over, they sat together for a while in front of the drawing-room fire, Rory pouring out his heart to her about Georgie's illness, his concern about her future welfare, his own inability to cope with a mentally disturbed invalid if, perchance, he was called upon to care for her, full-time, on her release from the psychiatric wing of the Hull Royal Infirmary.

'It may never come to that,' Lara assured him. 'No use crossing bridges before you come to them. Commonsensically, Georgie will remain in hospital until she is well enough to pick up the threads of her old life once more. Then, and only then, can you decide about your future together. Now, take my advice, go upstairs to bed, get a good night's sleep, and not to worry about tomorrow morning's crack of dawn. I'll make damn sure you'll get to work on time, with a full English breakfast inside you.'

Heeding her advice, getting up, he said, 'You'll never know how much this has meant to me, just being here, talking to you, enjoying the food you cooked for me, such a wonderful meal. You're a born homemaker, Lara.' He smiled. 'Know what? I think I'll sleep well tonight, the first time in ages, thanks to you.'

'I hope so, Rory. Goodnight.'

When he had gone, she went through to the kitchen to wash up their coffee cups, to make certain that all was safe and secure for the night: Buster settled in his basket, Cleo on her window sill. Then, bidding them goodnight, Lara went slowly upstairs to her own room, deeply aware of Rory's presence in the house, recalling his words, 'You're a born homemaker', and those of her mother, 'Food, given without love, has no flavour', thinking, as she got into bed, that in cooking for Rory she had expressed her love for him in the only way possible, the only way she knew how.

# Eleven

'If there's anyone I can't stand,' Ben complained bitterly, making inroads on the marmalade and butter, 'it's that bossy wumman, up yonder, gieing me orders, tellin' me ti shift me feet; treatin' me like muck, the miserable ould git, wi' a face as long as a fiddle an' that damn turban on her nut! Wot's up wi' 'er, ah should like ti know!

'Eh, wot a schemozzle when ah arsked 'er, point-blank, if she were a Muslin. Threated ti report me, she did, an' ah said, go on then, an' ah'll report you, missis 'igh an' mighty, fer mekkin' me life a misery, you an' that there bloody floor mop of yourn. Beggin' yer pardon, my lady, ah doesn't offen retort ti bad language, but that un'd mek a saint swear, allus whingein' an' whinin' 'bout this an' that, as if it were my fault 'er 'usband 'as a porely leg an' 'er granchilder's in trubble wi' t' perlice. Wot them needs is a good belt rahnd t' lughoiles, ah told 'er, an' wot *you* needs is a bit o' 'uman compashion!'

Iris Smith, Lara thought wryly. Ben was

talking about Iris Smith, who else? She'd have recognized the description anywhere; the turban, the mop, the bad temper, the whingeing and whining, the husband with the poorly leg, the troublesome grand-children. She said, changing the subject adroitely, 'Where's Beau today?'

'Oh, 'im? 'Avin' 'is brain-box examined, pore sod, but 'e'll be back termorrer.' Ben added mischieviously, 'Tekken quite a shine ti you, 'e 'as, my lady, beggin' yer pardon. Thinks the world o' you, 'e does. You an' that dog o' yourn. Allus on about it, 'e is.'

'Yes, well, that's as may be,' Lara said briskly. 'Now, if you've finished your break-fast, there's work to be done, so we'd best be getting on with it, hadn't we? The laundry man will be here directly, and I have silver to clean, paintwork to wash, rooms to vacuum...'

'Wot you needs 'ere, my lady,' Ben ventured on his way to the back door, 'is an 'elpin' 'and wi t' 'ousework. 'Tis a main big 'ouse fer one wumman ti see to. 'Appen ah cud put in a good word wi' that bossy wumman up yonder.'

'No thanks, Ben,' Lara replied fervently. 'I'd far rather you didn't. In fact, I abso-lutely forbid it! Do I make myself clear?'

The old man grinned wickedly. 'Ah wus ony jokin',' he said.

Jeff, the laundry man – spelt with a J not a

G – arrived at nine o'clock precisely to collect his bundle of washing. 'All right, are you?' he grinned boyishly, a pleasant, open-faced young man, ruddy-cheeked, with short fair hair.

And, 'Yes, I'm fine, thank you,' Lara replied, imagining him to be a happily married man with an adoring wife and several children, glad of a steady job, leading a blissfully uncomplicated life far different from her own. Drawing a bow at a venture, she asked, 'Have your children started school yet?'

'All except the youngest,' he supplied eagerly, 'who isn't quite old enough yet. He's only three, coming up four next month,' he added proudly. 'Now my wife's expecting again, and none too pleased about it neither, I might add, just when she thought of going back to work again, part-time.'

'Doing what, exactly?' Lara enquired. 'Sorry, I didn't mean to pry, but I'm in need of a home help at the moment, on a part-time basis. Nothing too arduous, just someone to come in three times a week to do a bit of light housework, dusting and polishing and cleaning the silver.' She smiled appealingly. 'Unless, of course, she has something better in mind.'

Jeff flushed to the roots of his hair. He said joyously, 'You mean...? Well, that's real kind of you, missis! And young Toby wouldn't be a problem once she's dropped him off at his playgroup. And Sadie's only four months gone; over her morning sickness, and she's a real good worker. You should see our house, as neat and clean as a pin. So I'll ask her to get in touch with you, shall I?' He added cannily, 'And Sadie's a real nice lass, nowt at all like that last home help of yours, that old misery guts, Iris Smith.'

Bidding Jeff goodbye, strange, Lara thought how often Iris Smith's identity kept on cropping up, obliquely or otherwise. Twice in one morning, as if the wretched woman still hovered over Stella Maris like a bird of prey.

Sadie Cogill proved to be a mild-mannered, pretty young woman, plainly dressed, with neat brown hair, a face devoid of make-up, and a nervous air about her, as if in awe of the sheer size of Stella Maris, and of her prospective employer. She asked anxiously, entering the kitchen, 'I suppose Jeff told you I'm four months pregnant?'

'Yes, of course he did. Why? Is that a problem?' Lara frowned worriedly. 'All I'm asking is someone to give me a hand with the housework three mornings a week. I don't own this house, by the way. I'm simply the housekeeper until September, by which time your baby will be due, and we'll be parting company anyway.' She paused. 'So, the job's yours, if you want it.'

'Even when I'm the size of a house end?' Sadie reminded her. 'Lumbering about the place like a baby elephant?'

'Apart from donkeys, a certain dog and a cat, baby elephants are my favourite animals,' Lara laughed. 'Now, tell me about your other children. I know about Toby, three coming up four next month. Do sit down, by the way. We might as well talk over a cup of tea.'

'Thank you.' Seating herself at the kitchen table: 'Well, apart from Toby, there's Thomas, he's eight, and Sarah, she's six, both at school and doing nicely. They're good kids, not a mite of trouble and never have been. Jeff and I are real proud of them. Mind you, it isn't easy bringing up a family on a housing estate, teaching them right from wrong. What I mean is, some of the neighbours' kids are forever into mischief – throwing stones, using bad language, vandalizing other folks' gardens – and worse – shop-lifting, and stealing money from old-age pensioners.' She sighed deeply, 'I often wish Jeff and I could afford to move away from the Cramer Estate, but we can't, not on his wages and with three children to clothe and feed, apart from ourselves.'

Handing Sadie a cup of tea, Lara said thoughtfully, 'But, forgive my asking, as an employed person with a good steady job, surely your husband could apply to his bank for a loan to cover the downpayment on a mortgage?'

Sadie shook her head. 'He's tried, believe me, but he has no collateral, you see? No savings, nothing apart from his wages and, things being what they are today, he may well be unemployed next week or the week after.' She smiled bravely. 'At least, as we are now, we have a roof over our heads, we're not starving, not in debt, and happy together, so I'd really like to accept the job you've offered me. A bit of extra income wouldn't come amiss right now.'

'In which case, how soon can you start?' Lara asked. 'Shall we say next Monday morning at ten o'clock?'

'Oh yes, that would suit me fine,' Sadie said gratefully. 'And I'll work hard, you'll see.' Rising to her feet: 'Well, thanks for the tea, Mrs Davenport. Jeff told me you were a real nice lady, and he was right. Working for you will be a pleasure, I'm sure.'

How soon, Lara wondered, when she had gone, before she could decently provide the Cogills with collateral sufficient to provide them with a new start in life? The Cramer Estate was no place to raise a family. But she must tread warily, get to know Sadie better before offering what might appear to be charity, or interference in their personal affairs. All that she could possibly do, for the time being, was pay Sadie well for her services, buy young Toby a present for his birthday, possibly organize a party for him and his siblings in the back garden of Stella Maris, with donkey rides, a Punch-and-Judy show, and lots of food – sandwiches, ice cream and jellies for the kids, a barbecue for the grown ups – herself, Jeff and Sadie, Ben Adam and, hopefully, Beauregard Jackson – even, possibly, Marcia Matthews of the Information Bureau?

All pie in the sky, perhaps, and she'd need to ask Joan Prewett's permission beforehand, but worthy of thought, a means of bringing happiness into other people's lives as well as her own. *Her* kind of people, not the Amanda Fieldings of this world. Too much to hope for that Rory might grace the occasion? Georgie, now discharged from hospital, had taken up temporary residence in the Windsor Hotel, to her infinite displeasure at being confined in what she had described to Rory as a 'second-rate boarding house', when she should be in a nursing home – to his infinite distress at being unable to afford a nursing home for her in his present straitened financial circumstances.

All this revealed in an early evening phone call, to Lara, subsequent to Georgie's removal from hospital to the hotel, when she had complained bitterly about everything from the view from the window to the awfulness of the food brought up to her room on a tray: inedible portions of steak-and-kidney pie, for instance, when what she really needed was smoked salmon and caviar, to tempt her appetite.

'I'm fighting a losing battle, Lara,' Rory had confided, sounding distraught, at the end of his tether. 'What to do about it, I haven't the faintest idea.'

Neither had Lara, at that precise moment. She'd said compassionately, yet practically, 'Try not to worry too much. Georgie is still a pretty sick, mentally disturbed lady. Why not have a quiet word or two with Johnny and Jill Carstairs? I'm certain they'd understand if you smuggled in a pack of smoked salmon or a tin or two of fish roes. Not caviar exactly, but as near to it as dammit is to swearing! What I'm getting at, they're all fish eggs, aren't they? Whether from a sturgeon or a cod! Would Georgie really know the difference? What I'm driving at: how often, during your marriage with Georgie, did *real* caviar appear on the menu, if ever?'

'You are absolutely right, Lara,' he'd replied, sounding happier all of a sudden. 'So, I'd best keep soldiering on, hadn't I? Making the best of a bad job?'

'I guess so, along with the rest of the world

and his wife,' Lara responded thoughtfully. Hanging up the phone, how long before Rory realized that Georgina was playing him for a fool, she wondered, as she had always done in the past, as she would continue to do in the future if he hadn't the sense to call her bluff, to tell her bluntly that if they had any kind of future ahead of them, she'd best stop acting as a spoilt child and begin behaving as a responsible human being. But then, what had love to do with common sense? The answer was, nothing. Nothing at all.

Rory's nightly excursions to Hull were over now, so no possibility of further detours to Carnelian Bay. His evenings would be spent at the Windsor, listening to Georgie's complaints. Smoked salmon and caviar indeed! But she mustn't judge the girl too harshly, or assume that Georgie would want to pick up the threads of her life with her former husband. In any case, what threads were left to pick up, from her viewpoint? Rory had sold their marital home she had disliked so much. Scarcely likely she would jump at the notion of living in a rented flat with a man she had so wantonly rejected in favour of another. Presumably a far richer man than Rory, able to provide her with the luxuries she craved. So, where was that man now? And why had he left her in the lurch so disgracefully?

Questions to which there were no clear answers, Lara realized, feeling that her mind was going round in circles.

Needing something positive to latch on to, one afternoon she had gone upstairs to the attics to reopen the cabin trunk, to withdraw from it the daguerrotype photographs of old Joshua Stonehouse, his wife and family, which she carried downstairs to the drawing room to examine more closely that evening, after supper.

The photographs, formally posed in the photographer's studio, revealed an unsmiling, frock-coated elderly gentleman, be-whiskered and holding a top hat beneath his right arm, standing next to a prim-looking lady wearing what appeared to be a black bombazine dress, high-collared, obviously his wife, also unsmiling, with wings of dark hair drawn back, uncompromisingly, from a high forehead, presumably into a bun at the nape of her neck.

Two young girls at the forefront of the photograph, and a slender youth – almost certainly their son and his sisters – also appeared ill-at-ease in the presence of a tri-pod camera within the confines of a studio chock-a-block with high-backed chairs, potted palms and aspidistras, in front of a canvas screen depicting a hazy landscape of hills and dales and flanked by pedestals surmounted with urns of arum lilies.

No wonder the poor girls and their brother looked nervous, Lara thought, imagining the scene, the fussy, obsequious photographer arranging his subjects to his satisfaction, ducking and diving now and then to view the angles beneath a velvet head cover, emerging to prime his flash light; beseeching them to keep still, not to move a muscle until he had counted to ten after the explosion of the flash. Above all, not to blink.

And so the Stonehouse family entire had emerged from the past into the present as a group of unsmiling zombies, staring fixedly at the camera, betraying nothing of their true identities, as if they had been frozen in a kind of timewarp, nervously anticipating the blinding flash of the photographer's 'gun', not daring to blink, not even to swallow lest the picture was ruined: the long-winded process about to begin all over again, to the displeasure of the pater familias, Joshua Stonehouse, a stern, crusty gentleman by the looks of him, Lara surmised, a Victorian despot whose word was law in his household, his castle by the sea.

The two girls were prettier than their mother: slender, wearing lighter-coloured dresses, possibly pale grey or lilac. Both were dark-haired but with softer hairstyles framing plump cheeked faces, full-lipped

181

and with rather lovely eyes beneath wing-like brows. Lara imagined them giggling together, out of earshot of their father, when the photographer had finished his work and they were free to smile, blink and swallow to their heart's content, saying how ghastly it had been awaiting the explosion of the flash light, and how ridiculous the man had looked beneath his velvet blanket with only his legs and his right hand showing – the one holding the flash – reverting to the silliness of youth when the ordeal was over.

Lara knew instinctively that their brother would not have joined in their conversation or their laughter. This was a serious-faced young man with lighter coloured hair falling forward on to a high forehead, not unlike Rupert Brooke in appearance, aesthetically handsome, with an aquiline nose, delicately fashioned lips and eyes betraying an inner sadness at odds with his youth. Perhaps he, like Rupert Brooke, had been a poet? A visionary forced by circumstances beyond his control into a role in life he had no wish to assume? To follow in his father's footsteps as the only son of a worldly, ambitious task master? A misfit? A dreamer of dreams in a world which had no time for dreamers, but only doers, especially not in the eyes of Joshua Stonehouse, a spinner not of dreams but of money.

★ ★ ★

Beau arrived early on Monday morning to continue his work, looking pale and shaken after his recent examination. Lara wondered, in view of his memory loss, presumably also the loss of his identity papers, how he had come by the name Beauregard Jackson? Was this a name dreamed up by the doctors 'up yonder', akin to the American 'John Doe' tag relevant to persons unidentified? If so, it was a nice name, with a ring of the Southern States of America about it, reminiscent of the American Civil War, of the film *Gone With the Wind* – Scarlett O' Hara, Tara and cottonwood trees – and it was obvious, by his accent, that Beau was no Yankee but a Southerner. In which case, why was his real name and identity so hard to establish?

Surely there must be recourse to army records of American servicemen missing in battle, according to where those battles had taken place, and when? Where exactly they had gone missing, from which unit or squadron. Which begged the question, if Beau had been an airman, not a soldier, his aircraft might well have been lost at sea, his survival an unrecorded miracle – missing, presumed dead, with no shred of evidence to prove otherwise.

Possibly, even now, a family in the Southern States of the USA were mourning the loss of a son who was still very much alive. If only, by some further miracle, *something* – even the smallest incident – might jog his memory to an awareness of his true identity, heralding his return home to his family – his loved ones.

Sadie arrived at ten o'clock precisely, to begin her new job, having taken Toby to his playground, preceded by her husband, who had called an hour earlier to pick up Lara's laundry.

First of all, Lara showed Sadie the cupboard under the stairs where the cleaning materials were kept, prior to showing her the rest of the house, remembering how lost she had felt, initially, when Joan Prewett had been too unwell to undertake that particular voyage of discovery.

'It's very big, isn't it?' Sadie said nervously, obviously out of her depth at the sight of so many rooms, so much space compared to her cramped semi-detached house on the Cramer Estate. She added wonderingly, 'Don't you mind being here all alone, especially after dark? I know I would.'

'It bothered me at first, but I'm getting used to it now,' Lara admitted. 'There's a good burglar alarm, or so I'm told. Thankfully I've never found out. Some of the rooms are kept safety-locked from the out-side. I live mainly in the kitchen and drawing room. Besides which, I have my guardian angels, Buster and Cleo, and there's usually plenty of company during the day.'

'Yes, I noticed a man doing the garden when I came in,' Sadie replied. 'Funny, I could have sworn I've seen him before, but I can't think where.'

Lara's heart skipped a beat. 'Perhaps it will come to you,' she said casually, not wanting to make an issue of it on Sadie's first morning, realizing that the girl was awaiting instruction, wondering what would be expected of her. Nothing too demanding, Lara decided, alloting her the task of cleaning the drawing-room silver, a sitting-down job easily performed at the kitchen table, where Lara judged correctly that Sadie would feel at home, near the warmth of the Aga, with herself washing up the breakfast pots and making light hearted conversation to make the girl feel at ease in her new surroundings.

'Take a break whenever you feel like it,' Lara advised her, glancing at her watch. 'Right now it's time to take Buster for a walk, if you'll excuse me for an hour or so. The kettle, the tea bags, the coffee jar, the mugs and so on are over yonder; the milk's in the fridge and, if, by the way, the gardener comes in to make himself a cup of coffee, not to worry if he ignores you. He's rather – shy.' Shy, but amazingly attractive,

Lara thought.

On her return to Stella Maris with Buster, Lara discovered, to her amazement, Sadie vacuuming the drawing-room carpet, the perfectly polished silverware in place, two empty coffee mugs on the kitchen draining board, and Cleo lapping a saucer of milk. 'Sadie, what on earth are you doing?' she asked bemusedly.

'The job I'm being paid to do,' Sadie replied, switching off the vacuum. 'I know you mean well, Mrs Davenport, but I'm not poorly, just pregnant, and I'll not be fobbed off with easy, sitting-down jobs that even a child could do! Begging your pardon, I'm sure.' Her face crumpled suddenly. Close to tears, she added, 'I'm not a charity case! And if you regard me as such, well, you'd best find someone else to work here!'

'But I don't want someone else, I want *you*,' Lara assured her gently. 'Moreover, I not only want you but *need* you! What more can I say? Never having been pregnant myself, I assumed, mistakenly perhaps, that a woman in your condition would be glad of a not-too-demanding job of work to do. Charity didn't enter into it, believe me. But if you wish to leave me, that must be your own decision entirely. I'll do nothing to prevent you, but I'll never forgive myself for having lost you through my own fault, not yours.'

Suddenly, Sadie was in Lara's arms, admitting the truth of the matter, sobbing as if her heart would break, saying how much she dreaded the thought of giving birth to a fourth child when she and her husband could barely support the three they already had.

'Oh, I'm sorry,' she gasped, drying her eyes. 'I don't know what came over me. I don't usually give way to self-pity. I should be thanking my lucky stars for such a good husband and lovely kids, not making a fool of myself, crying over nothing; throwing kindness in your face just cos you're doing your best to go easy with me.'

'It simply occurred to me that you must have been up and doing early to get your children ready for school, Jeff ready for work, making sure they all had a decent breakfast inside them before setting off, dressing Toby ready for his playgroup, making beds, washing up the breakfast pots, thinking what to give them for tea and supper. I'm right, aren't I?'

Sadie nodded. 'Yes, but...'

'But what? Please hear me out. You are young and strong, a good wife and mother, I know that. You are also four months pregnant, with more than enough on your plate to handle without my acting as a – a slave-driver – knowing that when you leave here to collect Toby from his kindergarten, you'll have your own housework, shopping, cleaning, washing and cooking to see to. The last thing I wanted was to overburden you with hard work, leaving you too exhausted to care for your own home, your family commitments. Far more important, in my view, than caring for the home of a comparative stranger. So, we'd best reach a compromise, hadn't we?'

'What kind of a – compromise?' Sadie asked uncertainly.

'Well, for one thing, you might care to make use of the Aga to do a bit of home cooking and baking for your family, to save you the trouble on your return home, say on Friday mornings, after you've done the shopping.'

'You mean, feed my family at your expense?'

'No, not exactly, but the Aga needs using, and you could make good use of it, I'm sure. Besides which, I'm rather partial to home cooking, often too idle to cook for myself.' Lara smiled reassuringly. 'So, you'd be doing me a favour. I am rather partial to steak-and-kidney pie, by the way, Lancashire hot-pot, or a chicken casserole with lots of vegetables, not to mention home-made cakes and apple crumble.' She paused. 'Of course, if you'd rather not...'

'Know what I think, Mrs Davenport?' Sadie uttered hoarsely. 'You are the kindest person I've ever met, and a bad liar into the bargain.'

'Right, then. So, having reached a compromise, how about a cup of coffee?' Lara suggested. 'To celebrate our – reunion!'

'I've already had one, with Beau,' Sadie told her. 'When you were exercising Buster. We got along just fine together, though I still can't for the life of me remember where I've seem him before, unless it was towards the end of the war, at an American airbase near Driffield, where I worked as a waitress, long before I met Jeff, of course.'

She sighed deeply. 'A funny thing, life, a bit like a lottery, a game of chance, or trying to pick the winner of the Grand National. I daresay I could have married an American, gone home with him as a GI bride, and spent the rest of my days regretting it, more than likely. Instead of which I met Jeff, and it was love at first sight.'

'An American airbase near Driffield, you say?' Lara mused thoughtfully. 'And you think it possible that Beau was stationed there during the war?'

'He could have been, I suppose, but there were hundreds of Yanks coming and going at the time, and they all looked pretty much alike to me, apart from one of them, who took quite a shine to me, gave me chocolates and nylon stockings and treated me to a meal once in a while, even offered me an engagement ring, would you believe? Just as well I turned him down, as it happened, cos the next day he was gone, and he never even bothered to write to me.'

She continued reflectively, 'In any case, when I mentioned Driffield to Beau, I drew a complete blank. The name of the airfield obviously meant nothing to him, so I must have been mistaken when I thought I recognized him, that I'd seen him somewhere before. In any case, does it really matter one way or another?'

'I suppose not,' Lara acquiesced, handing Sadie a freshly made mug of coffee, at the same time thinking that it might matter a great deal to Beau if he had once been stationed in Driffield. A starting point, perhaps, in establishing his true identity.

Jeff came whistling up the path on Friday morning. Paying him for the laundry, 'You sound happy,' Lara remarked. Jeff laughed. 'Why wouldn't I? Sadie's over the moon with her job, just a bit worried that she's not pulling her weight, not earning her wages.'

'I look forward to seeing her, and that means a lot to me. Frankly, I dreaded our friend, Mrs Smith, crossing the threshold,' Lara said. 'I was heavenly thankful when she upped and left.'

'Iris Smith is no friend of mine,' Jeff said, pulling a face. 'We had words only yesterday when I caught those grandchildren of hers pulling up my spring vegetables. Granted, it's not much of a plot, but I like to grow a few greens, lettuces and cabbages mainly, and there they were, uprooted and chucked about like so much rubbish. That's when I went round to see Iris, and what did I get? A mouthful of abuse, that's what. She couldn't have cared less; told me to get lost – or words to that effect. Told me to mind my own business, prefaced with a choice assortment of swear words which I wouldn't care to repeat. And, all the time, those kids of hers were standing behind her putting their tongues out at me.'

'You mean they live with her? But *why*? Where are their parents?' Lara frowned.

'Parents? Huh! As far as I can make out, their father's in prison and their mother's gone missing. Rumour has it she had a blazing row with her mother, packed her belongings and stormed out of the house, since when no one's seen egg nor shell of her, leaving Iris to look after her kids.' He added shamefacedly, 'I'm sorry, I suppose the kids are more to be pitied than blamed, having Iris Smith for a grandmother, letting them run riot the way they do; terrorizing the neighbourhood. I've warned Thomas and Sarah to steer well clear of them, and they have done so far, but they're at an impressionable age and I can't help worrying what the future holds in store for them on the Cramer Estate.'

'Then the sooner you leave there, find a decent place to live, the better,' Lara said firmly.

'Easier said than done.' Jeff shook his head. 'I haven't got the wherewithal.'

Taking her courage in both hands, 'Perhaps not, but *I* have. Now, here's what I want you to do. Find yourself a nice little house in a quiet residential area, and when you've found it, I'll provide the wherewithal for the mortgage, the cost of your removal and whatever else necessary to enable you to live in peace from now on.'

Jeff stared at her aghast. 'But I couldn't possibly! What I mean is, how could I accept money from a – a stranger?' Colouring to the roots of his hair: 'I'm sorry, Mrs Davenport, but it's just not on! In any case, why should you part with your money on my account?'

'But it wouldn't be entirely on your account, would it?' she reminded him. 'Look at it this way...' She paused briefly, wanting to convey her exact meaning. 'I've never had children of my own, but I do have a little money, and it would please me to think that I had been instrumental in giving yours a fair crack of the whip, far removed from the Cramer Housing Estate. As for Sadie, doesn't she deserve a home to be proud of? Space in which to breathe, especially with a new baby on the way?

'No need of an answer right away. All I ask is, think about it. Take your time, talk it over with your wife; simply rest assured that if your answer is yes, I shall feel more useful, much happier than I have done for many a long day. After all, what's the use of money if not to bring happiness to others – especially to children?'

Jeff's eyes filled with tears. He said huskily, 'I'll tell Sadie, talk things over with her, let you have an answer as soon as possible. Meanwhile I'd like to...'

'If you were about to thank me,' Lara interrupted forcefully, 'forget it! It's not thanks I'm after, simply a much happier existence for yourself, Sadie and your little ones. Now, if you'll excuse me, I have work to do.'

Closing the door behind her, standing with her back to it, Lara wondered what on earth had possessed her to rush in where angels might fear to tread, in offering financial aid to a man of Jeff Cogill's calibre: a proud man, a decent, honourable man intent on caring for his wife and family in his own way, reluctant to accept help from a – stranger such as herself, which appellation, from Jeff's lips, had wounded her deeply.

But, deep down, she knew why. Because of

Iris Smith and those blasted grandchildren of hers, who, in the fullness of time, might well influence and corrupt the Cogills' off-spring, Toby, Thomas and Sarah.

So how, in all conscience, could she not have offered financial aid to a cash-strapped family in desperate need of an escape route from the Cramer Estate?

Only time would tell, just as only time would tell Rory's future with Georgina, and Beauregard Jackson's battle to discover his identity, not to mention her own battle against a deep-seated sense of loneliness and loss without the presence in her life of the man she loved.

# Twelve

When Sadie arrived on Friday morning, Lara noted approvingly that the sensible young woman had brought with her a sizeable, flat-bottomed garden trug containing two empty casseroles and a tin box, which she placed on the kitchen table in readiness for her baking session.

Smilingly, Lara handed her a shopping list and a generous amount of money to pay for the chuck steak and chicken, carrots, onions, parsnips, celery and mushrooms she had listed. 'The Aga's all riddled, stoked up and ready and waiting,' she said cheerfully. 'Oh, and you might as well bring a pound of sausage meat, if your kids like sausage rolls, that is.'

'Like them? They love them,' Sadie replied bemusedly, 'but I'm not certain that I understand the transaction. What I mean is, I'll be using your cooker, cooking for my family in your time, so what will you get out of it?'

'Hopefully a few sausage rolls and fatty-cakes, plus small portions of beef and chicken stew,' Lara reminded her. 'Not to worry, by the way, about flour, sugar, short-ening and so on, I've a well-stocked larder.'

'Yes, but...' Sadie frowned. 'I must be allowed to pay my own way, Mrs Daven-port. You do see that, don't you?'

'Of course I do, but let's worry about that later, shall we?' She added, 'And would you mind very much calling me Lara from now on? Or Mrs D, if you prefer. Now, hop it up to the shops for the meat and veggies, whilst I fetch out the baking bowl and pastry board etcetera, otherwise we'll get nowhere in a hurry!'

'Well, if you say so – Mrs D,' Sadie responded eagerly. 'I'll be back in two shakes of a lamb's tail!'

So far, so good, Lara thought, but how

would Sadie react to her role as a bene-
factor, a patron, a patronizer, a do-gooder,
when she found out that she had offered her
husband a substantial amount of money as
a means of escape from the Cramer Housing Estate?

She liked Sadie and Jeff Cogill enormously, but did that give her the right to
interfere in their lives? By the same token,
did opening the lid of that trunk in the attic
give her the right to pry into the lives of
a generation of strangers, now dead and
gone?

At twelve thirty, when Sadie had quitted
the kitchen carrying in her trug two
casseroles containing beef and chicken stew
and a tin box full of sausage rolls, fatty and
fairy cakes, sitting down at the kitchen
table, Lara saw herself as a lonely, middle-
aged woman living vicariously on the fringes
of other people's lives, with no home, no
man to call her own, no real future ahead of
her.

Missing Rory, she felt that a joyous
interlude in her life had gone beyond recall.
Looking forward to his visits had given her
a sense of purpose. He still rang occasionally, usually after work on his way to see
Georgie, but his conversation centred on
her state of mind, her constant complaints
about the Windsor Hotel, despite the Carstairs' kindness towards her. Lara listened

sympathetically, knowing that all she could possibly do for him was to listen, feeling that they were drifting apart, slowly but inevitably losing touch with one another, facing the possibility that soon he might well stop ringing her altogether.

A bitter pill to swallow, but then he had made it abundantly clear to her all along that he was still in love with Georgina and would go on loving her, whether or not she loved him in return, and there was one hell of a difference between friendship and love. Thankfully, never at any time had Rory suspected her own feelings towards him, that she had foolishly allowed herself to fall in love with him, and it was better so. Far better to have clung to her pride and self-respect than to embarrass and burden him with overt signs of affection which he would not have wanted, nor, indeed, have responded to in any case.

But where to go from here? It was then that Lara returned once more to the trunk in the attic to derive comfort from the past if not the present, the dead if not the living, to learn more about the Stonehouse family, the original owner of Stella Maris, old Joshua Stonehouse, his wife, daughters, and his son, the pale, willowy youth depicted in the sepia photographs she had examined closely a few evenings ago, whom, mysteriously, she felt that she had met somewhere before, but who knew where or when?

Slowly, guiltily removing the bundle of letters from the trunk, she took them down-stairs to the drawing room to read later after supper, when she had taken Buster for his goodnight walk along the prom and he, and Cleo, had been safely settled for the night...

Suddenly, glancing about her nervously, Lara imagined that she was not alone in the room, and, 'Danny, is that you?' she whispered hoarsely. The only sound she heard was the sound of the sea coming in on the shore. Even so, she could have sworn that she had glimpsed, momentarily, the shadowy figure of a young man, in uniform, standing near the drawing-room window, looking out to sea. And *Danny Boy*, she thought. Yes, of course, for that was the name of Joshua Stonehouse's son. Daniel Stonehouse. She knew that now, and sud-denly she was no longer nervous or afraid, simply glad of his presence in her life.

She, after all, was the interloper, this had been his home. Or was she deluding herself, imagining things as an antidote to loneli-ness? She had convinced herself in her bed-room, recently, when she'd imagined Charles's disapproving presence, that the dead did not come back to haunt the living, and yet there were too many well-docu-mented, if not authenticated, stories of ghostly visitations to disregard them entirely. Owners of stately homes were proud of their spectres. In York, stories abounded of Roman legions disappearing into thin air through solidly built stone walls. In Scarborough, many local inhabitants had glimpsed the ghostly figure of a young girl in a pink crinoline, in the garden of an old house in St Nicholas Street, who had been there one minute, gone the next, like mist on a May morning.

Feeling suddenly cold and shivery, leaving the bundle of correspondence on the settee, switching off the fire and the lights, Lara went upstairs to bed.

Around midnight, startled by the sudden clamour of the burglar alarm, throwing on her dressing gown and hurrying downstairs to find out what was going on, and to soothe the shrill barking of a dog in distress, she saw, to her infinite relief, that the constabulary, quick to answer their summons, had apprehended the burglars: not hefty grown-up men but two squirming boys protesting loudly that they hadn't meant no harm. All they'd done was to throw stones at the windows for a bit of fun.

'What, at this time of night? Well, we'll see about that, young feller-me-lads,' the sergeant in charge of the miscreants uttered severely. 'Out damaging other folks' property when you should be at home in bed.

Well, I want to know the names of your parents, and where you live, so speak up, the pair of you!'

'We ain't got no parents,' the older of the two muttered sulkily. 'We lives wi' us grandma, Mrs Smith, on t' Cramer Housing Estate.'

Turning to Lara, 'I'm sorry you've been disturbed, ma'am,' the man said apologetically, adding, on a lighter note, 'At least you know that your burglar alarm is in good working order.'

'Yes, and thank you, Sergeant,' she replied shakily. 'But what about the boys?'

'That depends on the magistrates, not us,' he informed her. 'Frankly, in their own best interests, I'd like to see the pair of them far removed from the Cramer Housing Estate. The trouble they've caused there you wouldn't believe: breaking and entering, intimidating old-age pensioners; shoplifting, vandalization and so on. This is the first time we've caught them red-handed so to speak, with their pockets full of stones and running away from the scene of the crime.'

'Yes, I see that, but they *are* very young, aren't they?' Lara demurred, glimpsing their pale, frightened faces through the back of a police-car window, at the same time faced with the realization that she had done the right thing in offering Jeff and Sadie Cogill an escape route from the Cramer Housing

Estate, whether or not they chose to accept that offer.

Returning to bed after the contretemps, having soothed the hysterically barking Buster with a portion of Sadie's chicken casserole and a bowl of water and milk combined, at the same time caressing his ears and calling him a Good Boy, Lara lay wide awake till the early hours of next morning, trying to make sense of her life so far, without success. A bit of a mess, all told. An existence wihout rhyme or apparent reason: haunted, ghost-ridden and entirely worthless in her estimation. If only ... If only *what*? That question remained unanswered until, falling asleep at daybreak, she dreamed sweetly of herself and Rory standing together on a promontory overlooking Carnelian Bay, looking up at the stars above; his arms about her, his lips caressing her cheek; telling her he loved her.

Later, she awakened to the sound of rain lashing the windowpanes. Knowing that dreams had nothing to do with reality, she got up, bathed and dressed, and went downstairs to see to the Aga, to open the back door for Buster, to make herself a cup of tea and a slice of toast, destined to remain untasted at the sudden, urgent ringing of the front doorbell.

Jeff was on the doorstep, rain-soaked but smiling. He said eagerly, 'The answer is yes,

Mrs Davenport! Talking things over, Sadie and I have decided to move away from the Cramer Estate, to find another place to live, for the sake of our children. I've come to talk it over with you, if you don't mind, Saturday being my day off, and wanting to get things clear and straight between us, financially speaking, I mean to say – your rates of interest on the loan, and so on.'

Lara frowned. 'What loan? I'm sorry, I should have explained more clearly what I had in mind. But come in and sit down, take off your wet coat. I'll put it near the Aga to dry out.'

'Not much point, is there?' Jeff said dejectedly. 'If you've changed your mind, if you didn't mean what you said.'

'I haven't changed my mind, and I meant every word. Oh, come through to the kitchen and let me explain.' Leading the way: 'Now give me your coat. This is Buster, by the way, feeling a bit sorry for himself, poor dog. We had a bit of a scare last night, a visit from the Police no less, to do with the burglar alarm. Someone had been throwing stones at the drawing-room windows.'

'I know,' Jeff said. 'Word gets around. The Police were at the Smiths' house earlier this morning. That's what decided us – Sadie and me – to get away from the Cramer Estate, to find ourselves a decent place to live before it's too late. Now I don't know

202

what to think.'

'Then I'd best tell you what *I* think,' Lara said. 'Find yourself a house. When you've found something you like, let me know and I'll settle the mortgage. It's a straightfoward business deal. The deeds will be in my name, and you'll pay me so much rent per month, whatever you can afford. Then, if ever you lost your job, which I doubt, you'd still be certain of a roof over your heads.' She smiled reassuringly. 'So, now what do you think? Or perhaps you wouldn't fancy me as a landlady?'

'What do I think?' Jeff beamed. 'I think it's a wonderful idea. Honestly, Mrs Davenport, I can't begin to thank you...'

'Then *don't*,' Lara advised him. 'Just start house-hunting and leave the rest to me. We'll work out the details later. Now, how about a nice fresh pot of tea by way of celebration?'

Buster barked suddenly. 'Oh lord, that means he wants to go out for a walk,' Lara said wryly. 'I'd best wear my raincoat and take an umbrella.'

'No ma'am. Allow me,' Jeff said gallantly. 'I'll take him, if he'll let me, that is. I'm main wet as it is, and I wouldn't want you catching your death of cold. How far shall I take him?'

Lara laughed. 'Not to worry, *he*'ll take *you*!'

Making herself a fresh slice of toast, strange how things worked out, Lara thought. Her misfortune of last night had resulted in good fortune for Sadie, Jeff and their children. The arrival of a police car at the Smiths' that morning had galvanized them into a life-changing decision, and when they had found a more suitable house, she would settle the downpayment on the property and arrange to pay the mortgage from Charles's pension fund.

Meanwhile, she must ring a glazier to replace panes of glass cracked by Iris Smith's grandchildren in their stone-throwing escapade. More than likely they would be called upon to attend a juvenile court on a charge of wilful damage to other people's property. How Iris would react to more trouble, Lara shuddered to think, especially if the boys' court appearance was covered in print in the *Carnelian Bay Gazette*. Worse still, what if the boys were taken into care? Placed in a home for young delinquents? Iris branded as an unfit person to act as their guardian? Even more worrying, what if Iris blamed her, Lara, for this latest turn of misfortune in the Smith family saga? She wouldn't put it past her.

When Jeff returned with Buster, Lara switched on the kettle for a fresh pot of tea, put Jeff's coat near the Aga to steam gently, unearthed a towel to rub Buster as dry as possible after his outing in the rain, hampered by his utter refusal to stand upright, simply rolling over on his back, paws waving in the air, to have his tummy tickled. Jeff laughed, Lara joined in. 'Animals! Who'd have 'em?' she remarked, tongue-in-cheek.

'Toby would, for one,' Jeff replied lightheartedly. 'He's been on about having a "doggy", almost since he learned how to talk, an impossibility of course, on the Cramer Estate, but I – what I mean to say is...'

Reading his mind, handing him a cup of tea across the kitchen table, 'No need to worry, ownership of a "doggy" is every child's birthright,' Lara assured him. 'And when you've found the house you want, it will be my pleasure to grant his heart's desire, as a kind of house-warming present. A really splendid puppy complete with a basket and lots of squeaky toys besides, with two provisos. If it's a dog, you'll call it Buster; if it's a bitch, you won't name it after me!'

The rain seemed 'set-in' as Lara's mother was won't to say, ruefully, when visitors were hanging about the house staring out at the rainswept seafront, robbed of the expected sunshine of their summer holidays. 'Well, it can't be fine every day, can it?'

There was something especially depressing about wet Sundays, Lara thought, going downstairs to begin her daily chores: riddling the Aga ashes, taking Buster for his early morning walk, her macintosh buttoned up to her chin, wearing wellingtons and a sou'wester. Filling in time on a day like this would not be easy. Apart from attending Morning Service in St Mary's, afterwards warming up Sadie's beef casserole for lunch, washing up and listening to the one-o'clock news on the wireless, faced with a long, lonely afternoon and evening ahead of her, what could she possibly do to while away the hours until bedtime?

It was then she remembered the bundle of letters on the drawing-room sofa, which she later sat down to read, albeit guiltily, feeling like a voyeuse until, gradually, absorbed in the closely written pages, losing track of time, she experienced a strange sense of déjà-vu, as if she had slipped from the present into the past, when Stella Maris had been the home of the stern pater familias, Joshua Stonehouse, his wife, aptly named Patience, their daughters Mary-Anne and Dorothea, and their son Daniel.

Many of the letters were from friends and relations of the Stonehouses, thanking them for hospitality received during weekend visits to Stella Maris: praising the excellence of their accommodation, the food and wine, the many delightful excursions, so thought-fully arranged for them, to visit places of interest in the surrounding countryside.

Other letters, written to their parents by Mary-Anne and Dorothea from venues including Margate, London, Melton Mowbray and the Lake District, to which they had been invited, presumably, by close family relations of theirs, spoke glowingly of the picnics, concerts and tea parties they'd attended. They had, apparently, enjoyed London most of all: visits to the Tower of London, Regent's Park, St Paul's Cathedral and Westminster Abbey (suitably chaperon-ed, of course). No mention of flirtations along the way, of stolen kisses, of less formal letters written to secret admirers long after their chaperone of the day was fast asleep and snoring in her bedroom next to theirs.

Most intriguing and thought provoking of all was a letter, dated 14 July 1913, penned by Daniel Stonehouse to his father, which read:

Dear Papa,

I deeply regret the harsh words that passed between us last weekend and your cavalier treatment of Clara Foxton, the girl I love and intend to marry, with or without your permission, when I discover her present whereabouts.

Instant dismissal, without references,

of a young woman in your employ was both cruel and unjust, since she had done nothing wrong to warrant such treatment, views expressed when I came home from Huddersfield a week ago to discover her absence from the house, also that you held me responsible for entering a relationship with what you were pleased to call 'a gold-digging member of the lower classes'.

Money has always been your raison d'être. Thankfully it has never been mine. As your son and heir, I entered the family business at your insistence and against my own better judgement, and you allowed that to happen, even knowing that I was not cut out for the job alloted to me as a member of the 'illustrious' Stonehouse family, so called.

Now the time has come to make my own way in life. I have already taken steps to disclaim my inheritance and to quit the mill by the end of the month.

I shall, of course, keep in touch with my mother and sisters whenever possible. They, like Clara Foxton, have done nothing wrong. I love them all dearly, as I love Clara, a deep-seated affection which, sadly, no longer applies to yourself.

The letter was signed, 'Yours regretfully,

208

Daniel Stonehouse.' What it must have cost a sensitive human being such as Danny to have locked horns with his martinet father, to the extent of disclaiming his role as the inheritor of old Joshua's fortune, Lara could only surmise, at the same time rejoicing in his courage in standing up for his own beliefs and ideals in the face of so formidable an opponent as Joshua. So, how had the story ended?

Suddenly the doorbell rang. Confusedly, Lara rose to her feet to answer the summons.

Gareth Roberts was on the doorstep. And, 'What is it? What do you want?' she asked, far more involved in the past than the present, deeply resenting his appearance when her thoughts were centred, not on her own life, but on that of Daniel Stonehouse in particular, that gentle, ghostly presence in her life – or so she believed. A presence far more compelling than that of Dr Roberts.

He said quietly, 'A word in your ear, if you don't mind asking me in out of the rain.'

'Oh, is it still raining? I hadn't noticed,' she replied bemusedly. 'Sorry. Yes, of course, please do come in. Anything I can get you? A cup of coffee, perhaps?' – remembering that she had meant to write a note of apology to him after their disastrous lunch together at the Golf Club Hotel.

Leading the way to the drawing room,

'Forgive the clutter,' she said. 'I'm researching the history of Stella Maris. I came across a trunk in the attic full of documents, letters, photographs and so on.'

'And I'm intruding?' He smiled as Buster, stretched out in front of the fire, looked up, tail wagging faintly, then promptly fell asleep again. 'Don't worry, I shan't stay long. I came to apolgize for my behaviour at our last meeting. I shouldn't have been so outspoken, I can see that now. I'm sorry. Forgive me?'

'I'm sorry too,' Lara admitted. 'I meant to write to you but I didn't know what to say. You didn't behave badly, *I* did.'

'Does this mean you'd be willing to risk dining with me next Saturday evening?'

'Well, yes. But not at the Golf Club Hotel, if you don't mind.'

When he had gone, Lara wondered if she had done the right thing in accepting his invitation. On the other hand, he had taken the trouble to apologize for his outspokeness at their last meeting, so hardly likely he would repeat his mistake.

Returning to the drawing room after bidding him goodnight, Lara folded Daniel's letter to his father back in its envelope, her train of thought broken by Gareth Roberts' appearance on the doorstep, and sat staring into the fire for a while, mulling over the undertones of that letter: an angry young man coming home to discover that the girl he loved had been sent packing by his stern, judgemental parent.

But to continue reading on in her present state of mental and physical fatigue would be both foolish and unwise, when what she most longed for was the benison of sleep, an end to this long, rainy Sunday, Lara realized, switching off the lights and seeing to the animals before making her way upstairs to bed.

# Thirteen

Monday dawned fair and clear. When Jeff arrived to pick up the laundry, he said that he and Sadie had been out and about the day before to look at houses for sale, making a kind of game of it, the kids on the back seat of his old jalopy, playing at 'house-spotting'.

Lara laughed. 'And did you spot anything you fancied?'

'Yes, as a matter of fact, a nice little semi in a cul-de-sac on the far side of town, with a well-maintained front garden. I made a note of the estate agent's name and number – just in case. What I mean is, we wouldn't want to jump the gun, so to speak, without your permission. After all, it may not be what you had in mind for us, or yourself, come to that.'

'Why not ring the estate agent?' Lara suggested. 'Make an appointment to view, and I'll come with you. Do so now, if you like. The phone's in the drawing room, first door on the right. Meanwhile, I'll be in the kitchen, doing battle with the Aga.'

But Beau had beaten her to it. Entering the kitchen, she found him riddling ashes, a basket of kindling beside him. He said, respectfully, rising to his feet, 'Sorry ma'am, I figured I'd best make myself useful indoors, if that's OK? The grass being too wet to cut after the rain.'

And, 'Yes, of course, Beau,' she replied gently. 'That was very kind and thoughtful of you.'

Flushing slightly, thinking what an attractive lady she was, he continued, 'Next, with your permission, I'd like to clean up your garden shed, oil the mower, the secateurs and so on; after I've gotten rid of these ashes, that is.'

'Sounds fine to me,' Lara assured him, liking the man enormously, his proud bearing, good looks, above all his impeccably good manners inextricably linked to his innate shyness and charm, thinking how lucky she was to have broken through his initial barrier of reserve to the extent that he now regarded her, not as an enemy but a friend. Feeling shy herself, reading admiration in his eyes.

Jeff appeared at that moment, as Beau was about to leave the kitchen. 'So, what news?' Lara asked him. 'Have you made an appointment?'

'Yes, for tomorrow afternoon at two o'clock,' Jeff said. 'If that's all right with you? I can take a late lunch hour, Sadie will have picked Toby up from his playgroup, and Thomas and Sarah won't be home for tea till four o'clock.' He added apologetically, 'Toby will have to come with us, if you don't mind. But he's a good little lad, as a rule.'

'Of course I don't mind. So, shall I take a taxi?'

'No, Mrs D. I'll call for you at a quarter to two. The agent, a Mr Strong, said he'd be at the house at two o'clock sharp, to show us round; said there'd been a lot of other folk after it.'

Thinking of Rory, Lara said wistfully, 'In which case, if the house lives up to expectations, the sooner a firm offer is made for it, the better. But it's up to you and Sadie to decide. After all, it will be your home, not mine.'

It really was a charming house, Lara

decided at first glance: solidly built, with a tiled porch over the front doorstep, a curved bay window overlooking a small, tidily kept garden. Inside, a red-tiled vestibule leading to a spacious hall, staircase, and doors leading to a sizeable drawing room, a smaller living room, and a well-fitted kitchen giving access to a long rear garden with stout larch fencing, slim birch trees, and a stone-paved patio adjacent to the back door.

Sadie's face was a picture, a joy to behold as she caught sight of the dining alcove in the kitchen, something she had always dreamed of, where she, Jeff and the kids could have their meals together, en famille, without having to bustle food from the kitchen to the cramped living room of the council house on the Cramer Estate. It was then, at that precise moment in time, that Lara decided to buy the house, for Sadie's sake, to keep aglow that stunned expression of absolute joy on her face.

Leading the way upstairs, the estate agent, Mr Strong, opened the landing doors to reveal three bedrooms, a boxroom and a tiled bathroom complete with a large airing cupboard, boxed-in bath, hand basin and lavatory.

Standing back a little, with the air of a conjurer having produced a white rabbit from a top hat, 'Well, what do you think?' he asked.

'That rather depends on the asking price, and whether or not you are willing to lower it in favour of a quick sale,' Lara said winsomely. 'I realize, of course, that you are probably not the prime mover in this event. In which case, when you have had time to consult with your partners, perhaps you would care to contact me later this afternoon? Here is my name, address and telephone number.'

Glancing quickly at the scrap of paper she had given him, Mr Strong said, 'I'm sure some agreement can be reached, if you really are interested in buying the property.'

Lara smiled. 'Yes, I am. Extremely so.'

Sadie said ecstatically on the way home, 'If you do decide to lend us the mortgage money, Sarah could have her own room, Thomas could share with Toby, and that little room would make a lovely nursery for the new baby.'

'Don't get too excited,' Jeff warned her. 'It isn't cut and dried yet. It's up to Mrs D to decide.'

'Mrs D *has* decided,' Lara chuckled. 'All that taradiddle about a price reduction was just a bluff to keep Mr Strong on his toes. An estate agent friend of mine once told me never to appear overanxious to buy, and always to negotiate a deal of some kind, if possible.' Dear Rory, she thought, wishing he were here, now, to signify his approval of the property, and her astuteness in 'carrot-dangling' the urbane Mr Strong.

'You really *mean* it?' Sadie uttered, close to tears of happiness and relief, fiercely cuddling the child in her arms as a means of expressing her pent-up emotion. 'You're not just saying it to please Jeff and me? You really *do* like the house?'

'*Like* it? I love it!' Lara assured her. 'I knew, the minute I saw it, that it would be ideal for you and the children. No passing traffic to worry about, with a safe garden for them to play in, and that patio near the back door where you can eat out, if you feel like it!'

Jeff interposed huskily, 'With plenty of room for a nice little kitchen garden. I might try my hand at growing runner beans, peas and outdoor tomatoes.'

Dreaming aloud, Sadie broke in excitedly, 'I've always wanted a proper kitchen with a dining alcove and plenty of cupboard space, a nice bathroom, and a porch over the front door...'

A quiet feeling of joy invaded Lara's heart, because, by means of the money at her disposal, she could use a small part of it to bring happiness to others. Mortgage repayments would present no problem, deriving from Charles's pension paid monthly into her savings account, so far untouched since his death. Not that her dour, late husband would rejoice at the squandering of his pension on mortgage repayments in respect of the Cogill family's security. But Charles was dead and gone now. Life was for the living, especially decent people like the Cogills, in need of a good home in which to bring up their children.

Returning to Stella Maris, dismounting from Jeff's broken down jalopy, blowing kisses to Sadie and Toby through the back-seat window, 'I'll ring you this evening,' she promised. 'When I've heard from the estate agents.'

Jeff said pragmatically, 'Just our luck if someone else had got in ahead of us. Mr Strong did say there had been lots of folk after the house already.'

He was right, Lara thought dejectedly. What if she had done wrong in prevaricating, not putting a downpayment on the property there and then? Too late now to regret her tardiness. All she could possibly do, for the time being, was await, nervously, the phone call from the firm of Elleker, Messruther and Strong.

When it came at five thirty, 'Yes,' she said hoarsely. 'Mrs Davenport speaking ... Oh, I see ... So, what is your advice? ... Tomorrow morning at ten o'clock? ... Yes, of course ... Thank you for ringing!'

At six o'clock, when she had calmed down

a little, Lara rang the Cogills' phone number. Jeff answered the call. 'Mrs D?' he asked expectantly. 'So, what news? ... Really? Oh, thank God! Tomorrow morning you say, to sign the contract? No, I'm sure Sadie won't mind ... And they actually agreed to a price reduction? I'm sorry, Mrs D, to seem so stupid. The truth is, I scarcely know what to say – except thank you, and God bless you!'

Taking Buster for his accustomed early-evening walk along the prom, tired but happy, what an extraordinary day this has been, Lara thought reflectively. A kind of watershed during which she had acted independently for the first time in her life. What a wonderful ending if the phone rang, that evening, and she picked up the receiver to hear Rory's voice on the line, but his calls came less frequently nowadays than before, as she had suspected they might now that Georgie had re-entered his life so dramatically, insistent on leaving the Windsor Hotel and moving into his bachelor pad to live; annexing his bedroom, Lara imagined, forcing him to spend uncomfortable nights on his living-room sofa – unless, of course, they were sleeping together. Somehow, the thought was unbearable, but the truth often was just that, she thought wretchedly, her happiness dissipated suddenly at the very idea of a renewed intimacy between Rory and the woman he loved. Later, settling down in the drawing room, the animals for company, Lara returned to the Stonehouse correspondence. Uppermost came a letter from Mary-Anne to her sister Dorothea, which read:

Dear Thea,
   Mama and I are missing you so much, but I'm glad that I elected not to go with you to Melton Mowbray, leaving Mama on her own – apart from Papa – who we see little of nowadays since he refuses to dine with us and has taken to having his meals served in his study. An unhappy state of affairs resultant on Danny's decision to quit the Mill and make his own way in life, for which I blame Papa entirely. There, I've said it, and I'm glad, not sorry. If only I possessed the courage to tell him so, but I dare not, for Mama's sake, as well as my own. In his present mood, he would more than likely send us packing also, as he did poor Clara Foxton.
   What has become of Danny, no one knows. My own belief is that he has gone in search of Clara, who may be any-where, facing starvation for all Papa cares, having so cruelly dismissed her without references or a penny to her

name, just because Danny had fallen in love with her and wished to marry her. And who could blame him? Such a pretty, gentle girl, not well educated yet possessed of inborn kindness and sensitivity which far outweigh mere formal education; softly spoken, knowing instinctively how to behave in the presence of her so-called betters. Given the chance, Clara would have graced, not disgraced, the Stonehouse family name. But Papa could never accept Danny marrying beneath him, just as poor Clara could not accept marrying above her own station in life, because she told me so herself.

One evening, at bedtime, brushing my hair, she said, 'I'm very fond of your brother, Miss Mary, but he's a rich man, heir to a family fortune, and I am nothing more than a servant. I could never bring myself to marry into money.'

Well, my dear Thea, I must end this letter now. Trusting that you are enjoying your stay in Melton Mowbray with Aunt Felicity and Uncle Samuel. I remain, ever your loving sister,
    Mary-Anne.

Refolding the letter, Lara wondered if Danny had eventually discovered the whereabouts of his lost love. If so, and when she found out that he had refused his inheritance for her sake, would Clara Foxton have married Daniel Stonehouse after all? Lara hoped so, with all her heart, just as she wished, with all her heart, that the telephone beside her would ring. She would give the world to talk to Rory, to tell him about The Birches, the name of the house she intended buying, to find out how he was coping with Georgina. But the phone did not ring.

Up and doing early next morning in anticipation of her visit to the estate agents', ordering a taxi, she arrived at their offices at ten o'clock precisely. Mr Strong emerged from his sanctum to greet her. Smiling urbanely, he said, 'Please come this way, Mrs Davenport. This shouldn't take long. The contract is ready for you to sign, subject, of course, to—'

'I know what you are about to say, Mr Strong. Naturally you'll need confirmation of my financial status,' Lara said. 'One can't be too careful.' She smiled. 'Which is why I brought these–' laying on his desk her current bank books, statements and so forth. Referring in particular to her late husband's ongoing pension from his former employers, she continued, 'It is my intention to pay the mortgage, monthly, from this account by standing order, if that is acceptable. If so, perhaps you would care to ring up the bank on my behalf? Might as well settle the matter here and now, don't you agree? I don't mind waiting.'

Strong made the call. Waiting, Lara glanced round his office. He said, hanging up the receiver, looking pompous, 'All is well, you'll be pleased to know, Mrs Davenport.' Lara said serenely, 'I never doubted that for one moment, Mr Strong.'

At ten fifty that Wednesday morning, Lara signed the contract with a flourish, handed the agent a cheque, scooped up the keys to The Birches, tucked them into her handbag, and, bidding Mr Strong a not entirely fond farewell, walked out into the fresh air of an early May morning, a house-owner, a person in her own right at last!

This area of town was new to her. A far cry from the Cramer Estate, the thoroughfare in which the estate agents' offices were situated contained a variety of well-established shops with interesting window displays, including a jeweller's, a bookstore, florists, a chemist's, furniture showrooms, a boutique, two cafés, banks, bakeries, a supermarket and a lending library.

Entering a café, ordering coffee and a scone, seated at a window table, looking out at the passing parade of pedestrians, Lara thought of the Cogills, the pleasure Sadie would derive from her new environment, how much Jeff would enjoy creating a small kitchen garden, far removed from the destructive element of the Cramer Estate's juvenile delinquents.

What had happened to Iris Smith's grandchildren? she wondered. So far she had heard, read nothing of their appearance in court. Possibly the Police had let them off with a warning. She hoped so for Mrs Smith's sake, her own also, come to think of it. No way would she wish to press charges against a couple of youngsters deprived of parental upbringing and guidance, left in the charge of grandparents scarcely qualified to cope with their own lives, much less those of a pair of tearaway schoolchildren.

Finishing her scone and coffee, paying her bill and leaving the café, suddenly she remembered her Saturday dinner date with Gareth Roberts, wondering what on earth she should wear. Something neat but not gaudy. Certainly not her cocktail dress or one of her two-piece suits.

Entering the boutique, displaying rails of separates in all colours, shapes and sizes, the saleswoman led her unerringly towards a selection of ankle-length evening skirts and a bewildering choice of tops, ranging from the frilly and fabulous to the more mundane.

An hour later, Lara emerged from the shop having treated herself to a black, satin-lined, ankle-length grosgrain skirt and a long-sleeved, flame-coloured silk blouse, discreetly cut and opaque enough not to accentuate unduly what lay beneath, despite the saleswoman's assurances that 'Madam should feel proud of her figure'.

Oh hell, Lara thought wretchedly, quitting the boutique. What on earth had possessed her to part with money on clothes for a dinner date with a man she didn't want to dine with anyway? A matter of pride, of self-respect, perhaps?

But no, not entirely that, she reminded herself, rejoicing in the sunshine and fresh air about her as she recalled her recent visit to the estate agents', the signing of the contract, the handing over of the keys of The Birches. The clothes she had bought, the money she had squandered in the boutique, had nothing whatever to do with pride or self-respect. Everything to do with sunshine, fresh air. Pride, not in her appearance, but in her ability to help others less fortunate than herself. Self-respect, not because of a dinner date, but because she had been instrumental in helping a decent, ordinary family towards a better way of life.

Returning to Stella Maris, picking up the phone and dialling the Cogills' number,

224

'Sadie?' she said breathlessly. 'Mrs D here. Just ringing to let you know that all's well. The contract has been signed, and I have the keys of your new home in my possession. Could Jeff call this evening, after work, to collect them?' She paused anxiously. 'Sadie, are you all right? You're not crying, are you?'

'I always cry when I'm happy,' Sadie sniffed. 'And I'm so happy right now, I could – burst!'

Later, when the bell rang, Lara hurried to open the door, expecting to see Jeff on the step. But it wasn't Jeff, it was Iris Smith.

Face contorted with rage, she burst forth, 'I have a score to settle with you, my lady, and settle it I shall, here and now. I'm not leavin' till I've had my say.' Brushing past Lara, she stormed into the hall, slamming the door behind her. Nostrils flaring: 'Now just you listen to me! I'll get even with you for all the misery you've caused me if it's the last thing I do!'

Standing her ground, refusing to be intimidated, Lara said levelly, 'I suggest you leave now, otherwise I shall ring the Police.'

'Oh yes, you're good at that, ain't you?' Iris sneered. 'Like you did t'other night when my grandkids was havin' a bit of a lark out yonder, in t' garden: gettin' the pore little beggars arrested an' tekken down to t' p'lice station, for nowt more than a bit of innocent fun!'

Lara said quietly, 'I didn't ring the police. The alarm went off automatically when the drawing-room windows were hit by flying stones and your grandchildren were caught red-handed.'

'Oh, trust you to try to wriggle out of it,' Iris retorted. 'But you'll not wriggle out of what I have planned for you! Them kids have to appear in court next Tuesday, thanks to you, you evil bitch! God knows what'll happen to them afterwards, nor me neither if they takes them away from me, after all I've done to tek care of them. But I'm warning you, my fine lady, if that happens, you'll rue the day you was born!'

The front door, having been left on the latch, opened suddenly. Jeff came into the hall. Confronting Iris, he uttered disgustedly, 'Still up to your mischief-making, are you? Well, I overheard every word you said. Now take my advice and hop it while the going's good, unless you'd rather I throw you out neck and crop!'

Rounding on him fiercely, 'You lay a finger on me, Jeff Cogill, and I'll have you for assault an' – an' grievous bodily harm,' Iris spat back at him.

Lara interposed quietly, 'And if you don't do as Mr Cogill suggests, *I'll* have you up for trespass and threatening behaviour, is that perfectly clear?'

When Iris had gone, trembling violently, Lara burst into tears. Then, smiling valiantly, she said huskily, 'Not to worry, Jeff. I always cry when I'm happy.'

# Fourteen

Lara went to Whitby on Saturday morning, to have her hair done. Too late now to cancel her dinner engagement with Gareth Roberts, however much she regretted having made it in the first place.

Knowing he would arrive punctually at seven, she went upstairs to bathe and change into her 'finery' an hour beforehand. When the doorbell rang at half-six, Oh drat it, she thought, trust him to come early. Well, he'd have to wait in the drawing room till she was good and ready.

But it wasn't Gareth.

'Hello, Lara,' Rory said quietly. 'Sorry to call unannounced. I happened to be in the vicinity and decided to make a detour. Hope you don't mind.'

'*Mind*? Of course not!' Holding out her hands to him: 'Come in, my dear. How long can you stay? Overnight?'

'If only that were possible.' He smiled ruefully. 'But Georgie will be on tenter-hooks, wondering what's become of me.'

'I've been wondering the same thing myself,' Lara admitted. 'I miss your phone calls, talking things over with you. Sorry, I shouldn't have said that. Life must be pretty difficult for you at the moment.'

They were standing in the hall together, the front door slightly ajar, the scent of lilacs and sea air drifting in from the garden and the cliffs beyond.

Drawing in a sharp breath, 'Difficult? Impossible would be nearer the mark,' he confessed. 'Since Georgie came to live with me, I'm seldom alone nowadays. It's such a tiny flat, you see? She follows me from room to room, wanting to know what I'm doing, thinking, feeling, when I don't know myself half the time.'

Lara's heart went out to him, thinking how thin, strained and ill he looked, imagining the set-up: a sick, fretful woman in constant need of reassurance, draining the life out of him, leaving him little or no room to breathe within the confines of a two-roomed bachelor flat.

Breaking into her thoughts, he said, with a dawning awareness of her evening en-semble, long skirt and flame-silk blouse, 'Am I right in thinking that you have some-thing special planned for this evening?'

'I'm having dinner with Dr Roberts,' she said reluctantly.

'I see. And here am I making a darned nuisance of myself. I'm sorry, Lara, I shouldn't have turned up out of the blue the way I did. Forgive me?'

'You're not going already?' Her voice betrayed a note of anguish. 'But you've only just got here!'

'I know, but two's company, three's a crowd. I daresay Dr Roberts would agree with me, in which case I'd best make myself scarce before he appears on the scene, don't you think?'

'No, I don't as it happens! The fact is, I'd far rather stay here and talk to you than have dinner with him. I never know what to say to the wretched man anyway!'

'Then best say nothing. Let him do the talking,' Rory advised her, brushing her cheek with his lips before hurrying down the front steps towards the garden gate, where he paused, momentarily, to wave her goodbye.

Watching him leave, through tear-dimmed eyes, still standing on the top step, Lara scarcely noticed the arrival of Gareth Roberts.

'At the risk of having my head bitten off,' he said, 'may I say how charming you look.' He paused. 'Is anything the matter? You seem a little upset. Not bad news, I hope? I saw your friend getting into his car a few minutes ago.'

'No, not bad news. I'm just a bit concerned about him, that's all,' Lara explained awkwardly. 'He's ... That is to say ... What I mean is, he's been under a lot of pressure recently.'

Regarding her thoughtfully. 'You're very fond of him, aren't you?' Gareth asked bluntly.

'Yes, I am,' Lara admitted. 'Rory is a very dear friend of mine. Why? What of it?' Irritation coming uppermost at Dr Roberts' catechism. 'I'd rather not discuss it further, if you don't mind.'

Oh God, she thought mutinously, trust Gareth Roberts to rub her up the wrong way. Five minutes in his company and she was already on the defensive, wishing him far enough away; dreading the thought of the evening ahead of her, wanting it over and done with as quickly as possible.

In the event, it turned out far better than she had expected. The Feathers Hotel, ten miles inland from Carnelian Bay, where he had booked a table for two, was far less ostentatious than the Golf Club Hotel: Dickensian in character, solidly comfortable, with a coal fire in the lounge; sporting prints and a display cabinet filled with items of Victorian memorabilia.

'Oh, this is nice,' Lara said appreciatively, feeling more relaxed.

'I thought you might like it, which is why I chose it. How's your research coming on, by the way?'

Suddenly Lara found herself talking to Gareth quite naturally, telling him about the Stonehouse family, going on to explain her stewardship of Stella Maris and the role Rory had played in it.

Listening intently, he said, 'I've heard of Joan Prewett. Amanda has spoken of her more than once. Something of a recluse, one gathers. Not over fond of socializing with the neighbours. How about you?'

'I haven't met anyone else apart from the Fieldings. The other houses appear to be unoccupied at the moment. But no, I'm not a party-goer by nature. I have, however, rented a beach chalet for the summer.'

'Have you indeed? Well, that's a step in the right direction,' Gareth said. 'Ah, I think our table is ready. Shall we go through to the dining room?'

A young waitress showed them to a window table overlooking a discreetly floodlit garden. Handing them the menus, she said, 'Would you like anything to drink while you're making your minds up?'

Lara smiled at the girl. 'Just mineral water for me, please, with ice and a twist of lemon.'

'And I'll have a half of lager,' Gareth said easily. 'By the way, what is tonight's specialité de la maison?'

The girl looked flummoxed. 'Oh, if you mean what's on, well, there's some nice fresh trout, chicken in a cream sauce with mushrooms, roast lamb an'...' She stopped speaking abruptly, cheeks pink with embarrassment. 'Sorry, sir, I forget what else.'

'Not to worry, I'll settle for the trout and roast lamb,' Gareth said. 'And you, Lara?'

'I'll have the chicken,' she responded, intrigued by a fresh insight into her companion's character she had never seen before. Possibly because she had never bothered to look for it? And yet he had been kind to her following the death of her husband, she thought. So, why her former hostility towards him?

'A penny for your thoughts,' he said lightly.

'I'm not sure they're worth that much,' she replied. Changing the subject adroitly, glancing up at the night sky, 'Oh, look,' she said eagerly. 'There's a new moon.'

Despite her earlier misgivings, it had been a lovely evening, Lara decided on the return journey to Stella Maris. The food had been delicious, surprisingly well served by their trainee waitress, who had blushed scarlet at the size of the tip Gareth had given her.

Overwhelmed by his generosity, 'Oh lor, sir,' she'd blurted. 'Ta ever so! I'll be able to buy my brother a decent birthday present after all.'

Which reminded Lara that she would like to organize a garden party to coincide with Toby's birthday, with donkey rides, Punch and Judy, food and presents, plus a puppy and squeaky toys for the birthday boy. On an impulse, on her way out of the dining room, 'What's your name, by the way?' she asked the waitress. And, 'Clara Stonehouse,' the girl replied. 'An' my brother's name is Daniel.' She added proudly, 'We call him Danny for short, and he's a real good kid is Danny Boy!' Lara stared at her in amazement. This seemed incredible. Clara and Daniel Stonehouse?

Seated beside her in the car, 'Now what's on your mind?' Gareth asked her. 'Apart from the new moon? I know there's something!'

'Yes, but I need time to think about it,' Lara demurred. 'You see, it may be just a coincidence, a – fluke. Please don't ask me to explain, because I can't. Another time, perhaps, when I've had time to go into it more fully.'

'There will be another time, then?' he asked, escorting her to her front door.

'Well, yes, I think so.' Suddenly nervous and ill-at-ease with him again, aware of his closeness to her on the doorstep, uncertain how to deal with the situation, she said, 'Thank you for a lovely evening, and goodnight.'

'Goodnight, Lara,' he said softly. 'Sleep well, and sweet dreams!' And then he was gone, hurrying down the steps away from her, having made no attempt to kiss her goodbye, as she had feared that he might. Had he done so, how would she have responded to his embrace?

Going through to the kitchen, kneeling beside Buster's basket prior to letting him out to relieve his feelings, she said, at the touch of his rough, warm tongue on her cheek, 'I'll never know now, shall I? Well, they do say there's no fool like an old fool.'

Habitually, throughout her life so far, Lara had paused occasionally to take stock of whatever situation she was faced with – a kind of do-it-yourself clearing away of mental cobwebs, going so far as to write down lists of problems and their possible solutions. Not that cut-and-dried solutions were always forthcoming, especially during her marriage to Charles Davenport, and yet her attempts at self-analysis had given her a sense of direction akin to standing at a crossroads looking up at a signpost marked Past, Present and Future.

By the same token, during her Middlesbrough days, she had written endless shopping lists to ensure that she would forget nothing pertaining to Charles's comfort and well-being, making certain of a constant supply of toilet rolls; his favourite foods – breakfast cereal, bacon and eggs; fresh fruit and vegetables, a superabundance of potatoes in particular, plus plenty of lean meat, knowing his detestation of anything in the least bit fatty, or frozen. Above all, her inability to please him no matter how hard she tried.

Now, seated at Joan Prewett's elegant drawing-room escritoire, having rung Joan first to ask her permission for the garden party, Lara headed her list:

(a)   Hire beach donkeys; a Punch-and-Judy; a barbecue. Where from?

(b)   Food. Sausages, hamburgers, jacket potatoes, sandwiches, cakes, jellies? Ask Sadie's advice.

(c)   Presents. How about a bran tub? Ask Sadie's advice.

(d)   Where to purchase a puppy, a basket and squeaky toys? Seek Jeff's advice.

(e)   Have I bitten off more than I can chew? If so, it won't be the first time, nor, in all probability, the last.

Laying down her pen, staring out at the sea,

deep in thought, it occurred to Lara that her once-empty days were now so full that she could scarcely cope with them. Apart from the garden party, soon she would begin her occupancy of the beach chalet: taking down to it her portable radio, an ample supply of books, and food sufficient to her own needs, and Busters, as well as his drinking bowl, basket, toys, his favourite blanket, not to mention a tin-opener, a jar of coffee, packets of tea, milk, biscuits and so on. Her mind boggled momentarily, and yet a deep-seated sense of purpose and happiness lay within the heart of her, because she had, at last, been granted the gift of a life worth living. No longer a lonely, insular existence, but filled with renewed hope for a future based on bringing happiness to others – little Toby Cogill, for instance, and possibly 'Danny Boy', Clara Stonehouse's kid brother, who she intended to invite to the party, having received Joan's permission. There *must* be a family connection with old Joshua Stonehouse, she thought. Somehow, somewhere, Daniel must have met and married Clara Foxton. Thanks be to God had he done so, in defiance of his father's hostility towards poor Clara.

It must have taken a great deal of courage for young Daniel Stonehouse to have turned his back on a fortune, to make his own way in life for the sake of the girl he loved, knowing that if and when he found her again, they would be comparatively poor in all save love.

Possibly their wedding had been a simple affair in a country church, with merely a handful of Clara's close relations and friends present to witness the ceremony. No white wedding dress for the bride, no bridal bouquet, no Wedding March by Mendelsshon as Clara walked down the aisle towards her bridegroom. Afterwards, no sumptuous wedding reception, no speeches, no champagne, just a wedding cake, perhaps, made by the bride's mother, a few sandwiches and sausage rolls in the front parlour of Clara's home, before the happy couple, hands linked, starry-eyed, set off on honeymoon together to create a new lineage of the Stonehouse family.

And yes, Lara thought wistfully, it must have happened that way, the begetting of a family far poorer, financially, than the Stonehouses of Stella Maris, yet richer, by far, in happiness and love than they had ever been, recalling the present-day Clara Stonehouse's joy that the tip she'd received from Gareth Roberts would enable her to buy a decent birthday present for her brother Danny.

Ben Adams told Lara, over breakfast next morning, that the donkey man and the

Punch-and-Judy bloke were long standing pals of his from way back, who 'wuddn't mind in the least providin' entertainment for a kids party, jest so long as she made it worth their while by way of a few bottles of pale ale an' a quid or two ter grease the palms of their 'ands, so to speak'.

'Well, think on, Ben,' Lara told him. 'If they let me down on Saturday, I'll hold you responsible. In fact, I'll have your guts for garters! Is that clearly understood?'

'Yes'm,' Ben replied smartly. Then, 'Any chance of another cuppa 'n' a coupla more slices of toast, by the way? Ah'm feelin' main peckish this mornin', since all they give us for us brekfusts, up yonder, wus bleedin' rice crispies an' baked beans wi' plain bread an' margarine. Well, I asks you, missis, me guts feels like garters ony road, so what, if owt, hev ah got left ti lose?'

Lara laughed, but she needed to have everything cut and dried beforehand, hence her suggestion that Ben's pals should pay her a visit to settle the details as soon as possible, greasing palms and providing pale ale being a dodgy way of conducting business affairs to her way of thinking.

Ben looked aggrieved. 'Well, if y' dain't truss me,' he complained, all injured innocence. 'Ah'd best mek mesen scarce; start moaning the grass fer that there "fate" o' yourn!'

238

'Thanks, Ben, what a splendid idea,' Lara beamed reassuringly at him as he shuffled towards the door, hoping against hope that her party would not prove to be a fate worse than death.

Jeff appeared that evening, after work, to iron out the finer points of the celebration, bringing common sense to bear on the barbecue, for instance. 'No problem,' he said, seated at the kitchen table perusing the list he had brought with him. 'That's taken care of. A colleague of mine has agreed to lend me his, plus the accessories – fuel, tongs, skewers and so on, and I'll see to the cooking, if that's OK?

'Now, about the grub. Sadie's volunteered to make the jellies, cakes and sandwiches, to save you the trouble. She's baked Toby a smashing birthday cake, by the way. His favourite – chocolate cake with chocolate-drops on top!' Jeff grinned amiably. 'He'll be over the moon when he sees it! That just leaves the sausages, potatoes, hamburgers and breadcakes to see to in the food department, unless I've forgotten anything.'

'How about pickles, relishes and salad for the grown-ups?' Lara reminded him. 'And perhaps chicken portions? Oh, and ice cream! The kids are sure to want ice cream!' Jotting down ideas as they occurred: 'We'll need plates, cutlery, glasses too, for the drinks. Tea and coffee for the adults, lemonade, ginger beer and fruit juice for the children. What do you think?'

'Best go for paper plates, cups, and plastic cutlery,' Jeff advised her. 'In case of accidents.'

'Yes, of course. Thanks, Jeff,' she said gratefully. 'What does Sadie think of the bran-tub idea, by the way?'

The discussion continued, their lists growing longer by the minute as fresh ideas entered their minds, until finally arose the all-important question of Toby's present – the puppy, its basket and squeaky toys. Looking somewhat abashed, Jeff said hesitantly, 'For what it's worth, Mrs D, the lad has his heart set on a stray mutt he saw the other day, scrounging scraps of food from a dustbin. Came indoors brokenhearted, he did, wanting to give it his own dinner. He's even given the damn thing a name – "Ruff". Short for "Ruffian", I shouldn't wonder.' He sighed deeply. 'Now it's "Ruff" this, "Ruff" that. Poor little lad, I hadn't the heart to tell him that the last I saw of the dog was in the back of a council van on its way to the pound.'

'You mean...?' Lara looked stricken. 'You mean it's under sentence of death?'

'Afraid so. They keep them for seven days, then, if no one claims them, they're put to sleep, the poor little devils – quite painlessly, or so I'm told.'

'I see.' Lara's eyes filled with tears.

Jeff said quietly, 'Well, I'd best be on my way now. I can see that you're tired, but we've got things more or less sorted out, haven't we?'

'Yes, and thanks for coming. You've been a great help. You and Sadie.'

'How many folk are we expecting on Saturday?' he asked as an afterthought.

'I'm not quite certain,' she confessed. 'Twelve to fifteen in all, mainly adults. We could do with more children, that's for sure. Any bright ideas?'

'Come to think of it, there's an orphanage back of the veterans' hospital,' he supplied eagerly. 'A privately owned place, not very big, housing a dozen kids or so. I call there twice a week to pick up and deliver the laundry. I could put in a word with the owner, if you like.'

Lara smiled mistily. 'I'd like that very much, Jeff,' she responded warmly.

At that moment, Ben Adam, the donkey man and the Punch-and-Judy man appeared at the garden gate, and, 'Please come in, gentlemen,' she said expansively, leading the way to the kitchen and the several bottles of pale ale she had purchased, earlier on, to wet their whistles.

# Fifteen

Saturday dawned clear and fair. Up early, Lara lilted downstairs to see to the Aga and the animals, to check up on the garden, which bore, by way of several small tents erected by Jeff the night before, a strong resemblance to a village fête, due to begin at midday.

Sadie would be here an hour beforehand, bringing with her Toby's birthday cake, jam tarts, iced buns adorned with glacé cherries, egg and cress sandwiches, Scotch eggs, scones and cheese straws, apart from jellies and blancmanges.

Additions to the food had been necessary on the acceptance of Jeff's invitation by the head of St Jude's Orphanage on behalf of the twelve children in her care. Gladly, Lara had elected to help Sadie with the catering, to make sausage rolls, apple pies, fruit loaves and custard tarts to satisfy the appetites of the extra guests. It would be great for Sadie and Jeff's trio to have other kids to play with, just as it had been great fun buying extra presents for the bran tub – a large packing case that Beau had carried down from the attic for her, in which to place the soft toys, boxes of sweets, crayons and picture books Lara had brought home from a shopping expedition to Woolworths.

'Anything else I can do, ma'am?' Beau had asked, and, 'You could try your hand at wrapping up,' Lara had replied, sensing that he wanted to be involved in the celebrations. 'That would be a great help.'

'Sure thing.' He'd grinned happily.

'You could take charge of the bran tub, if you want to,' she'd added, smiling at his air of boyish enthusiasm, his obvious pleasure at feeling himself useful in even the smallest way. 'Help serve the food; organize a game of hide and seek, perhaps? We'll need all the help we can get with fifteen, possibly sixteen youngsters to look after.' Uncertain if Danny Stonehouse, his sister and parents would turn up.

'Besides which,' she'd continued, counting up on her fingers, 'there'll be Jeff, Sadie, Ben, a Miss Marcia Matthews from the Information Bureau, Miss Long, head of the children's home and her assistant, Miss Debenham, Bert Temple, the donkey man, Mr Punch-and-Judy. Gosh, quite a gathering! Let's hope the weather's fine and the food doesn't run out.'

Beau said quietly, 'The sun will always shine on you, ma'am.'

Deeply touched, she said, 'Thank you, Beau. What a nice thing to say,' aware of a frisson of happiness as his eyes met hers.

A feeling of nervousness chewed at Lara as she set about making pastry, wondering, as she rubbed fat into the flour, if all would go according to plan, pausing before she began the rolling-out process to check on the contents of the fridge to make certain that nothing had been forgotten or overlooked.

Jeff had trundled the barbecue into one of the tents the night before, in case of rain, and he would be here in good time to set it up on the lawn and get it going, as he termed it. She had Beau to thank for his suggestion of a trestle table on which to place the comestibles: chicken pieces, sausages, hamburgers, bread rolls and such. 'Not to worry, ma'am,' he'd added, interpreting correctly the blank expression on her face. 'There's one in the garden shed. I gave it a good wash the other day, when I was cleaning the mower.'

'Oh, *thanks*, Beau! What ever should I do without you?' What indeed? she wondered.

Now, he'd be here soon to set up the table, to see to the bran tub and to perform one very important, last-minute task she'd discussed with him yesterday, to which he had readily agreed, smiling as he did so, entering wholeheartedly into the surprise element of young Toby's birthday present, with an instant understanding of what would be required of him.

Now, all was set fair for a splendid party. The sun was shining, the garden looked lovely, her apple pies, custard tarts, sausage rolls, cooling in the pantry, were a joy to behold; Sadie had just arrived, via the kitchen door, lumping her trug of jellies and Toby's cake, blancmanges, held carefully level, plus carrier bags of tins containing cakes and sandwiches, scotch eggs and so forth.

'Here, let me help you!' Lara hurried to relieve Sadie of all save her trug. 'Sit down and catch your breath. I'll put the kettle on for a cup of tea. I've a plate ready for Toby's cake, dishes for the "wobblies". Tell me, does he know what's going on?'

Sadie laughed. 'No, not really, he's not quite old enough yet.' She added wistfully, 'Besides, he's a bit upset about a dog he took a fancy to, which disappeared all of a sudden. But I daresay he'll forget about it when he sees the puppy you've bought him. Is it a labrador?'

'No, it's a terrier, more suitable for a little boy to handle, I thought. Beau's collecting him from the pet shop this afternoon.'

'I can't believe all this is happening,' Sadie said joyously. 'The kids are wild with excitement. Truth to tell, so am I. Now, what shall we do first?'

Together they carried the food outdoors to one of the tents, on trays covered with clean tea towels, leaving the cakes and foil-wrapped sandwiches in their various tins, the 'wobblies' and the birthday cake indoors for the time being, along with the food in the pantry. And, 'Oh, a trestle table. That will come in handy,' Sadie remarked.

'We could do with a few smaller ones,' Lara conjectured. Putting on her thinking cap: 'I know! There's a couple of them in the pantry, two or three in the attic. I'll ask Beau to bring them outdoors for us!' She added proudly, 'He's been so helpful, so kind, so useful. He wrapped all the bran-tub presents himself, far better than I could have done. Not that it's a bran tub exactly, more of a tea chest. I wouldn't have known where to lay hands on bran anyway.'

Sadie giggled. 'You could have used cornflakes!'

Beau appeared at that moment, casually dressed in slacks, open-neck checked shirt, and wearing a Panama hat – as a means of hiding his face, Lara realized, from the eyes of strangers, rather than a means of shielding it from the sun. An intensely shy man, it wouldn't be easy for him to come into contact with so many people he had never seen before. A sheer impossibility, since, a few weeks ago, he had panicked and run away from even herself. At least that hurdle had been overcome. Hopefully, there would be more to follow in his acceptance of other fellow human beings as friends, not enemies. If only, by means of treatment received in hospital, his memory would begin to return, however slowly, along with his true identity. Memories of his home, his family, his loved ones.

Greeting him warmly, she mentioned the tables she needed from the pantry and the attic, and, 'Sure thing, ma'am,' he replied easily. 'Anything I can do to help, just ask.'

Lara laughed. 'That's a promise you may regret making when you find out what it entails. By the end of the day, you might well meet yourself coming back from where you've been, if you can remember that far back!' Then, filled with remorse at her thoughtless, joking remark, 'Oh, how insensitive of me,' she murmured. '*Please* forgive me! It was just a stupid utterance from a stupid woman without two ounces of brains in her head!'

Beau said quietly, 'No need to upset yourself, ma'am. I'm glad you said what you did.' He smiled. 'Memory loss isn't a disease, in no way infectious, not like measles or chickenpox. The worst thing about it is being treated as if it were – as a kind of leper. OK, so I can't remember who I am or where I came from, and perhaps I never shall. But there's nothing wrong with my short-term memory, and I have you to thank for all your kindness towards me, which I shall never, *ever* forget.'

He paused momentarily, then: 'Now, if you'll give me the key to the attic, I'll bring down those tables you need.'

Jeff arrived at twelve o'clock precisely, to set up the barbecue, bringing with him Thomas, Sarah and Toby, appearing somewhat nervous in a strange venue until, catching sight of their mother, they ran towards her ecstatically, into her arms, outspread to gather them into a warm embrace: Thomas, a dark-haired child, the spit and image of his father, Sarah a bonny little lass, brown-haired, the model of her mother, and the baby of the family, the dark, curly-haired Toby, a thick-set, solemn little boy who resembled neither parent in particular, to Lara's way of thinking. A birthday boy trying hard not to cry in unfamiliar surroundings, even with his mother's arms about him.

At a quarter past twelve, the contingent of youngsters from the orphanage and their guardians arrived on the scene, closely followed, thank God, Lara thought gratefully, by the donkey man and two patiently trotting donkeys, saddled and ready for action. Meanwhile, clouds of smoke were billowing forth from the barbecue on the lawn, herself and Sadie were busily engaged in setting out food on the tables Beau had manhandled to the scene of activity, along with the so-called bran tub, by which time Mr Punch-and-Judy had arrived to add to the confusion.

Oh lord, Lara thought desperately, why had she dreamed up this crazy venture in the first place? Moreover, what on earth had possessed her to invite Marcia Matthews from the Information Bureau to the wingding? This, after all, was turning out to be a children's party, and certainly the kids appeared to be enjoying themselves to the full, donkey riding and watching the Punch-and-Judy show, whilst the grown-ups, gathered about the barbecue, were tucking into hamburgers, chicken portions and bangers – especially Ben Adams, whose appetite far exceeded good taste, in Jeff's opinion.

'Hold on, Ben,' he said. 'Don't they feed you up yonder? The rate you're going there won't be enough left to go round. Now, hop it!'

'The kids from St Jude's are having a great time, aren't they?' Sadie remarked fondly. 'Just look at their little faces. Poor bairns. How awful for them living in a home, no parents to look after them. I bet they've never had a day like this before, though they're well cared for, or so Jeff tells me. Miss Long is very kind to them, and the home is spotless. Even so, an orphanage isn't a home in the true sense of the word, is it?'

'I suppose not,' Lara said wistfully, disappointed that the Stonehouse family had not put in an appearance, but possibly Clara was serving lunches at the Feathers.

'Are you all right, Mrs D?' Sadie asked gently. 'You seem a bit – worried.'

'No, I'm fine,' Lara assured her. 'It's just that I've never done anything like this before, and I do so want it to be a success.'

'Oh, is that all?' Sadie laughed. 'But it *is* a success! A howling success. The sun's shining, the garden looks a picture, the kids are having a whale of a time, there's food and to spare, so stop worrying.'

' "God's in His Heaven, all's right with the world",' Lara quoted softly, thinking about Rory, wishing he were here beside her right now to dispel a sudden feeling of loneliness without him.

When Bert Temple, the donkey man, decreed a rest period for his animals and put on their nosebags, and the Punch-and Judy man emerged from his cabinet to wet his whistle, a lull occurred, during which the children from St Jude's queued up for their plates of food, eyes bright with happiness and expectation at the sight of the cakes and jellies.

It was then Lara realized that this was the time to highlight the reason for the party as a birthday celebration in honour of the youngest child in their midst, Toby Cogill, aged four. A spontaneous round of applause from the grown-ups greeted her announcement. The shy birthday boy clung to his mother's skirts as Miss Debenham and Miss Long led a resounding chorus of the 'Happy Birthday' jingle. Jeff, the proud father, hurried forward to hoist his son shoulder-high, to the boy's bewilderment at the fuss being made of him, seemingly about to cry until he caught sight of his mother and siblings smiling up at him and felt the comforting clasp of his father's hands on his arms, the strength and firmness of his shoulders beneath his legs when suddenly he cried out, 'Gee up, Neddy!' – being well inured to pick-a-back rides astride his dad's shoulders.

Continuing her role as Mistress of Ceremonies, albeit nervously, Lara exhorted her guests to enjoy their lunch break now that the birthday boy had been returned to terra firma and his father had resumed his place at the barbecue. After which, she announced, when the donkeys had been fed and watered, the donkey riding would continue till mid-afternoon. In the meanwhile, all the youngsters present would be invited to gather round the bran tub to dip for small gifts to take home with them. And finally, around four o'clock, the birthday boy would receive his own present. And, ah, here came the bran tub now.

To Lara's amazement, Beau appeared, on cue, rolling on to the lawn, not a tea chest but a tub, a hefty barrel, bran-filled, with colourful streamers attached to each and every one of the presents it contained.

Approaching him, 'But *how*?' Lara gasped, 'And *why*?'

'Because, ma'am,' he replied, tongue-in-cheek, 'a tub is a tub, a tea chest is a tea chest, and never the twain shall meet. Kids aren't fools. I just didn't figure on disappointing them, that's all.' He smiled briefly. 'Now I reckon it's time I was heading to pick up Toby's pooch, if that's OK with you.'

And, 'Yes, of course,' she replied bemusedly, as the children came flocking towards the bran tub to tug at its many coloured streamers.

Turning suddenly, scarcely knowing if she was on her head or her heels, Lara saw, coming up the garden path towards her, Clara Stonehouse, her parents and her brother Danny. Hurrying towards them, hands outstretched to greet them, 'Oh, I'm so glad you came,' she said fervently. 'I thought you'd decided not to come after all.'

Edward Stonehouse, the father figure, a handsome man despite his greying hair and horn-rimmed glasses, said quietly, 'I reckon you know, then, that we have certain connections with this place – this house? But, forgive my asking, how do you fit into the picture?'

'I don't, not at all, strictly speaking,' Lara explained briefly. Edward nodded. 'This is my wife, Grace,' he said. 'Clara you've already met, and this is young Daniel, named after my great-grandparents. Unfortunately there was no love lost between my great-grandfather and his father, and although we live quite close to Carnelian Bay, this is the first time we've been to the house.'

'You're welcome to look round it later, if you like,' Lara said. 'Meanwhile, please help yourselves to food and so on. The party's mainly in celebration of young Toby Cogill's fourth birthday. His present is due any minute now.' Smiling at Danny and Clara: 'Why not join the queue at the bran tub? Now, if you'll excuse me, I believe Toby's present is on its way.'

Beau had appeared with a dog basket under one arm, leading a smartly trotting terrier wearing a red collar, to which was attached a matching leash. It was a handsome little dog, alert and eager, obviously well fed and cared for. Sadie said disbelievingly, 'It isn't, it *can't* be!' In a flurry of excitement: 'Where on earth has Toby got to? He was here a minute ago!'

Lara said mistily, 'Unless I'm much mistaken, he's on his way to renew an acquaintance with a special friend of his.'

Never till her dying day would she ever forget the expression of absolute joy on the little lad's face as he stumbled across the lawn towards his beloved Ruff, or the dog's reaction on seeing him again, the frantically wagging tail, the joyous barks of recognition as the dog, straining at its leash, covered Toby's face with kisses of the canine kind as the boy, kneeling beside it, cuddled the little creature in his arms, laughing delightedly at the touch of Ruff's warm tongue on his cheeks.

Watching the happy reunion between the child and his dog, it had all been worthwhile, Lara thought. In the first instance, her rescue of Ruff from the pound for unwanted animals under sentence of death. Secondly, her visit to a vet's to have the poor creature wormed, de-loused and innoculated against distemper. Finally, to have taken him to a pet parlour to have his fur de-matted, shampooed and set, his teeth descaled, claws manicured, to be fed and generally pampered and cared for in readiness for today.

In floods of tears, Sadie said gratefully, 'Thank you, and bless you, Mrs D, for giving Toby such a wonderful birthday present. A perfect end to a perfect day.'

But the day was not over and done with quite yet. There was clearing up to be done in the wake of departing guests, leftover food to be dealt with, tents to be dismantled, goodbyes to be said, especially to the St Jude's children and their guardians, the barbecue to be bundled into the back of the Cogill's ancient jalopy, alongside a dog basket, three exhausted youngsters and a sleeping dog.

The donkey man and Mr Punch-and-Judy had long since departed, as had everyone else apart from the Stonehouses and Beauregard, the latter about to remove the bran tub.

The words, 'Don't bother about that now, Beau,' were on her lips when suddenly, approaching Beau, she heard Edward Stonehouse's voice, his words uttered in a low tone. 'Forgive this intrusion, sir. You won't remember me, I daresay, but I remember you right enough. I was there, at Ringley, when your aircraft went missing. Terrible, that was.' He paused briefly. They sent out reconnaissance planes and air-sea rescue launches to search the Channel in the hope of finding you, or the Rosie Belle. Two full days, from dawn to dusk, the search went on for. The atmosphere was grim to say the least. No one feeling inclined to say much, not eating properly neither. And I don't mean just the Americans. We Brits, every man jack of us, the maintenance crews, cooks and stewards, felt pretty much the same.'

Another pause, then, 'I, for one, couldn't bring myself to believe that you were a goner. Not you, sir. It just didn't seem possible somehow, and I was right, thank God. Mind you, it came as a bit of a shock, seeing you again after all these years. My wife said I must be mistaken. Why, sir, is anything the matter?'

Beau was staring at the man unseeingly, or beyond him, into the past, Lara realized. Then, 'The Rosie Belle,' he uttered, as if the name meant something to him.

Lara held her breath, willing a miracle to happen.

The man said quietly, 'I'm sorry, sir. Perhaps my wife was right after all. Her name is Grace, mine is—'

'No, don't tell me,' Beau said huskily. 'Give me time to think, I must have time to think!'

Watching Beau's face intently, Lara noticed an almost imperceptible change of expression, a dawning awareness in his eyes, as if a long-extinguished light had been switched on inside him.

256

Clenching her hands till the knuckles showed white, pressing them to her lips in an agony of suspense, praying for that miracle to happen, she heard him say, in little more than a whisper, 'Your name is Ted Stonehouse, isn't it? Am I right?'

'Perfectly right, Captain Orlando,' Edward assured him, wringing Beau's hand. 'Fancy you remembering after all this time. Well, goodbye, Captain, and good luck.' Turning to Lara, 'Well, I reckon we'd best be off home now. Clara's on duty at six thirty. Perhaps we could come again some other time to look round the house?'

'Yes, of course,' Lara replied, unclenching her hands, feeling suddenly exhausted, emotionally and physically drained by the realization that the man she thought of as Beauregard Jackson no longer existed, that a stranger had taken his place.

Excusing herself abruptly, she hurried into the house and upstairs to her room, filled with the dawning realization of how much she would miss Beau's presence in her life when he went home to America.

# Sixteen

An hour later, she went downstairs to see to the animals. Beau was in the kitchen refuelling the Aga. He said, 'I've taken Buster for a walk, cleared away the bran tub, raked the lawn and brought the tables indoors, all except the trestle, which is back in the shed.' He spoke naturally, as if nothing untoward had happened.

Scarcely knowing how to handle the situation, fearing an intrusion into the delicate subject of his memory recall, she said, 'Tell me about the bran tub. Where on earth did you find it, not to mention the bran?'

'Oh, that.' Beau smiled. 'The tub was in the backyard of the Crown and Anchor; as for the bran, it came from a greengrocer's store. Apparently bunches of grapes come from abroad buried in the stuff. The greengrocer was mighty glad to get rid of it. So, there you have it in a nutshell.'

'Oh, I see.' Lara turned away, uncertain how to continue the conversation, afraid that if she continued to face him he would read, in her eyes, that he seemed as a stranger to her now.

He said quietly, 'No, I don't believe that you *do* see at all. Look at me, Lara.' He turned her to face him. 'OK, so my real name is Richard Orlando. I know that now, and believe me I'm beginning to wish that I did not, if it means the loss of your friendship. As if something had changed between us.'

'Everything *has* changed,' Lara said bleakly. 'Oh, don't think for one moment that I'm sorry, not glad that you have recovered your memory. I actually willed it to happen. Now that it has, I feel at a loss to know how to treat you. Not as a servant, that's for sure, expecting you to fetch and carry for me. I'm so ashamed of that now. I'm sorry, but that's the way I feel. I don't even know what to call you any more. Certainly not Beau, because that's not your real name, is it?'

'It is so far as you and I are concerned, ma'am,' he replied reassuringly, smiling down at her. 'I much prefer Beau to Richard any day of week and, so long as I remain here, until the powers that be have decided what to do with me, I'll continue to do your bidding. Walking the extra mile, so to speak. As a free man, not a slave, not because I have to, because I want to.'

Lara's spirits lifted. So he knew the

biblical story of the Roman centurion and his newly liberated slave who had chosen to walk the extra mile of a journey with his master of his own free will?

'In which case,' she said, 'I'd be glad of your help in carrying my belongings to the beach bungalow I've rented for the summer months. According to Miss Matthews of the Information Bureau, it is now ready for occupation.'

'Sure thing,' Beau replied easily, removing his hands from Lara's shoulders. 'Meanwhile I'll continue to tend the garden, shall I, and to keep an eye on Cleo?'

'Oh yes, by all means,' she said gratefully. 'Thanks – Beau!' Then, hesitantly, she asked him how soon the powers that be would come to a decision about his future, his return home to America, in view of his newly established identity.

'Heaven only knows,' he responded quietly, shrugging his shoulders. 'As soon as they've checked up on me, I guess; been in touch with the US Air Force; made certain sure that I am who I claim to be, not some kind of imposter with a criminal record a mile long; which may take months, even years.'

'But surely they'll allow you to communicate with your family? Your parents, your – wife and children?'

'Hopefully with my parents, my brothers

and sisters,' he said, tongue-in-cheek, 'since I have no recollection of a wife and children. Does that answer your question? To the best of my knowledge and belief, I am still foot-loose and fancy-free.' He added more seriously, 'Though I'd give the world to see my folks once more; to sleep in my own bed in Louisiana; taste my mother's cooking, her pot roast in particular.'

'Then may your wish come true as soon as possible,' Lara said softly, sincerely. 'Within weeks, not months or years.' She neglected to add how much she would miss him when he was gone. Not Captain Richard Orlando of the United States Air Force, but her dear companion and friend, Beauregard Jackson.

Glancing about her appreciatively at the interior of the beach bungalow, noticing the small cooker, stone sink, draining boards, fitted cupboards, tables and deckchairs, Lara knew that she was destined to enjoy this small home from home, this tiny haven of peace and quiet with the sea on its doorstep, the sound of waves washing in on the shore.

Beau was busy unpacking the various bags and boxes they had brought with them, arranging washing-up liquid, scouring powder and dish cloths on the draining board; placing tins of biscuits, jars of coffee, canisters of sugar and tea bags in a store cupboard, having found a place for Buster's bedding under the table; pleased that Lara had decided not to bring his basket after all, just his rubber bone, drinking bowl, tins of dog meat and Bonio's – and a tin-opener.

Fold-back doors led on to the verandah, where Lara was now standing, gazing out to sea, a slender figure casually dressed in slacks and a lightweight sweater. Thoughtfully, Beau unfolded a deckchair for her to sit in, and placed beside it a small table to accommodate her library books, portable radio, reading glasses and coffee mug, prior to his return to the veterans' hospital to begin a series of tests relevant to his present state of mental awareness.

He said, when all seemed shipshape, 'I've filled the kettle, put the milk in the refrigerator along with the butter and cheese, if that's OK? Now I'd best be on my way.'

'Surely not before you've had a cup of coffee?' Lara protested. 'You must be thirsty. I know I am! No, you sit down. I'll make the coffee. I insist! After all, you are my guest, not my – slave!'

'Touché,' he laughed, enjoying their shared camaraderie based on Lara's acceptance of his newly discovered identity, her quick understanding of his reference to 'walking the extra mile'.

He said, seated beside her on the verandah, sipping the mug of coffee she had made for him, 'Renting this bungalow for the summer was a wise decision on your part, Lara. A kind of bolt hole, an escape route, unless I'm much mistaken, far removed from the cares and responsibilities of Stella Maris, if you'll forgive my saying so. Oh, it's a lovely house, but tell me, what will you do when summertime is over, when autumn comes?'

'I don't know,' Lara admitted. 'I haven't decided. Impossible to think that far ahead. Who knows? I might look for a place of my own, in or near to Carnelian Bay; take a trip to Paris, or, more than likely, go back to the Windsor Hotel in Middlesbrough to live as a paying guest.' She paused momentarily, then: 'Or I may even consider the possibility of re-marriage as an alternative to ending my days alone and unloved. What do you think, Beau? Should I marry someone I'm not in love with for the sake of future security? A home of my own with a man who, I suspect, is no more in love with me than I am with him.'

'You and you alone must be the judge of that,' Beau said levelly, rising to his feet to rinse the coffee cups prior to his departure to the veterans' hospital. 'Frankly, from my own point of view, I'd rather spend the rest of my life alone than marry for security, not love.'

'Thanks, Beau! You are perfectly right, of course,' Lara said wistfully. Then more resolutely, 'Good luck for this afternoon. You will let me know how you get on, won't you?'

'Sure thing, ma'am,' he promised, striding away from her along the promenade to begin his uphill journey to face his afternoon inquisition at the hands of his doctors and, possibly, representatives of the US Air Force, gathered together to establish his credentials as the person he now knew himself to be, Captain Richard Orlando, whose aircraft, the Rosie Belle, had been shot down by enemy gunfire over the English Channel in the autumn of 1944.

Returning to Stella Maris around five o'clock that afternoon, having locked the doors of the chalet behind her, with Buster in tow, Lara thought what a happy day this had been, recalling the sense of freedom, a kind of holiday feeling in the sights and sounds of her newly discovered summer-time retreat. The eternal, soothing sound of the sea on the shore, for instance, followed by its retreat when the tide ebbed to reveal stretches of damp golden sand, moss and seaweed-covered rocks; children at play near the water's edge; dogs racing madly in search of thrown sticks, balls and pebbles; ears pricked, tails wagging, in which games she and Buster had eventually joined, to Buster's obvious delight, released from his collar and leash, spraying the air about him with showers of water as he emerged from the sea with his favourite rubber bone clenched firmly between his teeth.

It had been a tiring day, all told, with so much exercise and fresh air. After supper, Lara exchanged her outer clothing for a housecoat, her shoes for slippers, and went downstairs to continue reading the old Stonehouse correspondence, eager to learn more about the family, Danny and Clara in particular, and what had become of them in reality, not in her imagination. She had, after all, dreamed up the village church wedding, the front-room reception, their setting off on honeymoon together.

At least she knew for certain that they had married. Meeting their descendants had proved that to be true beyond a shadow of doubt. Edward Stonehouse had said as much at Saturday's garden party, and she had fully intended to show Edward, Grace and their offspring round Stella Maris when the party was over. Then suddenly time had run out following Edward's recognition of Beau and their subsequent conversation. The Stonehouses had perforce left the garden abruptly to ensure their daughter's return to work on time.

Deep in thought, mulling over the events

of that emotionally fraught garden party and its aftermath, Lara started nervously at the sound of the doorbell, wondering who on earth ... Oh damn, she thought irritably, getting up to answer the summons. *No rest for the wicked*, as her mother was wont to say when visitors came knocking at her sitting-room door when she had just nicely finished the washing-up and sat down to listen to her favourite wireless programme. Then, resignedly: *Ah well, I'd best see what they want, I'll not get a moment's peace of mind if I don't!*

Edward Stonehouse was on the doorstep. 'Sorry to disturb you, Mrs Davenport,' he said apologetically, 'but I'd really like to talk to you if at all possible.'

'Of course, Mr Stonehouse. Come in,' Lara said, understanding the man's need to cross the threshold of Stella Maris, to absorb something of its ambience, a fleeting impression of the past, perhaps, in things which had not changed perceptibly despite its modernization. The staircase, for instance, the deep skirting boards and Victorian ceiling rosettes; the stained glass landing window, the original mahogany panelled doors to left and right of the hall.

Edward said mistily, 'It's all pretty much as I imagined it would be. My late father talked about it a great deal, you see, in his latter years, memories gleaned mainly from my great-grandmother who once worked

here as a ladies' maid to Joshua Stonehouse's daughters, Dorothea and Mary-
Anne.'

'Your great-grandmother being Clara
Foxton?' Lara said gently. 'Before her mar-
riage to your great-grandfather, Daniel
Stonehouse?'

'Yes, but how did you come by my great-
grandmother's maiden name?'

'Come through to the drawing room, sit
down and I'll explain,' Lara said quietly,
leading the way.

It was Sadie who told Lara about Iris
Smith's grandsons. 'They've been taken
into care,' she said. 'One of those homes
for juvenile delinquents. The magistrates
reckoned they'd be better off there than
with Iris and that feckless husband of hers.'
Sadie sighed deeply. 'I just thank my lucky
stars we'll be well clear of the Cramer Estate
come next Tuesday. The removal men are
coming at nine o'clock, and Jeff's taken the
day off to lend them a hand. Oh, the relief
of not having neighbours like the Smiths to
contend with. Apparently Iris caused quite
an uproar in the courtroom when the kids
were taken into custody. The wonder is she
didn't end up in custody herself when she
started screaming and swearing at the magistrates. Well, you know Iris! Determined
to have her say, and the devil take the

hindmost! Making things worse for herself, not better. To be honest, I've often wondered if she's quite – all there. I'm just so glad, Mrs D, that you weren't asked to give evidence.'

'There was really no need,' Lara said, since the kids were caught red-handed by the police the night they threw stones at the drawing-room windows. I was questioned, of course, required to sign a statement pertaining to the events of that night, which the police accepted, thank God, as proof positive that I was in no way involved in calling out the constabulary.'

'I should think not, indeed!' Sadie said, knowing Lara's infinite capacity for kindness, not revenge. Then: 'Well. I'd best be getting on with my work. Anything special you want me to do first?'

'Well yes, as a matter of fact,' Lara said quietly. 'I'd like you to sit down and listen. You see, I have something rather important to tell you, concerning – Beauregard Jackson.'

'Well, that is good news, I must say,' Sadie beamed. 'He's a really nice person. How did he take it? Remembering, I mean.'

'Quite calmly, as I recall,' Lara replied.

'Even so, it must have come as a bit of a shock.'

'It did to me at any rate.' Lara smiled

268

wistfully. 'I'd been willing him to remember. When he did, I – ran away.'

'I'm not surprised,' Sadie said stalwartly. 'After all the running about you'd done during the day, organizing the garden party and suchlike; giving everyone such a wonderful time. You must have been tired out. I know I was. So was Jeff, so were the kids, not to mention Ruff. The poor little thing never moved a muscle all night long, neither did Toby. Needless to say, the dog slept on Toby's bed. I just hadn't the heart to separate the pair of them.'

Getting up from the kitchen table to begin work, struck by a sudden thought, frowning slightly, Sadie said, 'I suppose that, having recovered his memory, Beau will be leaving here soon? Going back to America?'

And, 'Yes, I imagine so,' Lara said tautly. 'At least, I hope so for his sake. He misses his family a great deal, you see.'

Sadie gained the distinct impression that Lara would also miss Beau a great deal when he went back to America. Perhaps more than she was prepared to admit?

Lara said, 'About next week, the removal, I mean. You'll need time off to see to things at The Birches, so take the whole week, or more time if necessary. And don't worry about your wages. Let's call it holiday pay, shall we?'

'Oh, I couldn't, Mrs D...'

'Don't be daft. I'll be out most of the time anyway, at the beach bungalow,' Lara interrupted kindly. 'And Beau will be coming in to feed Cleo, see to the Aga and so forth. I just don't want you to tire yourself out, that's all.' She added mischievously, 'After all, a woman in your delicate condition...'

'Delicate, my eye,' Sadie riposted happily. 'I'm as strong as a horse, and I've never felt better in my life!'

Sadie was upstairs vacuuming the bedrooms, when Beau appeared to impart the news that his interview had gone far better than he'd expected. Tests had proved conclusively that his amnesia was a thing of the past as he had recalled, in detail, memories of his past life, including his mother's maiden name and the dates of birth of his siblings, the schools he'd attended, even the names of his teachers.

'My doctors were delighted,' he said. 'And even the US Air Force officials were quite impressed when I recalled precisely my name, rank and number and filled them in on ... Well, I'd rather not go into that right now, if you don't mind.'

'No, of course not.' Understanding his reluctance to discuss events leading to his memory loss in the first place, Lara asked him the burning question uppermost in her mind. 'Does this mean that you'll be going home soon?'

'I guess so,' he replied quietly. 'Quite soon as a matter of fact. You see, ma'am, I'll be leaving the veterans' hospital the day after tomorrow. Everything's taken care of, transport to London, overnight accommodation, my flight tickets to New York the day after.'

He added obliquely, albeit painfully, 'The trouble is, I've begun to think of Carnelian Bay as my home. At least my home from home. I've known kindness here, help and support in my darkest hours. Need I say more?'

'What more is there to say?' Lara spoke cheerfully, for his sake. I'm glad you've been happy here, but your memories of Carnelian Bay will seem far less important, I daresay, when you are back where you belong, in Louisiana, in your own bed, having tasted your mother's pot roast at suppertime. After all, Beau, home is where the heart is, so I wish you all the joy and happiness in the world. Just think of it, Beau, a whole new future ahead of you.'

'I'll miss you, Lara,' he said hoarsely, knowing that he was in love with her.

'I'll miss you, too, Beau,' not daring to tell him how much.

'Then I guess it's time to say goodbye?'

'I'd much rather we didn't. Goodbye is a word I hate.' She smiled up at him, holding back tears. 'Let's make it au revoir, shall we?'

'Sure thing.' Picking up her hands, he kissed them gently in turn, returned her smile, and then he was gone, and that was it.

Watching from the kitchen window until he was out of sight, I shall never see him again, Lara thought bleakly. That thought seemed suddenly unbearable.

# Seventeen

She missed Beau intensely; wondered where he was and what he was doing. At the beach bungalow, she was glad of passers-by: occupants of the other chalets, who stopped occasionally to talk to her and make a fuss of Buster.

Not that they stayed long. They had their own lives to lead, children to see to, especially young parents with toddlers wanting to play on the beach with their buckets and spades.

Despite the comings and goings, the sight and sound of the sea close at hand, Lara felt isolated, lonelier than she had ever done before – an onlooker on life, not a part of it, somehow dispensable, a woman with no forseeable future ahead of her, come September, when her custodianship of Stella Maris would come to an end.

If only Rory had kept more closely in touch with her, but apart from his brief, infrequent phone calls, concerned mainly with Georgina's state of mind, she had never set eyes on him since he had come to Stella Maris on the evening of her dinner date with Gareth Roberts. If only she had possessed the courage to cancel her engagement with Dr Roberts at the last moment. If only, if only, if *only*! Too late now, she realized, to turn back the hands of time.

In the words of the poet Edward Fitzgerald's stanzas from the Rubaiyat of Omar Khayyam: 'Oh come with old Khayyam, and leave the Wise to talk; one thing is certain, that Life flies; One thing is certain, and the Rest is Lies: The Flower that once has blown for ever dies.'

Flower? What – flower? A one-sided love affair, non existent except in her imagination, born of a desperate need to find, to rediscover the kind of happiness she had lost when her parents died? Rory had re-kindled an ember of that lost happiness in the brief time they had spent together, restoring her self-confidence, bringing a sense of purpose into her life; warmth, laughter and friendship; affection on his part, certainly not – love.

At least Daniel Stonehouse had not searched in vain for the love of his life, she thought wistfully, in his discovery of the whereabouts of Clara Foxton, whom he had married despite his father's blank refusal to attend their wedding, so Edward Stonehouse had told Lara on the occasion of his evening visit to Stella Maris.

'The sour old devil wouldn't budge an inch from his high-handed principles.' Edward had grimaced, recounting the, to him, old familiar story of his great-great-grandfather's stiff-necked stubborness, his lack of humanity and forgiveness in not only turning down his son's wedding invitation but also in denying his wife and daughters their right to attend the ceremony.

'The pity of it is,' Edward continued heavily, 'that my great-grandparents' happiness was so short-lived. You see, Daniel Stonehouse met his death in the Battle of the Somme during the Great War, eleven months after his wedding to my great-grandmother, leaving her a widow, the mother of a month-old baby – a son, my grandfather.

'I'm so sorry, Mr Stonehouse,' Lara murmured compassionately. 'So very sorry. Poor Daniel, poor Clara, after all they'd been through ... It just doesn't seem fair, somehow, a couple deeply in love with one another to be separated in the full bloom of their youth and happiness.' She imagined the heartbreak of the situation.

'Yes, well, that's the way of the world, isn't it? Out of evil comes good, leastways to my way of thinking. Take my recognition of Captain Orlando, for instance. Nothing short of a miracle, I'd say, both of us being present in the same place at the same time – a million-to-one shot. Now, my being here under the roof of my great-great-grand-father's house where my great-grandfather once lived.' Suddenly, glancing about him somewhat nervously: 'Know what' – he shivered slightly – 'I have the strangest feel-ing that we are not entirely – alone.' Then, unexpectedly: 'Tell me, Mrs Davenport, do you believe in – ghosts?'

'If you mean, do I believe that every old house retains the spirits of its former occu-pants, well yes, I do,' Lara replied quietly, rising to her feet to escort her visitor to the front door. 'I didn't once upon a time, but I do now.'

Days later, Jeff called one evening to invite Lara to a housewarming party at The Birches. Smiling broadly, he said the re-moval had gone like a dream due to Sadie's careful labelling of boxes containing kitchen equipment, household china, ornaments and so on, to ensure she'd be able to lay her hands on the kettle, toaster, the children's

275

favourite mugs and suchlike, whilst he'd done the humping of furniture, laid carpets and hung up the curtains Sadie had made beforehand.

'Honest, Mrs D,' he said. 'When the kids came home from school, the kitchen was as neat as a pin, their tea was on the table, the beds made, and young Toby was in the garden playing a ball game with Ruff. Moreover, Sadie had been busy baking that afternoon: scones, cakes and apple pies, bless her.

'Afterwards, when the kids had been bathed and gone to bed as good as gold, Sadie suggested a bit of a housewarming party in your honour, tomorrow evening, if possible. So please say you'll come.'

'Of course I'll come,' Lara assured him. 'Wild horses wouldn't keep me away, just as long as Sadie doesn't go to too much trouble.'

It had been a delightful evening, fulfilling Lara's need of company, of fun and laughter: the antithesis of her recent loneliness and introspection. Seated at the kitchen table spread with a red and white gingham cloth, shining cutlery and with a centrepiece of double white lilacs – fresh from the garden – visible from the open patio doors, she had marvelled at her hostess's choice of a menu, the thought and care which had gone into the preparation of the prawn cocktails; the coq au vin, the summer pudding served with thick Jersey cream, followed by freshly-ground coffee and after dinner mints.

Then, when the meal was over, despite Sadie's protestations, helping her with the washing-up, Lara said quietly, 'You'll never know how much it means to me that you, Jeff and the children are so happy here. You and Jeff have done wonders in turning an empty house into a real home in so short a time.'

'We couldn't have done it without you, Mrs D,' Sadie replied, close to tears of happiness in her present surroundings, far removed from the squeezed confines of a council house on the Cramer Estate. 'Jeff, the kids and I bless the day you entered our lives, believe me.' She added mistily, 'In fact, when our new baby arrives, we'd feel so proud if you'd consider becoming its god-mother.'

'Really?' Lara's heart skipped a beat. 'Oh, Sadie, there's nothing in the world I'd like better.'

Later, in the lounge, seated in front of a simulated coal effect fire, the subject of Beauregard Jackson arose as a topic of conversation. Was it really true that, having recovered his memory, he was now on his way to a reunion with his loved ones in the

USA? Jeff asked innocently. If so, good luck to the bloke, a really nice man, in his opinion.

Lara could not have agreed more. She said, rising to her feet preparatory to leaving. 'Now, if you'll excuse me, I have a dog to exercise before bedtime.'

Driving her home, Jeff said, 'Tell me to mind my own business if you want to, but are you all right, Mrs D? You seem a bit down in the dumps. Or is it my imagination?'

'Not entirely,' she confessed.

'Any particular reason?' he ventured cautiously. 'You can trust me. I shan't let on.'

'That's just the trouble,' Lara sighed. 'There is no particular reason. I'd know how to tackle it otherwise.' She smiled faintly. 'At least, I think I would.'

'Could it be that you're on your own too much?' Jeff suggested perspicaciously. 'Happen you'll feel better when Sadie starts work again, come Monday. What you need is company. You were fine tonight until we got on to the subject of – Beauregard Jackson – or whatever his real name is – but you know who I mean.'

'Captain Richard Orlando,' Lara said quietly, as Jeff's battered jalopy drew up outside Stella Maris. 'But I can't think why you thought that speaking of him was

278

unwelcome.'

'Sorry, Mrs D,' Jeff said contritely, wishing he had held his tongue. 'It just occurred to me that you might be worried about the garden, with him gone and old Ben Adams none too well at the moment; confined to his bed up yonder.'

'Ben?' Lara asked concernedly. 'I had no idea! What's wrong with him?'

'That I don't know for sure,' Jeff said unhappily. 'All I know is, his condition is giving cause for concern, according to one of the nurses, who said as much when I called, last Monday, to pick up the laundry.'

In which case, Lara decided, she must visit the old man as soon as possible; take him flowers, grapes and so on, although, knowing Ben, he'd far sooner be given a packet of cigarettes, a box of matches and a few bottles of pale ale.

Getting out of the car, escorting Lara to the front steps of Stella Maris, feeling that he had somehow put his foot in it, not entirely certain how or why this had happened, Jeff said eagerly, 'Look, Mrs D, I'll take Buster for his bedtime walk, if you like.' He added earnestly, 'I'm truly sorry if I've upset you in any way; poked my nose into your affairs, said too much. If so, please will you forgive me?'

'On one condition,' Lara responded warmly. 'That when you've taken Buster for his walk, you'll drink a cup of tea with me, and stop talking nonsense! Agreed?'

Crossing the threshold of the veterans' hospital the next afternoon, Lara recoiled slightly at the smell of the place: an effluvium of boiled cabbage, floor polish and air-freshener, reminiscent of most hospitals, she imagined, a curious amalgamation of vegetable water, hygiene and old age.

Entering Ben's cubicle in the west wing of the building, clutching the bunch of flowers, the bag of grapes she had brought him, fearing the worst, to her amazement she discovered Ben Adams sitting bolt upright in his bed, apparently as bright as the proverbial button, displaying his near-toothless gums in a wide smile of recognition.

'Abaht time, too,' he grumbled amiably. 'Ah thowt as 'ow yer'd forgot me entirely, my lady. You, the donkey man, the Punch-an'-Judy man, an' all. Forgot all abaht a pore ole man on 'is death bed!'

Lara said crisply, 'If you're on your death bed, then I'm the Queen of Sheba! So what exactly is wrong with you?' Smiling, seating herself next to his bed, holding his heavily-veined hand in hers: 'I'd have come sooner had I known you were feeling poorly. But you'll be feeling much better soon, I daresay, when you've had a good rest, plenty of nourishing food inside you, and with so

280

many pretty young nurses to take care of you.'

'They ain't *all* purty,' Ben spat forth disgustedly. 'Not liken you, my lady. You'm been kind to me, my lady, an' that's summat I shan't niver forget. Jest promise me one thing, that when Ah'm dead an' gone, yer'll bury me decent in yon churchyard over-lookin' t' sea. Ah've allus fancied bein' laid ter rest there. An' it wain't cost yer nowt. Ah've an inshurance policy to tek care o' that.

'Jest mek sure, my lady, that someone'll sing "The Day Thou Gavest, Lord, is Ended". Promise me, my lady. Please, *promise*!'

'Yes, of course, Ben,' Lara assured him. 'You have my word, but that's a long way off! You see, I really need you to take care of the garden when you're feeling better.'

Ben shook his head. 'Nay, me gardenin' days is ovver an' done wi' now, ah'm think-in'. Seems like me 'eart ain't in it no more, not now Beau's gone. 'E were good ter me, wus Beau. Truth ter tell, ah knows sod all abaht gardenin'. Beau knew it an' all but 'e niver let on. It were 'im wot done t' 'ard graft. All ah iver done wus get in 'is way. It near bruk me 'eart when 'e said goodbye. That's when ah started feelin' porely like, as effen summat inside me 'ad gone missin' an' ah didn't want ti' go on livin'.'

'I know, Ben,' Lara said gently. 'I miss him too. But you mustn't give up on life. I meant what I said about needing your help in the garden. Not to worry, I'll lend you a hand. Not that I'm much of a gardener either, but I can at least mow the lawns and weed the borders. Between us, we can keep things shipshape and tidy till Mrs Prewett comes home in September. Well, what do you say, Ben? Shall we give it a try?'

'Aye, ah reckons so.' Ben's wrinkled face lit up suddenly. 'Effen yer'll gie me one of them nice breakfusts of yourn afore 'and. Sausages, a bit o' bacon an' a fried egg, ti line me stummick afore ah starts work.'

Lara smiled happily. 'That's settled, then,' she said, releasing his 'and. 'Now, just you concentrate on getting better. Try to sleep now while I find someone to put these flowers in water, and don't forget to eat those grapes I brought you.'

The old man pulled a face. 'Grapes,' he muttered, lying back against his pillows. 'Can't abide t' danged things. Ah niver knows wot ti do wi' t' pips!' Raising his head a little, 'Off now, are yer?' he asked breathlessly.

'Yes, but I'll come again tomorrow,' she promised. 'And every day until you're up and doing again.' On a sudden impulse, bending down, she kissed the old man's forehead. 'Remember, Ben,' she murmured.

'I really do need you.'

Picking up the flowers, she turned at the door to smile back at him. 'Sleep well, Ben,' she called to him softly. 'Until tomorrow.'

Ben nodded contentedly. 'Until termorrer, my lady,' he replied serenely, closing his eyes.

The doctor Lara spoke to next day was very kind, sympathetic and understanding. Mr Adams, he explained to her when she was seated in his office, had died peacefully in his sleep in the early hours of the morning, from heart failure.

Choking back tears, 'But he seemed much as usual when I saw him yesterday,' Lara murmured, recalling Ben's typical response to the grapes, his quirky gruffness of manner combined with an almost childlike innocence, his way of wheedling breakfast, beginning with a couple of slices of toast and a cuppa, ending up with a full English and a pot of tea, which she had found vastly amusing, somehow touching – as she had found equally touching his reference to her as 'my lady'. 'I'm sorry he's gone. I'll miss him.'

'We all shall,' the doctor said. 'He was quite a character.' He paused, then continued, 'I'm not certain if you know this, but Ben named you his next of kin during a recent conversation I had with him when, to speak bluntly, I felt it neccessary to find out...'

'It's all right, doctor, I understand what you're getting at.' Lara smiled faintly, seeing the man was upset, quite a young man, probably unused to dealing with situations of this nature. 'I had no idea he'd appointed me his next of kin, but when I saw him yesterday he mentioned an insurance policy to pay for his – funeral.'

Young Doctor Richards nodded, seemingly relieved that Lara knew about the policy. He said, 'Ben told me he wanted to have his policy paid to you; he signed a statement to that effect, and I called in one of the nurses to witness his signature.'

'Poor Ben!' Lara's eyes filled with tears. 'He asked to be buried in St Mary's churchyard.'

'Then may I leave the arrangements to you, Mrs Davenport?'

'Yes, of course, Doctor.'

'If there's insufficient money, the Hospital Board will be prepared to help out,' Dr Richards assured her.

'That won't be necessary.' Lara rose to her feet. Extending her hand: 'I'll let you know the time and date of the funeral, and there'll be food available after the service.' She smiled. 'Ben would like that, I know.'

Sadie helped Lara with the buffet, which

they set out in the conservatory on the marble-topped table which had once graced the Stella Maris dining room. Ben Adams' eyes would have twinkled at the sight of so much food, Lara thought. *Eh, that's wot I calls a spread*, he'd have said approvingly, longing to get stuck into the cold roast beef, chicken and salmon sandwiches, cucumber sandwiches; the home-made ham-and-egg pies, sausages on sticks, cheese scones, iced fairy cakes, maids of honour; the trifles and jellies and deep custard tarts so lovingly prepared in *his* honour. Not that he'd have gone a bundle on the bowls of salad.

When all was ready, Lara and Sadie walked together to St Mary's Church, carrying bunches of garden flowers: purple and white lilacs, laburnum blossoms, wallflowers and tulips, as a tribute to a – gardener – who, by his own admission, 'knew sod all about gardening'. But what did that matter? Ben's heart had been in the right place, and this was all that really mattered on the day of his funeral.

'Suppose nobody turns up?' Sadie ventured fearfully. 'Except us, Jeff, the parson and the funeral directors.'

Lara smiled mysteriously. Ben deserved a good send-off and she had taken steps, beforehand, to make certain he had just that.

Sadie gasped in amazement. Entering the

church, she noticed, first of all, the lighted candles and the magnificent display of white carnations and arum lilies gracing the altar; next the church choir, fully robed in their Sunday regalia – white surplices and blue velvet caps – occupying the choir stalls, awaiting the arrival of Ben's coffin. Finally, the number of mourners gathered together to pay their last respects to a poor old man who had scarcely known, during his lifetime, the depth of their feelings towards him, until his departure from this world to the next had brought about the realization of the empty spaces left in all their lives, now that he was gone.

And now the service was due to begin. Ben's flower adorned coffin was borne into the church to the solemn strains of the Nunc Dimittis, sung by the choir. 'Lord, now lettest thou thy servant depart in peace.' They later sang, by special request of the dear departed, 'The Day Thou Gavest, Lord, is Ended'.

But Lara had not envisaged Ben's departure from life as a gloomy occasion entirely, the reason why she had invited the children from St Jude's Orphanage to sing 'All Things Bright and Beautiful' as a fitting reminder of Ben's sense of fun, his quirky sense of humour, his love of all things bright and beautiful during his time on earth.

Dr Richards, several nurses in uniform,

other doctors and members of the Hospital Board had attended Ben's funeral. The donkey man and the Punch-and-Judy man had also been present, plus Jeff, who had escorted Lara and Sadie down the aisle in the wake of Ben's casket. There had been a number of hospital inmates, too, all of whom had fought in the armed forces in the first or second world wars, all of whom had known Ben, who had played cards and dominoes with them, watched sport with them on TV or spent time with them in the bar of their local pub; all of whom had been invited back to Stella Maris to partake of the buffet Lara and Sadie had provided for them.

'Will there be enough to go round?' Sadie enquired anxiously, switching on electric kettles for tea and coffee. 'I should have stayed behind to see to all this. And what about the children?'

'Not to worry, there's fruit juice, lemonade and ice cream in the fridge, and plenty of shop-bought food in the pantry, just in case. Veal-and-ham pies, extra bread, sausage rolls and chicken vol-au-vents.'

Inspecting the contents of the large iron kettle she had placed on the Aga before setting off for church, 'It's barely simmering,' Sadie panicked. 'Oh lord, no wonder. I should have stoked the fire, but the log basket was empty and I hadn't time to fill it.

I'm sorry, Mrs D, I should have *made* time!'

'No, I should have seen to it myself when I came downstairs this morning. I quite simply forgot, what with one thing and another. I just used up the logs in the basket, took Buster for a walk then got on with the sandwiches. Thank goodness I'd made most of the food the night before.'

'I'd best refill the log basket now then, hadn't I?' Sadie suggested.

'No need,' Lara said. 'I'll see to it later. I'd rather you make the tea and coffee while I see to the buffet, hand round plates and so on, if you don't mind.'

' 'Course not!' Sadie chuckled. 'What I mean is, his Reverence and those doctors from up yonder will think it a bit odd if you don't put in an appearance. Mind you, it mightn't be a bad idea to send the kids through here for their lemonade and ice cream. I daresay they won't be all that interested in sandwiches and suchlike.'

Later that evening, in her dressing gown and slippers, thinking over the events of the day, tired but contented, she felt that Ben had received the send-off he so richly deserved. His had been a lovely, heartwarming service. She could almost hear him saying, *Eh, ah niver thowt as 'ow there'd be so many fowk, so many flowers, an' that theer parson spoutin' on abaht me bein' a good an' faithful servant.*

*Jest as well 'e didna know me all that well, my lady, else 'e might hev tould the truth. Good? That I ain't nor iver has bin. More of a pain in t' arse like, beggin' yer pardon, my lady.*

On an impulse, picking up the phone, Lara rang The Birches. Sadie answered the call. 'Just to say goodnight, Sadie, and to thank you and Jeff for today. I couldn't have borne it without your help and support.'

'Our pleasure entirely,' Sadie reassured her. 'Everything went so well. Ben would have been over the moon at the nice things said about him, and all the flowers. More like a wedding than a funeral, if you know what I mean.'

Knowing exactly what she meant, Lara said, 'By the way, it was so kind, so thoughtful of you to refill the log basket before you went home.'

A slight pause occurred, then Sadie said thoughtfully, 'But I didn't. You told me not to, remember? Are you quite sure you didn't fill it yourself?'

'Perfectly sure! But if not you, who did?'

'Oh, it must have been that man I saw in the garden before Jeff brought me home,' Sadie responded eagerly. 'Yes, of course, now I remember. I asked him if he was lost, but he just shook his head and smiled at me. Then Jeff called to me to get a move on, and when I looked back, the man was gone.' Another pause, then Sadie said uneasily,

'Funny, come to think of it, I could have sworn I'd seen him before, but I couldn't for the life of me think where.'

'This man, how old would he have been?' Lara asked intently.

'Oh, quite young, in his early twenties, at a rough guess. He reminded me of someone, but I can't think who. Sorry, Mrs D, I must be losing my marbles.'

'More likely you're in need of a good night's sleep. So am I. See you on Monday?'

'Sure thing. Goodnight and God bless, Mrs D.'

Hanging up the phone, Lara went through to the kitchen. Gazing mistily at the basket of logs near the Aga, she whispered intently, 'Thank you, Ben. Well done, thou good and faithful servant.'

Smiling, she added, 'How does it feel to be young again?'

# Eighteen

Now that Sadie was back at work, Lara's sense of isolation had lifted considerably. Things were back to normal so far as the household chores were concerned. The garden was a different matter. Eventually, she rang Dr Richards to find out if anyone at the hospital would be willing to come in two or three times a week to cut the grass, weed the borders and bring in fuel for the Aga. In short, what she needed was a jobbing gardener-cum-handyman, preferably strong and reasonably mobile.

Dr Richards laughed and said he would see what he could do, which is how Lara came by a burly individual called Jack Fisher, taciturn but not unfriendly, an ex-boxer who had stopped a bullet at El-Alamein, as he put it, which had put paid to his boxing career, and other things too, including his ... Well, never mind what else. Lara had felt it expedient not to enquire too closely into the what else. His love life presumably.

★ ★ ★

Worried that she had not heard from Joan Prewett for some considerable time, one day, at the chalet, Lara wrote to tell her about the death of Ben Adams; Iris Smith's trials and tribulations leading to the appointment of Sadie Cogill as a home help; mentioning briefly that she had not been in touch with Rory McAllister of late due to his wife's illness.

A difficult letter to write on the whole, to Lara's way of thinking, sounding somewhat stilted and unnatural; factual, unemotional, betraying little or nothing of herself. More a report than a letter, she decided, sealing the envelope. Not a word about the flare-up between herself and Iris Smith, about the stone-throwing incident perpetrated by her grandchildren; the trunk in the attic, her discovery of old letters and photographs leading to her research into the Stone-houses' family history.

And yet she had felt so certain, meeting Joan Prewett for the first time, that here was a kindred spirit, a confidante. Possibly Joan's long silence had unnerved her to the extent of her inability to communicate with Joan more fully? Or was the woman ill? There was always that possibility, of course, a worsening of her condition. After all, a sick elderly lady, far from home ... And yet Joan had sounded fine during their brief phone conversation about the garden party.

One afternoon at the chalet, watching the passing parade of early summer visitors, beach donkeys trotting along the sand, children holding on to the reins, urging the animals to go faster, others crowding about the Punch-and-Judy show, screaming approval as naughty old Punch came face to face with the crocodile, Lara recalled her own childhood, those warm summer days of long ago when she had also revelled in donkey-riding and the comeuppance of the villainous Mr Punch on the sands of Scarborough's South Bay.

May had now slipped away imperceptibly to make way for the month of June, leaving in its wake scatterings of fallen blossoms, golden laburnum petals, white and mauve lilacs and the pink confetti of ornamental cherries, in favour of June's inheritance of burgeoning rose bushes, candled sycamores, upthrusting delphiniums and peonies; budding hydrangeas and fuchsias, rhododendrons and pink and white azaleas. The weather was warm, the sky blue, the sea calm, so why this persistent, niggling feeling that something of importance was missing from her life? Lara wondered, gazing out to sea at a flotilla of white-sailed yachts, flitting like white-winged butterflies on the waters of the bay.

Suddenly Buster, lying at her feet, half

asleep, lifting his head, scenting the air, lumbered to his feet, furiously barking and wagging his tail at the sound of familiar footsteps on the promenade.

Looking up from a kneeling position, cradling the ecstatic dog in his arms, then rising slowly to his feet, 'I was told that I might find you here,' Rory McAllister explained quietly. Then: 'Oh, Lara, it's so good to see you again!'

'You too, Rory,' Lara responded calmly, despite the swift beating of her heart at his sudden reappearance in her life. 'Can you stay a while, or is this another flying visit?'

Sensing her restraint, he said, 'I'm sorry I've been out of touch lately. Things have been difficult, but I'd like to stay overnight, if possible. If you want me to. If it's not too much trouble.'

'Of course not. You know you're welcome to stay any time, for as long as you want. Your room's ready and there's plenty of food in the house, which reminds me, it's almost tea time, so shall we be making a move?'

Lara made tea and ham sandwiches. Later she cooked chicken pieces, minted new potatoes and broad beans, cauliflower and cheese sauce, in her element at having someone to take care of, especially Rory. 'This is like old times,' she said, watching him tucking into the food she'd prepared for him, thinking that he seemed much quieter than usual, more preoccupied, as if he had a lot on his mind; something he wanted to say but didn't quite know how to begin.

'Let's have coffee in the drawing room, shall we?' she suggested. 'Then you can tell me what's troubling you, the reason why you're here. To do with Georgie, I imagine?'

'Yes, but there are other things, too. You see, Lara, I've found myself a new job...'

'The Cotswolds, you mean? But that's what you wanted, isn't it?' Lara interrupted eagerly, pleased that he had decided to take charge of his own destiny at last, to kiss the past goodbye and carve out a brand new future for himself.

'Well, no, not exactly,' he confessed awkwardly. 'The fact is, I'm moving to London to be with Georgie and her parents. She's with them now. I'll be joining them later when I've packed my belongings and worked out my time in Middlesbrough; put my personal affairs in order, so to speak, before starting my new job.'

'You mean you're planning to live with Georgina in her parents' home? Good God, Rory, are you out of your mind?' Never before had she spoken her thoughts so forcibly, so angrily. 'Have you any idea what you're letting yourself in for?'

'Of course I have,' he retorted defensively.

'You think I don't know? Do you really imagine that this was an easy decision for me to make? It simply occurred to me that living with Georgie in a two-room flat in Middlesbrough was the road to nowhere. She was getting worse, not better.'

'What puzzles me,' Lara flung back at him, 'is why you choose to live with her at all! A woman no longer your wife but a thorn in your flesh!'

'I thought that you, above all people, would understand why,' Rory responded grimly. 'Because she needed me, because I'm still in love with her!'

'I see. So you came here because you wanted a shoulder to cry on? An overnight caravanserai; a decent meal and a good night's sleep? Well, I'm sorry, Rory, it just won't wash! You are welcome to your good night's rest, just as you were welcome to the supper I cooked for you. But if you have the sense you were born with, which I have every reason to doubt, you'll leave here the first thing tomorrow morning. Do I make myself clear?'

Turning at the door, on her way upstairs to bed, she added, 'Goodnight, Rory and good luck. I have the feeling you're going to need all the luck you can get, living in London with your in-laws.'

'Wait, Lara!' He had never seen her like this before, coldly angry and upset. 'I'll leave now, if you like, but not like this, as enemies, not friends.'

'I'm not your enemy. I never have been.' Lara spoke wearily. 'To the extent of not wanting you to go head first into a no-win situation. I know you love Georgie, but wouldn't it have been better to find the job you wanted, in the Cotswolds, a place of your own to live?'

Standing at the foot of the stairs, looking up at Lara, he said, 'I tried, believe me, but Georgie wouldn't hear of it. In any case, it wouldn't have been an ideal situation for her, living in some quiet backwater, being alone all day, surely you can see that?'

'Oh yes, I can see that quite clearly. I can see everything quite clearly. Well, they do say the onlooker sees most of the game. Understanding or accepting what I see is a different matter entirely. As a friend, it's *you* I care about, your future happiness, not Georgie's or her parents'.' She paused. 'If that sounds harsh and uncompromising, I'm sorry. You once fought a battle on my behalf, remember, the day we confronted Iris Smith. Now I'm trying my best to fight a battle on your behalf. Unsuccessfully, it appears. But you can't blame me for trying, can you?'

'I can't, and I don't,' Rory responded quietly. 'I've always thought of you as the best, the dearest friend I've ever had, which is why I came here to talk things over with you; not for the sake of a meal and a night's sleep, as you suggested. What more can I say except I'm truly sorry that we fail to see eye-to-eye on my future with the woman I love. Georgie is no monster, believe me, just a very sick and sorry young woman in need of all the support, love and understanding I am capable of giving her, albeit to the detriment of my own plans for that pie-in-the-sky future in the Cotswolds.'

He continued sadly, 'If you had ever been in love yourself, Lara, you'd know exactly how I feel. The pity of it is that you married a man you were not in love with, with whom you spent – or should I say squandered – the best years of your life.' Drawing in a deep breath of resignation intermingled with despair and a tincture of self-pity, he said, 'Well, I'd best be on my way now.'

And, 'Yes, Rory,' Lara replied, with a proud uplifting of her head, knowing that her brief love affair of the heart with him was over and done with. 'Better that way, don't you think?'

He shrugged helplessly. 'No, I don't, but if that's what you want...'

'It was your idea, not mine.'

'Even so, I had hoped that you'd want me to stay, not to have me leave like a thief in the night, as if I had done something to be ashamed of in wanting to be with Georgina.

If so, I fail to understand why. What harm has she ever caused you?'

'It's the harm she has caused you that concerns me,' Lara said levelly, holding her emotion in check, needing to speak the truth, as she saw it, as dispassionately as possible. 'I haven't forgotten, if you have, the state you were in when she left you for another man – pregnant by him, carrying his child. And what happened afterwards? When she lost that child and the man she was in love with abandoned her, there you were, waiting in the wings to pick up the pieces. Fair enough. But has it ever occurred to you that Georgina made use of you? Do you really imagine that, if the man she really loves came back to her, she wouldn't drop you like a hot potato? Now here you are, on the verge of making the greatest mistake of your life, and wanting me to condone it. Well, I *can't*, Rory. I'm sorry, but that's the way it is.' She continued wearily, 'Now, if you'll forgive me, I'm on my way to bed. I'm certain you can find your own way out.'

Later, in her room, hearing the closure of the front door behind him, giving way to tears of regret, remembering all the good times they had shared together, the happiness of those moonlit walks along the promenade with Buster in tow; pausing to look up at the stars, the feel of the wind ruffling her hair, the way he had coaxed her into shedding her old dowdy image along with her dowdy old clothes, rebuilding her shattered self-confidence step by step along the way, was it really possible that she had sent him away so abruptly, without a word of farewell, a goodnight kiss, the touch of his lips on her cheek?

Too late now that he was gone away from her, for tears of regret that he might never come back to her, to Stella Maris, in need of her help and understanding, until it occurred to her, by dawn's early light, that she also had been made use of, to some extent, by a weak-minded man in need of a far stronger-minded person to cosset and take care of him, That *she* had been that person all along, to whom he had turned for comfort, good food and consolation, certainly not love born of a physical attraction towards her. She knew that now. A bitter pill to swallow, but swallow it she must if her future depended on self-reliance, not bittersweet memories of the past.

The last people she had expected to see were Johnny and Jill Carstairs, who appeared at the chalet one afternoon, a week later, saying they'd been told where they might find her by a thickset man with a broken nose engaged in lawn-mowing at Stella Maris.

'My word, you're looking good, Mrs Davenport,' Jill remarked admiringly, planting a warm kiss on Lara's cheek. Then, appealing to her husband: 'Doesn't she look well, Johnny?'

'I'll say she does,' Johnny enthused. 'Obviously sea air and freedom has done her a power of good after – Middlesbrough.' Speaking a little too enthusiastically, Lara thought, too expansively, as though he had something to hide, wondering why they had turned up out of the blue so unexpectedly.

Inviting them to sit down, making them coffee, she asked, 'Are you on holiday, or taking a day off from the hotel?'

'Ah well,' Jill laughed, accepting a cup of coffee. 'Neither one nor the other exactly. You see, we've sold the hotel, though we are still in residence there for the time being until the new owners take over. Honestly, you wouldn't believe how difficult things are at the moment, what with the new owners coming and going all the time; wanting everything changed in a hurry, with Johnny and me doing our best to winkle residential guests out of their rooms as kindly as possible.'

'People such as myself?' Lara suggested quietly. 'So, what you are really saying is that when I leave here in September, there'll be no room for me at the inn? Has quite a biblical ring to it, don't you think? So, if not long-term residents, what kind of a clientele are the new owners hoping to attract?'

'Commercial travellers,' Johnny confessed shamefacedly, 'and their ilk, once the ground floor bar has been established and the upper rooms carved up into overnight cubicles.' He added bitterly, 'We didn't want this to happen, believe me, but the Windsor, as a residential hotel in an offbeat town like Middlesbrough, was losing money hand over fist. The truth is, we had no other option than to sell it when the opportunity arose.'

'I see,' Lara said sympathetically. 'So, where do you intend to go, what will you do when the new tenants take over?'

Jill said decisively, 'One thing's for sure, we'll be leaving Middlesbrough for good and all. Johnny fancies a country pub some-where in the Yorkshire Dales, don't you, darling? So do I! An easier, more relaxed lifestyle. Running the Windsor Hotel was no picnic, believe me, catering for awkward guests, yourself excluded, had me at my wits' end at times, especially that spoilt young madam, Georgina McAllister, who flatly refused to eat anything save smoked salmon and caviar!' She added repentantly, 'Oh, sorry, Mrs Davenport, I'd forgotten that her husband was a friend of yours, but how the hell he put up with her shennani-gans, I'll never know. What that young madam needed was a lesson in manners. The way she spoke to the poor man was shocking. In fact, it was she who decided us to sell up, wasn't it, Johnny?'

'That it was,' her husband said grimly. 'Hotel-keeping's bad enough without folk like her to contend with. Well, put it this way, she was the last straw that broke the camel's back. Jill was tired out with all the work and worry. We were having a tough time financially, so, talking things over, we decided to call it a day. Early next morning, I went into town to put the hotel on the market. Soon after came an offer we'd have been mad to refuse, so now the deal has gone through.' He added, 'The reason we came was we wanted to explain the situation, to say goodbye to you personally, not to simply send you a letter, knowing you intended to return to us in September.'

Deeply touched, Lara said, 'Thank you. I appreciate that.'

Jill asked wistfully, 'Shall you find another hotel in Middlesbrough, or stay here in Carnelian Bay?'

'Impossible to say right now,' Lara admitted, glimpsing another hole in the fabric of her life, so far as the future was concerned. 'I'll need to think about it before reaching a decision.' Reaching a right decision would be crucial to her future happiness and peace of mind, she realized.

Happiness? Contentment, more likely, happiness having seemingly passed her by since her quarrel with Rory, the death of Ben Adams and Beau's return to America. Again came that feeling of spiritual loneliness, of expendability in the game of life.

Staying at the Windsor Hotel had never been the sea mark of her utmost sail. At least her return there, come September, would have given her time to recover from her summertime custodianship of Stella Maris, by no means as easy an option as she had been led to believe, involving not merely housekeeping, dog-walking and stoking the Aga, but personal human relationships which had drawn her deeply into the lives of people other than herself: the Cogills, the Stonehouses, Iris Smith, the Fieldings, Beauregard Jackson, Ben Adams; above all, Rory McAllister, whose hasty departure from her life she deeply regretted. Her own fault entirely. If only she had been more understanding, less harshly uncompromising towards him, she might at least have retained a foothold in his affection. The closing of the door behind him, without a sign of forgiveness on her part, had put paid to the possibility of further communication between them.

Bidding the Carstairs a fond farewell, sick at heart that they, also, would soon be gone from her life, when they had walked away from her along the promenade, turning back to wave to her till they were out of sight, closing the chalet, Lara returned, with Buster, to Stella Maris, dreading the silence of the house, the empty rooms, exacerbated by the emptiness of her heart.

That evening, Lara wandered into the garden. The air was cool and fresh, sweetly scented, the sea reflecting the trapped turquoise and gold of a dying summer day.

Shadows lay thick beneath the trees, there was the scent of newly turned earth from the flower beds and the herbaceous border, the intermingled perfume of early roses, stocks, and seaweed from the sands below, borne on the summer breeze.

At the click of the front gate, Buster, busily nosing the grass beneath a spinney of silver birches, lifted his head, barked shrilly and went to investigate. Lara followed suit. Gareth Roberts was halfway up the path to the front door.

'Hope I haven't startled you?' Gareth asked apologetically. 'I'm staying with the Fieldings for a few days, to recuperate.' Frowning slightly: 'You did get my message?'

'What message?' Lara stared at him uncomprehendingly. 'I haven't heard a word from you since our dinner engagement. I simply concluded that you had decided not

305

to keep in touch.' She spoke coldly, in the belief that she had made a fool of herself, that night, in imagining she had glimpsed a warmer side to his nature. Apparently she was wrong. Despite his hopefully uttered words, 'There will be another time, then?' he had not bothered to contact her again during the ensuing weeks, leaving her in a state of limbo until her common sense had warned her to put the incident behind her, to forget about the unpredictable Dr Roberts – a much less difficult task than she had supposed, with so many other matters to occupy her mind at the time.

Uttering an expletive, running his hands through his hair, 'I might have known this would happen,' he groaned. 'I suspected as much when you didn't reply to my message. When Amanda came to visit me in hospital, I asked her to let you know what had happened – about the accident, I mean.'

'*Accident*?'

'A road accident,' Gareth said impatiently. 'Some damn fool in a hurry to get to heaven ahead of time! The collision was inevitable, might have been fatal, head-on. Thank God I had my wits about me. Even so, I landed in a ditch, my car on top of me. A complete write-off, I might add. Next thing I knew I was in hospital with a broken collarbone, two cracked ribs, a ruptured spleen and concussion.'

'Oh, I'm so sorry,' Lara murmured sympathetically. 'I had no idea. You'd best come indoors and sit down.' Leading the way: 'I'll make some coffee.'

'No need,' he said impatiently. 'I'm on my way to the Golf Club Hotel to meet the Fieldings. Now you know what happened, perhaps we could have dinner together at The Feathers, tomorrow evening? Continue where we left off, so to speak. I'll call for you around seven. All right?'

'Yes,' Lara agreed, albeit uncertainly, glimpsing the harsher side of his nature once more, the side she disliked intensely; high-handedness for one thing, allied to his quixotic mood swings from charm to irritability in a matter of minutes. Here, after all, was a man she had successfully erased from her thoughts since their last meeting.

Things might have been different had he not said, accusingly, 'You don't sound too sure.'

Drawing in a deep breath, trusting in her own wisdom and common sense for once in her life, Lara said coolly, 'I'm not, if you really must know!'

'Why the hell not?' he demanded fiercely, startled by her response.

'I rather think you have answered your own question,' Lara said calmly. 'Think about it, Gareth. Frankly, you have been dipping your toes into a possible romantic liaison with me since you saw me on the doorstep of the Fieldings' house some time ago; struck by my new, less dowdy image, I daresay. By your own admission, in need of a new woman in your life to take the place of your wife. Apparently, you saw in me a solution to your own deep-seated emotional problems, just as I, possibly, saw in you, that evening at The Feathers, a solution to mine.'

Pausing momentarily, she continued, 'The truth is, as much as I long for love and security, right now – a home to call my own – I'd far rather face a future alone. Do I make myself clear?'

'Abundantly clear,' Roberts snapped back at her. 'And to think I was about to ask you to marry me! All I can possibly say is, thank God I found out in the nick of time what a shallow-minded person you really are!'

Turning away, marching down the garden path to the front gate, slamming it shut behind him, Lara watched him go without a trace of regret that she had finally rid herself of a presence in her life that she could well do without.

# Nineteen

Mist, known locally as 'fret', stole in silently from the sea, giving the impression of a grey gossamer veil shrouding the coastline. The foghorn near the harbour moaned intermittent warnings to ships at sea, imparting a feeling of unreality, a sense of isolation, as if Stella Maris, detached from its enclave of neighbouring houses, was floating on a fog bank, Lara thought, shivering slightly as she looked out of her bedroom window early one June morning.

Dressing and making her way downstairs to the kitchen, curiously the mist had invaded the house, she realized, feeling for the bannister. But surely this was not possible with doors and windows closed from the locking-up procedure of the night before? Even so, she appeared to be moving in a haze.

Listening intently, she could have sworn she heard movement, snatches of conversation, floating up to her from the downstairs rooms. The idea occurred that possibly Sadie had come in early to begin work, accompanied by Jeff. But this was Saturday. Sadie had come and gone yesterday, calling over her shoulder as she went, 'See you on Monday, as usual, Mrs D!'

So what was happening to her? Why this strange feeling of disorientation as if she had entered a time warp? Was it remotely possible that she was losing her grip on reality as she had done once before, following the death of her husband? Was she suffering the after-effects of bidding goodbye to Beau, Ben Adams, Rory McAllister, more recently to Gareth Roberts, to the detriment of her mental health and physical well-being, the stripping away, as it were, of the underpinnings of her life, leaving her emotionally vulnerable and bereft?

Were thoughts of the future so bleak that, unwillingly, she had turned to the past as a means of consolation? Was she asleep or awake? Had she really seen, or imagined she'd seen, someone entering the kitchen, not that room as she now knew it, but as it had been nigh on a hundred years ago? Was the cook preparing breakfast for the Stonehouse family on, not an Aga, but a coal-fired kitchen range, real or a figment of her overwrought state of mind?

Impossible to say on this mist-bound summer morning in which she felt herself to be a somnambulist, a sleepwalker surrounded by ghostly figures of the past, unaware of her presence as they went about their household duties of long ago.

From the room Joan Prewett regarded as her private sanctum came the sound of male voices raised in contention; words spoken in anger deadened by the door of what had once been Joshua Stonehouse's study.

Bemusedly, covering her ears with her hands, Lara stumbled across the hall to the drawing room. Standing on the threshold, glancing about her, she saw, with a mounting feeling of terror, that the windows were shrouded with heavy red velvet curtains and green, half-lowered venetian blinds with dangling ivory acorns, that the room was chock a-block with ponderous Victorian furniture, massive sideboards; high-backed chairs and a horsehair sofa grouped about the fireplace; chenille-covered tables displaying glass domes containing stuffed birds and waxen artificial flowers; oil lamps, brass-mounted, with dangling red lustres, and a plethora of silver-framed family photographs.

There were brass fire tongs in the tiled, brass-fendered hearth, a brass coal scuttle. Above the mantelpiece hung a gilt-framed head-and-shoulders portrait of a fierce-looking man wearing a high starched collar and a green silk cravat.

Uttering a low cry of horror, heart pounding, pushing her way through a seemingly impenetrable fog bank towards the stairs, suddenly Lara awoke from her nightmare to the realization that she was safely ensconced in her own bed, in her own room, that the sun was shining on the world beyond her bedroom window.

Yet, day-long, she could not rid herself of the feeling that all she had seen and heard during her nightmare was true. That, in her sleep, she had somehow entered another dimension.

Later, making her way to the attic, possessed of a burning desire to discover something relevant to her time-warp theory, dressed in her oldest clothes with Buster beside her nosing ecstatically in dusty corners, tail wagging in anticipation of finding a juicy bone among the mountains of junk cluttering Joan Prewett's repository of discarded household belongings, Lara scarcely knew where to begin her search. For what, specifically? She hadn't the faintest idea. Anything relevant to her so-called nightmare.

Little or no use delving into tea chests containing an accumulation of twentieth-century pots and pans, bundles of unwanted cutlery, discarded electrical equipment, old toasters, kettles, irons, table lamps and light switches, the leftovers from Joan's former home in Leeds.

Other chests contained bedding, sheets,

pillowcases and blankets, old-fashioned eiderdowns and candlewick counterpanes: Pyrex casseroles, incomplete tea sets, chipped teapots, long-disused and forgotten dinner services, lidless tureens and cracked gravy boats. Why Joan had felt it necessary to cling on to so much worthless household junk, Lara couldn't imagine, unless parting with it had seemed unbearable following the death of her husband and her daughter's defection to America soon afterwards.

Lara turned her attention to a wicker basket of sizeable proportions, fastened with cracked leather straps and rusted buckles which refused, at first, to yield to her attempts to open it. That it did so later was due to her fetching, from the kitchen, a bottle of olive oil to soften the straps and buckles until, eventually, opening the lid of the basket, she discovered a cache of brass-mounted Victorian oil lamps complete with lustres, a dozen or more family photographs in tarnished silver frames, two glass domes containing stuffed birds and waxen artificial flowers. Above all, at the bottom of the trunk, the head-and-shoulders portrait of a fierce-looking man wearing a high white collar and a green silk cravat.

Suddenly, Lara knew beyond a shadow of doubt that she was not alone in the attic, that someone was watching her. Not merely watching her, but watching over her, tenderly, lovingly, the shadowy presence in her life she had been aware of since she had first heard the strains of 'Danny Boy' in the air about her, when she had become the custodian of Stella Maris, with no clear idea of what that custodianship would entail.

She knew now!

Turning her head, she whispered breathlessly, 'I know you are there, Danny, but *why*? You should be at peace now, with your beloved Clara beside you. Or is that what's troubling you, that your graves are far apart from one another?'

Answer came there none. She was speaking into thin air, and yet Buster, whining softly, tail wagging, appeared to have glimpsed something far beyond her limited human vision to discern. Possibly a young man, in uniform, in search of peace.

Sadie arrived the following Wednesday, full of the latest troubles of the Smith family. Iris's husband was to face prosecution for fraudulently obtaining money from what Sadie termed, 'the Social', to which he was not entitled.

'Honestly!' Sadie said scathingly, unaware of the solecism. 'Some folk are so crooked they can't lie straight in their beds! Huh, he might have known he'd be found out sooner or later, the greedy old devil!' She paused. 'Wonder what they'll do to him? Lock him up, I shouldn't wonder. What do you think, Mrs D?'

Lara hadn't the faintest idea, and said so, at the same time wondering how this latest blow to her pride would affect Iris, volatile and unstable at the best of times, as she knew to her cost; sensing danger, though she could not for the life of her think why.

That evening, deep in thought, Lara walked slowly along the cliff top, pausing now and then to look out to sea. Darkness had fallen, the air was warm and still. The street lights of Carnelian Bay had sprung into bloom, outlining the harbour with its moored fishing vessels tethered to the quay. At sea, Lara noticed the slow passage of ships on the horizon, the twinkling of lights, like fireflies, pinpricking the dark velvet blue of the night sky, and heard the comforting wash of the incoming tide on the rocks below.

Her thoughts centred on Rory, she wondered how he was faring in London, whether or not he was happy living beneath his in-laws' roof, recalling the many times they had walked this way together, the wind in their hair, looking up at the stars, calling Buster to heel when he disappeared into his favourite spinney of trees overlooking the promenade. Which reminded her – where was Buster now? She hadn't seen him for some time, she realized, hurrying towards the spinney, calling out. 'Buster, where are you? Come here at once, you bad lad!'

A wild-eyed figure, that of a woman, smiling evilly, emerged from the spinney, holding a knife in her hand, a murderous expression on her face; hatred in her eyes. 'I've put paid to your dog, now I intend putting paid to you,' Iris Smith uttered wickedly.

Raising up her right arm, holding the knife aloft preparatory to a downward thrust into Lara's body, Lara knew, beyond a shadow of doubt, that this was a mad woman she was facing, that, in order to survive, she must summon up all the strength she possessed to disarm Iris of her weapon.

The thought of Buster, Iris's chilling words – 'I've put paid to your dog' – lent desperation to Lara's movements. Instinctively, seizing Iris's upraised arm by the wrist, she fought for possession of the knife.

Shocked by the suddenness of the attack, her mind in a turmoil, unable to think clearly, struggling ineffectually with her assailant, face-to-face with her, a leering face distorted by malice into a grinning, triumphant mask of hatred, Lara knew that to stand an earthly chance of survival against the much stronger woman, her existence depended on clear thinking.

At that moment, she remembered a playground trick of long ago, a form of torture known as an Indian burn, perpetrated by school bullies on their victims, comprising a twisting of the wrist two ways at the same time, causing considerable suffering to those singled out to endure the painful procedure.

Unhesitatingly, Lara applied the Indian burn to her assailant's wrist, twisting the flesh two ways until, screaming in agony, Iris dropped the knife, which Lara kicked aside into the long grass bordering the cliff edge.

Then, before Iris had time to recover from the pain in her wrist, Lara sent her sprawling backwards by means of a blow in the midriff.

But the fight was not over and done with yet. Regaining her breath, scrambling to her feet, Iris lunged towards Lara, no longer smiling that ghastly, mask-like smile of hers, but grim-faced, with murder in mind.

'So, you thought you could get the better of me, did you, my fine lady?' Iris uttered insanely, her hands about Lara's throat. 'Well, you'd best think again, hadn't you, you evil, sanctimonious bitch!'

With a superhuman effort, clawing and scratching Iris's hands and face, Lara could scarcely believe her sudden upsurge of energy, as if some unseen presence beside her was fighting this battle on her behalf, imbuing her with courage, guiding her every inch of the way in her struggle for survival.

Grunting with the pain of Lara's on-slaught on her face and hands, Iris relaxed her grip on Lara's throat. The moment that happened, Lara, gasping for breath, pushed Iris away from her, sending her spinning, causing her to fall heavily on her back, where she lay, panting heavily, winded for the time being, eyes closed and with blood flowing from the scratches on her face and hands.

Suddenly, to her infinite relief, Lara heard a voice calling her name, and saw the beam of a torch coming towards her from the direction of Stella Maris.

Sinking to her knees, with tears streaming down her face, when Edward Stonehouse asked her if she was all right, unable to reply, Lara merely nodded her head in response.

Blessedly, he had not come alone to her rescue. Raising her head, she saw that police cars and an ambulance had arrived at the scene of conflict.

She whispered hoarsely, 'Tell them to take care of Iris, to be gentle with her.' Rising unsteadily to her feet: 'Now I must find my dog. He's over yonder somewhere, in the spinney.'

'I'll come with you,' Edward said grimly, lending her a helping hand. 'Though you are really in no fit state to walk anywhere at the moment. You should be in hospital.'

'Not until I've found Buster. Iris had a knife, you see? Said she'd "put paid" to him. I'm not going anywhere until I've found him, seen with my own two eyes what she did to him, the poor creature.'

Approaching the spinney, Edward said kindly, 'You wait here, Lara. Let me take a look. A knife, you say? Where is that knife now?'

'Over there, in the long grass near the cliff edge. I managed to kick it out of harm's way.' Suddenly Lara felt intensely cold and vulnerable, worried sick about Buster, that close and dear companion she loved with all her heart. Only a mad woman would have inflicted injury, possibly death, on a harmless animal, she realized, watching intently as Edward entered the spinney alone.

Minutes seemed like hours until Edward emerged from the trees holding in his arms a bundle of yellow fur, eyes closed, with dangling paws and tail. He said, 'He's barely alive, I'm afraid.'

'Please, give him to me,' Lara said quietly, holding out her arms to receive the precious burden, far heavier than she had imagined it would be.

Sinking to her knees once more, cradling the dog in her arms, burying her face in its fur, 'Please, Buster, stay with me,' she whispered, wetting his fur with her tears. 'I love you so much. Besides, what would Cleo do without you?'

Glancing up at Edward, 'Please help me get him to the nearest vet's,' she said urgently. 'At least let us give him a fighting chance of survival!'

Lara had stubbornly refused medical help. 'I'm not injured,' she said. 'Besides, I want to be near the phone, just in case...'

'I'm sorry about your dog, ma'am,' the police sergeant told her sympathetically. 'It was a nasty, brutal attack on a fine animal. What did the vet say? Any chance of survival?'

'It's too soon to tell. I wanted to stay at the surgery but he advised me not to. He said he'd ring me as soon as possible.'

'Of course,' the man said awkwardly. 'A nasty business all round.' Glancing at his watch, rising to his feet: 'I'd best be getting back to the station. There's nothing more to be done tonight. We have your statement, the weapon has been secured, your attacker's in custody, under sedation for the time being. Happen we'll get a statement from her in the morning if she's up to it, which depends largely on the consultant's diagnosis of her mental state. Could be, more likely than not, that he'll recommend her removal to the psychiatric unit until he's got to the bottom of what ails her.'

Turning at the door: 'Well, goodnight,

Mrs Davenport, Mr Stonehouse. I'll see myself out.' He added, speaking to Edward, 'Things might have turned out a lot worse, a whole lot worse, if you hadn't called us when you did. "A gut feeling that Mrs Davenport was in danger", you said on the phone; "A kind of presentiment". Was that really true, or is there something you're not telling us?'

When the sergeant had gone, 'I've been wondering about that, too,' Lara confessed, frowning. 'Can you explain?'

Edward, who had accompanied Lara back to Stella Maris after leaving the vet's surgery, to keep her company and lend her his support following the traumatic events of the evening, shook his head bemusedly. 'I only wish I could. My wife and I were watching television, the kids were in bed, when all of a sudden...'

'Go on. I'm listening!' Lara smiled wistfully. 'On the other hand, there's really no need to explain. It was Danny, wasn't it? I know, because I felt his presence on the cliff top when I was out there fighting for my life. I *am* right, aren't I?'

'Yes,' Edward acknowledged, 'I felt his presence so strongly in the room; sensed danger so urgently, that I knew I must act quickly. That's when I rang the police station. They probably thought I was stark raving mad.' He grinned wryly. 'How I'll ever be able to convince them that I was acting on the advice of my great-grand-father who died in the First War, the lord only knows!'

Lara paraphrased softly, ' "There are more things in heaven and earth than are dreamt of in our philosophy".'

She added, 'Thank you for staying with me, for being here for me when I needed a shoulder to lean on. Thank you for saving my life. You – and Danny.'

Suddenly the phone rang. Lara hesitated momentarily before picking up the receiver. 'Yes,' she said. 'Lara Davenport speaking.' A pause, then, 'I see. Thank you for letting me know.' Slowly she replaced the receiver.

Standing near the door, heart in mouth, seeing the uprush of tears in Lara's eyes, 'Was that about – Buster?' Edward asked softly. 'Is he – all right?'

Facing him, tears running down her cheeks, 'Not exactly that, not yet, but he soon will be! Thanks be to God, he's going to pull through. He's going to get better! He's going to – *live*! My dog is going to live!'

# Twenty

The Sergeant had been right in surmising that Iris would be removed to the psychiatric unit of the local hospital. Making enquiries, Lara was told that Mrs Smith was being kept under observation for the time being. Visitors were not allowed. Not that Lara felt inclined to visit. Instead, she sent flowers from 'a well-wisher'.

Truth to tell, she felt deeply sorry for Iris despite their life-or-death struggle on the cliff top that evening when the woman's febrile state of mind had crossed the borderline between sanity and madness, when Iris's paranoid dislike of herself, apparent since their first encounter on the doorstep of Stella Maris, had turned to a bitter hatred, fed by jealousy of the person she held responsible for her misfortunes, the loss of her grandchildren, more recently the arrest of her husband on a charge of fraudulent conversion. Above all, the blow to her pride when she, Lara, had been awarded the custodianship of Stella Maris, a job which Iris felt should have been hers by right. And who could blame her?

'You're a blooming saint, you are,' Sadie opined when she heard of the traumatic cliff-top events of the weekend. 'Sending flowers to a woman who damn near put paid to yourself and Buster! Either that or stark raving mad! You'll be telling me next that you're not going to press charges against her for attempted murder!'

'I'm not,' Lara said mildly. 'Think about it, Sadie. There's been enough suffering as it is. Why add to it? My belief is that Iris will spend the rest of her life in some mental hospital or another, so what would be the point or purpose of my pressing a charge against her?'

'Yeah, I see what you mean,' Sadie agreed reluctantly. She sighed deeply. 'Even so, my blood runs cold at the thought of what might have happened to you if you hadn't got the better of her, if that nice Mr Stone-house hadn't arrived in the nick of time!' She paused, frowning. 'Why did he, by the way?'

'It's a long story,' Lara prevaricated. 'Which you probably wouldn't believe any-way. So, let's leave it at that, shall we? Now, shall I do the vacuuming whilst you polish the silver?'

To Lara's relief, Buster was on the road to recovery. His stab wounds were healing well, the vet had told her. Frankly, he had not anticipated the dog's survival, the state he was in following such a frenzied attack, but he was a fine, strong young animal who had responded well to treatment.

'How soon can I take him home?' Lara asked. The vet smiled. 'At the end of next week,' he responded warmly. 'If you are sure you can manage. He'll need rest and quiet, and he may not be very mobile to begin with, in need of help in getting out of his basket to answer calls of nature, and he's no lightweight, believe me.' He added, 'There could be messes to clean up, and it will be your responsibility to make certain he takes the pills I'll prescribe for him: painkillers and vitamin pills, antibiotics and so forth. In short, Mrs Davenport, caring for a sick animal is very much akin to caring for a sick child. His wounds will need bathing and dressing twice daily. On the other hand, you could leave him here at the clinic to be cared for by myself and my staff for another month or so until he regains his mobility. It's entirely up to you.'

Buster was lying down in his kennel at the time, looking up at Lara adoringly, faintly wagging his tail. She said, 'I rather think he'd like to come home. No need to worry, Mr Phillips, I'll take care of him just fine.'

'Good.' The vet, James Phillips, nodded his head approvingly. 'A wise decision. The poor lad certainly knows to whom he belongs. I'd go so far as to say that we might have lost him had it not been for your visits following that touch-and-go operation of his. Even semi-conscious, he sensed your presence, of that I am entirely certain.'

Leaving the vet's premises, the chilling thought occurred to Lara that Buster belonged, not to herself, but to Joan Prewett. And, oh God, she thought despairingly, when September came, how could she bear to leave behind her, not only Stella Maris, but also her beloved animals?

One day, towards the end of July, Lara answered the doorbell to discover, on the doorstep, a smartly dressed young woman carrying an overnight case, who said coolly yet pleasantly, 'You must be Lara Davenport. I am Rebecca Barnaby, Joan Prewett's daughter. May I come in?'

'Yes, of course,' Lara replied bemusedly. Then, 'I'm sorry, Mrs Barnaby, but I don't quite understand. There's nothing wrong, is there, with your mother, I mean?'

Becky sighed deeply. 'There's a lot wrong with her, which is why I'm here. But I can't talk about it now, I'm bone-tired and hungry, in need of a shower and a decent cup of coffee.'

'Then why not come upstairs, take a shower whilst I rustle up some food and make the coffee? I'll carry your case and show you the way to your room.'

'Sounds fine to me. Thanks, Mrs Davenport.'

'Please, call me Lara.' She smiled. 'All right if we eat in the kitchen? Come down when you're ready.'

Half an hour later: 'That coffee smells good.' Becky sniffed appreciatively. 'Freshly ground, if I'm not mistaken.'

Lara laughed. 'I usually drink instant. I keep a tin of beans handy for special occasions. Do you take milk and sugar?'

'Milk, no sugar.' Becky sat down at the kitchen table. Buster stood up in his basket, wagging his tail in greeting; Cleo jumped down from the window sill when the milk jug appeared from the fridge. 'I have to hand it to you, Lara,' Becky said warmly. 'You're a mighty fine housekeeper, everything in apple-pie order. A room ready and waiting for me, plenty of hot water, freshly ground coffee and – what's this? Glory be, a mushroom omelette, green salad, strawberries and cream! Sure you weren't expecting me?'

'Quite sure,' Lara said happily, pouring the coffee. 'Now, enjoy your meal while I take Buster for a stroll round the garden. Come on, old son, I'll lend you a hand.' Bending down, she lifted the dog from his basket on to the floor. On terra firma, the dog followed her, somewhat unsteadily, to the back door. 'I'll be back in a sec,' Lara called over her shoulder to Becky. 'He's not a hundred per cent fit yet, but he's making remarkably good progress.'

Becky stared after her anxiously, pondering the present situation, wishing to heaven that she had come to impart good news, not bad.

Later, in the drawing room, Becky explained that her mother had decided to stay on indefinitely in New York, to share the Greenwich Village house with herself, her husband and children. 'You see,' she explained sadly, 'Mummy has not been at all well, recently. Pretty ill, as a matter of fact. In no fit state to undertake the long journey back to England.'

'I had a feeling something was wrong,' Lara said. 'I knew she wasn't well when she went on holiday, which is why my coming here happened in a hurry. She was desperate to see you and her grandchildren while she was still reasonably mobile.'

Glancing about her, Becky said regretfully, 'Mum loves this house. It has style, elegance, an old-world charm about it. It was far too big for her, of course, an elderly person on her own. I tried to talk her out of buying it, but she wouldn't listen. You see, she thought I'd be living with her at the time. It came as a hell of a shock when I told her I was about to marry an American and was going to New York to live.

'Terribly selfish of me, I guess, but I was head-over-heels in love. Not that Mummy stood in my way. She liked Scott enormously. A remarkable lady, my mother.' Becky's eyes filled with tears. 'I count myself lucky that Scott and I are able to take care of her now, to visit her every day in hospital. It will break her heart to sell Stella Maris, but Mum's a realist, no self-pity.' She paused, then: 'The reason I'm here is to act on her behalf in putting the house on the market, along with its contents.'

She added, seeing the stricken look on Lara's face, 'I'm really sorry. I guess you love Stella Maris too. You seem to belong here, somehow, as if you had put down roots. But Mummy asked me to make it clear to you that you are to remain here till the end of September. If you want to, that is. If you have no other immediate plans in mind.'

'No, I haven't,' Lara said stiffly, afraid of revealing too much emotion in the face of Becky's devastating news regarding Joan Prewett's illness, the forthcoming sale of Stella Maris to strangers, the realization that soon, very soon now, she must reach firm decisions about her own future role in life. Where to go, what to do next when

September came.

Becky said understandingly, 'I'm so sorry, Lara. Tell me, is there any possibility of your staying on here as the new owner of Stella Maris?'

'Of buying the house and its contents, you mean?' Lara responded regretfully. 'I'm afraid not. I haven't that kind of money. My late husband left me well provided for, but I'm far from rich enough to afford a house of this size. You see, I've already invested in property for friends of mine, which ate into my small amount of capital. Not that I regret it, I don't!'

'But you do own that house, don't you?' Becky insisted. 'A form of collateral, wouldn't you say? Please, Lara, think about it!'

'I shall, Becky, believe me,' Lara replied. 'But not now, not tonight.' Feeling suddenly drained of energy, of hope and purpose, rising to her feet, she said, 'Now, if you'll excuse me, I'll just make certain that the house is securely locked for the night, that the animals are all right.'

'Anything I can do to help?' Becky called after her, to which there came no response. Lara must also be feeling tired, weary after a long day ending in bad news, she considered, glancing about the room, drawing to herself, momentarily, the essence of her mother in the charm of her surroundings, the sound of the sea on the rocks beneath the bay window, imagining she saw, for one brief moment in time, the outline of a young man, in uniform, near the window, looking out to sea.

Next morning, Lara was busy in the kitchen when Becky came down neatly but casually dressed in slacks and a cashmere sweater. 'Did you sleep well?' Lara asked, pouring coffee.

'Like a baby,' Becky said, cradling the cup. 'It was so peaceful, the sea sounded like a lullaby. I felt as if someone was watching over me. Must have been that young soldier I saw near the drawing-room window last night.'

'You – *saw* Danny?' Lara's face lit up.

'You don't mean...? I thought my eyes were playing tricks. So, you've seen him, too?' Becky looked bewildered.

'Not really, but I know he exists. He saved my life. He died in France during the first war. He's buried over there. My belief is that he wants to come home, to be near his wife. She worked here once, as a servant. They fell in love. Danny married her against his father's wishes.'

'Do go on. Tell me more.'

'It's a long story.'

'I'm not in a hurry. Please, Lara.'

'Not now, if you don't mind. Later per-haps. Tonight, in the drawing room. I'll show you his photograph and letters. Right now I have work to do, breakfast to cook – bacon and scrambled eggs OK?'

'Very much so. Then what?'

'I have Buster to see to. His wounds need bathing and dressing twice a day. Then I must go shopping, otherwise we'll run out of food.'

'May I come with you?' Becky asked.

'Of course, I'll be delighted,' Lara said warmly. 'That way you'll be able to choose what you want to eat for lunch and supper.'

'Fish! I want lots and lots of fish,' Becky said decisively. 'Lots of vegetables and fresh fruit. And you must let me give you a hand with the housework.'

'But you're a guest,' Lara protested, grilling bacon and scrambling eggs, making toast and helping Becky to more coffee.

'A guest, fiddlesticks! I wasn't invited, I just stuck my nose in without a word of warning; the bearer of bad tidings to boot.' She paused. 'Thanks, Lara,' as her hostess brought breakfast to the table. 'That looks marvellous, bacon nice and crisp, eggs creamy, not knobby and watery, toast piping hot. Have you ever thought of running a guest house, Lara, a haven of peace for the elderly? You're a born homemaker, nothing too much trouble.'

'Can't say the idea ever occurred to me,' Lara admitted, sitting down to eat her own breakfast. 'My parents once took in summer visitors for a living, in Scarborough, before the war. I enjoyed helping out once in a while, especially at weekends, but I wouldn't care to repeat the experience, even if it were possible.' She added wistfully, 'Perhaps, when I leave Stella Maris, I'll find myself another job as a housekeeper.' Staring into the void of the future ahead of her as she spoke.

Later, after Buster's wounds had been duly bathed and dressed, Lara and Becky set off on their food-shopping spree, Becky aching to ask how the dog's stab wounds had occurred, thinking it advisable not to ask; sensing a mystery, Lara's reluctance to discuss the subject. A private, somewhat inhibited person, she realized, to whom she had quickly formed a strong attachment by reason of her commitment to caring for Stella Maris the way she obviously had done, on her mother's behalf.

It grieved Becky to think she was here in Carnelian Bay to sell her mother's property, at least to alert estate agents to its availability, come September. Frankly, she hated the thought of parting with it, not merely because of its links with her mother but due to its prime position overlooking the sea and the fishing village below the cliffs, which she longed to explore once she had set the wheels of the sale in motion.

Over lunch – grilled plaice served with knobs of butter and lemon juice, she asked Lara about Rory McAllister, the estate agent who had been so helpful to her mother regarding the purchase of Stella Maris.

'Mum took quite a shine to him,' she said. 'Have you any idea of his address?'

'I'm sorry, I haven't,' Lara replied. 'He's living in London. His wife had been ill, you see...' Her voice faltered suddenly. 'I haven't the faintest idea whereabouts in London.'

'You mean he simply went away without leaving a forwarding address? That seems a bit odd, doesn't it? I know that Mum and he were the best of friends. I naturally assumed that you and he were close friends also, since it was Rory who persuaded you to come here as Mum's housekeeper.'

On edge, sick and tired of being questioned, of prevarication, Lara said tautly, 'Very well, if you must know, Rory and I *were* friends. *Close* friends. He turned to me for help at a time of crisis in his life. His wife had left him for another man, whose child she was carrying, I did my best to help him through that crisis, and yes, God help me, I fell in love with him, so now you know! Any more questions?'

'Oh, Lara,' Becky murmured hoarsely. 'I'm so sorry. I didn't mean to pry. Please forgive me! Me and my big mouth!'

Lara continued, 'To set the record straight, Rory was no more in love with me than the Man in the Moon. It was his wife he loved. Not me. It was Georgina who haunted his dreams, not I. I simply provided good food, a shoulder to cry on. The last time he came here in need of sympathy and understanding, when he told me that he was moving to London to live with Georgina beneath the roof of his in-laws, I told him to leave Stella Maris, which he did. I have neither seen nor heard of him from that day to this!'

Standing up. 'Now, if you've finished eating, I'd best start the washing-up. No, don't bother to apologize further. Just leave me alone to get on with my life in my own way. Meanwhile, if you feel inclined for a breath of sea air, here are the keys to a chalet I rented for the summer, on the promenade. A waste of money, as it happens, since I've seldom been there to make the most of it.'

Becky said quietly, 'I know that you are very angry and upset, Lara, that it's all my fault; but I really am truly sorry to have caused you so much pain. If you feel unable to forgive me, at least let us try to be civil to one another, shall we?'

Her anger forgotten, liking Becky enormously – very much her mother's daughter

335

– throwing her arms about her in a warm embrace, 'Of course I forgive you,' Lara assured her. 'So, let's take it from here, shall we, as friends, not polite strangers?'

They had fish pie for supper, a combination of fresh and smoked haddock nestled in folds of parsley-and-egg sauce and crowned with a coronet of creamy mashed potatoes and grated cheese, nicely browned and bubbling, served with new potatoes and glazed carrots.

Laying down her cutlery, 'That was absolutely delicious!' Becky told Lara. 'One of the best meals I've ever tasted in my life. Who on earth taught you to cook like that?'

'My mother,' Lara replied simply.

Becky listened intently to Lara's story concerning the Stonehouse family, and watched her rapt expression, speaking of Danny and Clara in particular, thinking what a surprising person Lara was, a woman of depth and discernment, and she wished she knew more about her background, more about her abortive love affair with Rory McAllister.

When the Stonehouse letters and photographs had been put aside, Becky said hesitantly, 'You told me Danny had saved your life. How did that come about? Don't answer if you'd rather not. It's not idle curiosity, I'd really like to know.'

It was then Lara told her about Iris Smith's vendetta against her, culminating in the cliff-top battle which had nearly cost Buster his life, the strong feeling she'd had that she was not fighting the battle alone, that some mysterious force had been with her. Certainly Danny had been instrumental in alerting Edward Stonehouse to her plight.

'How terrifying for you. And that poor dog – you mean to say the Smith woman really meant to kill him? You too? But that's monstrous!' Becky shuddered. 'But what possible reason could the woman have had for wanting to kill you?'

'She was jealous because she felt she should have been left in charge of Stella Maris,' Lara explained reluctantly. 'You see, she adored your mother.'

'Good grief! Is that *all*?' Becky looked shocked.

'Not quite all. She'd got it into her head that Rory and I were having an – affair – a physical relationship, that I was a drug addict.'

'But that's ridiculous!'

'I know, but when Rory was unwell, he spent a week here with me, and I *was* dependent on pills at the time. I hadn't been well myself, after the sudden death of my husband. Which is why Rory persuaded me to come to Carnelian Bay for a change of scene, and thinking the fresh air, plus a job of work, would do me good. And he was right! I'd stopped caring about myself, my appearance, life in general. Then, when he came along, suddenly things changed for the better. Falling in love with him was the last thing I intended. It just happened. But perhaps it wasn't love at all, just a kind of – elderly schoolgirl crush – because he'd been good to me.'

'For what it's worth, Mum had quite a crush on him too,' Becky said thoughtfully.

Lara advised Becky to try Whitby or Scarborough for an estate agent of the calibre needed to offer for sale a prestigious property – preferably Scarborough.

Asked if she would care to go with her to Scarborough, 'I'd like to,' Lara said, 'but I have Buster to see to, and Sadie will be here soon.'

'Sadie?' Becky queried, buttering a slice of toast. 'Your home help?'

'More of a friend really. An ally. She's expecting her fourth child, so we kind of share the housework. I don't want her to get over-tired.'

'I see you have a gardener too,' Becky commented, sipping coffee. 'A useful-looking chap to have around. I've got to hand it to you, Lara, the way you've handled your responsibilities. It can't have been easy for you running a house of this size with so little help.'

'I had two gardeners to begin with,' Lara said wistfully. 'One of whom died recently, the other who went to America to live. I haven't heard from him since.' Her voice faltered, remembering both of them. Missing them so much.

Sadie arrived at that moment. 'Sorry I'm late,' she said breathlessly, 'but things are a bit fraught now the kids have broken up for the school holidays. Thank goodness for nice neighbours. Mrs Dunsmore, two doors away, will take care of them just fine.' She stopped speaking abruptly. 'Oh, sorry, Mrs D, I didn't realize you had company.'

'Hi, Sadie,' Becky said warmly. 'I'm Mrs Prewett's daughter, Rebecca Barnaby. Call me Becky.' Glancing at her wristwatch: 'Well, I'd better get going to catch the bus to Scarborough. Expect me when you see me, around suppertime, I guess. What are we having, by the way?'

'Fish! What else?' Lara said resignedly.

When Becky had gone, 'Who on earth is she, and what's she doing here?' Sadie demanded, staring after her. 'And why is she going to Scarborough?'

'Sit down, Sadie, and I'll explain,' Lara said. 'It's a long story.'

When the story had been told, 'You really

mean she's putting Stella Maris on the market?' Sadie burst forth indignantly. 'But where will that leave you?'

'I'm not quite sure at the moment,' Lara confessed. 'But I knew all along that I'd be leaving here in September, so it's up to me to find another job, somewhere else to live.'

'Another job? But I thought you intended going back to Middlesbrough to live at – what's its name – the Windsor Hotel!'

'That's gone by the board now,' Lara explained. 'And I'm not sorry. I need something to occupy my time, let alone my hands and mind. A place to call my own, a cottage or a flat, perhaps. I haven't thought it through yet.'

'But what about the animals? Come September, what about Buster and Cleo?'

'I really don't know! I imagine, at least I hope, that Becky will take them back to New York with her, either that or find new homes for them here in England. The subject has not arisen so far. There's been so little time, you see?'

Sadie saw right enough. She said forthrightly, 'But you love those animals, and they love you. This is their home. My God, what kind of a set-up is this? Becky Barnaby should feel damn well ashamed of herself coming here to upset the applecart!'

'It isn't her fault,' Lara explained sadly. 'She is simply acting on her mother's behalf;

following her instructions. Mrs Prewett fully intended to return to Carnelian Bay in September, of that I'm certain. Now, due to illness, that return home is no longer possible. The poor woman is ill, the reason why she is so anxious to settle her affairs to the extent of selling Stella Maris, presumably to do so while she is still in full possession of her mental faculties. To do with her will, I imagine. How should I know? In any case, it's none of my business, is it?'

'I'd make it your business if I were you,' Sadie advised tautly, getting up to begin work. 'Especially about the animals!' She added waspishly, 'It don't bear thinking about, Buster and Cleo being crated up and flown abroad to live. Either that or being found new homes. No sir, it doesn't bear thinking about!'

Supper was ready and waiting for Becky when she returned home from Scarborough at six o'clock that evening, tired and hungry yet agog with news about her visits to various estate agents and full of praise for the beauty of the resort in which she had spent the day. 'Have you ever been there, Lara?' she asked, tucking into cold poached salmon and salad.

'Yes. I was born there,' Lara said coolly. 'I left there when I was eighteen, after the death of my parents, when I went to

Middlesbrough to live.'

'Really? Why Middlesbrough?' Becky frowned slightly. 'In no way comparable with Scarborough, I guess, according to my guidebook. A dreary place by all accounts. Weren't you happy in Scarborough?'

'Yes I was, very happy, but the man I married lived in Middlesbrough,' Lara said off-handedly. 'So, I was bound to go there whether I wanted to or not.'

'Oh God!' Becky sighed deeply. 'I've done it again, haven't I? Poked my nose into your business? I'm sorry, I didn't mean to. After all, I should know. I went to New York to live with the man I love. Guess it doesn't matter much where you live, as long as you're happy.'

Happy? Clearing away the supper dishes preparatory to washing up, pondering the meaning of the word, Lara doubted her ability to ever feel happy again in view of her present circumstances, the loss of Rory's friendship, the death of Ben Adams, Beauregard Jackson's lack of communication since his return to America, Joan Prewett's illness, the imminent loss of Stella Maris to the highest bidder. Above all, the loss of her beloved animals, Buster and Cleo.

'What is it, Lara? What's wrong?' Becky asked her concernedly. 'A foolish question, perhaps, but I'd like to know what's really bugging you. It's more than just the sale of the house, isn't it?'

'Yes,' Lara acknowledged. 'I can't bear the thought of losing the animals!'

'I see,' Becky said thoughtfully. 'In which case, I'll do my best to persuade Mummy to leave them here with you.'

Suddenly the phone in the drawing room rang. Hurrying through to pick up the receiver, realizing by a burble of voices and signals on the line that this was a long-distance call from America, she called out, 'It's for you, Becky.'

'About time, too,' she replied airily. 'I thought that husband of mine had forgotten my existence.' Cradling the receiver: 'Hello, Scott darling, is that you?'

In the kitchen, putting away the supper dishes, about to make coffee, minutes later Lara turned her head to see Becky, a forlorn figure, standing on the threshold, tears streaming down her cheeks.

'Becky, my dear, what is it?' Lara asked quietly. 'Not – bad news?'

'The worst possible news,' Becky sobbed. 'Scott rang to tell me that Mummy died early this morning, of a heart attack. I must go home as quickly as possible!'

# Twenty-One

In a state of shock, Becky would have left Carnelian Bay there and then, hired a taxi to London, most probably have stayed up till the crack of dawn awaiting a cancellation on the first available plane to New York, if Lara had not persuaded her to begin her journey when she was feeling calmer.

'I guess you're right, she conceded. 'It's just that I can't bear to think I wasn't with Mummy at – the end.'

'I know, love. I'm sorry too,' Lara murmured sympathetically, recalling the shock horror of that accident which had robbed her of both her parents at the same time, culminating in her hasty decision to marry Charles Davenport, which she had lived to regret. If only she had given herself more time to think things through calmly and sensibly, she might well have not spent – wasted – twenty-odd years of her life with a man she had grown to loathe, not love.

She said, 'Why not ring New York? Talk to Scott. Find out exactly what happened. Tell him you'll be on your way home tomorrow.

Then ring the airport, or vice-versa. Yes, that would be best. Book your flight, then ring Scott. Sorry, I'm not thinking too clearly myself at the moment. Meanwhile, I'll be in the kitchen if you need me.'

Joan Prewett's death had come as a shock to her also. Lara realized – a woman she had both liked and admired from the moment they'd met. A brave, humourous woman, a kindred spirit, a friend worth having.

Fortunately, Becky had secured a flight cancellation at noon the next day, where-upon Lara advised her to take a taxi to York station, from there to London by an early morning train to King's Cross. She would need to set off early, but at least she would have time to compose herself beforehand, to bathe, apply her make-up and have a bite to eat before starting her journey.

'I can't thank you enough, Lara, for all you've done for me,' Becky said tearfully, next morning. 'I'll be in touch very soon, I promise. Meanwhile, if various estate agents come to look over the house, just show them round, explain my absence, and tell them to contact me in New York. I'll take it from there.'

She added, 'And try not to worry too much, I'm sure everything will work out fine in the end. About the animals, I mean.'

At least, Lara thought, she had been given

time enough to begin her search for a new job of work to do, to start answering adverts for cook housekeepers, companions or whatever, to start looking for a small cottage or a flat to call her own, come September. Living with strangers was not the seamark of her utmost sail. She would need a bolt hole of some kind when she left Stella Maris, however small it might be, just as long as it belonged to her and to no one else; preferably in Carnelian Bay, with a view of the sea from its windows.

Up late that night, delving into her financial affairs, strange, she thought, how quickly capital dwindled away, not that she regretted for one moment the hefty lump sum she had parted with in her purchase of The Birches, nor the entailment of Charles's pension in mortgage repayments on the property. She did marginally regret, however, the money she had squandered as a paying guest at the Windsor Hotel, being cosseted and waited on hand and foot when, had she possessed the sense she was born with, she should have rented a bed-sitting room and taken care of herself.

All in the past now, Weighing up her present financial situation, she was still comfortably off, she realized. Neither rich nor poor, although the purchase of another property, however small, in need of furnishing, might well swallow up the dwindling amount of capital at her disposal, when she would certainly stand in need of paid employment to keep the wolf from the door.

'Where's your visitor?' Sadie asked, on Friday morning. When Lara explained what had happened, 'Oh, that's bad news,' Sadie said. 'I suppose that'll make a difference, won't it? What I mean is, Mrs Prewett's bound to have left her estate to her daughter, so Becky's bound to want rid of it as soon as possible, on her own behalf, not her mother's. On the other hand, she may have to hang on a bit till the will's proved, in which case she might want you to stay on indefinitely. Now, wouldn't that be fine?'

'Not necessarily,' Lara demurred. 'I'd far rather know where I stand, make my own plans. So far as I'm concerned, I'll be leaving here in September, according to my agreement with Mrs Prewett, nothing whatever to do with Becky.'

'Plans? What plans?' Sadie looked shocked. 'Is there something you're not telling me? Oh, Mrs D, you're not thinking of leaving Carnelian Bay, are you?'

'No, on the contrary, I intend to stay on here, to find a place of my own to live.'

She smiled mysteriously. Checking her finances in the early hours of that morning,

Lara had earmarked a certain sum of money in the pursuance of a long held dream of hers – that holiday in Paris to see, with her own eyes, the Sacré Coeur, the River Seine by moonlight, the bookstalls on the Left Bank, the Cimetière au du Père Lachaise, the Arc de Triomphe, the Latin Quarter, the Tuileries Gardens in autumn, affordable if she stayed in cheap accommodation in the student quarter near the Sorbonne. A chance which, missed, might never come again during her lifetime. She had already waited far too long for the realization of that dream; waiting longer, it might never happen at all.

'So what is it you're after?' Sadie asked prosaically. 'A semi-detached, a bungalow? There's plenty on the market right now.'

'No, not really, I'd prefer a cottage, just a two-up, two down, near the harbour, with a pantiled roof, and a backyard, if possible.'

'Well I never!' Sadie exclaimed disbelievingly. 'You, above all people, in a fisherman's cottage! After Stella Maris! Why, you wouldn't have room to swing a cat!' She sighed deeply. 'Still, if that's what you want, I'll ask Jeff to keep his ear to the ground. He knows lots of people, does Jeff. Mind you, I'm not promising! Fishermen's cottages for sale are rarer than hen's teeth nowadays! Now, where do you want me to start, upstairs or down?'

Cooking days were a thing of the past now that Sadie had a well-equipped kitchen of her own to preside over. This Friday morning, Lara elected to see to the bedrooms and bathrooms, asking Sadie to clean the drawing-room silver, not wanting to burden her with too much heavy work in the seventh month of her pregnancy. She said teasingly, 'The laundry man will be here soon. The money's on the hall table, if you wouldn't mind paying him.'

Sadie chuckled, Lara went upstairs, carrying the vacuum cleaner. The bell rang. Turning to bid Jeff a cheery good morning, she saw Sadie, on her way to open the front door, stumble suddenly before sinking to her knees, clutching her stomach and crying out in pain.

Dropping the vacuum, Lara raced down to help Sadie, thanking God that Jeff was at hand to take charge of the situation. 'I'd best get her to hospital,' he said tautly, noticing a bloodstain on her clothing.

'I'll phone for an ambulance,' Lara said, hurrying to the drawing room. 'Don't try to move her, just stay with her till it arrives.'

Returning to the hall, she found Jeff, ashen-faced, cradling his wife in his arms, murmuring words of comfort, telling her not to worry, that help was on its way.

Looking up at Lara beseechingly, he uttered bleakly, 'I've just started my round.

What the hell shall I do? I can't just leave the van where it is, unattended.'

When the ambulancemen arrived, Lara said briskly, 'Never mind about the van, I'll phone the laundry, tell them what's happened, ask them to send a replacement man. Your place is beside Sadie in the ambulance.'

'But what about the kids?'

'I'll see to the kids! If necessary, I'll bring them here for lunch, take them to the beach bungalow for the afternoon. I'll think of something. You just concentrate on Sadie; let me know what's happening. I'll wait here till twelve o'clock then scoot up to The Birches; take it from there!' Lara smiled encouragingly. 'All right?'

'Yeah, I guess so,' he replied shakily, getting into the ambulance in the wake of his wife's stretcher. 'Thanks, Mrs D.'

At midday, Lara took a taxi to The Birches, and went next door but one to collect Thomas, Sarah, Toby and Ruff. Following a brief word or two with the Cogills' neighbour, Mrs Dunsmore, to explain her own presence, instead of Sadie's, 'Come along, kids,' she said gaily. 'We're going for a picnic on the beach!'

Lara had spent the morning making sausage rolls, peanut-butter sandwiches, cheese straws, biscuits piped with funny faces, fairy cakes adorned with pink icing and glacé cherries, thinking it best not to intimidate her guests with a cooked meal eaten indoors. A picnic on the beach would be far more acceptable, far more relaxed, she had realized, adding to the picnic hamper several packets of crisps, bananas, apples, plus bottles of ginger beer and lemonade.

The children's joyous acceptance of this unexpected treat came as a relief to Lara as they gazed in delight at the interior of the beach bungalow and awaited, excitedly, the unpacking of the hamper, thrilled by the novelty of this curious little house with its verandah and steps leading down to the sand and the sea beyond. Above all, at the prospect of eating in the open air, swinging their legs from the verandah.

'It's just like Hansel and Gretel's ginger-bread house,' Sarah remarked, starry-eyed, tucking into a warm sausage roll. Then: 'Oh look! Donkeys! What are they doing, Mrs D?'

'Having their lunch, the same as you,' Lara laughed, handing round the peanut-butter sandwiches and pouring out mugs of lemonade.

'I wouldn't mind having a donkey ride when they've had their lunch,' Thomas said solemnly. 'If they aren't too full to trot.'

'An' me ud like an ice-cream cornet,' Toby

said decisively. 'So would Ruff!'

'Wish I had a bucket and spade,' Sarah sighed wistfully. 'An' a shrimping net.'

In due course, when the children had finished eating, locking up the chalet, feeling like a female Pied Piper of Hamelin with her contingent of youngsters in tow, walking along the beach towards a little parade of shops near the harbour, she bought three sets of buckets, spades and shrimping nets – 'One each apiece, all round,' as her mother was wont to say when it came to doling out leftover Yorkshire puddings at Sunday dinner.

By the same token, she treated her trio to ice-cream cornets, later to donkey rides, including Ruff, since Toby had utterly refused to board a donkey without him. 'Now listen here, I ain't takin' no mutt donkey ridin' and that's flat,' the donkey man demurred, until, pressing a silver coin into the palm of his hand, with an appealingly uttered, 'Please, just this once?' Lara breathed a sigh of relief when the man replied, with a twinkle, 'All right then, missis, you win. But just this once, think on!'

Returning to the chalet to collect the picnic hamper, keeping a wary eye on her charges making sandcastles on the beach, close to exhaustion from the day's traumas and activities, now what? Lara wondered.

The tide was coming in and she desperately needed to go home to attend to Buster, from whom she had been absent since midday. The time was now four thirty. The kids must be feeling pretty tired too, she reckoned, after hours spent in the fresh air.

Finishing the clearing up, standing on the verandah, she called out to them that it was home time. They came reluctantly, dragging their feet, until, 'Daddy!' Sarah cried out ecstatically to Jeff, whom she had spied hurrying down the cliff path towards them. 'Tommy, Toby, it's Daddy!'

On their way to Stella Maris, where Jeff's jalopy was parked in readiness for his family's return journey to The Birches, he said gratefully, 'I can't thank you enough for all you've done for us today.'

'Oh, never mind that. How's Sadie?'

'Doing fine, thank God! The baby's safe, and so is she.'

'The – baby? I don't quite understand. You mean she's had the baby?'

'Yes, a little girl. Lara Louise, born at two o'clock this afternoon. Sadie's still in hospital and the baby's very tiny, bless her. They are both doing...'

'Fine?' Lara supplied tenderly, tongue-in-cheek. 'Oh, Jeff, I'm so pleased, so happy for you. And not to worry about Thomas, Sarah and Toby, they are welcome to spend their afternoons with me, at the chalet, until Sadie and the baby leave hospital. Indefinitely, so far as I'm concerned. I just hope they've enjoyed my company as much as I have theirs.'

The day prior to Sadie's homecoming, Lara took the kids to the beach for a final picnic. She was on the verandah afterwards, keeping her eye on them making sandcastles, thinking how quickly time sped by – July had slipped into August, unnoticed – she'd been so busy with her adoptive family, shopping, cooking, tending Buster and visiting Sadie in hospital to bother about the passage of time.

There had been a letter from Becky, enclosed with an order of service used at her mother's funeral, saying she would write more fully when she felt up to it. She'd added a PS. 'Things pretty chaotic here at the moment, with Mummy's personal effects to sort out. I am now the new owner of Stella Maris, by the way, but more re this later.'

Deep in thought, Lara scarcely noticed the man coming towards her along the promenade. Mark Fielding, of all people.

He said, 'Hope I'm not disturbing you?'

'No, of course not. Do sit down, I'll make you some coffee.'

He smiled bleakly. 'No need. I've just had

354

lunch. But I'd like to talk to you, if I may.'

'Why? Is anything the matter?' Lara asked, sensing the man's distress.

'A great deal, I'm afraid,' he admitted, sitting next to her. 'I've come to say good-bye. I'm leaving Carnelian Bay tomorrow, you see.'

'Oh? I'm sorry to hear that,' Lara replied uncertainly, wondering why Fielding, a man she scarcely knew, had felt it necessary to bid her a personal farewell. 'May I ask why? What I mean is' – scarcely knowing what she meant – 'why your sudden decision to leave Carnelian Bay?'

'Because of – Amanda,' he said briefly.

'*Amanda*?' She recalled memories of Mark Fielding's alcoholic wife, whom she had steered well clear of since that ghastly social gathering at the Fieldings' house what seemed like a lifetime ago. 'Why? Doesn't she like living here?'

'The present tense is no longer applicable,' Fielding said tautly. 'Apparently she did not, which is why she left me, recently, for another man – an old flame of hers, she assured me, with whom she'd been conducting a clandestine affair even during his wife's lifetime. A man I'd regarded as a friend, a trusted colleague of mine.'

'You mean – Gareth Roberts?'

'Yes, but – how did you know?'

'I didn't. I merely guessed. I'm sorry. It

must have come as a shock to you.'

'It did. The reason why I decided to leave Carnelian Bay, to sell my house and another property I own. A small cottage near the harbour. Fortunately, the house sold quickly. Not so the cottage, which was meant as a bolt hole when I'd got around to having it made habitable.'

'You did say a cottage near the harbour?'

'Yes. Why?' Mark looked puzzled.

'Because I desperately need somewhere to live,' Lara explained, with a fast-beating heart. 'You see, Joan Prewett, the owner of Stella Maris, died recently. The house is up for sale, and I must leave there by the end of September.'

'I'm sorry. I had no idea. But, my dear girl, I meant what I said. The cottage is in a sad state of disrepair. The roof leaks, there's no bathroom, no electricity, no hot and cold running water, and the kitchen resembles something from the pages of a Charles Dickens novel.'

'Even so, I'd like to look at it,' Lara said. 'To gauge its potential and to weigh up the financial pros and cons of the cost involved in making it fit for habitation.'

'Very well, then.' Mark nodded, touched by Lara's need of a home to call her own. 'How about this evening? Say six o'clock? I'll call for you. Show you the way.' Rising to his feet: 'Now, if you'll excuse me,

I have rather a lot on my plate at the moment.'

Lara fell in love with the cottage the moment she crossed the threshold into a surprisingly spacious living room with an inglenook fireplace. A flight of narrow stairs led to the upstairs rooms. So what if the roof leaked and the kitchen contained a rusted iron range, a shallow stone sink with wooden draining boards? There was a happy atmosphere about the place.

'I'd planned to have the kitchen completely modernized,' Mark said, watching Lara intently as she looked out of the window at the cobbled yard. 'Also to have a bathroom installed. Not that I'd have spent much time here.' He smiled ruefully. 'I just needed a – retreat – if you like. Somewhere to call my soul my own. Amanda knew nothing about it. I never intended that she should.

'We'd been living separate lives for some time before she broke the news of her departure to Middlesbrough to join her – lover. Of course, I was deeply shocked and upset at the time. I knew that she and Gareth were friends. I never suspected that they were far more than that. Indeed, I had reason to believe that it was *you*, not Amanda, he had his sights set on.'

'So he had,' Lara admitted, 'inasmuch as he invited me to dine with him on two occasions, so far as I can remember. But I never really cottoned on to him.'

'Thank God you didn't,' Mark said fervently. 'The man's a womanizer, plain and simple! I just pray to heaven that he won't let Amanda down in the long run.' He paused, then: 'But we're here to discuss the cottage, not my personal problems. So how do you feel about it? Could you be happy, living here?'

'Oh, yes,' Lara replied. 'Utterly and completely happy.'

'Then why the worried frown?' Mark asked quietly.

'Because, in my present financial circumstances, I doubt if I could afford the cottage, let alone having the roof fixed. Well, maybe the cottage, at a pinch, but not the repair work.' She added reluctantly, 'I'm sorry to have wasted your time. You see, I'm a bit strapped for cash at the moment. Not exactly on my beam ends, as yet, but having to think ahead, taking everything into account, not wanting to bite off more than I can chew.'

Making up his mind in an instant, liking Lara enormously, Mark said, 'But as the present owner of the cottage, it is up to me to make it fit for habitation, which I intend to do, on your behalf. As I intended to do on my own behalf, given the time and the opportunity. So if you really want the cottage, it's yours.' He added charmingly, 'Frankly, it seemed likely, recently, that I'd have to pay someone to live in it, not vice-versa. So is it a deal, or not?'

'Yes, if you say so.' Regarding Mark Fielding with shining eyes. 'But only if you're sure that I'm not taking advantage of you.'

'Far from,' he assured her. 'It will gladden my heart to think of you, safely ensconced here, in my bolt hole, when I'm far away from Carnelian Bay, carving out a new future for myself in a London hospital.' Escorting Lara back to Stella Maris, when everything had been settled between them, opening the gate for her, 'Well, goodnight, Lara,' Mark said fondly. 'And may the future hold for you all the good luck and happiness you so richly deserve.'

'You too, Mark,' Lara replied. 'And thank you so much for making that future possible for me. For turning a pipe dream into reality.'

When he had gone, a slight, brisk figure walking away from her towards his own home, deep in thought, bemused by the events of the day and its scarcely credible outcome, Lara did not notice, at first, the shadowy figure of a man, near the front door, awaiting her arrival, until, about to fit her key into the lock, she looked up, startled, into a familiar face, smiling down at her.

'Rory,' she murmured hoarsely. 'What on earth are you doing here?'

# Twenty-Two

'You were right all along,' Rory admitted over sandwiches and coffee. 'You warned me that things wouldn't work out with my in-laws. They didn't!'

'So now what?' Lara asked wearily. It had been a long day, and she was tired after all the excitement, pleasurably so, not sleepy but needing time to herself to think about the cottage.

'I'm taking that job in the Cotswolds,' he said. 'Thankfully it was still available. Moreover, I've found myself somewhere to live, a small bungalow, well maintained, in a picture-postcard village near Northleach.'

'Well, that *is* good news,' Lara responded quietly, pleased that he had taken control of his own destiny at last, wondering at the same time how he had managed to talk Georgie into living in a bungalow in a village, however picturesque.

As if reading her mind, he said regretfully, 'It's the end of the line for Georgie and me, I'm afraid. Our divorce is going ahead after all. She utterly refused to leave her parents, you see. Of course, they were on her side entirely. Not that I'm sorry! They had never wanted their precious daughter to marry me in the first place. I quickly discovered there was no room for me in that tasteless mansion of theirs, where I was treated as an interloper, a – nonentity!'

'Oh, Rory, I'm so sorry!' Lara meant what she said, remembering that she had once believed herself to be in love with him. 'But I'm sure you've done the right thing in looking ahead to the future, not dwelling in the past.' She added sympathetically, 'You are welcome to your old room for a couple of nights, if you like, for old times' sake. Now, if you'll excuse me, I *am* rather tired.'

Rising swiftly to his feet, placing his hands on her shoulders, Rory said hoarsely, 'You don't understand, Lara, how could you?'

'Understand – *what*?' she asked bemusedly, staring up at him.

'How much you mean to me! How much I need you, have always needed your presence in my life, from the first day we met! Which is why I'm here, to beg you to come with me to the Cotswolds, to share your future with me! Is the idea so impossible?'

Lara smiled faintly. 'In what capacity? As a housekeeper, a mother figure?' Gently removing his hands from her shoulders: 'Think about it, Rory. You must know as well as I do that what you suggest is – pie in the sky. Now you have your own life to live, just as I have mine. Let's leave it at that, shall we?'

'There's someone else, isn't there?' he said, drawing a bow at a venture. 'That doctor friend of yours?'

'Gareth Roberts? No, far from! What ever gave you that idea? I dislike the man intensely.'

'If not Roberts, then who?' he demanded. 'I know there's someone. I really thought that someone might be me! Apparently I was wrong in thinking you – loved me.'

'Was it so obvious?' Lara murmured shamefacedly.

'It was to me,' he confessed, loathe to let go of her.

'And yet you never said a word! You simply watched me making a damn fool of myself?'

'It wasn't like that at all, Lara, and you know it! What *could* I have said? You see, I had Georgie to consider at the time, a sick woman in need of my help and support.'

'With whom you were then, still are, and always will be head over heels in love, unless I'm much mistaken,' Lara reminded him. 'Oh, come on, Rory, admit it! Chances are you'll come together again sooner or later. So, if I were foolish enough to go with you to the Cotswolds, as your housekeeper or whatever, if you and Georgie ironed out your differences, where exactly would I fit into the picture in a ménage à trois? Cooking and cleaning for the pair of you, I shouldn't wonder.'

'You mistake my motives entirely,' Rory persisted. 'I'm asking you to marry me, Lara, as soon as my divorce is finalized. To come to the Cotswolds with me as my fiancée, soon to become my wife. What more can I say?'

'Nothing, I imagine,' Lara conceded gently, smiling up at him. 'Except that I am no longer in love with you, that you have never ever been in love with me. So, my answer is no. When – *if* I ever marry again, it will be to a man who not only needs me, but wants me with every fibre of his being, if such a man exists. And, if he does not, I'll be no worse off than I am right now!'

So saying, she went slowly upstairs to her room, close to tears of regret at turning down an offer which, once upon a time, would have meant the world to her. For what precisely? A broken-down cottage and a phantom lover whose presence in her life might – never materialize? Next morning, Lara discovered an envelope enclosing a set of keys and a letter from Mark Fielding on the doormat. 'Dear Lara,' she read,

I meant to give you the keys of your kingdom last night, and to give you the

name of a reliable builder to carry out the repair work, an elderly, self-employed man aptly named Fred Wiseman – slow but thorough, who will not, in present-day parlance, make his teeth meet, whom I suggest that you contact as soon as possible, if, as I suspect, you want the work completed by September. Good luck, and all best wishes.
Yours sincerely,
Mark.

Rory came downstairs at that moment, looking subdued. Lara said, leading the way to the kitchen. 'Please sit down, and listen. I have a great deal to say to you, a lot of explaining to do concerning my present situation, which has a bearing on your own, beginning the day you persuaded me to come here, to Stella Maris, as Joan Prewett's housekeeper. A fairly easy job, or so I imagined at first. I was wrong! Had I realized, at the time, what I was letting myself in for, I'd have run a mile!'

Rory listened intently as the story unfolded. When it was finished, he murmured, deeply shocked by her revelations pertaining to her life-or-death battle with Iris Smith, the near-fatal injuries inflicted on an innocent animal, the sad news of Joan Prewett's death, of which he had heard nothing until now. 'Oh God, Lara, I'm so sorry. So desperately sorry that you had to face all this alone. That I didn't keep in closer touch with you all along, as I promised I would. I was just too wrapped up in my own problems to give a damn about other people's.'

He continued hoarsely, 'I knew all along that ours was a very special relationship, that you were in love with me, and I took advantage of that, God forgive me, assuming that you would always be there for me, offering a convenient shoulder for me to cry on, as and when necessary. It came as a blow to my ego that night you told me exactly what you thought of my decision to live with Georgina and her parents.

'Now, here you are, faced with leaving Stella Maris within weeks, about to make your own way in life, no longer in need of anyone's help or support, especially not mine. Standing strong and proud on your own two feet.'

He smiled lopsidedly. 'I felt so certain that you would leap at my proposal of marriage that I bought you this.' He unearthed a red velvet box containing a solitaire diamond ring from his jacket pocket and revealed its contents. 'More fool I! I might have known that you, above all people, would not be so easily seduced into believing that your future happiness lay with a man you had lost faith in long ago, who had never even bothered to keep in touch with you at a time when not only Georgina but *you*, Lara needed a shoulder to lean on.'

Lara said wistfully, 'All in the past now, Rory. For what it's worth, there will always be a corner of my heart reserved for you alone. Now, what do you want for breakfast? The usual, bacon, sausages and fried eggs? If so, you'd best take Buster for a walk along the prom until it's ready!'

Later that morning, accompanied by Rory, Lara met up with Fred Wiseman to discuss the work necessary to restore her new home to a state of live-ability.

' 'Course, the roof needs seeing to,' he supplied, stating the obvious, stabbing a blunt pencil on the pages of a well-thumbed notebook. But there's no dry rot, thank the Lord. Mind you, the staircase is a bit dodgy in places, but nowt to worry about unduly; and modernizing the kitchen, getting shot of that old sink and draining board – and that there range. Wain't be too much of a problem, though having electricity installed might set you back a bit, not ter mention a new bathroom-cum-toilet, but that's my sons' look-see, not mine. My eldest, Ted, is an electrician by trade, my youngest, Alfie, is a plumber. The one in between, Les, is a painter and decorator. The four of us work just fine together. So now, missis, you just

366

tell me what you want done, an' it'll be done in two shakes of a lamb's tail!'

Lara, who had not so far ventured up the 'dodgy' staircase leading to the upper rooms, saw, with delight, that they were reasonably spacious, that a boxroom sandwiched between the two master bedrooms would easily convert to use as a bathroom.

'Where does that door lead to?' she asked, gazing at a rough wooden edifice adorned with a metal sneck, of Victorian vintage, similar to the one in the backyard.

'The attics,' Fred Wiseman told her. 'I shouldn't venture, if I was you, it's main mucky up yon; spiders as big as your fist.'

'Perhaps Les could give it a coat of paint when you've finished the roof?' Lara suggested mistily.

Fred looked surprised. 'What iver for? Not thinking of tekkin' in visitors, are you?'

'What was all that about?' Rory wanted to know when Fred had duly noted Lara's requirements in his dog-eared notebook, and they were walking downhill together. 'Look, Lara, I hope you haven't paid through the nose for the property,' his estate-agent instincts coming uppermost. 'It's worth next to nothing. Do you mind my asking how much?'

'Next to nothing,' she replied.

At least, Lara thought, on the point of his

departure for pastures new, she and Rory had recaptured something of their old rapport in the two days they had spent together. Yet, bidding him goodbye, she experienced no feeling of regret that she had turned down his offer of marriage, cohabitation of his bungalow in the Cotswolds – a consummation not devoutly to be wished.

That afternoon, she went to the library in the precinct, remembering Amanda Fielding as she did so, glad of her absence, her overwhelming, gossipy, glamorous presence, so at odds with the peace and quietude necessary when it came to browsing, the choosing of books in a peaceful, relaxed atmosphere.

To her dismay, Lara walked into a far-from-relaxed atmosphere. Chaotic, to put it mildly. The counter, littered, end-to end with books which no one had had time to return to the shelves, appeared to be in the charge of an elderly woman wearing pince-nez glasses, grey-faced and anxious, trying her best to cope, albeit unsuccessfully, with a queue of people waiting impatiently to have their books stamped.

Taking in the situation at a glance and feeling sorry for the woman, 'Would it help if I put these books back on the shelves?' Lara asked her. 'I used to work in a library, so I know the ropes.' She added, to establish her credentials, 'I live locally, my name is Lara Davenport.'

'Oh yes, I've seen you in church. I sing in the choir. I'm Margaret Johnstone.' The woman's face appeared more animated. 'If you really wouldn't mind helping, I'll be most grateful. The book trolley is there somewhere.'

'Leave it to me, Miss Johnstone.' Lara smiled encouragingly, happy to be of use, doing something she really enjoyed; handling books, loving the feel of them as she deftly stacked the trolley and set about returning them to their correct places on the shelves.

This accomplished, returning to the counter, she asked the beleagured Miss Johnstone if she could do with a cup of tea. 'Oh yes,' Margaret replied earnestly. 'Milk, one sugar. The staff room's through there,' indicating a door behind the counter. 'If you really don't mind.'

Lara didn't mind at all. In her element, she made the tea, then with a whispered word in the woman's ear that it was ready, knowing that it would never do for a librarian to be seen drinking tea in public: 'Not to worry, I'll stand in for you while you drink your tea. No need to hurry. I cut my eye teeth rubber-stamping books and filing library tickets.'

When Miss Johnstone returned to the fray,

the 'fray' had disappeared as if by magic. Everything was back to normal, people were browsing contentedly, and Lara was date-stamping a copy of *The Browning Version*.

Miss Johnstone confided that she was a secretary by profession, a town-hall employee elected to take charge of the library until a replacement for Mrs Fielding had been appointed.

'You mean they're seeking applicants for the job?' Lara's pulse quickened imperceptibly.

'Why? Are you interested?' Margaret asked, sensing her excitement.

'Very much so. In fact, I'm on the lookout for a job at the moment, and this would suit me down to the ground.'

'In which case, you'd best fill in an application form here and now. Ah, here we are!' Delving into a drawer: 'I knew I'd put them somewhere! You'll need two referees. No problem there, I imagine. I'm sure the vicar will oblige for one, and I'll be happy to do so – *and* put in a good word for you, for what that's worth! You see, my boss happens to be the town clerk, in charge of the Appointments Board.' She smiled conspiratorially. 'The dear man will be glad of a shove in the right direction!'

'Now hang on just a sec,' Lara demurred. 'If I get the job, I'd rather be given it by reason of merit, not favouritism, friends in high places.'

'Oh, go on with you, you'll walk it!' Margaret assured her calmly. 'With or without my help. I happen to know there have been only three applicants so far, a sixteen-year-old student still wet behind the ears, a former headmistress with a personality problem, and a socialist poet with a penchant for stirring up trouble. The kind of man who could start a fight in an empty room.'

'Thanks, Margaret,' Lara responded gratefully. 'In which case, I'll fill in the application form right away!' The task completed: 'How soon before I know the outcome?'

'Let me see!' Riffling the pages of the desk calendar: 'By the end of the month. Of course, there'll be an interview beforehand, but just you turn up looking as cool, calm and collected as you did today, and you haven't a worry in the world.'

Not a worry in the world? Had she been out of her mind to fill in that application form? Of course, she could always turn down the job, if by any chance she succeeded in passing the interview. Turn down a job she really wanted? Why did life have to be so complicated? Not for the first time she felt that it was running away with her like an express train.

Realistically, how could she leave Stella Maris until she knew for certain what was to become of Buster and Cleo? How could she go to Paris until work on the cottage was completed? Despite Fred Wiseman's assurances that it would be ready for her to move into by the end of August, she had doubts about that. The place was still in a state of chaos, although the roof had been repaired, the stairs fixed and the plumbing started on.

Her mind in a turmoil, if only she had someone to turn to for advice, a shoulder to lean on, someone close and dear to her to rely on, to take her by the hand and lead her out of the mess she was in. There had been such a person once, she realized, a strong comforting presence in her life, but he was long gone. Not Rory, but someone else. Someone...

Busy about the kitchen one day a week later, preparing a simple meal for herself, worrying about her interview at the town hall, due to take place at ten o'clock tomorow morning, suddenly the doorbell rang. Pushing aside the pan of scrambled eggs out of harm's way, answering the summons, wondering who the hell it could be, opening the door to an unexpected visitor, 'Becky!' she said weakly, with an upsurge of tears born of relief at seeing her again. 'I was beginning to think that—'

'I had forgotten you?' Becky replied warmly. 'No way! Oh Lara, it's so good to see you again. May I come in?'

Blinking back her tears: 'Why not? After all, this *is* your house, not mine,' Lara reminded her, leading the way to the kitchen.

'An inheritance I'd far rather have done without.' Becky said quietly, sitting down at the table. 'Knowing how much it means to you. But Mummy remembered that too.' She paused momentarily. 'I, of course, was her sole beneficiary so far as the house is concerned, but she made it abundantly clear to my husband, before she – died – during my absence here in England, that you were to be granted sole custody of her beloved animals. He wrote down everything she said at the time, read it back to her, and she signed it. So it is all perfectly legal and above board. I have it here. Shall I read it to you? Well, here goes.

'I bequeath to my friend, Lara Davenport, my dear companions Buster and Cleo, also the painting of Paris above the drawing-room mantelpiece, my escritoire and the marble table in the conservatory, along with my gratitude for making possible my visit to New York and my heartfelt good wishes for her future happiness.

★ ★ ★

373

'So there you have it in a nutshell.'

Becky handed the letter to Lara. She said, 'About your future, have you any plans in mind?' She smiled. 'It goes without saying that you are welcome to stay on here until the house is sold.'

'Thanks, Becky, but I'll be moving into a cottage near the harbour when the repair work has been completed. I've applied for a job as a librarian, though the outcome is uncertain. I'd planned a trip to Paris the first week in September, which I've decided to cancel.'

'But *why?*' Becky frowned slightly. 'A holiday would do you a world of good.'

'Because the time isn't right,' Lara explained. 'I'm in such a muddle right now, I scarcely know if I'm coming or going. All I can do is wait and see what happens next.' She smiled wistfully, fingering the letter Becky had given her. 'This means the world to me. More than you'll ever know.'

Getting up from the table, 'Now, how about lunch?' she asked, reverting to her role as cook/housekeeper. Inspecting the contents of the egg pan, pulling a face: 'The choice is yours. Either congealed, cold scrambled eggs or cold salmon and salad.'

Becky laughed. 'Cold scrambled eggs by all means. Might as well live dangerously or not at all, as Mum was wont to say.

★ ★ ★

The interview had gone along the usual lines, the interviewees – eight in all – painfully aware of each others' presence in a town-hall antechamber, apart from the socialist poet and the ex-headmistress with the personality problem, which appeared to be a hectoring tone of voice used to full advantage at being kept waiting. After all, a woman with her qualifications...

'How did it go?' Becky asked later, making a pot of tea.

'I don't stand an earthly.' Lara sighed deeply. 'I sat on the edge of the chair and – babbled!'

'Oh, you never know,' Becky said cheerfully. Adding to Lara's distress, she went on, 'By the way, I've had a letter from the Scarborough estate agents containing a firm offer for Stella Maris. Less than I expected, but at least an offer. Now, how about a bite to eat? I'll do the cooking.'

'Thanks, but I'm not hungry. I think I'll go down to the cottage, see how Mr Wiseman's getting on.'

'Mind if I come with you? I'd love to see it for myself,' Becky said brightly.

Crossing the threshold, 'But this is charming,' Becky enthused. 'Not in the least bit poky.' Looking about her at the sizeable living room, taking in the staircase near the front door, and the inglenook fireplace. 'You must have a log fire! Why, it's positively Dickensian!'

'So is the kitchen,' Lara remarked. 'At least it was the last time I saw it.'

She was in for a pleasant surprise. The rusted range had been removed, so had the stone sink and wooden draining boards. Alfie, the plumber, was on his knees beside gaping holes in the floorboards, whistling between his teeth. The tune he was whistling was 'Danny Boy'.

Looking up, grinning broadly, 'How do, missis,' he said engagingly. 'I've just nicely finished the bathroom, and I'll have your new sink unit in place by tea time. It's out in the yard if you want to take a gander. Ted's upstairs wiring the bedrooms, Les is painting the attic, and Dad's gone down to the fish shop for us dinners.'

'That's marvellous,' Lara said gratefully, as one glimpsing light at the end of a tunnel. 'Oh, just one thing I forgot to mention, I shall need a cat flap in the back door.'

'Oh, got a cat, have you?' Alfie asked conversationally, sitting back on his heels. 'Nice animals, cats. I have two of 'em myself, and a dog.'

'Mrs Davenport also has a dog.' Becky exchanged conspiratorial glances with Lara. 'A golden labrador who will adore that inglenook fireplace in the living room.'

'Is that so? Well, missis, you'll not be short

of company, especially when your visitor takes up residence in the attic.'

Frowning slightly, intrigued, 'Visitor? What – visitor?' Becky asked.

'No one. No one at all. Mr Wiseman was joking. When I mentioned having the attic made habitable, he put two and two together and came up with the wrong answer, that's all.'

Becky said perspicaciously, 'It strikes me that it's high time a new home was found for that old trunk in Mum's attic, plus any other bits and bobs you might need to make – a visitor – if any – feel at home.'

'You think I'm mad, don't you?' Lara said on their way downhill to the harbour.

'Not at all,' Becky responded thoughtfully. 'Though I had rather hoped that you would find – sorry, forgive me – someone like Rory to keep you company, a flesh-and-blood man to love you as you deserve to be loved.'

'Not Rory! That's out of the question now, I'm afraid. You see, I'm not in love with him. I thought I was, but I'm not.'

Probing gently: 'But you *are* in love with – someone, aren't you?'

'Another mistake on my part,' Lara admitted dejectedly. 'Now, I'd sooner drop the subject if you don't mind! A penchant of mine, apparently, bestowing my heart where it isn't wanted. But never again! Never ever again!'

# Twenty-Three

The cottage was finished at last. Becky had received a better offer for Stella Maris, which she had accepted.

Sick at heart, Lara turned her back on a house which had come to mean so much to her during the past six months, her meagre personal belongings contained in a small removal van: her clothes, the cabin trunk from the attic, various items of silverware, Joan Prewett's escritoire, the painting of Paris by night.

At least, she thought, bidding a silent farewell to The Star of the Sea, she had a new home to go to, a job to look foward to, having, to her surprise, been appointed as the new custodian of the Carnelian Bay library commencing the second week in September.

She had, moreover, furnished, carpeted and curtained her cottage to the best of her ability, mainly from salerooms and job-lot warehouses offering cut-price rolls of carpet at half their normal price, not wanting to overstretch her limited budget.

Becky had been more than kind in offering her tea chests filled with her mother's cast-aside household equipment, gathering dust in the attics, including pots and pans, pudding basins and mixing bowls, stainless-steel cutlery, table lamps and bedside rugs, which Lara had gladly accepted as a means of saving money until she could afford to buy new.

Sadie and Jeff had offered to take care of Buster and Cleo for her until she'd had time to settle into her new abode, at the same time inviting her to a christening party to be held the first Sunday in September, to celebrate the baptism of her god-daughter, Lara Louise Cogill.

'Nowt fancy,' Jeff had advised her. 'Just a few friends and a bit of a buffet at The Birches afterwards – the Church ceremony, I mean. If you're not too tired, that is, with all you've had on your plate recently. Above all, leaving Stella Maris, knowing how much it meant to you.' A decent, caring human being, unused to expressing himself in other than simple down-to-earth terms, he said, 'But life goes on, and we must learn to make the best of it, to be thankful for small mercies.'

'I know.' Lara smiled wistfully. 'And I am thankful, believe me, above all for your friendship and Sadie's, all the help and support you've given me. Now it's up to me to make the best of the future.'

'Sadie and I have talked things over, and she'll be happy to spend tonight with you at the cottage,' he said. 'In case you feel lonely on your own in a strange place.'

'Thanks, Jeff, but I'll be quite all right. The cottage is not isolated. I can see the harbour from my bedroom window; I'll see lights from other windows, street lamps too, I shouldn't wonder, when darkness falls. There'll be passers-by, the sound of the sea against the harbour walls, so I'll be perfectly content. In fact, I'll probably fall fast asleep the moment my head touches the pillow.'

'Well, if you're sure.'

She could not have told anyone, at that moment, how much she longed to be alone in her new home, to think her own thoughts, to say goodbye, in her heart, to Stella Maris, to come to terms with her changed circumstances, to lay aside dreams of what might have been if only ... If only – *what*?

She slept soundly at first. At midnight she awoke suddenly to unfamiliar sounds from the street below, laughter and snatches of conversation. Looking up, she saw strange light patterns dappling the ceiling of her room.

Getting up, opening the window, leaning her arms on the window sill, she noticed the shore lights of the harbour twinkling against the enfolding darkness of a warm autumn night lit with a myriad stars and a slip of a moon shining down on the still, dark waters of Carnelian Bay.

It was then she heard, as one in a dream, the haunting refrain of 'Danny Boy' played softly on a mouth organ, presumably by a sailor from one of the fishing vessels harboured near the quay, snatching a brief moment's respite before setting forth to the fishing grounds beyond the harbour mouth, and heard a faint movement from the attic overhead, a sound she had heard once before, from the attics of Stella Maris.

So, Danny, her champion and defender, that overwhelming presence in her life, had not deserted her after all, as she had feared he might when she left The Star of the Sea. Or was this all in her mind? A fanciful delusion born of loneliness and fatigue? If so, it was a comforting delusion. But deep inside, in her heart of hearts, she knew that it was not a delusion, that somewhere, in another time, another place, they had met before, recalling Jeff's prophetic words: 'Life goes on.'

Of course it did, it must, into infinity, for all eternity. Life and Love. As one. Indivisible.

Cleo had quickly weighed up the advantages of life as an alleycat rather than as a cliff-top cat. There were mysterious ginnels to explore, roofs to sit on, whisker-twitching smells issuing forth from the nearby fish shop, tasty scraps of batter lodged between cobblestones.

Buster had arrived at the cottage, made a quick tour of inspection, discovered his basket in the inglenook, and taken up residence.

'Oh, the place does look lovely,' Sadie said, standing back to admire the painting of Paris on the long wall near the fireplace, beneath the marble side table on which Lara had placed a pink-shaded lamp, a blue and green lustre bowl and a vase of pink dahlias, thinking how clever of Lara to have had the walls coloured a creamy off-white, not to detract from the dramatic impact of the painting.

'And your desk looks just right between the windows.' She turned to survey the wall opposite: the escritoire standing between floor-length rose velvet curtains hanging from brass rods; taking in, at the same time, various other items of furniture accumulated, by Lara, to complement her sitting room: a bookcase, a small gate-legged table, two easy chairs with rose velvet covers, and four small dining chairs surrounding the polished surface of the gate-legged table.

'I'm glad you approve,' Lara said shyly.

'*Approve?* I think it's perfect! Quite perfect!'

'Well, no, it isn't,' Lara demurred. 'There are snags which I hadn't anticipated beforehand!'

'Such as?' Sadie wanted to know, speaking anxiously, furrowing her forehead.

'Buster, for one thing,' Lara explained. 'No way can I leave him here alone all day when I start my new job.'

'Oh, is *that* all?' Sadie's brow cleared as if by magic. 'In which case, what's to prevent your taking him to work with you? He'll be as right as rain in a corner of the staff room. There *is* a staff room up yonder, isn't there?'

'Yes, of course!' Lara breathed a sigh of relief. 'Now, why didn't I think of that?'

And so, when Lara presented herself at her place of employment the following Monday morning, she did so with Buster in tow. And if the powers that be didn't like it, they must lump it, she thought mutinously, as if they, the powers that be; would be on the forecourt awaiting her arrival, not having fully assimilated the fact that she alone was now responsible for the smooth running of the Carnelian Bay branch library, and if she, as the newly appointed custodian of the shelves, wished to bring her dog to work with her, who, if anyone, could prevent her doing so?

In the event, there was no welcoming – or otherwise – committee from the town hall to mark her entry into the building, merely two young girls, Naomi and Deborah, her assistants, on the doorstep, both as thin as herring and appearing decidedly nervous at the advent of their new superintendent. They fell immediately in love with Buster, as he did with them.

'Is this your dog?' Naomi piped up admiringly. 'Oh, isn't he lovely?'

Deborah added enthusiastically, 'I was dreading this morning, but I'm not now! Working under a new boss, I mean.' Her face paled significantly. 'I'm sorry, ma'am, you're it, aren't you? Our new boss?'

Lara smiled indulgently. 'That I am! My name is Davenport, and this is my dog, Buster. Now, let's get inside, shall we, and begin work? If you can bear to drag yourselves away from Buster, that is! I shall want everything in apple-pie order by ten o'clock, the shelves dusted, every book in place, the staff room immaculate – and the kettle on for a nice hot cup of tea.'

The man had not had an easy time of it, of late. Accorded a hero's welcome on his return home to America, he'd been overwhelmed by the adulation heaped on him, leaving him little or no time to himself. And yet, as regularly as clockwork, every night when darkness fell and he was alone in his room, he had written, in diary form, his thoughts and feelings for the woman he loved, and would go on loving from here to eternity.

Whether or not the woman he loved would ever receive that written affirmation of his feelings for her, he had no way of knowing. And even if she did, how could he be sure that she would wish to be reminded of a man whose brief presence in her life had scarcely mattered at all?

Yet somehow, now that he was on his way to England once more, he must, at least, try to get in touch with her again.

Little Lara Louise's christening, in St Mary's Church, when Lara, her godmother, had tenderly held the babe in her arms, had touched her deeply to an awareness of how different her life might have been had she been awarded the accolade of giving birth to a child of her own. Still not physically too late, she realized, had she not dismissed Rory McAllister and Gareth Roberts so wantonly from her life, by either of whom she might well have become pregnant, had she cared enough for either of them to even contemplate taking such a step in the wrong direction.

Children should be born of love, not of expedience or self-gratification, she thought, looking down at the precious bundle in her arms, loving the child as dearly as she would have done children born of her loveless marriage to Charles, had she been lucky enough to have any.

There was something wrong, the man thought wearily. He recognized the trees, borders, flower beds, the lawns, the house itself, yet everything seemed dream-like, vaguely unreal, the way it had done before he had recovered his memory.

He was tired. Going home had been emotionally exhausting. Inured to privacy, a simple pattern of life, working with his hands, close to nature, he had been un-prepared for notoriety, welcome-home celebrations, endless parties in his honour, reporters and press photographers demand-ing interviews, wanting to know how it felt to be back in the land of the living, as one brash reporter had put it. 'My name is Orlando, not Lazarus,' he'd uttered scorn-fully, not that the newshound had a clue what he meant.

When the letter bearing a Washington postmark arrived, his mother said she'd had a funny feeling about it the moment she saw it. It looked so official, the embossed envelope, the typewritten address, the instruction on the back of the envelope, 'If undelivered, return to the State Department, Washington DC.'

'What is it, son?' she asked nervously when he'd finished reading the letter.

'A job offer,' he said. 'Here, see for yourself.' Watching her face as she read, anticipating her reaction to the news it contained, knowing his mother so well, her sense of honour and fair play, that she would never stand in the way of his happiness, at whatever cost to herself. 'It's only an offer, Mom, not a directive.'

'I know, son. Even so, it's quite an honour, isn't it, to have been chosen for so important a job. What does it say? To lead a team ... to establish camps for the care of homeless men, women and children, on an international basis? That means refugees, I guess. Am I right?'

'Perfectly right, Mom.' He smiled at her affectionately. 'It also means my leaving home, if I decide to accept the offer.'

His mother sighed deeply. 'I know that too, son. I also know that you are not happy here. Not root-and-branch happy, as you should be. I have the feeling there's someone you've taken a shine to in England. What happened?'

'Nothing. That's the trouble. There wasn't much time. I don't even know how she feels about me.'

'Then take my advice, find out before it's too late.'

Now, looking up at the house he remembered so well, it seemed likely that he *had* left it too late, after all. There was no sign of life, no welcoming bark of recognition from an ecstatic bundle of yellow fur.

Crossing the front lawn, he saw that the garden shed and the side door leading to the kitchen were closed and locked. It was then he noticed an uprooted For Sale sign, on its side, near the shed. It didn't need a mastermind to work out the implication of that notice, the house had been sold, and Lara might well have left Carnelian Bay when her summertime tenancy of Stella Maris had come to an end. If so, he had left it too late. Little hope of finding her now. Tomorrow he'd be on his way to London to begin the first leg of his journey to Africa with his team of doctors, nurses, caterers and surveyors, to establish the first of the international refugee camps funded by the US Government, of which team he, God help him, was in charge. A man not even in charge of his own destiny, he thought wryly, returning the way he had come, retracing his steps across the front lawn.

At the library, Buster, half asleep in his staff-room basket, suddenly lifted his head, nose aquiver. Wide awake, scenting the air, uttering a shrill, joyous bark, quitting his basket, he made a beeline for the main entrance and raced madly across the fore-court towards the private roadway opposite, fairly upskittling a couple of pensioners on their way to the library to renew their bag-full of overdue books.

'Well, *really*,' they muttered, in unison. 'It's coming to something when...'

'Mrs Davenport,' Naomi reported urgently. 'You'd best come quick! Buster's gone AWOL! He was lying in his basket as quiet as a mouse one minute, the next he was gone!'

'*Gone*? Where to?'

'Across the car park. Running like the devil was after him!'

'Thanks, love, I'll see to it right away!' Quitting the reception desk, quickly Lara went in search of her recalcitrant animal, wondering what on earth had possessed him to attempt such a mad dash for freedom: totally out of character with the dog she knew and loved so well – or thought she did. Unless...

Standing at the gate of Stella Maris, close to tears of joy, she saw the back view of a man, kneeling on the grass, his arms clasped about the neck of a softly whining dog whose face, resting serenely on the man's shoulder, spoke volumes about love, the love of a dog for a human being, and vice versa.

Then, moving towards them, recognizing

389

in an instant the set of the man's shoulders, a certain elegance and grace about him, a gentleness, the strength of his arms about the dog, the tilt of his head, his quiet composure, a kind of inate humility about him, 'Beau,' she whispered softly. 'Thank God you're here, that you've come back to us.'

At the sound of her voice, turning his head, he smiled up at her. 'I had to,' he said simply. 'My life was empty without you.'

Rising to his feet, taking her in his arms, he kissed her, slowly and deeply, with the air of a man, weary of wandering, who had found his way home at last.

Tracing the outlines of his face with her fingertips, knowing that this was the man she had been waiting for all the days of her life, she said gently, 'I love you, Beau, more than you'll ever know. Now and for ever.'

'As I love you, Lara,' he responded gently, holding her closer than she had ever been held before. 'So you will marry me, won't you?'

# Epilogue

They had opted for a simple church wedding. The groom had been granted a short spell of compassionate leave from his unit, to which he must return early in the new year.

Beau was in US Air Force uniform, Lara wearing a long cream wool skirt, a matching jacket and carrying a bouquet of early spring flowers which, on leaving the church amid a flurry of confetti and snowflakes, she placed on Ben Adams' grave.

The church hall, brightly decorated for Christmas, had been the scene of much laughter and merrymaking. Sadie had made and decorated the wedding cake and organized the buffet, fearful as usual that there wouldn't be enough food to go round. Hugging her, Lara told her not to worry, it had been a wonderful reception. She added, 'Don't forget that you are coming to us on Boxing Day.'

'Forget? We wouldn't miss it for the world, would we, Jeff?'

Lara had planned the little housewarming

party well in advance, to which she had also invited the Stonehouses and their children: taking infinite pleasure in decorating the Christmas tree in the living room with fairy lights and coloured baubles.

'There's something magical about this cottage,' Beau remarked when they were alone together in front the inglenook fire. 'I can't quite put a finger on it, the feeling I have of a loving presence close at hand. Tell me, darling, do you sense it too?'

It was then, by fire glow, with evening shadows fast falling on the world outside, on this, the night before Christmas Eve, their wedding night, that Lara told Beau about Danny, the benign unseen presence in her life.

When she had finished speaking, 'I guess you mean that little soldier boy I saw occasionally at Stella Maris, Beau said thoughtfully.'

'You *saw* him? You saw Danny Boy?'

'Reckon I must have done. He would stand near the drawing-room window looking out to sea. I thought my mind was playing tricks at first. No big deal in my case. Then Ben told me he'd seen him too, that he was 'nowt to be scared on', in Ben's parlance, just a poor lad who had lost his way in the dark. A feeling I knew only too well.'

Lara shivered involuntarily. 'Ben was right. Poor Danny. My belief is he'll never be at peace until he's laid to rest near his wife. It doesn't seem much to ask.'

Beau said gently, '*Has* anyone asked? If not, someone should. Ted Stonehouse, for instance, as his kith and kin.' He paused. 'Why not have a word with him on Boxing Day?'

Lara spent Boxing Day morning preparing food for the housewarming party, aided and abetted by Beau, who set the table, helped with the washing-up, brought in logs for the fire, polished glasses for the champagne he'd provided, sniffed the air appreciatively at the aroma of cooking as Lara produced trays of vol-au-vent cases, quiches and other savouries from her brand new cooker; made roast beef and turkey sandwiches, washed lettuce, tomatoes and cucumber in readiness for the cut-glass bowl of salad to accompany the meal, the bowl, plus a lace-edged linen tablecloth and matching napkins, which had been a wedding present from America, along with the many congratulatory cards and telegrams they'd received on their wedding day.

When all was ready, glancing up at the painting of Paris above the marble side table, 'That sure is a lovely picture,' Beau remarked, his arm about Lara's waist. 'Tell me about it.' He listened intently as she told him about her girlhood dream of long ago, which had never come to fruition.

At that moment, their guests had arrived, laughing and bearing housewarming presents wrapped in brightly coloured paper – a pair of oven gloves from Thomas, Sarah and Toby Cogill; a framed portrait of Lara Louise from their parents; silver pastry forks, a bottle of Bollinger champagne and a bouquet of red roses from the Stonehouses.

Choosing his moment for a quiet word in Ted Stonehouse's ear, it would take a long time, Beau considered quietly, a great deal of string-pulling, the cutting through of miles of red tape, to bring Lara's beloved Danny Boy home to England, but he would do his damnedest to pave the way for that particular homecoming.

Sadly, he was not present on that occasion when it finally happened, but Lara had written a long letter to him, detailing the events of that day, which he read over and over again in a refugee encampment near the Somalian border; picturing the scene in his mind's eye.

'It was a cold day,' she had written,

'with flurries of rain. The Stonehouses, Sadie and Jeff Cogill and I were huddled together in the churchyard, awaiting the arrival of the coffin, not knowing what to expect. The organist was playing Handel's 'Sheep May Safely Graze'. We were all tense, very nervous, deeply aware of the solemnity of the occasion, dreading the arrival of the coffin.

I'm not ashamed to say, I wept when I saw it, draped with a Union Jack and surmounted with a wreath of white lilies from the Red Cross Association, bearing the inscription, 'For Valour'.

The coffin was borne into the church by six pallbearers in khaki uniform of First-World-War vintage, and placed reverently in front of the altar. The service began with the hymn 'O, Valiant Hearts', which seemed so right, so appropriate somehow, especially the words: 'Tranquil you lie, your knightly virtue proved; Your memory hallowed in the land you loved.'

Beau, darling, I could scarcely believe the number of people gathered together to pay tribute to Danny Boy: Red Cross nurses, government officials, First-World War veterans and villagers alike.

Impossible to describe my feelings at that moment, knowing that Danny was home at last, his memory hallowed in the land he loved.

Then, mounting to the pulpit, the parson spoke warmly of human love and endeavour, ending with the words, 'Here he lies, where he longed to be. Home is the sailor, home from sea, and the hunter home from the hill.'

And so Danny was finally laid to rest. Buglers sounded 'The Last Post' as his coffin was lowered into the ground, and it seemed to me, at that moment, that my little soldier boy was safely home at last. No longer alone in the dark, but finally at peace with the world, God rest him.'

She'd added a PS: 'Please come home to me soon. My life seems empty without you.'

And yes, Beau realized, high time he went home, back to the woman he loved, drawing towards him an application form for his leave of absence, to which, following the many weary months he had spent without her, he felt fully entitled.

It was early spring. Beau's letter was in the pocket of her anorak, his loving words branded on her heart. He was coming home. A few days at the cottage first, then Paris for their long-awaited honeymoon. Two whole weeks in the world's most romantic city.

She fairly ran down the hill to the sands, Buster lolloping along beside her. She felt like singing, dancing near the sea's edge on the firm tawny sand left by the receding tide. Footprints on the sands of time, she thought. How did the stanza go? 'Lives of great men all remind us We can make our lives sublime, And, departing, leave behind us Footprints on the sands of time.'

Happiness appeared to be contagious today. Ahead of her she spied a young couple walking hand in hand, possibly a waiter and waitress about to go on early morning duty at one of the hotels already open in anticipation of the Easter weekend, judging by the girl's long dark skirt and high-necked white blouse. Not that Lara could see clearly from a distance, it simply struck her that the girl must feel chilly without a jacket. Or perhaps young people in love didn't feel the cold?

Suddenly, breaking apart, arms outstretched and crossed, they began skitter-scattering in the sand, laughing, the girl's head flung back, her golden hair tossing in the breeze, spurts of sand flying up from their joyously circling footsteps.

Distracted momentarily by Buster's shrill bark, indicative of his desire to play a game entailing a mad dash into the sea to retrieve the ball she was carrying. 'Oh, very well then,' she laughed. 'Get wet! Rather you than me!' His eager claw marks turned up the sand as went after the ball.

Seconds later, looking ahead, she saw that

the young couple had disappeared from view. Possibly time had caught up with them? Fearing they'd be late for work if they didn't hurry, abandoning their childish game of skitter-scattering, had they hastened towards the promenade, their footprints in the sand the only reminders of that joyous dance she had witnessed?

It was then Lara realized, with a swiftly beating heart, that apart from her own, and Buster's, there were no other footprints in the sand.